DYING FOR STRAWBERRIES

The front door opened. I spun about and ran for one of the guest bedrooms overlooking the back-yard. I tried to see if I could spy Tess anywhere out-side, but she must have taken off for the empty lots next door.

Uncertain what to do next, I kept an ear cocked for the sound of Cole downstairs. I heard nothing but birdsong. Was that coming through the open front door? If so, why hadn't Cole entered the house yet? The next sound I heard was a car starting up, then pulling away.

Barely breathing, I tiptoed out of the bedroom and back to the top of the stairs. Had Cole come back for something quick, like a file from his office? Maybe he'd already retrieved what he wanted and was on his way back to the store. I stood motionless for several excruciating minutes, listening for any sound downstairs. Again, I heard nothing but bird-song.

Holding my breath, I crept down the stairs. When I reached the bottom step, I peeked over in the di-rection of the front door. The door had been left wide open, sunlight streaming inside. I gasped and almost toppled over in shock.

A body lay sprawled across the open threshold . . .

Dying for
Strawberries

SHARON FARROW

_k_

KENSINGTON PUBLISHING CORP.

http://www.kensingtonbooks.com

KENSINGTON BOOKS are published by

Kensington Publishing Corp.
119 West 40th Street
New York, NY 10018

All Kensington Titles, Imprints, and Distributed Lines are
available at special quantity discounts for bulk purchases for
sales promotions, premiums, fund-raising, and educational or
institutional use.

Special book excerpts or customized printings can also be
created to fit specific needs. For details, write or phone the
office of the Kensington special sales manager: Kensington
Publishing Corp., 119 West 40th Street, New York, NY 10018,
attn: Special Sales Department, Phone: 1-800-221-2647.

Kensington and the K logo Reg. U.S. Pat & TM Off.

ISBN-13: 978-1-4967-0486-3
ISBN-10: 1-4967-0486-X
First Kensington Mass Market Edition: November 2016

eISBN-13: 978-1-4967-0487-0
eISBN-10: 1-4967-0487-8
First Kensington Electronic Edition: November 2016

10 9 8 7 6 5 4 3 2 1

Printed in the United States of America

To Emma Blair,
Who loves this magical lakeshore as much as I do.
And Minnie,
The best little parrot in the world. You are missed.

Chapter 1

"I was buried in strawberries up to my neck!"

The customer at the counter looked behind her in alarm. I signaled to my friend Natasha Bowman to keep her voice down.

Unfortunately, Natasha always got far too worked up about her dreams, especially if they included food. "I could not even see my arms, just giant strawberries everywhere!" She slapped her hand on the café table for emphasis, causing half the contents of her iced tea to spill over. "And I could not move! Not an inch. I looked in my dream dictionaries, but there is nothing about such a terrible thing. You are the berry expert, Marlee. Tell me. *Pozhalujsta!* Please!"

Busy bagging two jars of gooseberry jam, a dozen strawberry muffins, and a bottle of blueberry salsa, I couldn't do more than answer, "I'm a store owner, Natasha, not a seer. If you want your dreams interpreted, head down the street to Gemini Rising."

Gemini Rising was the town's New Age bookstore, which was owned by Drake Woodhill, a former Olympic runner and longtime astrologer.

"May all my hair fall out before I set foot in his store again!" To emphasize she meant business, Natasha shook her gorgeous almond-brown tresses. "My husband is right. Drake Woodhill is a liar and a fraud."

As I handed the shopping bag to my customer at the cash register, I shot Natasha a warning look. Memorial Day was two weeks ago, and tourist season had officially begun in our charming lakeshore village. At least six out-of-towners were milling about the store, with dozens more strolling along Lyall Street. It was an unspoken rule that business owners did not disparage fellow shopkeepers when outsiders were within earshot. Since Natasha and her husband ran a culinary supply store called Kitchen Cellar three blocks over, she should have known better.

"Enjoy the rest of your stay in Oriole Point," I said to the woman at the counter. She accepted the bag with one hand, while keeping a firm grip on her restless toddler with the other.

I waited until they had left before joining Natasha at one of the bistro tables scattered near the ice cream counter. I had a few moments to spare. My other customers were trying to decide between berry-scented candles and a boxed set of organic cranberry tea.

"You can't go around saying Drake is a fraud, especially in front of tourists. That could hurt his business." After grabbing a napkin, I mopped up the tea she had spilled.

"But he is," she replied in a mercifully lowered voice. "I went to him last week for my horoscope. He told me I was going to die. And soon, too."

"I don't believe that. He makes a point of not

telling anyone bad news. That's his policy. Nothing negative. Why do you think his blog is called *The Affable Astrologer*?"

"I don't know what this 'affable' means."

"Pleasant. Friendly."

She made a face. "He was not so pleasant when he read my chart. And the whole time, he stared at me with those pale blue eyes. Eyes like a ghost, he has. And he talks strange, too."

I bit back a chuckle. Drake was an urbane British gentleman from Yorkshire who had moved to Michigan ten years ago. He possessed a mischievous smile, excellent manners, and a dry sense of humor. And while Natasha spoke nearly perfect English, her own accent became far more pronounced than Drake's when she was upset or excited—which was most of the time.

"I can't see him warning you that you'll die soon. You must have misunderstood. After all, you look pretty fit and healthy. And you're two years younger than me."

Indeed, Natasha displayed more nervous energy than a room full of poodles. She was also attractive enough to have snagged the title of Miss Russia when she was twenty. The crown, her looks, and her ambition enabled her to move to the United States, where she quickly became the wife of a wealthy man twice her age. She once more flung her head back, calling attention to her long, wavy hair. All that hair, combined with her enormous brown eyes and lush figure, brought to mind the character of Jasmine in the Disney film *Aladdin*. Given how animated she usually was, it made sense that she often seemed like an animated character to me.

"I hear Drake is maybe a sorcerer," Natasha said. "Or a druid. You know, someone who talks to trees."

"Drake's not a sorcerer, a druid, or even a wizard. It might be a lot more exciting around here if he was. He's just a quiet Englishman who knows a lot about astrology. And don't listen to rumors. After tourism, gossip is the main occupation in town." I threw her a sly look. "There are still a few whispers about the beauty queen who married a rich Chicago developer."

"*Ne oskorblyaj menya.*"

"What?"

"I say, 'Do not insult me.' Do I look like a greedy girl who marries for money?" I was glad she didn't wait for my answer. "If I want a rich man, I stay in Russia and marry the idiot son of the minister of culture. Or the minister himself. Both of them are nicer than the man I did marry."

"That I believe. Even the Grinch is more agreeable than your husband."

"But Cole is like Prince Charming in the beginning. And he treated me as if I am his princess. I had only to ask for something, and he would see it was done like that." She snapped her fingers. "I do not know what happened. It is confusing."

I was confused, too. That description sounded nothing like the unpleasant Cole Bowman I knew. "First, it was a mistake to marry a man you'd known less than six weeks. Second, he was twice your age. Third, he was Cole Bowman."

"I like older men. They are easier to control." She shrugged. "But Cole ended up being not so easy."

"Let's not explore your marriage right now. As for Drake Woodhill, you're the first person to say an unkind thing about him."

She leaned closer. "He tells me Mars is transiting my eighth house."

"What does that mean?"

"I don't know. But I do not like it. He says I must get my affairs in order as soon as possible. And I should avoid arguments with angry men."

"Seems like good advice. Especially for someone married to Cole."

Natasha lowered her voice even more. "Drake knows how much we fight. Especially after Cole choked me on Valentine's Day. That was embarrassing."

"And painful, I imagine." Although embarrassment had probably factored in since the incident occurred in front of sixty other diners at the restaurant San Sebastian. A quick-thinking waiter had pulled Cole away from Natasha before he caused her to black out—or worse.

"Honestly, what does that husband of yours have to do before you divorce him? The man was strangling you."

"Oh, he just grabs my throat. If the waiter had not come, I would have scratched his eyes out with these." She held up her hands, which boasted long acrylic nails. "They are sharp like knives. Also, I know about his Achilles' foot."

"I think you mean his Achilles' heel."

"For Cole, that heel is in his head. His uncle tells me how Cole fell down the stairs when he was a boy and cracked open his skull. There is a spot right here"—she pointed to just above her left temple—"that doctors say means big trouble for him if it gets hit again. If he goes too far, I will smack him there. I tried once." Her expression turned icy. "One winter in Chicago, Cole threw me against a wall so hard, he breaks my arm. I want to hit him with a wine bottle using my other arm. But I am too slow." She shook her head. "That night, he almost breaks both arms."

My mouth fell open. I always feared the Bowman marriage was abusive, but I had never known for certain how bad things really were. "You must leave him. If you stay, he'll kill you! Listen to me. I have firsthand experience with marriages that end in murder."

She waved a dismissive hand. "You think too much about the silly woman on that *Sugar and Spice* show. She and her husband were *sumashedshiye*. They were crazy. Cole and I are not like that."

"The only difference is that you and Cole are alive and well, while Evangeline Chaplin is in prison. And John Chaplin is dead." I sighed with frustration. "It's dangerous to remain in your marriage. Eventually, one of those fights will go too far. If any man treated me the way Cole treats you, I'd smash him over both sides of his head!"

I looked up to see several tourists staring at us with obvious concern. At that moment, three more women entered the shop and made a beeline for the section displaying blackberry and blueberry wine. I couldn't spend more time today on Natasha's problems, especially since tomorrow was the big Strawberry Moon Bash. I still had to assemble the boxes of berry items I planned to sell at my booth along the river. Normally, Gillian would be helping me, but I'd sent her to the post office to ship out several large online orders.

"There are too many people in the store," I said in a voice barely above a whisper. "We shouldn't be talking about this. But please leave him before either of you come to blows again. There's a women's shelter in the county. I'll contact them for you."

"You do not understand, Marlee. It is not simple to walk away. Maybe if we are still in Chicago, Cole will not mind so much if I go. But after he loses his money, he says he will not part with anything else. And that includes me." Her face grew somber.

I took her hand. "The next time he tries to hurt you, you must come to me. I swear I will do everything I can to keep you safe."

"My brave berry girl. You should smother him with your strawberries." Natasha gave a rueful laugh. "Who knows? Maybe my dream means my angry husband will be killed by strawberries. And if he learns how much my horoscope cost, I would be the one who might be killed. Cole thinks about money all the time. Like Old Man Bowman thinks about Bigfoot."

Cole Bowman was enough of an unsavory topic of conversation. No way was I going to discuss his nutty uncle. Time for a change of subject.

"Are you going to the OPBA meeting tonight?" Every month, the Oriole Point Business Association met to discuss the town's retail interests. I was invited to join the board five months ago, when Kim Banks, the membership chairperson, moved to St. Joseph.

"Why should I go? Cole is on the board, not me."

"You're a business owner. Anyone who owns a business in Oriole Point is welcome."

"Kitchen Cellar is Cole's store. Only, he insists I must work there. He calls me the window dressing." She shuddered. "As if I care about waffle irons. It is a spa I want to open, but Cole holds on to money like it is glued to his fingers."

"That probably explains why he's the board treasurer."

"But you must go to the meeting tonight." The chorus of Katy Perry's "Roar" suddenly sounded, and Natasha fished her cell phone out of her handbag. Swiping at the phone, she looked down to see who was calling. "I think it will be interesting."

"What do you mean?" Before Natasha could reply, one of my customers held up what looked like a small metal baton.

"Excuse me, but what is this used for?" she asked.

"That's a muddler, which is basically a long pestle." I got to my feet and went over to her. "They range in length from nine to twelve inches. As you can see, I carry them in stainless steel and cherrywood." I held up one of each as the woman and her friends gathered around me. "Bartenders use them to mash herbs and fruit for drinks. If you've ever had a mint julep or a mojito, then you've enjoyed a concoction made with a muddler."

"I thought bartenders used blenders," one of them said.

"They do for a lot of drinks. However, some drink recipes specifically call for mashed berries. The bartender at San Sebastian makes a drink called a Dessert Fizz. If you watch him, you'll see he uses a muddler to mash strawberries with lemon juice and agave nectar." I smiled at the ladies. "If you haven't eaten at San Sebastian yet, you really should. It's the best restaurant in all of west Michigan."

A woman in the group held up a strawberry huller. "Can you show us how this works?"

To my left stood a butcher-block table displaying small containers of fresh strawberries. I grabbed one of the red and green hullers and proceeded to remove the leaves and stems from several strawberries with its steel claw.

"You can also hull strawberries with a plastic straw. Insert the straw at the tip of the berry and push it through until it comes out at the top, where the leaf is." I brought over several strawberry slicers. "These can also be used to slice eggs or mushrooms."

After a few moments, I let the women play about with the hullers, muddlers, and slicers without my hovering over them. I walked back to where Natasha sat. I would have apologized for leaving her alone, but whenever I'd glanced her way, she'd been busy texting on her phone. Even when I sat across from her once more, her thumbs continued to fly over the phone keyboard.

"Sorry that took so long."

Natasha kept her eyes on the phone. "You are a good saleswoman. Cole has hullers in our store, but he is lazy and does not show people how to use them. We do not sell many."

"It's time for me to get back to work. Piper's coming here later to talk about what I'm bringing to the Bash."

She finally tossed the phone into her white straw bag. "Oh, that Piper. She makes my head ache with this Strawberry Moon stuff. I bet she made the whole thing up."

"I thought so, too, until I did a little research. A Strawberry Moon occurs whenever a full moon in June falls on Friday the thirteenth. The next one won't take place for decades."

"Why strawberry? Will the moon look red?"

"No. But according to some Native American tribes, every full moon is named after something related to that month. For example, April has a full Pink Moon, since one of the first wildflowers to bloom then is pink phlox. Because the short harvest season for strawberries occurs now, the full moon for this month is often called the Strawberry Moon."

Natasha wagged her finger at me. "See, you are a strawberry expert."

"I just sell the berries. I don't grow them."

"But this winter you will marry one of those sexy men who run Zellar Orchards. And you know all about these pretty berry things." She gestured at the items in my sun-filled shop. "Who in town knows more about strawberries? *Nikto.* No one. You are the berry person."

She had me there. I was the owner of The Berry Basket, which sold berries, fresh and frozen, as well as anything made from berries. This included ice cream, muffins, jams, syrups, bread mixes, smoothies, coffees, and much more. I also carried an array of products tied to berries, from mugs and T-shirts stamped with our logo to actual berry baskets hand-woven in nearby Allegan County. In just two years, The Berry Basket had become one of the most successful small businesses in town. If it continued to grow, I hoped to be able to buy the building I rented in another three or four years. After that, I had plans for franchising The Berry Basket. Natasha was right. Aside from my fiancé and his family, I was the go-to person for berries in Oriole Point.

"Please tell me about my strawberry dream,

Marlee. Should I stay away from strawberries? Am I in danger?"

I took a deep breath before launching into my strawberry tutorial. "Strawberries generally represent happiness and purity. But in dreams, strawberries can mean that a person desires 'forbidden fruit' or that someone close to them has a secret wish. And if you pick the fruit in your dreams, it may symbolize repressed sexual desire."

Natasha looked worried. I hoped her ongoing marital troubles didn't include illicit affairs or perverse sexual practices.

Their arms filled with store items, the ladies who had asked about the muddlers made their way to the cash register at the same time another customer entered the store.

I stood up. "However, the Cherokee regard the strawberry as a good luck symbol. They often keep it in their homes as a reminder not to argue. So being buried in strawberries seems like a pretty great dream, symbolically speaking." I hurried over to cash my customers out.

Natasha got to her feet as well. Several of the women at the counter threw envious glances her way. I didn't blame them. Few females could compare with the former beauty queen. While I didn't regard myself as unattractive, compared to Natasha, I was just an average-looking brunette with a nice smile. Standing there in four-inch espadrille sandals, with her wavy hair spilling about her tanned shoulders, she looked as if she could once again take Miss Russia's crown. And her midriff-baring pink summer top and short pink skirt made her look as if she was still twenty years old. Small wonder Cole was insecure and jealous. He was a vicious troll who had somehow enthralled a sexy fairy queen.

"Ladies, the owner of the store over there is Marlee Jacob," Natasha called out to the customers at the register. "A few years ago, she lives in New York City and produces programs for the Gourmet Living Network." She smiled. "Famous ones, too. They still talk about her shows on TV and in magazines."

I shook my head at Natasha. The last thing I wanted to discuss was my six years at the Gourmet Living Network.

"Last fall *Vogue* mentions her homemade syrups. They are *ochen' vkusnye.* That means 'very delicious' in Russian." Natasha threw a last dazzling smile before leaving the store.

I hadn't finished bagging the organic teas before three of the women hurried to add bottles of blueberry syrup to their impressive pile on the counter. I owed Natasha a dinner at San Sebastian for that one, along with my best interpretation of the next dream she had about berries. And if she left Cole, I'd throw in an expensive bottle of wine.

With luck, she would leave before he tried to strangle her again.

Chapter 2

Tomorrow was the thirteenth of June, which fell on a Friday this year. Not that I was superstitious or dreaded the extra hours I'd be devoting to the Strawberry Moon Bash. In fact, I made certain to distract myself by working even harder than usual. And I wasn't surprised my store had been bustling all morning. Each summer Oriole Point attracted hordes of visitors drawn to Lake Michigan's sandy beaches, the surrounding vineyards and orchards, and our downtown shops and galleries.

But whenever I had a free moment, I remembered that tomorrow was the three-year anniversary of the end of my career at the Gourmet Living Network. Also known as the day when the star of the cooking show I had produced murdered her husband. As my old boyfriend liked to remind me, I might have had a checkered career in television, but at least it was never dull. I snuck a peek at my wall calendar during the hectic afternoon. Maybe everyone had gotten it wrong. Maybe today was Friday the thirteenth. There was no other explanation for how strange the day was turning out to be.

Two chattering customers accidentally broke a ceramic mug set, along with an expensive glass pitcher hand painted with raspberries. Next, a hyperactive child knocked over a towering display of bread mixes. Bees then found their way into the store and had hovered near my open pots of berry-flavored honey. This sent a woman into hysterics when she was almost stung.

An hour later, Aunt Vicki rushed into the shop. I was always happy to see my aunt, even if she did try to get me to foster or adopt one rescue animal after another. She ran an animal shelter called Humane Hearts and was always on the lookout for loving homes for her endangered strays. At last count, her son in Traverse City was the owner of six rescue dogs. I had no intention of following suit.

Before she could say a word, I held up my hand. "I can't take another animal right now. High season has just begun, and I won't have time to look after anything but myself." I aimed a warning look at her. "And no more ferrets. The last one I fostered bit me four times."

She took a napkin from one of the bistro tables and wiped her damp forehead. "I'm here because there's a stray Doberman puppy on Lyall Street. I've been trying to catch the little thing for over an hour, but I'm not quick enough. I'm terrified some tourist will run the pup over with their car. One nearly did about five minutes ago."

"Stay here. Gillian will get you an iced tea." I slipped off my blue chef apron. "I'll see what I can do."

Forty-five minutes later, I returned with a puppy and a scraped knee. It was a toss-up as to which of us was more exhausted. Who knew such little legs could run so fast?

"You're an angel," Aunt Vicki said as she took the puppy from me. "This poor little baby was seen yesterday, too. Imagine how hungry and tired he must be."

"I know how he feels." I scratched the puppy behind his ears.

Like many shop owners in Oriole Point, we kept a water bowl out front for thirsty dogs. Gillian brought it over now. The pup lapped up the water as if he hadn't drunk in days.

"I think we've got some dog biscuits behind the counter," Gillian said.

"Thanks, but there's puppy chow back at my house, along with a nice basket and blanket for him to curl up in. What he needs now is some peace and quiet." Aunt Vicki smiled. "Last week I had a call from a family interested in adopting a Doberman or a German shepherd. I'll probably be able to place him before I leave for the animal rights rally tomorrow."

After a quick kiss for my aunt and one for the puppy, I waved them off.

"You need some cold water yourself," Gillian said. "And a bandage for that knee."

But I barely finished downing my water bottle before someone yelled from outside our open door, "We need help here! Please hurry! He can't breathe!"

Gillian and I raced out front. A frantic girl was bent over a teenage boy sitting on the curbside bench in front of my store. They had been in my shop earlier. I remembered them since both had pale blond hair and wore identical running clothes.

"Is he allergic to strawberries?" I asked the girl whose cries had brought us running. A half-eaten strawberry muffin lay on the bench beside them.

But I didn't need her desperate nod to realize the boy was in the throes of anaphylaxis. My maternal grandfather had been severely allergic to strawberries and died after eating a pie he mistakenly thought was raspberry rhubarb. Ironically, my fiancé, Ryan, was also allergic, but to bee venom. I knew how to recognize the danger signs of a serious allergic reaction.

"Do you have an EpiPen with you?" I asked the young man.

His eyes were filled with fear. "I forgot it," he gasped.

A rash had spread over his bare arms, and I could see that it also covered his torso beneath his T-shirt. But rashes and hives weren't what I was worried about. It was his obvious struggle to breathe that frightened me; it meant his airway was beginning to swell up. A crowd of people gathered around us, and I heard someone call 911 on their cell.

I turned to Gillian. "Get the EpiPen I keep in the inside zippered pocket of my purse." With my family history, I had learned to be prepared. Last summer I'd been terrified after a bee stung Ryan during a family picnic at the Zellar Orchards. Three of his relatives carried their own EpiPens for exactly this sort of emergency. Since then, I had carried one, too.

As soon as Gillian left, a woman muscled her way through the crowd. "I've called EMS, Marlee." It was Denise Redfern, owner of the Tonguish Spirit Gallery next door.

Gillian was back in a flash and handed me the EpiPen. I needed to get the epinephrine into him as quickly as possible. Most allergies to strawberries were mild, no more than a rash or hives, maybe a little itching. But this poor kid was one of the few—like my grandfather—who was highly allergic to the fruit.

Taking the gray activation cap off the top of the pen, I gripped it in my fist with the black tip pointing down. Fortunately, the boy wore running shorts, which left most of his legs exposed. I positioned the black tip of the pen over his upper thigh. With a gentle but firm motion, I jabbed the black tip of the pen into his thigh. The young blond girl sobbed while I held the pen in place for the requisite ten seconds. After removing the pen, I massaged the injection area. In the distance I heard the siren of an ambulance. Oriole Point Hospital was only three miles away.

Holding it up to the sunlight, I examined the tip of the pen. I sighed with relief when I saw the needle was exposed, indicating the dose of epinephrine had been delivered. By this time, the EMS van had squealed to a stop in front of the store.

When the attendants rushed out with a stretcher, I explained to them what I had done. The boy, thankfully, seemed to be breathing a bit better.

"What did your brother eat?" I asked the weeping girl as I recapped the EpiPen tube.

"He's my boyfriend, not my brother. I bought strawberry muffins in your shop, and Alec wanted to taste one. He had told me earlier that he was allergic to strawberries, and I reminded him of that." She took a deep breath, trying to calm down. "But he said it was only fresh strawberries he had a problem with."

I squeezed her trembling hand. "All our products are made from fresh berries. And with an allergy that severe, he shouldn't get within five feet of anything with strawberries in it."

Tears rolled down her cheeks, and I gave her a quick hug.

"He's going to be fine," I reassured her, but I looked over my shoulder at one of the EMS attendants, who nodded. "They'll take you both to the hospital to make certain everything is okay." I stood up as she followed them to the ambulance. "And throw away those muffins."

"You're a lifesaver," Denise said with a smile.

"Nah. The EMS guys would have gotten here in time even if I didn't have the EpiPen." I gave the pen a slight toss. "I always keep one around because of Ryan. But every shopkeeper should have an EpiPen, especially during the summer."

Denise patted my shoulder, sending the silver bracelets on her wrist jangling. "I like your modesty, but you still helped save his life."

"She's right." Gillian linked arms with me as we returned to the store. "I bet someone in town will report the incident to the *Oriole Point Herald*. It could be next week's headline."

"Don't even think about it. I've had enough publicity to last me for a lifetime."

The store phone rang, and Gillian went to answer it. But I was going to make certain she did not go to the local weekly paper with this, even if the editor was her father.

When I glanced at the clock, I groaned. I hadn't

yet packed up the boxes for the Bash, even though I
had worked so hard today that I proved the truth of
my idiosyncratic name. After all, not many thirty-
year-old females were named after Jacob Marley, the
partner of Ebenezer Scrooge.

Blame my mother for such a whimsical decision.
She'd read Dickens throughout her pregnancy, while
working on her Ph.D. in English literature. It would
have been lovely had she chosen to name me Nell,
Estella, or even Dorrit. But my sudden appearance
on Christmas Eve had prompted a nod to *A Christmas
Carol*, which was aided by our last name of Jacob. I
would forever have to tolerate the amused reaction
of strangers who put the reversed name together.
And while I hoped I never became as selfish and as
greedy as Dickens's character, there were times when
I suspected my work ethic rivaled his.

Today was one of those days. For the next three
hours, the shop saw a steady stream of customers,
with one tour group buying a startling amount of
blueberry coffee. When we had a free moment,
Gillian and I unpacked a shipment of berry-scented
soaps. We also selected the strawberry-themed products for the Strawberry Moon Bash. I made certain to
include colorful posters listing fun facts about strawberries. My favorite: eating only eight strawberries
daily reportedly lowers blood pressure, reduces in-
flammation, improves cardiovascular health, and
reduces the risk of cancer.

With the weather growing warm, we whipped up a
dizzying number of strawberry smoothies. And the
taste for strawberries went beyond frosty drinks. By
closing time, every strawberry muffin, pie, cupcake,
and cookie had been sold. This did not surprise me.

Theo Foster was my resident baker, and I'd match his pastries against the finest patisserie in Paris. However, he did have a few quirks. Theo interacted so rarely with the residents of our village, we referred to him as the Phantom. A diligent employee, he arrived before dawn to bake in my shop and left by the time we opened at ten. Aside from that, he rarely left his cottage along the Oriole River. If I hadn't interviewed him for the job, I'd suspect a real phantom baked for me. But the soft-spoken fellow possessed a real gift for creating berry pastries. Although he wasn't responsible for the fruit pies. Those arrived fresh each day from Zellar Orchards, often delivered personally by my fiancé.

As for my culinary contribution, I had mysteriously acquired a talent for making syrups and jams. Both my homemade blueberry syrup flavored with lavender and my strawberry syrup infused with rosemary and basil had been featured in *Vogue*'s monthly What People Are Talking About section. It didn't hurt that an assistant editor at the magazine was an old roommate of mine from NYU. Whatever the reason, I was grateful for her friendship and her mentioning my syrups in the magazine. Online sales had been through the roof ever since. This year I planned to unveil a raspberry and ginger version.

Gillian stifled a yawn. A full-time student at Grand Valley State University, she spent most of her waking hours during the summer at The Berry Basket. The dynamic duo of Andrew and Dean Cabot rounded out the rest of my sales staff.

"It's after five, Gillian. Go home."

"Thanks. I'm meeting friends tonight for sushi." With a sigh of relief, she pulled off the band that held her ponytail in place. Gillian's curly blond hair spilled down her back. As someone named after a literary character, I liked to match people I met with their fictional equivalents. Gillian Kaminski's long blond hair, earnest expression, and fondness for the colors blue and white always brought to mind the heroine of *Alice in Wonderland*. Only Gillian's wire-rimmed glasses made her differ from Tenniel's famous illustrations of the intrepid Alice.

After flipping the CLOSED sign on the front door, we were headed for the shop's back room when someone knocked on the window.

I shook my head. "That has to be Piper. Leave it to her to wait until the last minute."

But the person banging on the window was not Piper Lyall-Pierce. I unlocked the door and stuck my head out. "Max, why are you knocking on the window instead of the door?"

Max Riordan walked over. "You have too many posters on the door. I can't see inside."

I stepped out to meet him. As soon as I did, a roll of thunder sounded from the direction of the lake. In the past hour, the skies had gone from hazy sunlight to dark, windswept clouds. Out of habit, I glanced down Lyall Street, which ended blocks away on the sandy shores of Lake Michigan. A mere fifteen-minute stroll along the Oriole River and the marina took you right onto the beach. Even from my storefront, I could enjoy the lake vista, along with the white lighthouse that guarded the entry to the Oriole River. I didn't think there was a more scenic downtown anywhere on the lakeshore. Although at the moment, the dark skies and flashes of lightning made the vista a bit ominous.

"What's going on?" I asked.

"Is Natasha here? I heard she came into your shop."

"She left hours ago. Is something wrong?" That worrisome horoscope flashed into my head, which was silly. Natasha loved to pop in and out of every shop on Lyall Street; if she spent more than an hour in her own store every day, I would be shocked.

Max ran a hand through his mop of red hair. A true ginger, he reminded me of the freckled, red-haired character of Ron Weasley in the Harry Potter novels, although he was a good ten to twelve years older. He was even tall, lanky, and had oversize feet. But as far as I knew, he possessed no magical powers.

"No one's seen her since around four," he said. "That's when the big fight happened."

"What big fight?" Gillian joined us by the door.

"I thought everyone downtown heard Natasha and Cole arguing."

"We turned the air on because it was getting too warm," I said. "Once I shut the door, we can't hear much from outside. How did you hear them blocks away at the harbor?"

Max owned the charter fishing and outfitter store on Oriole Point's pier. No matter how much the Bowmans screamed at each other, he couldn't have heard anything from that far away, unless the couple had exchanged gunfire.

"I was sitting for Carson at his gallery. He had the door open, and we heard them yelling." Carson White was a celebrated artist who had relocated to Oriole Point from Chicago twenty-five years ago. He'd recently launched a project where he promised to paint the portrait of each full-time resident. I wasn't scheduled to sit for him until September.

"How's the portrait going?" Gillian asked.

"I'll let you know when he's had longer than an hour to work on it. Look, I only want to know where Natasha's gone. It sounded like a pretty serious argument."

"How bad was it?" I asked, getting a sick feeling in my stomach.

"Bad enough for Odette to call the police."

Odette Henderson owned Lakeshore Holiday, a popular holiday-themed store that sold nutcrackers, Christmas ornaments, and Halloween decorations year-round.

My anxiety grew. "Did he hurt Natasha? Is she okay?"

"Odette saw her leave their store after the fight. She said Natasha looked upset but didn't seem hurt. The police showed up a few minutes later."

"Thank God," I said. "I hope they arrested Cole."

"Don't know why they would. He's the one who was injured. Cole claims Natasha hit him with a pizzelle maker."

"What!" I suddenly recalled Natasha explaining what part of his head she would strike if things got too violent during their arguments. "Where did she hit him? What part of his head?"

Max gave me a curious look. "I don't know. I wasn't there. And Natasha was gone by the time the police arrived."

"Who told you Natasha was in my store?"

"Drake said Hiram from The Wiley Perch heard from Sheila at Sweet Dreams that Anne at Michigan

Mudworks saw Natasha walk out of The Berry Basket earlier."

The next person to add to that would probably have been Colonel Mustard in the drawing room.

"Odette claims the police went to Natasha's house, but she wasn't there," Max continued.

It was on the tip of my tongue to mention how I had advised Natasha to come to me after their next big fight, but I thought better of it. If she had hit Cole during an argument today, he would want to strike back at her—literally. Until I got her to a safe house, I'd better keep quiet.

"I don't see what the big deal is, Max. Those two had another fight, and this time Cole got hurt instead of Natasha. Remember she briefly had a restraining order after Valentine's Day."

"Both of them should be restrained from even looking at each other," Gillian added.

"I agree. Did they take Cole to the hospital?"

Max shook his head. "He refused to go. But he's mad as hell."

"That's probably the end of the Bowman fireworks for today, unless Old Man Bowman shows up. Then all bets are off."

"I heard he went up north," Gillian said. "He told my dad he was off to catch bluefish. But everyone knows it's time for his annual summer hunt for Bigfoot."

"There are times I think he is Bigfoot," I said.

Gillian smiled. "Maybe Old Man Bowman can track down Natasha."

"Anyway, Cole is pressing charges against her," Max said.

"Are you kidding me? After the terrible way he's

treated her? I'm tempted to hit Cole myself, only with a kitchen appliance of my choosing."

"Try a toaster," Gillian suggested. "That should knock him right out."

"I'm serious, ladies. Cole is spitting mad. I wish he were in the hospital, for Natasha's sake. If he finds her before the police do, she might get hurt."

This whole thing could spiral out of control. Maybe it already had. I thought a moment. "Does anyone know what started the fight today?"

Max shrugged. "I think part of the fight was about strawberries. We heard the word *strawberry* being yelled a few times. That's why I thought about your store, marzipan."

Back in high school, "marzipan" had been Max's nickname for me. I noticed he had started to call me that again during the past year. This did not sit well with my fiancé.

Gillian looked over at me. "Why would they fight about strawberries?"

The whole incident seemed as senseless as the Bowman marriage. "Natasha dreamed she was buried in strawberries. She asked me this morning what it symbolized," I said.

"I hope it doesn't symbolize disaster." Max brushed back his unruly hair once more. "Anyway, if you hear anything about Natasha, let me know."

"I think he's got a thing for you," Gillian said after he left. "If you weren't engaged, I bet Max would go after you big-time."

"No way." I laughed, as if the idea of Max wanting me was silly. But I suspected she was right. "We dated in high school but broke up the day before prom night. That should tell you how well things turned out. We're just friends now. And not friends with benefits, either."

Before Gillian could reply, someone banged on the door.

"What now?"

When I opened the door once more, Piper Lyall-Pierce brushed past me as if I was a doorman letting her into the building. A striking blond woman in her late forties, Piper was always as well groomed as a privileged Edith Wharton character. She possessed the same entitled view of life as well.

"This Bash will be the death of me." She plopped herself down on a bistro chair, while flinging an overstuffed Birkin bag onto the table. "I've been running around since seven in the morning, coordinating all the booths and tents. One of the bands tried to cancel on me. Something about the lead singer's wife being about to go into labor. I told them we signed a contract for all five members of the Oriole River Band. And if all five don't show up for the Bash, there will be a nice breach of contract lawsuit to go with their baby announcements."

I fought to keep a straight face, while Gillian giggled.

"Then there's the OPBA meeting tonight. We should have rescheduled. At least I can get everyone up to snuff on how the Bash is progressing. But I'll never get any sleep at this rate." Another roll of thunder sounded overhead. She pointed at the ceiling. "Now we have this ridiculous storm front. I checked my phone's weather app. It says it might rain through tomorrow night. Well, not if I have anything to say about it. The full moon must be completely visible for the Bash, and I insist on clear skies for the fireworks. I won't accept anything less."

"Your connections are more impressive than I thought." I walked over to the pile of boxes in front of the counter. "By the way, I've already packed up what I intend to sell at my booth tomorrow night."

She slid her tablet from the green leather Birkin. "I need a list of everything to make certain it's strawberry related."

"Already e-mailed the file to you." After two years of being a business owner in Oriole Point, I knew enough to be one step ahead of Piper, otherwise you would forever be marked as a shiftless fool. "And I talked to the electrician about running a line to our booth so we can blend smoothies and drinks."

"I can't believe you got us permission to serve alcoholic drinks," Gillian said.

"Just make certain to check for IDs." Piper read for a moment. "I see you're bringing strawberry-themed teas, candy, jam, jewelry, mugs. It's smart that you're including strawberry slicers, muddlers, and hullers. I might buy a huller myself."

I wasn't certain why she would need a huller. Not only were the Lyalls the richest family in town, but she was also married to a wealthy retired executive. The only reason she would need a strawberry huller was if her personal chef had requested one.

"Did you hear about the big fight between Natasha and Cole?" Gillian asked.

"Those dimwits. I heard them screaming at the top of their lungs when I was talking to Cindy at the cheese shop. I have no idea what the fight was about. Half of it was in Croatian."

"Natasha's Russian, not Croatian."

Piper threw me an exasperated look. "What does it matter? She was yelling so loud, they probably heard her back in St. Petersburg. Assuming that's where Miss Beauty Queen is really from. I find some of her dramatic stories hard to believe."

"You've always disliked her," I protested. "I have no idea why."

"I don't trust her. And I don't trust Cole, either." She put her tablet back into her bag. "I've never met a more tiresome couple in my life."

"I hope Natasha's okay," I said. "No one's seen her since the argument."

"I wouldn't worry about that young woman. Natasha would survive a tsunami." Another deafening roll of thunder sounded overhead. "Which is what this absurd storm sounds like."

Before Piper could gather her things, the front door to the shop flew open. Cole Bowman stood framed in the doorway. If this were a movie, a crash of lightning would have sounded while the camera panned over his sullen face, dark beetle brows, and slicked-back thinning hair. For years, I'd tried to imagine what fictional character he reminded me of, but the only image that came to mind was a bipedal lizard.

He threw his briefcase onto the display table where my jars of flavored honey were stacked. Several fell over, but he paid no attention. "Where's my wife, Marlee?"

Now that he stood before me, I could see that Natasha had swung the pizzelle maker at his nose. In fact, his nose was so swollen and bruised, it made his already unnerving features even more sinister. I gave a sigh of relief that Natasha had not tried to strike him anywhere near his left temple. At least she hadn't meant to kill him.

"How would I know where Natasha is?" I asked.

"She was here. Everyone saw her come into your store."

"That was hours ago. And she left before noon. I don't know where she went after the two of you fought."

"Don't give me that. You think I don't know how you lying females stick together? If I find out you're protecting Natasha, you'll regret it. I never wanted her to be friends with you, anyway. You're a bad influence. Too bad Ryan doesn't know how to keep you in line." Before I could say anything, he turned to Piper. "And you're even worse."

Piper stood up, looking her most imperious. As a descendant of one of the founding families of Oriole Point, as well as the wife of the mayor, Piper Lyall-Pierce quailed before no man. "Stop all this posturing. You've already been run out of Chicago. If you keep this up, Oriole Point will no longer be the right fit for you, either."

He narrowed his eyes at her. "I'm as much a native of Oriole Point as you are. Certainly, I'm more of a native than your husband. You've had things your own way far too long. Time to let someone else take charge. I'd run this place a hell of a lot better than you and Lionel have."

"The same way you ran your company in Chicago?" She lifted a beautifully arched eyebrow. "I hardly think we need to drive our town into bankruptcy."

I could almost see the steam rising off him as his anger grew. "At least, I've actually gone out and earned money."

"And lost it all, too. By the way, don't accuse me of not working. I've spent the past fifteen years running the visitors bureau."

"You don't even take a salary for that." Cole smirked. "Of course, why should you take a salary? You spend most of your time drinking lattes at Coffee by Crystal and planning useless things like this Bash for everyone to waste their time and money on."

"You know perfectly well a percentage of the proceeds from the Bash goes to local charities. Which is the only way to wring a penny out of a greedy miser like you."

"How dare you call me a miser, you rich hag!"

I held up my hand. "Okay, guys. I want to close up the store, and I don't have time for whatever this is."

But they weren't listening to me.

"The Lyalls haven't put in an honest day's work since that ancestor of yours opened up the lumber mill," Cole continued. "Since then, the whole pack of you has done little else but lobby for everything in town to be named after you."

That was the wrong thing to say to Piper. "There wouldn't even be an Oriole Point if not for my family. As for the Bowmans, none of you have had a single worthwhile idea, except for your uncle who invented that silly contraption. And he's been mad as a hatter ever since. The rest of you have been living off his fortune." She sniffed. "Or, in your case, losing that fortune. I see now why your mother divorced your dad and left town as soon as she could."

Cole's sallow face flushed crimson, and I saw his fists clench. "If you were a man, I'd beat you to the ground. If you don't keep your tongue under control, I still might."

I hurried to stand between them. "You need to leave, Cole. Otherwise you're going to be embroiled in your second fight today. And I don't think you want another blow to the head."

He now turned his ire in my direction. "I don't like people threatening me."

"Who does? Now leave my store, or I'm calling the police."

He gave me a cold stare. "Did Natasha mention anything about the strawberry fields?"

"Strawberries? Do you mean her dream about the strawberries?"

"Dream? What are you talking about? I don't give a damn about her stupid dreams. It's the strawberry fields she's bothering me about. Don't play dumb with me."

"I think the blow to your head has made you even more irrational than usual. Go home and lie down. By the time you wake up, Natasha will have returned, and the two of you can fight about strawberries all you want."

He pointed a finger at me. "If she doesn't come back, Marlee, I'm going to blame you. Or do you think I don't know you're always telling her to divorce me? Bad enough you're meddling in our marriage. I won't stand for either you or Natasha interfering in business matters."

With a last seething look at Piper, Cole turned on his heel and left. Although the storm hadn't started yet, it had kicked up strong winds, and I struggled to close the door behind him.

Piper slung her bulging purse onto her shoulder.

"If he does anything to upset my Strawberry Moon Bash, I may have to run him down with Lionel's Hummer."

I sighed. "I don't know why you still own that Hummer. It gets no mileage at all."

"It suits us." What was left unspoken was that she and her husband could afford it.

"Did either of you understand what Cole was saying about strawberries?" Gillian looked puzzled. "Maybe the head injury's worse than anyone thought."

"I don't know how bad his injury is," I said. "But this is the first time I ever suspected Cole Bowman might be as crazy as his uncle."

As soon as I turned from the door, I spied Cole's leather briefcase lying on the table where the honey pots sat. "He forgot his briefcase."

Piper's eyes widened with interest. "We should open it up. I've always wondered what he carries in that thing. I wouldn't be surprised if he's got a handgun in there."

"Don't be ridiculous. We're not looking inside. Let me see if I can catch him before he gets too far." Ignoring Piper's disappointed expression, I grabbed his briefcase and left.

The sky roiled with wild black clouds, while the wind whipped my hair about my face so hard, my cheeks stung. I figured Cole would be heading in the direction of his shop, since that was where his car would be parked. I saw him about a block ahead, walking with his head down. Thunder rumbled once more, followed by several fearsome flashes of lightning. The rain would be coming down any second, and it promised to be a doozy.

Everyone else must have thought so, too. I saw only three other people out on the streets, and they were running for shelter.

"Cole, wait!" But my shout was lost among the howling wind and the thunder. He had crossed to the other side of the street.

At that moment, a car zoomed from around the corner several blocks ahead. I hurried across the street, assuming the car would continue down Lyall. Instead, it made another sharp turn. Even with the thunder, I heard the piercing squeal of the tires. So did Cole, who swiveled his head in that direction. For a second, he stood frozen in the middle of the intersection of Lyall and Iroquois. I was only a few feet behind him and stopped short as well.

The car barreled straight toward him, and I let out a strangled cry. Cole threw himself onto the sidewalk as the car sped past, missing him by inches. When I reached him, Cole lay spread-eagled on the pavement. I knelt down and touched his shoulder.

"Cole, are you okay? Were you hit?"

He didn't move for a moment. "I'm fine," he muttered. "I'm fine."

"Are you sure? I saw the whole thing. I swear that car looked like it was deliberately trying to hit you." I helped him to his feet. "Did you see who was driving?"

Cole shook off my hand. "Don't be an idiot. That car wasn't trying to run me down. It was just going too fast."

"The police should know about this. You could have been killed!"

His expression turned as dark as the skies. "We don't need to call the police because some drunk driver was speeding. And why are you following me, anyway?"

I held up his briefcase. "You left this behind at the store. I wanted to give it back to you."

Cole snatched it from me without a word of thanks.

I stifled the impulse to kick him in the shins for being such an ill-mannered pig. "Whoever was driving that car meant to run you down. You should report it."

"I don't have time for this lunacy." After giving a tug to his rumpled shirt, Cole marched away from me. He cast one last look over his shoulder. "And tell Natasha to get back home!"

The first raindrops began to fall as I headed back to my store. By now my mood was as dark as Cole's. I didn't care how much Cole tried to deny it; the driver of that car had tried to run him over. And of all the people who might want Cole Bowman dead, Natasha was at the top of the list. Only I didn't want to believe my friend had just tried to murder her husband.

Chapter 3

By the time I ran down the block to The Wiley Perch, the storm had approached *Wizard of Oz* proportions. Despite the downpour, I didn't drive. I wouldn't have been able to find a parking space along Lyall Street during tourist season anyway. Still, my rain poncho had done little to keep my capri pants from getting soaked. But I wisely chose to run barefoot down the street, having stowed my sandals in the tote bag I was taking to the OPBA meeting.

Ryan greeted me at the restaurant door, where he swooped me up for a kiss and an embrace.

"Now you're as wet as I am," I said when we broke apart. My rain poncho had soaked the front of his T-shirt and jeans.

"It was worth it." He helped me take off my poncho, then handed it off to Amber, the restaurant hostess. "Besides, I wanted to be the first to kiss the heroine of the day."

"We heard how you saved that boy's life, Marlee," Amber said as she led us to our favorite booth by the window. "My dad said drinks and dessert are on the house tonight." Amber Wasserman was the eighteen-year-old daughter of The Wiley Perch's owner, Hiram, and spent her summers working at the family restaurant.

"I only did what any person would who had an EpiPen handy. It was nothing out of the ordinary. So we're paying for everything." I nodded toward Ryan. "Actually, he's paying."

"She's worth the money, too, as long as she doesn't order dessert." Ryan winked at Amber, who blushed. I didn't blame her.

Ryan Zellar gave off a sexy country boy vibe. His muscles came from working at the orchards, not the gym, and he was brown from the sun even in winter. In fact, all the Zellar boys were tall, cute, and had honey-blond hair that was as soft as corn silk. I found it ironic that my favorite Zellar was named Ryan, as he bore a striking resemblance to movie hunk Ryan Gosling. When our engagement became public knowledge this past January, you could practically hear the hearts breaking all over the county. For some, it was especially depressing since Ryan had gotten divorced six years ago. More than a few single women in Oriole Point had hoped to be the one to catch him on the rebound, with no success. But as soon as I moved back to town, Ryan had quickly moved in on me. Looking back, it seemed I had very little to do with it. Ryan Zellar had fastened on me, and that was that. I wasn't complaining. Although there were times when I wondered how long it would last. I was notoriously unlucky in the romance department.

Six months into my first serious romance in college, my boyfriend was deported back to Bolivia, where he rejoined the young wife he had neglected to mention. Even my first date as an anxious fifteen-year-old went awry when my equally nervous escort left me sitting alone in the movie theater while he called his older brother to take him home. Once I realized he wasn't coming back, I settled in to enjoy the rest of *Harry Potter and the Chamber of Secrets* before alerting my mom and dad of the aborted dating attempt. I didn't go out on another date for two years. Small wonder I kept waiting for the other shoe to drop with Ryan.

"Do you need menus, or are you having the usual?" Amber asked.

Ryan and I looked at each other.

"The usual," I replied. "Except I need a cold beer tonight instead of iced tea. I'll have any Michigan pale ale."

"Sounds great to me. Make that two, Amber."

She smiled. "I'm serving you tonight to make sure you get special treatment, Marlee."

"Don't fight it, Florence Nightingale," Ryan teased after she walked away.

"With luck, everyone will forget about this by to-morrow." I dug my sandals out of my tote bag and slipped them on. As a local, I was allowed to do certain things that tourists weren't, but being bare-foot in a restaurant wasn't one of them.

Ryan sat back in the booth seat with a puzzled ex-pression. "What's with the cold beer? I can hardly get you to drink on New Year's Eve, let alone the middle of June."

"Today was crazy. The poor boy with the allergic reaction was the least of it. Right after I closed the store, Piper and Cole decided to show up at the same time. That didn't go well."

"I heard Cole and Natasha had another big fight at their store."

"I won't ask how you found out about that at your orchards, but yes, they went at it again. This time the police were called." I stared out the window in the direction of the lake. No matter how stressed out I got, the sight of my favorite Great Lake always re-laxed me. Even through the pouring rain, I could see the Oriole River and the marina just below us. Up ahead were the green channel markers, and past them stood the white stone lighthouse, already blink-ing at the end of the point. Beyond that were the storm-tossed waters of Lake Michigan.

I sighed. "The whole day feels off. Bad enough tomorrow is the anniversary of when Evangeline Chaplin killed her husband. You and I both know the cable shows will be dredging up the story again, like they've done every year since it happened."

"You can't blame them. I mean, how many other celebrity chefs have put arsenic in their husband's cake?"

Since I had been called as a witness at the Chaplin trial, I knew far too well the notorious details of that murder. "I'm still shocked Evangeline actually killed him. Then Natasha has this huge fight with Cole today, which only makes me think about the Chap-lins. Not that I need reminding. To top everything off, a speeding car almost killed Cole about an hour ago."

Ryan looked startled. "You're kidding."

I described the car racing down Lyall Street.

"Sounds like a drunk driver," he said when I was done.

"That's what Cole thought, but he's wrong. The car made a sharp turn before heading right for him. If he hadn't thrown himself out of the way, Cole Bowman would be lying in the morgue tonight. And before you ask, I can't tell you anything about the car except it was a dark color and was moving fast."

"I know she's your friend. But be honest. Who has a better reason to want Cole dead than Natasha?"

I shook my head. "It doesn't seem like something Natasha would do. She's too impulsive. If she wanted to kill him, she'd do it in the middle of one of their fights. Not seven hours later." I sighed. "I don't want to end the day discussing people who murder their spouses. If only there wasn't an OPBA meeting tonight. I'd like nothing more than to go home and soak in my tub, surrounded by about ten scented candles."

Ryan rubbed his foot up against my bare ankle. "Your tub or mine?"

"Mine. I'm the one with the claw-foot tub big enough for both of us."

"Your house, it is. I'll have the candles lit by the time you get back from the meeting."

"You could come to the meeting, too."

He made a face. "No way. The only one I went to last year put me to sleep. That's one of the reasons I like not owning a downtown business."

Unlike Ryan, I felt compelled to show up. Oriole Point's main source of income was tourism, which meant an enormous amount of time and effort was focused on the sixty-plus stores and restaurants in the downtown area. Like the village of Saugatuck directly to the north of us, Oriole Point had also become an art colony in the early years of the twentieth century. This explained the large number of galleries and art studios found on every block. And even though a little over four thousand people lived here year-round, our annual tourists often numbered in the millions.

The presence of so many artists—along with a large influx of people moving here from Chicago—also meant Oriole Point was not your typical small town. Our politics tended to be liberal, a Broadway director ran the summer theater, and rainbow flags were a common sight in front of homes and churches. Oriole Point had been a great place to grow up, and I was happy to discover it was an even better place to move back to. That still didn't make me look forward to another OPBA meeting tonight.

We sat back as our drinks and appetizers arrived at the table. For a few moments, we enjoyed the cold beer and hot batter-dipped mushrooms in silence.

After the food gave me some much-needed energy, I felt ready for conversation again. "Piper's going to talk about the Strawberry Moon Bash at the meeting. Since Zellar Orchards will have a booth there, you might want to hear what she has to say."

"Another reason not to go."

"I heard she purchased special fireworks." To be honest, I was surprised she hadn't arranged for fighter pilots to fly over in formation. Piper did nothing in half measures.

Ryan stared over my shoulder. "Your boyfriend's coming this way."

"My boyfriend?" I turned to see Max heading in our direction from the rear dining room. The restaurant was crowded, and he had to weave his way through the tables. "I can't believe you're still jealous I dated Max back in high school. Jeff Couch took me on my first date when I was fifteen. Why aren't you jealous of Jeff? He's still in town." I neglected to mention how that disastrous movie date had turned out.

Ryan snorted. "Like I'd be jealous of a thirty-year-old puppeteer who lives with his mother."

"Hey, marzipan," Max said. "I heard you saved a teenager who was having an anaphylactic attack. You should have told me when I came by your shop."

"It was no big deal. I mean, it was a big deal to the boy, but it's like using the Heimlich maneuver. If you're there when someone's in trouble, you do what you can."

He gently mussed my hair, and I saw Ryan narrow his eyes at us. "Anyway, I wanted to let you know I think something funny is going down at the meeting tonight."

"Funnier than usual?" Ryan asked.

Max didn't bother to look at him. This thing between the two of them had to stop.

"What do you mean?" I asked.

"I bumped into Keith VanderHoff an hour ago. I told him I planned to skip the meeting, but he said it was crucial everyone in OPBA be there. He has troubling news to impart. Those were his exact words. He's sent every OPBA member an e-mail about coming."

Keith VanderHoff was an attorney who served as the board's legal counsel. This didn't sound promising. "Troubling? He didn't tell you anything more?"

"Nope." He finally looked over at Ryan. "I'll let the two of you get on with dinner. Your perch and smashed potatoes should be almost done."

"Know what our favorites are, do you?" Ryan asked.

"A wild guess. Perch strips and smashed garlic potatoes are everyone's favorites here." He smiled at me. "See you at the meeting, marzipan."

Ryan watched him depart. "He can't wait for us to break up. And I wish he'd stop calling you that stupid name."

"And I'm waiting for you to stop being so silly about him." I caught sight of Amber heading our way. "Although it looks like Max was right about our food being ready."

"Here you are." Amber put down the plates of perch and potatoes with a flourish. "Let me know if I can get you anything else." She turned to go, then stopped. "Oh, and Max Riordan paid for your dinner, Marlee. He said it was the least he could do for someone who saved a life today." She beamed at me before hurrying off.

Ryan's frown deepened. "The man is way too interested in you. And I've changed my mind. I *will* go to the OPBA meeting tonight. Just to keep an eye on you two."

I was not in the mood for this today. And after I'd lived through the Chaplin trial, any hint of jealousy or possessiveness was enough to send me running for the hills. "Look, I have no patience with this suspicious boyfriend thing. It's insulting. I'm sorry your first wife cheated on you, but I'm not going to be the one who pays for it. I was dragged into a murder case brought on by jealousy, and I have zero tolerance for it. I'm serious. If you don't trust me, Ryan, we can call it quits any time."

His expression turned alarmed and a little fearful. He grabbed my hand and held it tight. "I do trust you. One hundred percent. It's Harbor Max I don't trust."

My only response was to finish off my beer. Now Ryan would be bringing up Max all night. Then there was the mystery news at the OPBA meeting. And all my calls to Natasha had gone straight to voice mail. I didn't know where she was or what condition she was in.

Yep, it felt like Friday the thirteenth to me.

Chapter 4

The worst of the storm had passed by the time the OPBA meeting began, but the mood in the room seemed as surly as the skies. It could be because we met in city hall, which did not have air-conditioning. The official reason for our lack of cooled air was that it was a historic building, and local historians wished to preserve the integrity of the original structure. Most of us assumed the town officials were simply too cheap to pay for air-conditioning.

Usually, this wasn't a problem. The lake breezes coming through the wide windows kept things tolerable, along with several table fans. But on a muggy summer evening, with rain preventing the windows from being fully open, it felt like we'd all been stuffed into a giant plastic bag. As a board member, I sat at a long table on the upraised stage in the meeting hall. The windows were cracked open to allow in some fresh air, but they also let in the rain. Deciding I'd rather be wet than die from heatstroke, I took a seat at the end of the table, by the window.

When she arrived, Tess Nakamura grabbed the

chair next to me. Tess and I had been best friends since fifth grade, when both of us made history by tying for first place at the regional spelling bee competition.

"A tornado touched down in Kalamazoo." Tess shrugged off her raincoat. "And parts of M-89 are flooded. I got soaked running here from the car. I look like a drowned rat."

"Oh, please. Not even a monsoon would ruin your hair."

Tess wore her short black hair in a sleek asymmetrical cut that seemed impervious to the weather. In contrast, my own hair had turned so frizzy from the humidity, I looked as if I had stuck my finger in a light socket.

"Good thing the storm hit today and not tomorrow," Tess said. "Piper will have a seizure if the skies aren't clear for the Bash. I'm relieved David and I won't have to operate a booth. I've never been happier that we sell only glass stuff."

Tess was being modest. She and her longtime boyfriend, David Reese, were graduates of the Rhode Island School of Design. Their store on Iroquois Street was part showroom, part studio, where customers watched the duo create breathtaking pieces of blown glass. I regarded them as the local successors to that glassworking master Dale Chihuly.

I sat back, waving a file folder in front of my face. "It feels like a lagoon in here."

Tess opened her laptop. As OPBA secretary, it was her responsibility to transcribe the minutes. Looking around, I noticed that all the board members were now sitting at the table.

Diego Theroux, owner/chef of San Sebastian,

waved at me from the other side of the table. Our restaurant representative, Diego was a jaw-droppingly handsome man, only two or three years older than me. He always treated the meetings as a lark and spent most of the time catching a brief nap or playing on his phone. No one complained. Most of the women—and some of the men—wanted only an extended opportunity to gaze upon him.

I leaned closer to Tess. "Did you hear about the fight between Natasha and Cole?"

She pursed her lips. "Since our studio is right behind their store, I literally heard them. I couldn't understand what they were screaming about though. Honestly, I can't believe those two. How embarrassing to behave like that in front of customers. They have no sense of what is appropriate behavior."

As soon as I read *Sense and Sensibility* when I was a teenager, I had pegged Tess as a modern-day version of the cool and collected Elinor Dashwood. Good to know the adult Tess hadn't changed since then.

Piper stood up from her seat at the center of the table. On one side sat her husband, Lionel Pierce, also known as our mayor. He was an attractive, barrel-chested man of sixty. A former top executive with Fleming Appliance in Grand Rapids, he had retired early after making a considerable fortune. Their marriage initially sparked some surprise since Lionel was African American and Piper seemed the epitome of WASP privilege. But they were well matched; indeed, Lionel had a manner nearly as patrician as Piper's. And both Pierces were two of the most politically conservative residents of Oriole Point. I liked them, anyway.

On the other side of Lionel Pierce sat Juliet

Haller, president of OPBA and owner of Neverland, a children's toy and bookstore. By rights, Juliet should be at the center of the table since Piper was only OPBA's events coordinator, but everyone knew that OPBA—and maybe all of Oriole Point itself—was Piper's domain.

"It's showtime," I murmured to Tess.

Piper scanned the room from the stage until everyone quieted down. I was surprised to see so many people sitting on the wooden chairs out front. Usually, only shopkeepers with a request or a grievance bothered to show up for an OPBA meeting, but tonight it seemed as if half the business community was in attendance. Keith VanderHoff's e-mails had been effective.

"Before Juliet calls the OPBA meeting to order, I want to remind everyone the Strawberry Moon Bash begins promptly at ten tomorrow morning with the craft fair at River Park. Because we are catering to families and children during the day, I've contracted for an inflatable bounce house, a dunk tank, and a hot shooter."

"What in heaven's name is a hot shooter?" Drake Woodhill seemed out of sorts, but as the board's vice president, he had little choice but to show up or face Piper's wrath.

"A basketball hoop with netting," the mayor replied. No one in Oriole Point had a more deep and melodious voice. A shame he'd spent most of his professional life as an executive. With a voice as rich as his, he could have been a great operatic baritone.

Piper stepped back from the table. Despite the storm's humidity, Piper appeared as sharp and put together as she had earlier in my shop. She could have posed for a Ralph Lauren ad in her ankle-length white linen dress. And when she moved to stand in front of the table, I realized that her gold heels exactly matched the dress's gold braided belt. Even more enviable, her chin-length blond bob was smooth as glass, without a single wave or snarl to show it had suffered from the storm-tossed winds.

"As I was saying, there will be amusements for the children during the day, as well as vendors selling cotton candy, popcorn, and as many strawberry drinks and foods as possible."

I fanned myself even faster. She was telling us things we already knew. Piper had convened Strawberry Moon Bash meetings every month since February, when the idea of a Bash first occurred to her.

"Of course, those of you selling drinks or food products will be manning your booths from noon until the start of the fireworks."

A chorus of protests rang out.

I raised my hand. "Excuse me, Piper, but my understanding was that except for kiddie vendors and craft fair participants, everyone else would work their booth from five o'clock on."

Several shopkeepers vehemently agreed with me. Piper frowned, which caused a rare wrinkle to appear on her unlined forehead. "Very well. Open your booths at five, but I find it mystifying that any of you would turn down business during the day."

"We run our shops during the day," Michael Gerringer, our public relations chair, reminded her. He owned Muffins and More on Lyall Street. Most of us called him Muffin Mike, but not to his face.

"We're lucky this Strawberry Moon comes only twice a century," I whispered to Tess.

Piper now shot us an ominous smile. "Although

tomorrow is a special Strawberry Moon, since it falls on Friday the thirteenth, there's no reason we can't repeat the event annually."

Drake Woodhill muttered, "Bloody hell."

"After all, our research has revealed that every June full moon is called a Strawberry Moon. Think what a wonderful way this is to bring in more tourists during the month." Piper's smile grew even brighter. "No other lakeshore town holds a full moon festival. We'll be the first, therefore we must make it as memorable as possible. So I want everyone focused on the task ahead. Tomorrow we launch a great new tradition in Oriole Point with our first Annual Strawberry Moon Bash!"

A glum silence was the only response, along with a distant roll of thunder.

"Exactly how expensive is this Bash going to be?" asked Max, who sat in the second row.

"I'm not certain of the exact numbers." Piper looked over her shoulder to where Cole sat slumped behind the table. "How much is this all costing, Mr. Treasurer?"

"Too much," Cole snarled.

Piper's expression turned venomous.

"If we're done discussing the Bash, I'd like to start the business meeting," Juliet Haller said. A no-nonsense woman in her early fifties, Juliet was elected to her position because she was the only person willing to be the OPBA president after Piper was forced to vacate the office after serving three consecutive terms.

Tess read aloud the minutes of the last meeting. As membership chair, I introduced our latest member and newest shopkeeper, Gareth Holmes, a seventy-year-old woodworker who had recently opened a store selling hand-painted duck decoys. He was a sweet-natured gentleman who sported a lush white beard and mustache, along with a jolly manner worthy of his appearance as a modern-day Kris Kringle. However, I didn't know how much of a demand there was for duck decoys. I hoped he had another source of income. Or a solid retirement plan.

After that, the usual litany began. Someone reported the latest broken street lamp. Muffin Mike complained that the smell from the nearby barbecue joint was overpowering the aroma of his fresh baked muffins. Yvette from Foulards et Bijoux informed us there were too many birds visiting the fountain near her French accessories boutique. I looked at Max, and we rolled our eyes at each other. Too late, I remembered that Ryan was also here, and glanced over at him in the front row. He smiled at me, but it seemed forced.

To no one's surprise, Jerry and Sheila Sawyer, owners of Sweet Dreams, got to their collective feet next. Ideally, people who ran a candy store should be lighthearted and fun, but the Sawyers possessed all the charm of public executioners. They had owned Sweet Dreams for nine years and had been seen to smile perhaps once during all that time. With long-suffering expressions, they now faced the board members. First, they agreed about all those nasty chickadees splashing about the waters of that diabolical fountain. I couldn't believe I was listening to this when I could have been soaking in my tub with Ryan right now.

Pulling out my cell phone, I proceeded to text Natasha once again. Why wasn't she answering my calls or texts? When I looked up, I found Cole staring back at me. In the overhead light, his black-and-blue nose looked even more swollen. I wondered again what had made Natasha strike him. His gaze shifted to the cell phone in my hand. He probably believed his wife and I were in constant contact. I quickly put my phone away.

"And we would also like to know why Marlee Jacob has suddenly decided to sell candy," I heard Jerry Sawyer say in a ringing voice.

Startled, I looked at the couple. "Are you talking about me?"

Sheila frowned. "Perhaps the ambitious Miss Jacob has forgotten there has been a successful candy store in Oriole Point for almost a decade. We do not need another."

"What's the problem with my selling candy? The brand I purchased is not sold by anyone else in Oriole Point. I made certain of that."

"*We* are the candy store in town," Jerry said. "Everyone knows that. If a visitor wants candy, they come to Sweet Dreams. Then you show up two years ago and open a shop that is supposed to sell berries. But since then you've been including anything even remotely connected to berries. Soaps, teas, coffee, wine. Even chef aprons and T-shirts."

"And candy!" Sheila said, chiming in. "You're moving in on territory that we've carved out as our own. I demand OPBA see that you remove all candy products from your store."

I had my mouth open to reply when Max let out a loud laugh. "That's ridiculous," he said. "At least seven downtown shops sell candy. Maybe more. Are we supposed to send the candy police in to remove all the candy from every business but yours?"

"He's right," Tess added. "I sell glassware, but so do ten other stores. There are about eight places in town that sell ice cream, four shops that sell cookies. I could go on, but I think we've wasted enough of the board's time with this."

I sent grateful looks to both Tess and Max.

"Exactly," Lionel Pierce agreed in a booming voice. "By the way, if someone did want to sell the same brand of product, there is nothing legally to prevent it. Jerry and Sheila, your complaints have been noted and rejected." He added under his breath. "Again."

Piper shook her head at the Sawyers, who sat down with martyred expressions.

To my surprise, Cole got to his feet next. "I'm sure news of the argument today between my wife and me has become common knowledge. No doubt some of you would like to believe I am to blame for the altercation, which resulted in the police being called. But everyone should be aware that it was my unstable wife who caused the fight, not me."

"Where is this going?" Tess whispered.

I shrugged.

Juliet cleared her throat. "Cole, I don't see how an argument between you and your wife has any relevance to this business meeting."

"It has a great deal of relevance," he said. "Natasha assaulted me today and then fled the scene. She has not returned home, nor has she taken her car. Therefore, she is somewhere in Oriole Point. And since she spends her free time gossiping with everyone in their shops, one of you was the last person to see her." He looked at me accusingly. "Some misguided fool is hiding her, and I suspect that person is in this room.

I want to warn whoever it is that I've filed formal charges against my wife. If you are concealing her from me, then you're harboring a criminal. One who is violent and mentally unbalanced."

This was too much. "Natasha is not a criminal," I said. "That's a ridiculous thing to say, and you know it."

"Damn it, Marlee. You always take her side. But your friend struck me in the face with a metal object. She could have killed me! And I plan to bring charges of assault and attempted murder against her."

I shook my head in disbelief. "Are you insane?"

He slammed his fist on the table. "Are you hiding her?"

The faces out front gazed up at the stage as if we were actors in a play.

"No, I am not hiding her. But if she came to me for help, I'd do everything I could to protect her from you. Or do you think we've forgotten you tried to choke her on Valentine's Day at San Sebastian?"

Diego, who had been dozing, woke up with a start when he heard the name of his restaurant.

"How dare you bring that up?" Cole said. "You weren't even there!"

"And if she really wanted to kill you," I continued, "she wouldn't have smacked you on your nose. She would have hit you on your left temple."

Cole's mouth dropped open, while every person in the room now turned toward me. "What in the world are you talking about, Marlee?" Piper asked.

Okay, maybe I shouldn't have said anything, but I had gone too far now. "Natasha told me Cole suffered a head injury when he was a child. His left temple has been especially vulnerable since then.

Therefore, if Natasha really wanted to finish Cole off, she would have hit him on his left temple. But she whacked him on the nose instead. . . ." My voice trailed off. "Obviously, she didn't really want to kill him."

Ryan gazed at me in open amusement. At least this was one OPBA meeting he wouldn't doze off in.

"It's worse than I thought." Cole pointed at me. "The two of you are conspiring to kill me!"

"That's not what I said!" I heard Tess typing away on her laptop beside me. "Tess, you're not putting this into the minutes, are you?"

"Of course I am. It's my job to record everything brought up at the meeting."

Juliet rapped her gavel on the table. "That's enough about the Bowman marriage and how best to kill Cole. Hopefully, no one in the audience will act on this information." This elicited laughter from the people out front. "Please take your seat, Cole. If you want to continue this discussion, I suggest you consult a divorce lawyer. Or a bodyguard."

Cole sat down, glaring at both Juliet and me.

"Before we adjourn," she went on, "Keith Vander-Hoff, who serves as OPBA's legal counsel, has something he wants to bring before us."

Keith got to his feet. He held a sheaf of papers in his hands and wore an unhappy expression. "Earlier today I received information I feel is of importance to every business owner in Oriole Point," he began.

The meeting hall grew completely still; the only sound was the whirring of the electric fans.

"First, I have confirmed that the Fields property has been purchased."

Piper sat up as if she had been jabbed with an electric cattle prod. "Impossible!"

"I'm afraid it's true, Piper. The transaction took place last year, in fact."

She turned to her husband. "Do you know about this? Have you kept this from me?"

"Of course not." He seemed insulted she would even think such a thing.

"Is there anyone here besides Keith who knows about this?" she demanded of the board members around the table.

Some of us shook our heads, but I noticed that Drake, Cole, Muffin Mike, and Juliet avoided meeting Piper's gaze.

I didn't understand why everyone seemed so upset. The Fields property was a big piece of land on the border of town. It had been owned since the nineteenth century by the Fields family, and for as long as I could remember, Miss Hortense Fields had lived in the rambling Gothic Revival house that sat in the middle of acres of overgrown fields. She was a hardy little thing who had never married or had children. Hortense stayed there with a housekeeper/companion until she was moved to a nursing home three years ago. It was the end of an era when she died this past winter at the age of one hundred and five, having outlived the rest of her relatives.

As for the Fields property, I assumed it would be sold to a developer who would turn it into a subdivision of new homes. At one time, it had been a successful working farm, but as the Fields relatives died or moved away, the land and crops were neglected and had turned wild. Technically known as the Fields property, we often called it different things depending on what was blooming that month. In October we referred to it as the Pumpkin Fields, in

July it was the Blueberry Fields, and in June we called it Strawberry Fields.

I sat back with a start. *Strawberry Fields!* That was what Cole had been talking about today. He thought Natasha had told me about the sale of the Fields property. Which probably meant that either he had bought the land or he knew who did.

"Everyone in Oriole Point is well aware that I planned to buy the property myself once Hortense died," Piper said in a voice trembling with anger. "My ancestors Benjamin and Ellen Lyall built the first home in Oriole Point, and it stood on that very land."

"Hallowed ground," Tess murmured.

"And I have been in discussion with the historical committee for years about turning those acres into a living history museum—"

"Wait a minute," Jerry Sawyer interrupted. "Are you telling us all that prime real estate is going to be devoted to your family?"

"Not now," Cole said with an evil grin.

Piper directed her anger at Jerry. "Of course the property was not going to be devoted to my family alone, even though this town would not exist without the Lyalls."

Muffin Mike buried his head in his hands. We all knew what was coming.

"Let's not forget my family was the first to settle here," she said.

"Not exactly the first," Denise Redfern said, piping up from the rear of the hall. "Mine were here long before yours."

Piper had the good grace to blush. "Yes, your people were here first, Denise, but that was before there was a town called Oriole Point. And it didn't have a lumber mill or a post office or a general store. Those were established by the Lyalls." She gave a conciliatory nod to Ruth Barlow, who sat near Ryan. "I understand other families have also been important to our history, and I plan to include their contributions as well. It is my intention to reconstruct parts of the nineteenth-century town of Oriole Point on that land. It will be like our own Greenfield Village. Only not as large, of course."

I'd been to Henry Ford's Greenfield Village on the other side of the state. It was one of the finest living history museums in the country, on a par with Williamsburg. If Piper thought she could even begin to build anything to rival that, her dreams had officially turned into delusions of grandeur.

"The property is far too valuable to become a theme park devoted to three or four families," Jerry said.

"I agree," Sheila Sawyer added. "A developer could fit dozens of homes on that piece of land. And the town could certainly use the property tax revenue."

"This is not why I asked you all here." The young attorney had been ignored in the ensuing fracas, but he seemed determined to take back the floor. "The Fields property was acquired last year by a real estate holding company known as the Taylor Investment Group."

This announcement made me uneasy. For two years, I had paid rent for my retail space to this same investment group.

"In addition, the Taylor Investment Group has contracted Fitzgerald Developers of Chicago to oversee the property. I spoke with their office this afternoon and confirmed that the development of the Fields land will not be residential. Instead, the entire thirty acres have been rezoned for commercial."

Yet another uproar erupted in the meeting hall, with everyone talking at once. Acres of new businesses spelled trouble for the ones currently existing downtown.

"How did you learn all this?" the mayor asked.

"I received a call today from an interested party," Keith replied. "This individual, who wishes to remain anonymous, supplied me with the pertinent details and instructions as to whom I should contact in Chicago."

My concern about Natasha's safety grew. I remembered her texting away this morning in my store. Was she the one who gave all this information to the lawyer?

"Impossible!" the mayor said, his voice easily being heard over the din. "How could the zoning commission do this without my knowledge?"

"There's more." Keith's expression grew even grimmer. "The commission has also agreed to permit nationwide chains to open stores on the property."

All hell broke loose. Not allowing franchises and chains within the borders of Oriole Point had been one of its shining achievements. When tourists visited our lakeshore resort, they ate at local restaurants, not fast-food chains; shopped at unique stores and galleries, not Walmart; and drank their cappuccinos at Coffee by Crystal, not Starbucks. All those chains and franchises could be found in nearby Holland or South Haven, but everyone in Oriole Point worked hard to fight against the intrusion of the Big

Boys, who would—intentionally or not—ruin the charm of our small town. Not to mention the revenue for local shopkeepers.

"This is unspeakable!" Piper looked positively stricken.

Even Max and Ryan seemed startled by this latest news.

Juliet stopped the cacophony of voices by rapping her gavel on the table. "Let's have order here. This is an official business meeting, not the Sandy Shoals Saloon."

"Why would the zoning commission agree to something like this after all these years?" I asked Keith VanderHoff when everyone had quieted down.

He sighed. "Why don't you ask them? Most of them are sitting at this table."

Keith was right. I'd forgotten how incestuous Oriole Point was. Invariably, the same dozen or so people sat on most of the boards and committees in town, and that included the OPBA board and the zoning commission.

Piper threw outraged looks at Drake Woodhill, Juliet Haller, and Muffin Mike, all members of the OPBA board as well as the zoning commission. Then she turned to the front row and stared at Crystal Appeldoorn, the owner of Coffee by Crystal and a member of the zoning commission. Crystal seemed to shrink about three inches under Piper's gaze.

"Either every one of you has been bought off or you've all gone mad!" Piper said in a voice as loud as her husband's. "No other reason can explain your decision to rezone this property for commercial use. And how could you have the gall to include national chains? Everyone here, especially me, deserves an explanation."

The zoning commission members remained silent.

After a long tense moment, Drake said, "It made good business sense."

"He's right," Juliet added in a shaky voice. "Both tourists and residents will appreciate not having to drive ten miles whenever they want to visit a chain drugstore or restaurant."

Muffin Mike tapped his pencil on the table. "We have to keep up with the times. People want charm, as well as convenience. This way, Oriole Point will be able to provide both."

"Let's see how charming the town remains when the small businesses start to lose money." Piper seemed enervated by an icy calm now, which made her even more intimidating. "And do the members of this Taylor Investment Group have faces and names? I insist on speaking to their chairman as soon as possible. How quickly can you arrange a meeting?"

"Tonight, if you like," Keith said. "As of this past April, Mr. Bowman has served as their chairman."

A hint of a smile appeared on Cole's face as everyone turned to him.

"Don't be ridiculous. Cole doesn't have the cash to become part of a real estate holding company," Piper protested. "Not after his misadventures in Chicago."

Cole's smile grew. "Ah, but you forget that my mother died this past spring."

"Are you saying an inheritance is funding this? I wasn't aware Jessica Bowman had any money. Especially after she divorced your father. And he left nothing but debts after he died."

"She remarried fifteen years ago. And although she was widowed again, it left her more solvent than you know. You also seem to have forgotten that her maiden name was Taylor."

I gasped at the same time Piper did. "Your mother was the Taylor Investment Group?" she asked.

Cole nodded. "I convinced her to buy the Fields property and place it in a holding company. After she passed away, leadership of the company fell to my half brother Alan and me. Since Mother lived these past twenty years in Atlanta, Alan is overseeing the southern holdings, while I am in control of our properties in the Midwest. This has been in the works since I moved back from Chicago. Unlike most people in this town, my mother wanted to see me get back on my feet. Both of us knew developing the Fields property would be key."

Piper shook her head. "The Fields estate would not part with that land cheap. If your mother's liquidity was so impressive, she would have saved your Chicago company years ago. What did you use as collateral?"

"My buildings in downtown Oriole Point, of course. After my mother died, I inherited all her properties, which included Hortense's thirty acres."

I felt sick. For two years I had paid rent to the Taylor Investment Group. I never asked who actually owned the company, nor had I cared. My rent was reasonable, and I was about to sign another lease, as my present one expired at the end of the month. But if what he was saying was true, Cole Bowman was now my landlord. And I bet my rent was about to skyrocket.

Piper looked as if the wind had been knocked out

of her. Lionel apparently thought so, as well. He patted her bare arm. "Maybe you should sit down, sweetheart. You don't look well."

She shook off his hand. "What are you saying? Are you going to raise the rent on all your properties to pay for this venture?"

I tensed up in preparation for his answer.

"Don't be absurd. I'm going to sell the buildings." Exasperated, Cole smoothed back what little hair he had left. "I've humored all of you far too much tonight. None of this is anyone's concern but my own."

"The prospect of dozens of new businesses in town—especially franchises—concerns everyone!" Odette from Lakeshore Holiday called out. "There won't be a business left unaffected by *your* business decisions. And since I lease one of your buildings, I'd like to know what I can expect from this sale."

"Me too," I chimed in. Several others echoed this.

He picked off imaginary pieces of lint from his blue polo shirt before answering. Cole knew he was in control. "I have no interest in continuing to lease space in downtown Oriole Point," he said finally. "I'll have my hands full helping to develop the Fields property."

"Are we going to be kicked out of our stores?" I asked.

Cole turned to face me. "I don't know about the others, but *you* most certainly will be. And I doubt you'll have an easy time finding another building to sell your little berry things in." He paused. "By the way, where you're concerned, Marlee, this is not business. It's personal."

At this moment, my anger surpassed whatever Piper was feeling. "You plan to ruin my business because I've been a good friend to your wife?" Now it was my turn to stand up. "I think Piper was right. The only way you could have gotten permission to rezone that land was if you bribed the commission. Or blackmailed them! Which was it? Drake, Michael? Do you want to tell us? Juliet, how about you?" I turned to Crystal out front. "What did he pay you, Crystal? If not that, then what does Cole Bowman know about all of you that you would sell out this town?"

Tess yanked me down to my seat. "Are you out of your mind?"

Piper gazed at me with an almost parental pride.

Drake put his face in his hands, while Crystal flushed beet red. Muffin Mike looked straight out at the audience, his expression stony. Juliet seemed close to tears.

Cole appeared to be enjoying the drama. As Piper had done earlier, he decided to literally take center stage and went to stand in front of the table where the board members sat. "I'd like to finish what I was saying before the melodramatic Miss Jacob interrupted me. Since I plan to develop the Fields property, I will have neither the time to play landlord nor the interest in doing so. As for my downtown properties, I've been in negotiation with entrepreneurs in Chicago and have secured a prospective buyer for each of my buildings."

The buzz in the audience almost drowned out what he was saying.

"I understand many of you have been renting those spaces for years," Cole went on. "Therefore, I will allow those who currently lease my properties to purchase the property at the same price offered to me by the interested Chicago parties."

Tess looked over at me in concern. The historic buildings in downtown Oriole Point were prime real estate. The last time someone bought a store on Lyall Street, the price was five hundred thousand dollars. Of course, even if I had the money, it wouldn't matter. Cole would not let me stay. But once I was kicked out of my shop in the middle of tourist season, where would I go? Every downtown retail space was already taken. And if Cole made good on his threat, at least a dozen other shopkeepers in Oriole Point were going to be competing for the next available retail space. Who knew when that would turn up?

Piper marched over to where Cole stood. "You're nothing but a damn carpetbagger!"

He chuckled. "Wasn't that what your great-great-uncle Josiah was? Oh, wait, he couldn't have been. He was jailed for voter fraud after he cheated his way to a Democratic Senate seat."

Cole didn't have time to enjoy his gibe. Piper reached back with her fist and landed a punch that sent Cole flying.

We all jumped to our feet to see Cole moaning on the floor, one hand cradling his face.

"I always knew Cole was a sneaky bastard," I said to Tess as the meeting hall erupted once more. "But who guessed Piper had an ancestor who was a Democrat?"

Chapter 5

Despite the bad news—and fisticuffs—of the night before, I woke refreshed the next morning. I did finally soak in my expansive claw-foot tub with Ryan. And he did his best to help me forget my troubles, at least for the rest of the night. Armed with my yoga mat, I was about to set off for a session of yoga on the beach. Afterward, Ryan promised to whip up his famous Eggs Benedict for me. I should then be ready to face Friday the thirteenth.

But I'd barely enjoyed a quick sip of juice when my cell rang. Maybe it was my parents calling from New Zealand, where they were vacationing. When I grabbed the phone, it was Tess's name that flashed on the screen.

"Isn't this a little early for you? I thought you didn't get moving until nine."

"Marlee, put your TV on." She sounded grim. "And turn to *Wake Up, America*."

"Has something awful happened?" I fumbled for the remote as Ryan looked up from where he sat sprawled on the living room couch. "Is someone we know dead? What!"

A second later, I stared at the hosts of the most popular morning show in the nation. My heart stopped when I recognized the person they were interviewing.

"What is April doing on TV?" This was a rhetorical question. There was only one reason April Byrne would be interviewed today of all days. She was there to talk about the murder of her former lover, John Chaplin. Something she hadn't done since the end of the trial.

My knees buckled, and I found myself on the floor, staring at the TV in shock.

"So, Miss Byrne, it has been three years since John Chaplin was poisoned by his wife," said the boyishly handsome male host. "The public has heard nothing from you since Evangeline Chaplin was sentenced to life in prison. Why are you going public now?"

Exactly my question, I thought.

April took a deep breath, as if fighting for composure. She didn't look much different than she had three years ago. Her shoulder-length brown hair boasted a few more highlights than before, and she looked as if she had lost about ten pounds. But April still gave one the impression of a twentysomething Lolita.

Looking back, I didn't know why I had been so shocked when I discovered she and John Chaplin were lovers. Her round baby face had always made her look like an adolescent, even if parts of her body were surgically enhanced. She had used that girlish appearance to her advantage by playing the demure, inexperienced intern a good year after she had been working on *Sugar and Spice*. Because I was her immediate superior, she'd treated me with exaggerated deference, so much so that I had suspected her sincerity and considered transferring her to another show. If only I had. I didn't realize until too late that she was turning that sly nymphet charm on the male half of *Sugar and Spice*.

"As you know, the media revisits the Chaplin murder trial every June," April began. "Since John and I were in love, this time of year is difficult for me. I'm still heartbroken by his death. But I can no longer keep silent about the recent announcement that Evangeline is trying to get her sentence reduced. It's deeply upsetting to watch her being portrayed as the pitiful wronged woman who killed her husband in a fit of jealousy."

"But isn't that what happened?"

"Before John was brutally taken from me, he had every intention of leaving his wife. The Chaplin marriage was a sham, as anyone who knew them could attest."

"She's exaggerating," I told Ryan. "They were like any other couple married for twenty years. Sometimes great, sometimes not."

"In fact, the week he died, John gave me an engagement ring." Tears filled April's eyes as she lifted her hand to the camera. A large diamond solitaire twinkled on her finger.

I shook my head. "This is news to me. He and Evangeline were about to renew a contract for their series. John was well aware that no one would want Spice without Sugar. And this is the first anyone has heard of an engagement ring. She never mentioned it at the trial."

Ryan sat down on the floor next to me. "You know, I forgot what she looked like." He shrugged. "Eh. Nothing to write home about."

April seemed to fight back tears. "It is unacceptable to me that Evangeline Chaplin can destroy two lives—John's and my own—then spend her time giving malicious interviews from prison. I'm told dozens of people write her every week to express their sympathy and support. Now there's talk of yet another appeal and a shortened prison sentence. For that reason, I decided to write a book, *Sugar, Spice, and Vice: The True Story of the Chaplin Murder.*"

"A book! She's written a book?"

As if she heard me, April held up a hardcover book with that dreadful title on it.

"And what will we learn from this book that we didn't hear during the trial three years ago?" the host asked.

April looked straight at the camera. "The public will understand what a wonderful man John Chaplin was. Kind, honest, loving. They will also learn his wife was an egomaniac who cared only about her cookbooks, her show, and her celebrity. Evangeline was nothing like the image she projected of a folksy Tennessee housewife. And they will learn how everyone on the *Sugar and Spice* show conspired to keep that farce of a marriage going."

My living room seemed to tilt for a moment.

"Uh-oh," Ryan said.

The female co-host threw her a cool smile. "But you can't blame the show's staff for the murder of John Chaplin."

"Yes I can." The expression on her baby face grew hard. "It was they who informed Evangeline Chaplin that John and I were together. If not for executive producer Elliot Flynn and producer Marlee Jacob, John might still be alive today."

"Am I really hearing this?" I was so stunned, I wasn't even certain I asked this aloud.

"That's a serious allegation," the female co-host replied. It was clear that at least she wasn't buying April's performance.

"Murder is a serious act," April continued. "If we had been left to tell Evangeline in our own way and in our own time, I don't believe John would have been killed. But the producers interfered. As far as I'm concerned, they have John Chaplin's blood on their hands."

"I think I'm going to be sick."

Ryan grabbed my hand. "She's only out to make a quick buck and get some more publicity. This will all soon blow over."

I suddenly remembered Tess was still on speakerphone. "You see, Tess. This is why I hate the thirteenth of June. Nothing good will happen on this day again. Ever!"

"But today's the Strawberry Moon Bash. You know you're looking forward to that."

"Tess!"

"Just kidding," she said quickly. "Look, no one is going to buy her stupid book. And no one will remember the one time she mentioned your name this morning."

"She's right," Ryan said. "Forget about April and the Chaplins. And get going, before you're late for beach yoga."

"No way. If I go anywhere near the lake, I'll keep swimming until I reach Wisconsin." A wave of self-pity swept over me. "Or until I drown. Whichever comes first."

I didn't have the heart to face Oriole Point for hours. I literally hid in my back office at The Berry Basket while Andrew waited on customers. Since he and his brother Dean had watched April's interview this morning, he had a million lurid questions. And the Oriole Point grapevine soon spread the news that local shopkeeper Marlee Jacob was again being associated with the Chaplin murder. Then, out of no-where, I received a gift from the social media gods.

When Gillian and Dean burst into the store hours before their shifts, I knew something was up.

"Piper is officially famous," Dean announced.

"Someone at city hall used their phone to film the last part of the OPBA meeting and put it on YouTube an hour ago," Gillian said. "She's gone viral."

"You're kidding!"

"Piper Lyall-Pierce is a star." Dean pulled his phone from the front pocket of his jeans.

Andrew, Gillian, and I crowded around as Dean brought up a video captioned "Mayor's wife attacks small-town developer." A few minutes later, we all let out a yell at the same time when Piper punched Cole in the face.

"He went down like a ton of bricks," Andrew said after we watched it a fourth time. "I'm surprised he didn't crack the back of his skull open."

While I was grateful Piper's punch had diverted

attention from me, I couldn't help but be worried that whoever had filmed the fight at the OBPA meeting also filmed my argument with Cole. I didn't need that video to go viral. But for now, I felt relief that the spotlight was turned on someone else. Piper's left hook had effectively knocked April's accusations out of the picture.

By noon, the YouTube video had turned Piper into the heroine of Oriole Point. Instead of the arrogant rich lady telling everyone what to do, she was now viewed as our own Joan of Arc, battling the Chicago developers and their hit man, Cole Bowman. I caught sight of her parading past my store window, surrounded by an entourage of at least a dozen people. The only thing missing were the paparazzi.

Of course, I was still worried about Natasha, as well as the fresh publicity about my involvement in the Chaplin murder. I was also upset about being kicked out of my store in two weeks. I'd spent my savings setting the business up. Fortunately, The Berry Basket was in the black this year, but I'd plowed all my profits back into the store. Now I would lose the entire season's revenue while I searched for another space to rent. I refused to go to my parents for another loan; they'd already helped me out with The Berry Basket. And I had no intention of selling the lake house. It was a part of the family, our anchor in Oriole Point.

The Jacobs had lived in Oriole Point for generations, but over the years many relatives, including my parents, had moved away. We relocated to Chicago when I was eighteen. The same year, my application to New York University was accepted, and I moved to the Big Apple. For the next ten years, I'd returned only for holidays or friends' weddings. Not that any of us ever forgot Oriole Point. And we cherished our beautiful Queen Anne house overlooking Lake Michigan, where we hosted family reunions whenever enough Jacobs were in the area.

My parents made the two-hour drive from Chicago when they could, but Mom was a tenured professor at Northwestern, and Dad managed a successful boutique hotel on State Street. Their home was in Chicago. Until I moved back, they visited Oriole Point only four or five times a year, and they were grateful I was now here to take care of the lake house. It was also our one remaining financial asset.

Although it needed renovation, an historic Painted Lady on Lake Michigan was worth big money. My great-great-grandfather Philip Jacob built the three-story house in 1895 as a wedding gift for his bride, Lotte. He had even painted it robin's egg blue, Lotte's favorite color. Every Jacob since then had kept it the same beguiling hue. The gabled house with a corner turret had become a local landmark along the lake, and I adored every balustrade and creaking floorboard. I couldn't ask my parents to sell it. As an only child, I was accustomed to being indulged and lavished with affection, and I knew they would do anything for me. But I was thirty years old. Time to act like an adult. And asking them to sell the ancestral home wasn't the way to do it.

"I wish I'd gone to the meeting," Gillian said as I blended another smoothie at our Strawberry Moon

Bash booth. Hours later, she couldn't stop talking about the Cole-Piper fight. We were so busy, conversation was often impossible. But whenever there was a lull, Gillian wanted to discuss the OPBA drama.

"You're always telling me how much everyone fights at those things, but I didn't know they really fought!" she continued.

"Usually, it's just verbal. Although, at the May meeting, Yvette poured a water bottle over Jerry's head when he accused her of stealing his sandwich board." I handed the smoothies to a father and son waiting eagerly for them. I didn't blame them. The humidity had gone down since yesterday, but the temperature was still in the eighties, even though it was evening.

I wiped my damp face with my chef apron. "Be honest. I look terrible, don't I?"

"You look fine. By the way, I like the whole French braid thing. I don't think I've seen you wear your hair in a French braid before."

I reached back and touched the thick braid that hung down my back. "I thought a braid would be cooler than a ponytail. My other option was to cut it all off."

Someone tugged that braid, and I turned around. Ryan stood on the other side of my booth table. "How are the booth brats doing?" he asked, leaning over for a kiss.

"We've learned Gillian can make a killer strawberry mojito. How about you?"

"People don't come to an event like this to buy fresh strawberries. We're closing early."

I gazed out at the booths scattered on the grass

along the Oriole River. A band played live music under the nearby gazebo. Visitors sat on blankets under the trees or strolled along the boardwalk that led from the marina and pier out to the lighthouse. All the kiddie attractions closed at five. However, the stands selling cotton candy, elephant ears, and popcorn were still doing a booming business, as were the downtown bars and restaurants just up the street. The whole thing had a carnival feel to it, which suited a summertime event. Piper's relentless promotion of the Bash had paid off.

"When Piper throws next year's Bash, the OPBA board should remind her to sell only food and drink in the park. The shops don't need to set up their own booths. It's a waste of time."

"I'm sure you'll see she remembers," Ryan said with a grin.

My heart sank at his words. "I doubt I'll even be an OPBA member next year. You need to be a business owner. And it looks like I'm about to lose mine."

"Don't be pessimistic," Gillian protested. "You'll be able to find another space to rent. Besides, the other shopkeepers are so angry at Cole, they'll find a way to stop him."

"No matter what, he is my landlord, and he's pushing me out of that store in two weeks."

"Sweetheart, we're getting married." Ryan stroked my cheek. "That makes you officially part of Zellar Orchards. And we're a commercial powerhouse. Let Cole sell his overpriced buildings. Who needs The Berry Basket, anyway? You'll be part of *our* business."

Gillian beamed at us, and I tried to smile back. In truth, he had depressed me even more. His family had reason to be proud of Zellar Orchards, which included peaches, berries, pumpkins, and apples. But I would be joining a virtual tribe of Zellars, all of whom owned a piece of the orchards and farmland. They also owned two restaurants in South Haven and Saugatuck, which carried simple country fare, along with pies and tarts baked with their orchard fruits. It was no secret the Zellars hoped to expand the restaurants all along the Lake Michigan coast, eventually making inroads into the Chicago area. Thus it was a given that anyone who married into the Zellars was expected to work for the family business.

Because I ran The Berry Basket, I had not yet felt under any pressure to abandon my own business in order to concentrate on theirs. But if I lost the store, Ryan would expect me to help the Zellars market and expand their product and brand—and all from a farmhouse out in the country. From the moment we became engaged, Ryan had wanted to buy a place with at least six acres farther inland for us. I kept trying to convince him to look at houses closer to the lake, preferably my own family home in Oriole Point. So far, it was a stalemate.

"Ryan, we need the keys to the truck!" His brother Jim waved from the Zellar booth.

"Got to go. We have to haul all this fresh fruit back to the orchards."

"You'll be back in time for the fireworks?" I asked.

"Promise. Where do you want to meet?"

"Everyone will be pressed like sardines leading down to the beach. Let's watch the fireworks from one of the slips at the marina."

"Text me the number of the slip." After another kiss, he ran off to join his brothers.

"He's such a great guy," Gillian said. "You're lucky. And you're much nicer than his first wife. Of course, that's what he gets for marrying someone who's not from around here."

"I hardly think her birthplace was what caused the marriage to fail." I didn't want to talk about Ryan's first marriage, any more than I wanted to think about my last boyfriend in New York City. After four years of living together, I arrived home to find he had packed up and moved. And not just to another Upper West Side apartment. He was on his way to London for a job with a global investment firm. Accompanying him was a woman called Claire, who, he claimed, wasn't a crazed workaholic like me. Since his working hours were even more insane than mine, I found the accusation unfair. And unkind.

Gillian looked around. "People are shutting the booths early. If Piper finds out, she'll probably punch someone else out."

"I doubt it. She and Lionel are busy holding court on their yacht." I pointed to one of the biggest yachts at the marina. Even in the growing dusk, I could see Piper moving among her guests on deck in a flowing yellow dress.

"I can't believe Cole had the nerve to charge Piper with assault. After all, she's the mayor's wife. But she doesn't seem upset."

"It's because she's famous . . . at least for a day or two." I sighed. "If she's lucky, everyone will forget about it by next week. Celebrity isn't what it's cracked up to be."

"I guess you don't want to talk about the book by that April woman."

I shook my head as a couple came up to the booth

and asked for our most popular alcoholic drink of the day: the strawberry-basil refresher.

"Has anyone seen Cole tonight?" I grabbed a stainless-steel muddler to play bartender when Gillian went to help other customers interested in the last of our strawberry tarts.

"I heard he decided not to set up a booth for the Bash. No surprise there."

"He was probably afraid he'd run into Piper. Or her fist."

After dividing the strawberries into two glasses, I added strawberry syrup, several fresh basil leaves, and lemon juice. I mashed the ingredients together with the muddler before pouring in rum, soda water, and crushed ice from our cooler.

"Because of what happened at the meeting, Natasha's been forgotten. I'm worried sick about her. I've called and texted her a dozen times, but nothing. Where do you think she is?"

"Hiding from Cole," Gillian said. "If Natasha's smart, she'll lay low for a while."

After garnishing the drinks with a strawberry and sprigs of fresh mint, I handed the plastic glasses to the waiting couple. When I was done, I turned to Gillian. "I don't care how angry Cole is, it's not like Natasha to just disappear. I hope he hasn't done anything to her. She was probably the one to tell VanderHoff about the Fields property sale."

"She should go to the police."

"Except Cole charged her with assault and attempted murder. Maybe she's hiding because of that. And I bet Natasha knows something. Like why did so many people on the zoning commission allow Cole to rezone the property for chains and franchises?"

"I hate to say it, but my friends and I would kill to have a Sonic Drive-In here."

"I'd still like to know how he got the zoning commission to give him what he wants. Maybe I should smack him over the head with this until he tells me." I held up the steel muddler.

When I turned to toss the muddler onto the cutting board, I saw a man move from behind a tree that stood near my booth. He walked away with his head down. By the time he reached the boardwalk, I lost sight of him in the crowd. But I caught a quick glimpse of a bruised and swollen nose. It was Cole Bowman.

Although I wanted to close my booth early, word of our strawberry mojitos, margaritas, and strawberry-basil refreshers must have spread, because we were suddenly swamped with customers waving IDs and demanding a drink. Somewhere along the way, I decided to mix a few drinks for myself. Blame the stress over April's interview that morning, along with the prospect of losing my store, but I downed three strawberry mojitos in the next hour. I was reaching for a fourth when Gillian took the rum bottle out of my hands.

She gave me a warning look. "Marlee, I'm cutting you off. I know it's been a rough day, but passing out drunk won't make you feel any better."

I burped. Maybe she was right. And I did feel a little woozy.

Gillian made the drinks from then on, while I sat in a slight stupor on a nearby stool. By the time our "bar rush" ended, it was after nine thirty. The evening breezes from the lake had cleared my head a little. I didn't have the heart to keep Gillian any longer and told her to find her friends in time for the fireworks. Meanwhile, I packed up, but slower than I normally would. I also texted Ryan once I realized I needed his help to haul everything back to the shop.

"What are you still doing here?" I looked up to see Max wandering over with two of his friends, who also worked for him at the harbor. They all wore Riordan Outfitters T-shirts.

"Waiting for Ryan to answer my text messages. I need his truck so I can take these boxes back to the store."

"No problem. Louis has his SUV parked by the harbormaster. We can all grab some boxes, load 'em up, and drive it over to your shop."

"Thanks. That would be great." I handed boxes to the three guys. "How did you get such a great parking spot during the Bash? This place is wall-to-wall people."

"I'm parked illegally." Louis chuckled. "But don't worry. I'm dating Janelle."

Janelle Davenport was an Oriole Pointe police officer who spent most of her time handing our tickets for traffic violations, except to those she was apparently dating. I wasn't about to take the moral high ground over it. Especially since my store was three blocks away.

Within minutes, we had loaded the boxes in the SUV and were slowly driving through the crowd streaming en masse toward the beach. I figured I had about twenty minutes before the fireworks began. After parking behind my store, the four of us trooped inside and set down the boxes on the storage room floor.

"Should we drop you off at the beach?" Max asked when we were on our way back.

"No. I told Ryan I'd meet him at one of the boat slips at the marina. It will be less crowded there." I hiccupped.

Max looked closer at me. "Are you drunk, marzipan?"

I pushed him away. "I never get drunk. You know that."

"Liar." Louis looked at me over his shoulder from the driver's seat. "I was at your booth earlier to buy a margarita. You were throwing back mojitos like Lindsay Lohan."

Vince, Max's other friend, laughed. "I didn't know you liked to party, Marlee."

"Leave her alone, guys." Max took my hand and gave it a squeeze. "The fireworks are due to start. Why don't you come with us and watch the show from in front of my shop?"

"Janelle's bringing a couple of friends for Vince and Max," Louis added.

"I'm not crashing your dates. Besides, I have a date of my own. I just have to find him,"

"Are you sure?" Max asked me. "I'd hate for you to watch the fireworks alone." He paused. "Besides, I don't think you should be walking around by yourself. It may not be safe."

"He's afraid you might pass out drunk," Louis said.

"I didn't say that!"

"Look, I'm fine. Just a little buzzed." I hopped out

of the SUV as soon as Louis parked illegally in the harbormaster's space. "Thanks for the lift and the irritating comments about my drinking problem. But I've got a fiancé to track down."

Max put a hand on my shoulder. "If you change your mind, call me. I'll come get you."

After giving a final wave, I headed for the marina while texting Ryan once again. The fresh air helped clear my head, although I took greater care than usual in the simple act of walking. Once I reached the boardwalk, I decided to go as far down as possible while still being able to get a good view of the fireworks.

Although most of the boat slips were filled, several owners had taken their vessels out onto the water to get a closer view of the fireworks, which would be set off from a barge on the lake. It shouldn't be hard to find at least one empty slip among all the cabin cruisers and yachts. With a smile, I sent Max a text that said, Thanks again for the ride. And I'm not as drunk as you think I am.

I stopped before a wide slip that was empty. An impressive cruiser named *Lady of the Lake* docked there, memorable for its image of a medieval princess on its white prow. Since I had seen this boat heading out for the lake earlier in the evening, Ryan and I would have the space to ourselves. I looked at the number on the piling, then texted Ryan, I'm at slip #481. Best place to see fireworks. Join me when you can. But hurry.

Who knows if he would get this message in time? Maybe something had happened at the orchards. There were always a few Zellars running about their acres, barns, and greenhouses. No doubt he'd been diverted by yet another orchard emergency. I walked out to the end of the slip, where the river lapped against the pilings below. It was lovely here. The lanterns lining the boardwalk illuminated the happy crowd—tourists, families, couples, groups of teenagers, all waiting for the fireworks. I felt much better and hardly dizzy at all.

I set my purse down by one of the wooden posts. The band had stopped playing at the gazebo; the sound of boat horns and excited laughter filled the air. Standing at the edge of the dock, I watched the red beam of the lighthouse make its familiar rotation. Overhead was the reason for this event: that glorious full moon. I had to give it to Piper. The moon even had a reddish cast to it, as if even a celestial body knew better than to not give Piper what she wanted.

Thinking of Piper's iron determination to always get her way, I took heart that she—if no one else—might be able to put a crimp in Cole Bowman's plans. I simply couldn't bear to lose The Berry Basket, along with my future plans for the business.

The wood boards beneath my feet creaked, and I felt the pressure of someone walking toward me. "About time you showed up, hon," I said. "Another minute and you were going to miss the fireworks."

The first firework suddenly burst overhead, lighting up the sky with glittering gold stars. I was about to turn around and greet Ryan when a shadow fell across my face. Before I could say anything, something hard struck my head. I staggered to the right, reeling from the impact. What in the world had hit me? This didn't make sense. Without warning, a second blow slammed against my temple, much stronger this time. Yelling with pain, I fought to stay on my feet. Just as my knees were about to buckle, I felt a hand on my back. Whoever was behind me now shoved with great force. I lost my balance and pitched forward off the dock. With a strangled cry of horror, I plunged into the river below.

Panicked, I tried to scream. But water poured into my mouth and nose as I began to choke. My lungs threatened to explode. I flailed about in the dark water, desperately looking for the surface.

Then everything went black.

Chapter 6

I wasn't sure if I was drunk or dead. Most likely drunk, since I suddenly heard the theme song from *Gilligan's Island*. I doubted old TV shows were available for viewing in the afterlife. If so, I intended to request a show that was far more recent. Or were the baby boomers going to control everything there, as well?

"Put that away," a female voice said sharply. "Cell phones must be turned off while inside the hospital. If I hear one more ringtone, I'll have a nurse confiscate all of them."

I must be in the hospital. But how did I get here? And why did my skull throb so much? The last thing I remembered was looking up at the fireworks. With great effort, I opened my eyes. The overhead light blinded me, and I immediately shut them. My head felt as if the Oriole Point lighthouse had fallen on top of me.

"I think she opened her eyes." I recognized this latest voice. It belonged to Tess.

"Marlee, sweetheart." This voice was Ryan's. "Are

you awake? We're all worried about you. Can you say something so we know you're all right?"

When I opened my eyes this time, I did it in stages. Slowly peeking out from beneath my lashes, I saw Ryan and Tess staring down at me on one side, while a tall woman in a white lab coat stood to my left. They all seemed equally concerned. I also heard the beeping of a monitor and smelled antiseptic. Yes, I was lying in a hospital bed. Except for a moment, I couldn't remember why. Then, in a flash, I recalled falling into the water.

"My head," I murmured. "It hurts."

The woman in the lab coat whipped out a pen-light, which she aimed at my eyes. I fought back a sudden wave of nausea. After a few moments, she mercifully shut off the light. "I'm Dr. Sankar. And I'm not surprised your head hurts, Miss Jacob. You've suffered a mild concussion, along with several scalp lacerations. Although you were bleeding profusely when EMS arrived, that's common with such injuries. It often looks worse than it is. We clamped the blood vessels, and subsequent X-rays show no skull fractures. However, you did swallow a great deal of river water. You may feel sick to your stomach for the next twenty-four hours."

This was a lot to take in, especially since I suddenly remembered the sound of a siren, voices shouting, people poking at me. And the feeling of being submerged in dark water.

"Hey, marzipan. Glad you finally woke up." Max waved at me from the foot of the bed. He looked disheveled and wore a white sweatshirt that spelled out I LOVE LAKE MICHIGAN. This only added to my confusion. At the Bash, I had a dim recollection of Max and his friends all sporting blue Riordan Outfitters shirts. Exactly how many days had I been unconscious?

"How long have I been here?" My voice sounded hoarse and weak. And there was a funny taste in my mouth.

"About two hours." Dr. Sankar began to probe my skull. I tried not to wince too much. "You've come in and out of consciousness several times. But I think you'll stay awake now." She patted me on my partially bare shoulder, which made me realize I wore a hospital gown. "And since you have a concussion, we won't let you sleep as long as you'd like tonight."

"We'll camp out here and keep you awake," Dean said, grinning at me from behind the doctor. "Andrew and I can regale you with all sorts of stories from our trip to Brazil. Some of them are quite scandalous."

"He's right." His brother winked at me. "There's gossip we haven't begun to reveal to anyone in Oriole Point yet. You'll be the first."

"Forget about the gossip right now." Gillian peeked over Andrew's shoulder. Her eyes were red and swollen, as if she had been crying. "How do you feel, Marlee?"

At the sound of so many familiar voices, I took my first good look and realized the small room was crammed with people. Tess and Ryan stood on one side of the bed; Andrew, Dean, Gillian, and the doctor on the other. Behind them I glimpsed the spiked hair of Tess's boyfriend, David. And at the foot of the bed were Max, Piper, and Lionel Pierce. I was grateful Aunt Vicki was at an animal rights rally out of town. There would have been no room for her here.

I tried to sit up, but a wave of dizziness and pain told me to lie still. "I feel confused."

"I don't blame you, my dear." Piper gave an exaggerated sigh. "But what you should be is grateful. You might have drowned. And I blame myself for this. It was my idea to have you and Gillian sell alcohol tonight. That was a mistake. Although I never thought you'd get drunk and fall right off the dock. I credited you with more self-control."

"Wait a minute." I might have been confused, but I wasn't demented. "You think I fell into the water because I drank too much?"

Everyone looked at each other.

"You drank three strawberry mojitos. Don't you remember?" Gillian said. "I finally had to cut you off. I only wish I'd stopped you sooner."

"Don't feel embarrassed, young woman," Lionel said in a voice so loud, it set my head to pounding even harder. "It proves you're a teetotaler unaccustomed to hard liquor. I abstain myself. If I had drunk as much as you tonight, I might have toppled right off our yacht."

"Lionel, really." Piper sniffed. "As if I would ever permit such a thing to happen."

"I didn't fall into the water because I was drunk. I—I think I was pushed. In fact, I'm pretty sure someone hit me, too. It's just that things are a little fuzzy right now."

Ryan kissed me. "Hon, it looks like you got dizzy and lost your balance."

"But someone hit me on the head." A bandage covered part of my right ear, which felt sore, but not as sore as the lemon-sized lump just above it. "I think I was hit twice. Give me your hand, Ryan, and I'll show you where I must have been struck." I gently guided his hand to the two throbbing injuries. "Here, at the top of my ear, and then just above."

His gaze was filled with pity, which made me feel even worse. Granted, I was still unclear about exactly what had happened, but I remembered enough to know I hadn't been drunk when I was watching the fireworks. Tipsy, maybe. But not drunk enough to career off a dock without a little sinister assistance.

"You must have hit your head on one of the wooden pilings when you lost your balance," Tess said. "I've never known you to be able to handle more than one drink. And several people saw you walking along the marina shortly before you landed in the river. They all claim you were a little unsteady."

"You walked past our yacht, Marlee. We even called out a greeting, but you kept right on going," Piper said. "And you did seem to be weaving from side to side. I thought it was because you were tired. I never imagined you were drunk."

"Hold on. I was not drunk. I wasn't." I turned to Max. "Tell them. I was perfectly fine after you and the guys dropped me off at the harbormaster."

Max's smile was kind. "Maybe you were a tiny bit wobbly, but not enough that I thought you needed an escort. Of course, given what happened, I should never have let you out of my—"

"Hey, no one blames you for having a few drinks and trying to relax," Ryan interrupted him. "A lot happened yesterday and today. Most of it pretty upsetting for you."

"I'm pretty upset now, too." Indeed, I was fighting back the urge to burst into tears.

"Don't worry, Miss Jacob. I'll see to it no one

upsets you for the remainder of your time here. Or they'll answer to me." Dr. Sankar bent down to listen with her stethoscope to my racing heart.

With her striking good looks, commanding presence, and cropped hair, Dr. Sankar seemed like a Bollywood version of Lieutenant Ripley from *Alien*. And if I was a tentacled monster waiting to burst out of someone's intestines, I'd hesitate before tangling with her.

"Miss Jacob does not need any more excitement tonight," she said after listening to my heart. "Most of you will have to leave."

"I'm already excited and upset." And if someone didn't believe me, I was going to get a lot more upset. "Look, I can feel two lumps on my skull. If I passed out and hit one of the wooden posts, how did I manage to hit my head *twice*? Explain that if you can."

"The police believe you lost your balance and hit your head on one of the wooden pilings," Ryan said. "Then you probably hit your head again on the edge of the dock as you fell into the water."

"The police?" This time I did manage to sit upright. For a moment, the room swam before my eyes, and Dr. Sankar laid a steadying hand on my shoulder. When the room righted itself, I spied Officer Janelle Davenport, along with two uniformed policemen.

"About time you woke up, Marlee." Janelle wriggled between Piper and Lionel, neither of whom seemed pleased at being jostled aside. She nodded to the two policemen behind her. "Me and the boys are glad to see you've recovered, but we do have questions." She held up a hand as the doctor began to protest. "I promise we won't tire her, Dr. Sankar, but we need to know a few things as soon as possible."

"It's all right," I told the doctor. "I have to figure out exactly what's going on, or I'll never be able to rest." I turned back to Janelle. "I don't care what everyone is telling you. I wasn't drunk. A little light-headed, for sure, but not enough to knock myself out and fall into the river. That's completely ridiculous."

An aide suddenly rushed in and signaled to the doctor. "If you'll excuse me, I need to step out of the room," Dr. Sankar said. "But I'll be sending a nurse in with pain meds for Miss Jacob. I'll allow two people to stay with her, but not a single person more." The doctor patted my arm before threading her way through the mob around my bed.

While everyone seemed to relax once the doctor was gone, I was sorry to see her go.

"Look, I wasn't drunk," I said with as much force as possible. "I was waiting for Ryan to join me at the slip that belongs to *Lady of the Lake.*" I paused, trying to recall exactly what had happened. "The fireworks had begun. I remember looking up at them. And . . . and I think I heard someone walk up behind me. I assumed whoever was behind me must be Ryan. He was the only one who knew exactly where I was."

Ryan and Max exchanged furtive glances.

"How did Ryan know you were at that particular slip?" Janelle's partner asked.

"I texted him as soon as I got there."

"You texted your fiancé? You're sure of that?" Janelle frowned.

"Of course I'm not sure. My head is pounding right now, and I could have sworn Max was wearing something else tonight." I pointed at his sweatshirt. "But I'm pretty certain I texted Ryan." This was probably what amnesiacs felt like. How could I not grab on to the memory of something that had occurred only a few short hours ago?

Ryan took a deep breath before announcing, "You never texted me, Marlee."

A wave of dizziness swept over me once more. "Check my phone. I put it back in my purse after I sent you the message. Unless my purse went into the water with me. Look at my messages. You'll see I'm right." I looked around for my personal belongings. "Did anyone take my purse from the dock?"

"We've got it." Tess handed me my leather messenger bag.

As I searched for my phone, Max cleared his throat. "You texted *me*, Marlee, not Ryan. In fact, I got two messages from you. One telling me to enjoy the fireworks, and another a few minutes later, asking me to join you on the pier."

"No way. I texted Ryan." But as soon as I turned on my phone and searched my messages, I realized they were right. I had mistakenly sent the text to Max. No wonder Ryan looked irritated. "I could have sworn I texted Ryan."

"You suffered a serious blow to the head tonight and nearly drowned," Tess said. "No one expects you to remember everything that happened. The doctor told us that confusion and temporary amnesia are typical even with a mild concussion."

"If you can't recall who you sent a message to," Piper added, "perhaps you aren't remembering what happened on the dock correctly, either."

"Someone hit me. Twice." I threw my phone back

into my purse. "The one thing I don't remember is what happened after I fell into the water."

"Good thing you did text Max." Gillian clapped him on the shoulder. "He got that message you sent and arrived just in time to save your life."

I looked at Max in disbelief. "You saved my life?"

He blushed. "Yeah."

I was speechless for a moment. "Thank you, but—but I don't understand how all this happened."

"When you sent me that message," Max said, "I thought you decided you wanted company after all. But when I got there, the only thing on the dock was your purse. I walked to the end of the slip and saw your body floating facedown in the water. Scared the crap out of me. I jumped right in and pulled you out." He nodded down at his sweatshirt. "I needed dry clothes afterward, and Ginger gave me jeans and a sweatshirt from her beach store."

"And Max gave *you* CPR," Andrew added. "It was extremely dramatic. Max yelling for help, people running down the boardwalk toward the two of you. You were bleeding as if you'd been beheaded, Marlee. I've never seen so much blood in my life. A couple of onlookers got sick. Anyone who was there will never forget it. I bet you a few kids will have nightmares."

"That's quite enough," Piper said with a warning look. "Although, he's right about one thing. It was a memorable ending to the Bash, although not in the way I had hoped."

"Sorry," I muttered. "But things didn't end the way I planned, either." I looked over at Max. "Thank you again. I owe you a lifetime supply of anything you want from my store."

Max smiled at me, while Ryan tightened his grip on my hand.

Tess cleared her throat. "Everyone should get out of here and leave Marlee alone."

"I'm not leaving," Ryan said.

"Neither am I." Tess moved even closer to me, forcing Ryan to take a step back.

"Guys, I just have a concussion. I didn't even break any bones. I'll be fine. What I'm not fine with is everyone thinking I got dizzy and hit my head. I was attacked."

The room grew quiet, with only the beeping hospital monitors making any noise. "Who do you think attacked you?" Janelle asked.

"I don't know. But someone hit me on the head. Twice."

"The motive wasn't robbery, Marlee," Janelle said. "We looked through your purse, and it appears your money and credit cards are all there. Of course, you're the only one who can tell us if anything is missing."

I thought a moment. "If my attacker wanted to rob me, why not just grab my purse and run off into the crowd? No. Whoever it was wanted to kill me."

"But why?" Max asked.

"Maybe it was that dreadful April woman, who was on TV this morning, hawking her book about the Chaplin murder." Piper looked worried, if those frown lines were any indication. Her Botox must be wearing off. "Do you think she had anything to do with this, Marlee? I watched the interview, and she seems to harbor a great deal of anger toward you."

Before I could answer, Ryan said, "April was interviewed live this morning in New York City. She'd have had to fly to Chicago immediately, rent a car, drive two hours up here, then figure out exactly where Marlee was standing on the dock. All this in the middle of a huge crowd and at night. That doesn't seem likely."

"And why would April try to murder Marlee?" Tess asked. "She's already getting her revenge by writing that book. So who else would want to hurt Marlee? No one that I can think of."

"Cole Bowman." I wasn't aware I was going to say this, but once I had, it made perfect sense. "Anyone at the OPBA meeting last night could attest that he and I hate each other."

Lionel shook his head. "Almost everyone who belongs to OPBA hates him now."

"And let's not forget I was the one who punched him last night," Piper said. "If he was going to kill anyone, it should be me. Why in the world would he bother with you?"

I should have known that in Piper's stratified world, there was a waiting list for everything, including being a murder victim.

"We're aware of the events at last night's OPBA meeting," Janelle said. "Given those events, Mr. Bowman would be a prime suspect in any attack on you or Mrs. Lyall-Pierce. However, during the time of your fall into the river, Mr. Bowman was in full view of a number of people, including Max Riordan,

Vincent Gianopoulus, Louis Rojas." She paused. "And myself."

"What?" This news came as an unpleasant surprise.

"It's true," Max said. "Cole was standing about twenty feet away from us. He was talking to the Sawyers. You couldn't miss him, not with that swollen nose Natasha gave him. He was still there when I got your text and left."

"And he didn't follow Max," Janelle said. "We were standing only a few feet away."

I took a deep breath. The doctor was right. The sooner everyone cleared out so I could be alone with my thoughts, the better. Someone had attacked me. But if it wasn't Cole, then who?

"Maybe it was one of the zoning commission members," I said finally. "After all, I got angry at them during the meeting, too. One of them might have wanted to kill me."

"Because you got pissed they rezoned the Fields property and okayed franchises?" Ryan looked skeptical. "Every OPBA member is out for their blood right now. What is this so-called killer going to do? Knock off the entire membership?"

"But—"

Tess pushed past Ryan and bent over me. "Marlee, you got dizzy and hit your head on the post. Then, as you were falling, you smacked your head again on the dock. You had a terrible accident tonight and almost died. Thank God Max got there before you drowned. But no one tried to kill you." She kissed my cheek as if I was a fretful child that needed soothing. "It was an accident, nothing more. You're going to be fine now. That's all that matters." She smiled. "And we all love you."

This was echoed by a chorus of "We love you, Marlee." I managed a weak smile in return. It would be pointless and exhausting to argue any further tonight. But as soon as I got out of here, I'd launch my own investigation. Someone tried to kill me tonight. I didn't plan to wait around until the murderer decided to strike again.

Chapter 7

I had never taken enough time off from work to realize that a little leisure time can get one into a lot of trouble. After my release from the hospital the following morning, I was ordered to spend a few days resting at home. Since my stomach was still rebelling from all the river water I'd swallowed and my head throbbed if I sat up too fast, I agreed to take it easy. But within twenty-four hours, I'd cleaned out the pantry, done all my quarterly billing, and redesigned the front page of The Berry Basket website.

Even if I wanted to rest, the constant visits from Tess, Max, Ryan, Gillian, and Piper prevented me from relaxing. I was relieved Aunt Vicki had left Friday morning to attend an animal rights rally in Washington, D.C. If she were here, she'd haul me off to her farmhouse to tend to me as she did the numerous animals in need of care at the shelter she ran. Fortunately, the tribe of Italian relatives on my mom's side of the family lived in metro Detroit and rarely ventured west of Lansing. However that didn't stop them from texting me nonstop. Not that I was ungrateful for everyone's concern, but all the attention only added to my stress over Natasha's disappearance, the loss of my store, and the attack on Friday night.

To make matters worse, YouTube struck again. When word got around that I was dragged out of the river unconscious, whoever had filmed Piper punching Cole at the OPBA meeting decided I was newsworthy as well. It was the only explanation I could find for footage of me describing how best to hit Cole over the head popping up on YouTube. I assumed the same person was responsible for posting footage of both Piper and me from that meeting. Then again, everyone had a cell phone with a video camera now. For all I knew, each of us was filmed as soon as we left the house every morning. Privacy had become no more than a quaint notion from a bygone age, like curtsying.

By Sunday afternoon, I was sick of pretending to rest and recover. I decided to go into work, only to have Gillian and Dean literally chase me out the door of The Berry Basket. Gillian even threatened to call my parents in New Zealand if I didn't go home and binge watch some cable show I had missed.

Instead, I headed for the police station, hoping Officer Janelle Davenport was on duty. It was tourist season in Oriole Point. That meant our small police force was either off giving speeding tickets or sitting in the white clapboard building on Lyall Street, waiting for the next frantic call over some tourist doing something stupid on the river or the lake. At night, the complaints shifted to tourists doing something stupid at the Sandy Shoals Saloon. Violent crime was rare in our village. Maybe the fact that our police chief, Gene Hitchcock, shared the same last name as the famous director of *Psycho* caused potential criminals to think twice.

When I walked inside the station, the first person I saw was Suzanne Cabot, the receptionist. No one in Oriole Point was the fount of more rumors, gossip, and secrets, not even her sons Andrew and Dean. I wondered if she might have any ideas as to where Natasha had gone to, but at the moment she was trying to calm down two young men in surfer shorts. From what I could hear, some guy on a WaveRunner had knocked them off their paddleboards directly in the path of Oriole Point's chain ferry.

When Suzanne glanced over, I mouthed "Janelle?"

"Crystal's," she said before returning her attention to the two guys.

An intense police officer called Bruno Wykoff now joined the group, and everyone grew even more animated and loud. My head threatened to burst from the noise, and I gladly left. If Janelle was relaxing at Coffee by Crystal, it meant she would be in a receptive mood for my latest theory. Janelle loved her lattes and cappuccinos, and there was no better time to approach her than when she was sipping some highly caffeinated drink.

Five minutes later, I surprised Janelle as she sat at one of the sidewalk tables scattered on the front terrace of Coffee by Crystal, Oriole Point's favorite coffee hangout. The off-duty officer seemed engrossed in both her enormous iced coffee and a paperback thriller. When I sat across from her, she looked up with a surprised smile.

"I thought the doctor told you to rest at home for a few days." She closed her book.

"Hard to rest when someone has tried to kill you."

"Are we back to that again?" Janelle took a long sip of her coffee.

She wore a white tank top and jeans, which made her look a good ten years younger than she did when in uniform. As always, her impressive well-toned upper arms, aviator sunglasses, and lean, angled face brought to mind the warrior mom Sarah Connor in *Terminator 2.* It remained something of a mystery why she had chosen our lakeshore village to continue her career in law enforcement. With such a formidable demeanor, Janelle seemed a more natural fit for the mean streets of Chicago and Detroit.

I moved to New York City a good four years before she came to Oriole Point to join the police force. When I returned, Janelle was already pegged as Chief Hitchcock's favorite, no surprise considering the often casual policing of his other officers. All I really knew about her was that she hailed from Wisconsin, was divorced with two kids, and that she was respected by the locals. But in a small town like Oriole Point, a person who had lived here only eight years was still on probation. One never knew how much to trust an outsider, especially if that outsider carried a gun.

"I still have a headache, but my memory's improved." I had struggled to recall the details of what happened on the dock all day Saturday, but it was like trying to glimpse an image with blurry vision. However, when I woke up this morning, everything snapped into focus.

She raised an eyebrow. "So you remember what happened that night?"

"It was like I told everyone on Friday. Someone hit me on the head twice, then pushed me into the river."

"Did you see who struck you?"

"No, but I felt their weight on the wooden dock when they walked up behind me."

"You never looked around to see who it was?"

"I assumed it was Ryan. I even said something like 'About time you got here.' I started to turn around and saw a shadow out of the corner of my eye. It had to have been whatever I was struck with. I didn't have time to do much after that before I was hit again."

"And that's when you lost your balance and fell into the water?"

"I never lost my balance. How many times do I have to say this? My attacker shoved me off the dock. I remember feeling their hand on my back. And once I hit the water, I blacked out. But I was struck twice and pushed into the river. I know that for a fact. Which means someone tried to kill me."

"But you have no idea who would want to kill you." Janelle seemed as unmoved by this story as she had been on Friday night.

"Look, I'm not the police officer. You are. I assume crime solving is part of your job description."

She took a long sip of coffee. "And I assume that someone who was bashed on the head two days ago might have a few problems with her memory."

I counted to ten before answering. "My memory is fine now. And it tells me this may have been the second time an attempt was made on my life."

At last I spied a spark of interest on Janelle's face. "When was the other attempt?"

"Thursday, right before the big storm hit. Cole came to my store at closing time. He thought I was hiding Natasha and got pissed off when I told him I didn't know where she was. When he left, he forgot his briefcase, and I ran after him to give it back. But right before I got to him, this car came squealing around the corner and headed straight for us. It barely missed hitting Cole, and I thought the whole time that he was the target." I paused. "I even was afraid Natasha might be the driver. After all, she has more than enough reasons to want her husband dead. But now I think the driver may have been trying to kill me."

Janelle threw up her hands. "And this is the first the police hear about it? Or don't you think we need to know there's a crazed motorist careening through downtown, trying to run people over?" Luckily, not only were the nearby tables empty, but two leashed dogs yapping at each other on the sidewalk drowned out her raised voice.

"What are you getting angry at me for? I thought Cole was the intended victim, and told him to report it to the police. But he thought it wasn't worth reporting."

"You should have reported it, regardless."

"Yes, it probably would have done as much good as reporting the disappearance of Natasha Bowman. Which I did on Friday morning. And exactly how much information have you turned up since she disappeared?"

Janelle whipped off her sunglasses. "Odette Henderson saw Natasha leave the Kitchen Cellar store immediately following her argument with Cole. Odette swears Natasha was not bleeding or bruised, nor did she seem to have any problem walking down the street. Therefore, we can probably dismiss the possibility of broken bones. From where I sit, it appears Natasha took off after the fight with her husband on Thursday and plans to stay away for a few days. Which wouldn't be the first time she has done so."

I shook my head. "Except the last time she did this, she went to Chicago to stay with that former Miss Belgium who competed in Miss World with her. And the time before that, she hid out at my house. Natasha doesn't vanish into thin air after she has a big fight with Cole. This time is different."

"Yes, it is. This time she was the one who injured Cole. He's pressing charges, and we issued a warrant for her arrest. If you ask me, that's pretty strong motivation for her to remain out of sight, at least until Cole's temper cools down."

My headache was growing worse. "Cole is a violent and possessive husband. I don't know how anyone can blame Natasha for finally fighting back."

"I don't blame her. But Cole is the one who was assaulted by Natasha. And he has every right to press charges. What happens after she's arrested is up to the courts and whatever strange mood Cole is in at the time."

This further irritated me, because Janelle was right. Natasha was my friend, but how many times had I warned her to leave that creep of a husband? She had waited too long to take action and had done it in the worst possible way when she did.

"There should be bulletins on the news asking people if they've seen her," I persisted. "She could be lying hurt somewhere. Or dead. Maybe Cole tracked her down later. For all we know, her body is in the basement of the Bowman house."

"Either you took too much Vicodin today or you need to go home and take some more. But let me assure you, there is no dead body in the Bowman basement." Janelle chuckled at the thought, which only pissed me off more.

"How do you know that?"

"Do you really think someone would disappear and we wouldn't question the spouse or bother to search their residence? Yes, Marlee, we went through the Bowman house—with Cole's blessing, by the way—and found nothing suspicious."

"Nothing of Natasha's was missing?"

"Not according to her husband."

I sat back in disbelief. "You can't believe anything Cole says, especially where his wife is concerned. Let me go in there with the police and look around. I've been to their house dozens of times. I could tell you if anything of hers was missing or disturbed."

"That is so not going to happen." Janelle put her sunglasses back on.

"Am I the only person in Oriole Point who is worried about Natasha?"

She shrugged. "You do seem to be her only real friend. As far as we know, you are the only person in town who ever visited her at home or had her over to your own place. That doesn't speak well for Miss Russia. Why wasn't she welcomed by the people in town?"

"Lots of reasons. Small-town prejudice against out-siders. Also, she was married to Cole, who everyone knows is a disgusting pig. Even the gossip about how abusive her marriage was made people shy away. It didn't help that Cole's financial meltdown in Chicago was so public. People don't like to borrow trouble."

"None of that bothered you, though."

"Why should it? I like Natasha. And I sympathized with her. It can't have been easy when she and Cole moved here three years ago. Until I moved back a year later, I'll bet hardly anyone said two words to her. All people knew was that she was a beauty queen from Russia who married Cole weeks after meeting him. And that she was half his age. The whole thing screamed 'gold digger.'"

"If the shoe fits . . ."

I rolled my eyes. "Oh, please. There are lots of big houses on the lake owned by rich men from Chicago with much younger wives. The difference is they keep a low profile. Cole was almost as famous as Donald Trump for a while. I'm sure the two of them attracted a lot of attention when he moved back. Believe me, if I wasn't born and raised in Oriole Point, people would have treated me differently when I came back, too." Indeed, being involved in a notorious murder case was much worse than having a real estate company go belly up, at least if you were trying to make a home for yourself in our lakeshore village.

"The Chaplin murder did stay in the news for the better part of a year," Janelle said wryly. "I'm not surprised you returned here to regroup. Do you intend to go back to New York and work in television again? Or maybe L.A.?"

"I never meant to work in television in the first place. My goal was to get into marketing after I graduated from NYU. That's why my first internship was in the marketing department at Dean & DeLuca. I was surprised at how much I enjoyed working with food when I was there. So when that internship ended and one at the Gourmet Living Network was offered, I took it." I looked off into the distance. "Things didn't work out as planned."

That was an understatement. My first job at the network was interning on a popular cooking show called *Tandoori Delight,* starring Johar Bhaduri. He was a jocular chef from Bengal who cooked for his live audience while entertaining them with jokes and personal anecdotes, sort of an Indian version of Emeril. It was all great fun until the day he made the chicken vindaloo that gave everyone in the studio audience a serious case of food poisoning; three people wound up in intensive care. Bhaduri's contract was not renewed, and he went off to land himself another cooking show, this one in New Delhi.

After another year of working at the network, I was thrilled to land an assistant producer job on *The Amish Kitchen.* No live audience here, just a demure young woman called Hannah Miller, who left her Amish community in Indiana with little more than the clothes on her back and a wealth of Amish recipes. Both the show and Hannah had a homespun charm that connected so well with viewers that I convinced the network to have Hannah release a cookbook to launch her second season. My marketing plans and national promotion for the cookbook were too successful. Within a month, we learned that our shy Amish Hannah was actually a former stripper from Saskatchewan called Tiffany. We quickly pulled *The Amish Kitchen* off the schedule. Last I heard, Hannah/Tiffany had appeared on three different reality shows; one of them involved her experiences in rehab.

I soon redeemed myself with the network when I discovered the Chaplins at a food expo in Nashville. The married couple's affectionate banter, combined with her fabulous pastries and his Southern recipes, seemed tailor made for a cooking show. For the next three years, I was producer and creator of *Sugar and Spice*, the most popular show on the network. So popular that it spawned two cookbooks, a set of Chaplin enameled cookware, and boxed cake and bread mixes bearing the *Sugar and Spice* name. We were on track for food superstardom until an intern called April wriggled onto our set. Fourteen months later, Evangeline Chaplin baked an arsenic-filled anniversary cake for her philandering husband. And that was the end of both John Chaplin and my career in television.

"I followed that trial like everyone else in the country," Janelle said. "I never understood why you and the other producer told the wife about the affair."

"We didn't have much choice. John and April were indiscreet. My fellow producer and I talked to them privately about cooling things down for a while. We even tried to get April transferred to another show, but John refused to let us take April away. And April was fastened on him like a parasite. Then we got a call from the *New York Post*, saying they had photos of John and April all over each other at a club in Soho. The story was hitting the newsstands the next day. We had no choice but to go to Evangeline that night." I sighed. "She was in the middle of cooking an anniversary dinner for just the two of them, which included John's favorite cake."

Janelle finished off her coffee. "With a surprise ingredient of arsenic."

"Yeah, that surprised all of us." I gave her a penetrating look. "This is why I'm so concerned about Natasha. Cole has a violent temper, and he must be furious Natasha struck him. I think she's probably terrified."

"We have a warrant out for her arrest, and we've questioned Cole twice and searched his house. I don't know what else you expect us to do."

"Don't you find it suspicious that Natasha disappears but seems to have taken nothing with her? Not even her car. How did she leave town? Unless the police think she levitated out of Oriole Point."

Janelle adjusted her sunglasses. "Natasha found friends to help her during previous fights with Cole. It's likely she's done so again."

"Wow. What does it take to get the police to do their job? A woman disappears, and everyone sits around, drinking coffee."

"Be careful, Marlee. I'll let you and your head injury go only so far."

"Yes, because being deferential around the police is what's really important. Is your friend missing? Relax. Don't worry. Did you get bashed over the head and shoved into the river? Go home and take a Vicodin. And you wonder why I didn't report the driver of that car." I leaned forward. "You know, being a police officer in this town sometimes requires more than handing out tickets to reckless kayakers."

"I know my job."

"And I know my friend is missing. I also know someone tried to kill me."

She held up a finger. "You *suspect* someone tried to

kill you. You don't know anything. And we've already questioned people who were at the marina on Friday night. No one reported seeing anything suspicious."

"When there are fireworks on the lake, everyone is pointed toward the beach and looking up at the sky. Why should someone bother to pay attention to the boat slips?"

"What more do you want the police to do? We're also in the process of questioning the members of the zoning commission, since it appears you threatened to uncover some dastardly secrets about them during the meeting." She laughed. "I saw that YouTube clip of you describing how best to land a lethal blow to Cole's head. I can't believe some of the ridiculous things civilians say in public."

I was about to make a caustic reply when my lacerations sent a jolt of pain along my skull. Pain must have registered on my face, and Janelle's mocking expression turned serious.

"Marlee, you should be home, taking it easy. Head injuries are serious business." She got to her feet. "Stay here. I think you need something to drink. What would you like?"

I cradled my head in my hands. "Iced tea. Thanks."

When Janelle returned with the drink, I felt less angry but far more frustrated. And afraid. This must have been apparent to Janelle since she patted me on the shoulder.

"It's been a rough couple of days for you," she said while I took grateful sips of iced tea. "I heard what happened at the OPBA meeting. I know Cole plans to shut your store down."

"I still haven't figured out what to do about that." Between Natasha going missing, April's exposé of

Sugar and Spice, and being assaulted on the dock, the imminent demise of my business had actually taken a backseat. It was one hell of a bad week when financial ruin was the least unpleasant thing on the list. "I'd do anything to save The Berry Basket, only I can't figure out what to do. Whatever it is, I better do it quick. My lease runs out at the end of the month."

Janelle cocked her head at me. "Why berries?"

"What do you mean?"

"Why did you decide to sell berry products? You could have opened up a gallery or a wine-tasting room. Even a boutique. Why berries? I've heard the Jacobs once owned berry fields that rivaled the Zellars or Crane Orchards in Allegan County. But your family got out of the fruit-growing business. Why go back in?"

No doubt Janelle had heard the entire story about how we had lost our land, but she obviously wanted to distract me from Natasha and the assault on the dock.

"We didn't get out of the business. We lost the business. The Jacobs have been farmers and fruit growers in Oriole County since my great-great-grandparents. Even back in the Netherlands, the family grew berries and pears. They had a gift for it, a passion. But things fell apart when my dad and his sister Vicki took over the business. Neither of them inherited the Jacob agricultural gene. Within five years of Grandpa's death, we lost the orchards to the bank."

I didn't add that the loss of the family business through mismanagement and laziness was why I had developed such a fanatical work ethic. Not that it appeared to have done much good. Despite working nonstop at The Berry Basket over the past two years and at the Gourmet Living Network before that, it looked like I might end up as bankrupt as my father.

I tipped back my iced tea and drained it. I set the glass back down on the table with an audible sigh. "After the orchards were sold, the Jacobs went to seek their fortune in the big city. Chicago for them, New York for me."

"But you came back and decided to sell berries."

"It felt right. I grew up playing in the family orchards and berry fields. My grandparents taught me everything they knew about fruit growing, and I gravitated toward the raspberries and blueberries, not the fruit trees. I think it's my need for immediate gratification. Trees take a long time to mature, but berry bushes start producing within a few years." I smiled. "Plus, I genuinely enjoy working with the berry growers, creating recipes, discovering new products tied to the fruit. I'm good at it. And it seems fitting that five generations in a row have been in the business of selling berries. That's important to me. More important than I realized."

"You're marrying a fruit grower, as well. Was that intentional?"

I stiffened. "Of course not. I've known the Zellar family since I was born. I went to school with Ryan's younger brother. The Zellar boys were like Oriole Point's version of the Baldwin brothers. Every girl had their heart set on one of them. I got lucky. But none of us cared about what they did for a living. We just thought the Zellars were cute."

Janelle rattled the ice in her plastic coffee cup. "Seems providential to me. Two fruit-growing families being joined together through marriage. Your grandfather would be pleased."

"Don't know how pleased he'd be. The Zellars were one of the orchards that bought the Jacob properties from the bank."

"That's even more perfect. By marrying Ryan Zellar, you'll be taking back part of what your family lost."

"I'm not marrying him for anything like that," I muttered. "We love each other."

"Of course you do. But it's an unexpected benefit. Talk about coming full circle."

"Speaking of full circle, how long does Natasha have to be gone before a full-scale bloodhound search is launched for her?"

"As soon as we have evidence of foul play." At my muttered curse, Janelle said, "Hey, we were getting along so well. Let's not go back to arguing about Miss Russia again."

"Just because Natasha was a beauty queen doesn't mean her disappearance should be treated lightly. It's not Natasha's fault she's gorgeous."

"I don't care what she looks like. But what I've learned about her in the past few days is not endearing. Did you know her uncle Leonid emigrated to America twelve years ago? He operated a cocaine-smuggling ring out of Miami. At least until he was put in prison for shooting two businessmen. Although, we aren't sure exactly what business they were in."

Although startled by this news, I was determined not to get sidetracked. "I don't see how we can blame someone for what their relative does."

"I'm not blaming Natasha, but I'm suspicious. We know very little about her background, aside from the fact that she won a lot of beauty contests in

Eastern Europe. And that she came in ninth in the Miss World Contest when it was held in Chicago." She peeked over the sunglasses to give me a cynical look. "Where real estate magnate Cole Bowman just happened to be one of the judges. And they got married six weeks later."

"Stop the presses. 'Rich older man marries beautiful young woman.' That's about as startling as 'Rock star marries supermodel.'"

"I only want to remind you that Natasha Rostova is a survivor. Her family tree is filled with other characters nearly as colorful as Uncle Leonid. Be realistic. You met her only two years ago, Marlee. How much do you really know about her?"

"I know she was afraid of Cole. With reason." I thought a moment. "When did you search the Bowman house?"

"Friday morning. Cole called to ask if the police had learned anything about Natasha. We asked if we could go through her belongings for a clue as to her whereabouts. He agreed."

"Then you haven't been in the house for two days?" She shook her head.

"Maybe Cole tracked her down later. Maybe he brought her back to the house after the police search. Maybe Natasha is there right now, bound and gagged."

"Maybe your head injury has caused you to believe Hannibal Lecter is now living in Oriole Point."

I wasn't certain what my head injury was responsible for, aside from the occasional sharp jabs of pain. "All right. Maybe she isn't trussed up in the Bowman basement. But she could be in trouble. Have you tracked down the signal on her cell phone?"

"Don't have to. Natasha's cell phone was lying on her night table in the bedroom."

I grew dizzy for a moment, and it wasn't only because of my lacerated skull. "Natasha never goes anywhere without her cell phone. Literally. I've been to the gym with her. She puts her phone in a ziplock bag and brings it with her into the shower. If Natasha left her phone behind, things are really ominous."

"Or maybe she didn't want anyone to track her down, which we could easily do if she'd taken the phone." Janelle sighed. "Marlee, I'm trying to humor you because of what happened on Friday. Also, I know you're upset about your friend and losing your store. But this is a police investigation, and you have no business interfering. Now get some rest, like the doctor ordered."

I slowly got to my feet. "You don't believe I was attacked on the dock, do you?"

She had the grace to look sheepish. "No. I believe you had too much to drink, got dizzy, and hit your head on the wood pilings."

"Great. I guess I can go home and relax, confident there will be no further attempts on my life. Apparently, I hallucinated everything that happened last week."

"Go home," she said in an unfriendly tone. "And I hope someone is staying with you. You shouldn't be alone until you've recovered. You clearly need a little help right now."

I didn't tell her that Ryan planned to stay at my house for as long as I wanted him there. "I have friends who want to help me, which is a lot more than the police are willing to do. I suppose I could wait until Chief Hitchcock gets back from Seattle and demand action from him, but either Natasha or I could be dead by then. That means I'll have to handle things on my own."

"Stay out of police business, Marlee."

"Actually, I think you're the one staying out of it." Before she could come up with a rejoinder, I stalked off. I had no time to lie around and recuperate from the attack on the dock. I needed to find out what had happened to Natasha, while trying to figure out who wanted me dead.

Despite my aching skull, I spent the rest of the day driving around Oriole Point, hoping to recognize the car that had nearly run Cole and me down. Since I recalled only that it was a dark color, it was a useless effort, but I needed to keep busy. Cole never worked at his store on Sundays and invariably spent the day at home. That meant I had to wait until tomorrow before I could break into his house.

Chapter 8

"Did you hit your head again, Marlee?" Tess asked. "Because it's the only thing that justifies asking me to break into Cole Bowman's house."

"I'm not asking you to break into Cole's house. I only need you to play lookout for me while I break in." When I drove my bike up the driveway to the house Tess shared with David, she was out back, filling the oriole feeders. David had already left to open their glassworks studio, which meant I didn't have to keep our conversation discreet.

Tess pursed her lips in disapproval while pouring sugar water into one of the feeders. "It looks like you suffered a more serious concussion than we realized. You aren't thinking rationally. In fact, you're not thinking at all. Janelle was right. This is police business. Let them handle it." She glanced over at my mountain bike. "And you shouldn't be riding your bike with a concussion. You have no sense of balance, physically or emotionally. But since I'm not unbalanced, I've no intention of helping you bust into Cole's house."

"If only you weren't such a trigrymate."

"I may be your female companion, but I'm hardly idle. If only you were a dysaniac. You wouldn't be bothering me this early in the morning if you were."

We looked at each other and laughed. As two former spelling bee champions, Tess and I possessed an extensive vocabulary. Since most people were unaware of the full richness of the English language, it was as if we shared access to a secret code.

"Tess, I need to search the house. I don't trust the police to even know what to look for. For one thing, they aren't concerned that Natasha didn't take her phone."

Even she looked troubled by this news. "I know. She never lets it out of her sight. David once saw Natasha texting while she was paddleboarding."

"Exactly. If she's safe, why wouldn't she take her phone with her? I'm telling you, there's something fishy about all this. I need to see what else is in the house that I know she never would have left behind. At least not willingly."

Tess hung the last feeder back up. Several orioles sat in the nearby maples, waiting for us to leave. "I agree none of this sounds good. But breaking and entering isn't the solution. For one thing, how are you planning to get inside?"

"The Bowman house has three outer doors, and the one to the Florida room is often left unlocked. Natasha goes there to smoke. If Cole's home, he yells at her for smoking, so she finishes her cigarette out on the patio. I've been with her when that happens. She usually forgets to latch the door when we go back in."

"You have thought this through," Tess said as we

walked to the garden shed. "But have you thought about what will happen if Cole catches you trespassing?"

"No problem. Before I came here, I biked through downtown. I kept circling Iroquois and Lyall until I saw Cole hang up his OPEN flag outside the store. If we head over to the house right now, there will be no chance of getting caught. He'll be at his shop."

Tess disappeared into the garden shed. When she emerged again, she gave me a pitying look. "I know you're worried about Natasha. We all are. But I can't help you break the law."

I had expected this. In response, I took my bike helmet, which was hanging from the handlebars, and replaced it gingerly on my still aching head. "Fine. I'll do it without a proper lookout. But if I get caught, let it be on your conscience." I hopped on my bike and prepared to pedal away.

"At least I have a conscience."

"Conscience? Where was that conscience when I took the fall for you in tenth grade, after you set all the dissection frogs free? I did six months of after-school detention for your noble but furtive deed. And my punishment included missing a class trip to Mackinac Island."

Her expression went from pained to guilt-stricken. I resorted to the biology frog misadventure only when absolutely necessary. "When are you going to let me forget that?"

I smiled. "After I no longer need a favor from you."

She glared at me. Tess was Japanese American, and when she was irritated, her fierce expression brought to mind a female samurai. "Fine. But if I do this, I never want to hear about those ridiculous frogs again."

As she stomped off to the garage, where her own bike was kept, Tess shouted back at me, "And you have become quite the rantipole!"

Chuckling, I readjusted my helmet. Wild and reckless I might be, but sometimes that was the only way to get things done.

Even though the Bowman house was only twelve blocks away, it felt a lot farther. My head throbbed beneath the bike helmet, and a rivulet of perspiration ran down my face from the already steamy morning. I was glad I'd worn my thinnest cotton shorts and a tank top. Heat waves usually occurred later in the summer, but this was turning out to be an unusual June in more ways than one.

When we turned onto the winding road where the Bowmans lived, I breathed a sigh of relief. Numerous tall trees lined the street, offering welcome shade and privacy. Houses were set back from the road, most of them half hidden by beach grass, shrubbery, and rhododendron bushes now gloriously in bloom. It was an upscale neighborhood, but by no means the most affluent. The grandest houses were found on or near Lakeshore Drive. After Cole's ruinous career in Chicago, he could no longer afford one of those costly addresses.

We cycled up his driveway, and my heart sank to see Natasha's red Subaru still sitting before their three-car garage. I pedaled up to the side of the vehicle. The doors were locked, but I looked inside, trying to spot anything unusual. I tried the garage next, but it was locked, too.

Tess watched while I walked up the front steps and

rang the bell. "You don't really expect anyone to answer, do you?"

"Never hurts to try. Besides, it helps to know the house is empty before breaking in."

"I really do not like this."

"Neither do I. But I don't like that Natasha's disappeared. And I'd do the same if you up and vanished." When the last door chime faded away, I commenced knocking.

"You're making too much noise," Tess warned.

I tried the door. As expected, it was locked. "No one's likely to hear. The houses aren't close together, and the trees and vegetation keep us hidden from view. But let's take the bikes into the backyard. In case someone does drive up, I don't want them to see our bikes sitting out front."

Tess muttered under her breath as we walked around the house and into the half-acre yard. The Bowmans had no interest in gardening, but some professional landscaper had made a decent job of planting little islands of birches, ferns, and perennials about their property. A koi pond sat beside their flagstone patio, while a gas grill roughly the size of a train locomotive stood guard a few yards way. Everything seemed normal, although the mint-green cushions on the lawn furniture were in disarray, probably a result of the violent storm that hit the lakeshore last week.

I was certain the back door was locked, but I tried anyway.

"This makes me very nervous," Tess said in a low voice. "Honestly, I don't care how you suffered over those frogs. I don't think I can be part of this."

"All you have to do is let me know if anyone drives up."

"How do I do that? Text you?"

"Yeah. I'll set my phone to vibrate." I rummaged through my messenger bag and pulled my phone out. I tried to turn it on. "Great. I forgot to recharge it last night."

"Then how can I let you know if someone's coming?"

Looking around, I spotted a tall ornate lamppost. From one of its black iron bars hung enormous aluminum wind chimes. "Rattle the chimes. Believe me, I'll hear them."

Tess still seemed uneasy, and I regretting involving her in this. Sometimes I forgot just how circumspect she was. "Tess, if you get too scared, take your bike and go through those holly bushes. Keep going straight, and you'll hit a new subdivision called Trillium Trail. The only thing you have to worry about is avoiding the Sawyers. They bought a house there last month with money Jerry got from some lawsuit with his brother-in-law."

"How do you know all this?"

"I work with Andrew and Dean. They know everything." I took off my helmet and handed it to her. "Okay. I'm going in."

I marched over to the door to the Florida room and pulled on the handle. It was locked. I yanked harder. Nothing. I was not pleased about this.

Tess came up beside me. "That's it, then." Her relief was obvious. "If all the doors are locked, we may as well leave."

When I scanned the back of the house, I could see the windows were shut tight, as well. On such a warm day, the central air would be on full blast. I was prepared for this.

"Let's go," Tess said.

Ignoring her, I hurried over to the patio and grabbed one of the lawn chairs. Yes, the window over the kitchen sink would do nicely.

Tess followed me as I dragged the chair over to the window. "Sneaking in through an unlocked door is bad enough. But you can't break a window. That is an actual crime."

"Calm down. I'm not going to break the window. I'm simply going to lift the window and screen out of their tracks." I opened my messenger bag and retrieved a small felt pouch. Inside were the screwdriver and clamp I had packed.

"Tools? You brought tools to break into the house?"

"Looked all this up on the Internet last night." I climbed onto the chair. "I should be able to pop out the screen. Then I'll slightly lift out the window, after which I will gently—"

"This is insane, Marlee. You have to stop right now. It's illegal *and* dangerous. You could cut yourself on the glass or fall or—" There was more to Tess's litany, but I was too engrossed in my task to listen or care.

When I finally crawled through the open window and eased myself onto the kitchen counter, I felt as victorious as Edmund Hilary scaling Everest. I stuck my head out the window. "I'm going to put the window back in, then run over to the Florida room and unlock the door. This way, if someone does surprise me, I'll simply say the back door was open."

Tess looked even more distressed. "When did you turn into Catwoman?"

But I didn't have time to reassure my hyperventilating friend. I was too busy snapping the window and the screen back into place. After a quick trip to the Florida room to unlock the door, I raced back to the kitchen. Only then did I feel a wave of uneasiness.

The house was quiet, and I found the silence unnerving. What if Cole *had* killed his wife? It was a real possibility. He was a violent, brutish man. And the high-maintenance Natasha was not a good match for him. Of course, no woman aside from Lizzie Borden would be a good candidate for Mrs. Bowman. I turned slowly and looked about the kitchen. The granite countertops were clear of clutter. Except for the partially filled coffeemaker pot, nothing in the kitchen looked as if it had been used in the past few days. Not that the kitchen ever looked used. Natasha was a great one for carryout.

I was torn between looking for what Natasha might have left behind upstairs and searching for her possible remains. My head swam again, and I fought back a wave of dizziness and alarm. I feared Natasha was dead. If she was, the man who had killed her was most likely her husband . . . whose house I was standing in. Nope. Too late to back down now. I had to take advantage of this opportunity to search the premises. Unlike the police, I had been friends with Natasha for two years. And like all friends, we'd been to each other's homes a number of times. I knew this place pretty well.

Taking a deep breath, I headed for the basement first. It was a large daylight basement filled with little more than daylight, Cole's rowing machine, and scattered pieces of furniture that had once been in their Chicago penthouse. No place to hide a body here. I went back up to the kitchen and examined the walk-in pantry. The living room and family room were next; both were a collection of unattractive contemporary furniture surrounded by stacks of magazines. The front closet held nothing but coats and an absurd number of golf jackets.

Tess was probably frantic, if she wasn't long gone. Next, I headed for the office, which was little more than a cubby. Cole's computer sat on the desk, but I bet he was wary enough to use a password. I sat before the large monitor and clicked on the computer. I was right. If secrets were hidden on his hard drive, I wouldn't be able to retrieve them.

A glance around the small room told me there were few opportunities for snooping. The two file cabinets were locked; I thought briefly about using my tools to break into them, but I hadn't read up on how to disable a cabinet lock.

A stack of mail lay on his desk, and I thumbed through it: bills, correspondence with Fitzgerald Developers in Chicago, sale flyers. I was about to put them back when I spied a business envelope that hadn't been opened. The return address, North Yorkshire, England, caught my eye. I knew only one person from Yorkshire: Drake Woodhill. And Drake was a member of the zoning commission. I held the envelope up to the window but couldn't see anything.

When I gave it a shake, the contents seemed to shift as one, as if a booklet was inside or a sheaf of papers stapled together. The sender was a V. Sanderton, which meant nothing to me.

Next, I rifled through a notepad on his desk, but the only thing that jumped out at me were the letters *S, A, M, H, A, I,* and *N* written on one of the pages. I knew Samhain was a Celtic word for Halloween, not a subject I imagined Cole would be interested in.

After replacing the mail, I scanned the bookshelves, most of which were filled with biographies and memoirs of business moguls: Sam Walton, Lee Iacocca, Jack Welch, Steve Jobs. The other books were about real estate investment and development, except for one shelf devoted to Tom Clancy novels. I was about to call my search of the office quits when I spied the faded spine of a slim volume tucked beside a copy of *The 7 Habits of Highly Effective People.* I pulled it out and was surprised by the title: *Romuva.*

As a spelling bee champion since the age of eight, I possessed an endless compendium of archaic words. And this one seemed vaguely familiar, something to do with the pre-Christian religion of the Baltic people. Opening it up told me little, since the script resembled Russian. It probably belonged to Natasha. I replaced the book and hurried upstairs.

There were four bedrooms. I decided to go through the guest bedrooms first and searched under the beds, in the closets, and in the dressers and highboys. The house lacked an attic, so that left only the bathrooms and the master bedroom, which I kept for last. The master was yet another room filled with sleek contemporary furniture, which was not my style. I loved distressed, vintage, old, and quirky. I preferred character in my furniture and my

friends. Since Natasha loved anything plush and
bordered with gilt, it was obvious the entire house
was the domain of her overbearing husband.

In fact, except for the high-fashion contents of
her walk-in closet and the framed photos of her
beauty pageant career on the walls, the house held
no sign of Natasha Rostova at all. I rifled through
her dresser drawers, hunted through her shoe racks,
even peeked inside the satin-lined boxes of designer
handbags, yet nothing seemed to be missing. Not a
single hanger was empty, all the shoe racks were
filled, and her dresser drawers were stuffed to bursting. And Natasha's cell phone was nowhere to be
seen. The police had probably confiscated it.

Depressed, I sat on the plush carpeting and
leaned back against the king-size bed. There was no
sign Natasha had taken anything with her. That
somehow didn't trouble the police, who believed she
was hiding from her angry husband. But Natasha
never traveled light. We once spent a girls' weekend
in Chicago, and she had brought three pieces of
luggage and a carry-on.

This search confirmed my worst fears. It was
Monday morning, and she'd been missing since
Thursday afternoon. No one had seen her since she
left Kitchen Cellar following her big argument with
Cole, an argument about the strawberry fields. Cole
was already furious at her for whacking him in the
nose with a pizzelle maker. And it seemed likely
Natasha was the one who had informed Keith
VanderHoff that same day about Cole's plans for
the Fields property.

Of course, all of us would have learned about his
plans fairly soon. Especially since my lease ran out in

two weeks. But by breaking the news early, Natasha might have made things more difficult for Cole. Perhaps someone in the Oriole Point business community could throw a monkey wrench in his plans. Cole must have been in a black fury Thursday evening, no doubt made even fouler after Piper punched him in front of half the town. Did Natasha come back home that night only to find her husband more out of control and violent than usual?

With a mournful sigh, I got to my feet. This had been a futile effort, along with a dispiriting one. Natasha had disappeared with no signs of a struggle, but she hadn't taken a single possession with her. My friend was most likely dead. The realization suddenly brought me to tears, and I had a good cry for myself. After about ten minutes, I got myself under control.

It was time to leave, especially since I had no idea how long I'd been searching. About to shut off the light in the walk-in closet, I paused to straighten one of Natasha's photos on the wall. I felt on the verge of tears once more at the sight of Natasha's favorite books stacked on top of her scarf drawers: a Russian translation of the *Outlander* series, a biography of Marilyn Monroe, coffee table volumes on cosmetics and fashion. My eyes suddenly widened. I grabbed the books and rifled through each one to make sure I wasn't mistaken.

Natasha's dream dictionaries were gone! Doing a fist pump, I let out a whoop of joy. Natasha was a huge believer in the significance of dreams. She had three well-thumbed dream dictionaries, which she referred to constantly. Natasha also wrote down her dreams in a notebook as soon as she woke each morning, after which she immediately grabbed her dream dictionaries and scrambled to interpret them. I'd lost count of how many times I'd been drafted to help her figure out what her latest dream meant. Even when we took that weekend trip to Chicago, Natasha had brought the dictionaries with her. I ran to the night table beside the bed and searched both drawers. Her dream notebook was gone, too.

I burst out laughing. Natasha was alive! Leave it to that crazy, dream-obsessed beauty queen to make her getaway with just the clothes on her back—and her dream dictionaries and notebook. I felt like a leaden weight had lifted off my shoulders. But I didn't have time to savor my relief. Something clanged outside. It was the wind chimes on the patio. Tess was signaling me that someone was coming to the house!

I hurriedly replaced the books on the scarf drawers, shut off the closet light, and ran for the stairs. But before I could take another step, I heard the key in the front door, followed by the sound of Cole's voice. He was speaking to someone. I swore under my breath. There was no way I could race down the stairs before he entered the house. The front door led right into a wide hallway in the center of which was the stairway. He couldn't avoid seeing me.

The front door opened. I spun about and ran for one of the guest bedrooms overlooking the backyard. I tried to see if I could spy Tess anywhere outside, but she must have taken off for that new subdivision just on the other side of the holly bushes.

Uncertain what to do next, I kept an ear cocked for the sound of Cole downstairs. I heard nothing but birdsong. Was that coming through the open front door? If so, why hadn't Cole entered the house yet? The next sound I heard was a car starting up, then pulling away.

Barely breathing, I tiptoed out of the bedroom and returned to the top of the stairs. Had Cole come back for something quick, like a file from his office? Maybe he had already retrieved what he wanted and was on his way back to the store. I stood motionless for several excruciating minutes, listening for any sound downstairs. Again, I heard nothing but bird-song.

Holding my breath, I crept down the stairs. When I reached the bottom step, I peeked over in the direction of the front door. The door had been left wide open, and sunlight was streaming inside. I gasped and almost toppled over in shock.

A body lay sprawled across the open threshold.

After a second of paralyzing fear, I ran over and knelt beside the motionless body. It was Cole, the left side of his head covered in blood. Not knowing what else to do, I shouted for help. Although no one could help Cole now. He was dead.

Chapter 9

For the first time in our twenty-year friendship, I saw Tess's cool demeanor shatter. Given the circumstances, it was understandable. After I found Cole, I shouted her name so loud, they probably heard me in Milwaukee. By the time she had raced around the corner of the house, I was speechless with shock. Tess made up for my stunned silence by letting out an unnerving series of screams.

"I don't have my phone with me," I said when Tess finally quieted down. "Use yours to call the police. Now!"

Meanwhile, I worked up the nerve to look closer at the body. As I thought, Cole had been killed by a blow to the head. Given the amount of blood covering both his face and the welcome mat before his front door, I suspected multiple blows. At least one of them had gashed open his skin with the impact. I shuddered to see that Cole's eyes were wide open. Had he been looking at his killer when he was struck?

"This is terrible!" Tess said after she made the call.

"A murderer was just here. A murderer! What are we going to do?"

"We've called the police. There's nothing more we can do."

Tess looked white as chalk, and I felt terrible for involving her. I went over and wrapped an arm about her trembling shoulders. "The police will be here soon."

Tess closed her eyes, unable to look at Cole's body. "I heard someone drive up a few minutes ago. That's why I rang the chimes to warn you. Did you see who did it?"

"No. I was upstairs, in Natasha's bedroom. I tried to run downstairs, but the front door opened, and I heard Cole talking to somebody. I went back upstairs to hide."

She nodded. "I heard two car doors slam. Cole wasn't alone."

"Obviously." I sighed.

Tess peeked at Cole's body, then shut her eyes again. "Marlee, it looks like he was hit on the left side of the head. Didn't you say at the OPBA meeting that his left temple was injured when he was younger? And that Natasha said if she wanted to kill him, she could hit him there?"

"Yes." I cursed myself for revealing in public what Natasha had told me.

"What if Natasha killed him?" she whispered.

I didn't want to think about that, not when I still felt relief about Natasha being alive. "No one liked Cole. It could have been anyone. Maybe now people will believe me when I say I was bashed over the head Friday night."

Tess's fearful expression turned to horror. "I'm

sorry for not believing you, Marlee. This is worse than I thought. The same person who murdered Cole tried to murder you! We have to do something before the killer strikes again!" She began to tremble.

I was trying to calm my friend down when two police cars pulled into the driveway. Janelle Davenport got out of one car, the sunlight glinting off her aviator glasses. I regretted once more that Chief Hitchcock was still in Seattle. Janelle didn't look any happier to see me as she and the other officers hurried to where Tess and I stood by the body. We both tried to explain what had happened, but Janelle's attention was more focused on securing the crime scene. A third police car soon arrived, along with an ambulance.

Tess and I stood off to one side, our arms around each other for support. Finally, Janelle walked over with a stern expression.

"Who found the body? And one at a time please. I couldn't understand half of what the two of you were saying when we got here."

I stepped forward. "I found the body."

When I explained how I was on the stairs when the front door opened, Janelle held up her hand. "Hold on. Why were you in the Bowman house?"

My cheeks grew hot. "I wanted to check things out for myself. Like I told you yesterday, I needed to see if anything of Natasha's was missing."

Her expression grew even more forbidding. "How did you get in?"

"Natasha usually keeps the door to the Florida room open. I entered through there." I felt bad about lying, but I'd feel a lot worse if Janelle arrested me for breaking and entering.

Janelle looked over at Tess. "And you. Were you inside the house, too?"

"No. I waited out back. Marlee shouted for me when she found the body." Tess's voice was shaking as much as she was. I hoped she wasn't about to go into shock.

"Don't blame Tess. This is all my fault. She was only doing me a favor, because she knew how worried I was about Natasha."

"Officer Wykoff!" Janelle waved to a policeman by one of the patrol cars. "Take these two women to the station. They're going to be charged with breaking and entering."

My heart sank.

"No!" Tess grew even paler, and I feared she might pass out.

"Leave Tess out of this," I insisted.

"You involved her, not me." She shook her head. "And count yourself lucky that you're not being arrested for murder. Not yet, anyway."

At that, both of us set up such a commotion, it took two officers to lead us away and stow us in one of the patrol cars. Tess began to cry. If I had felt bad before about involving Tess, I felt positively evil now. I knew only one thing for certain. I would never make Tess feel guilty about those damn biology frogs again.

Despite my guilt at involving my friend, things would have been a lot worse if Tess hadn't been with me. Her brother Mitchell was married to a well-known criminal attorney in Grand Rapids. Despite being only thirty-six, Elaine Snow had gained national attention for several high-profile cases, all of which she had won. I was relieved when Tess called Elaine before we even reached the police station on Lyall Street. Officer Wykoff ordered her to put the phone away, but for the first time in her life, Tess Nakamura seemed bent on breaking the rules.

When we arrived at the station, it was pandemonium. News travels fast in our village, but this time, word of Cole's death must have spread by telepathy. Although after one look at the excitement on the police receptionist's face, I had no doubt Suzanne had been making her own calls while fielding the ones from the officers at the Bowman house.

We were quickly ushered into a room at the back of the station house. Unlike the windowless interrogation rooms in TV shows, this one held a barred window that looked out on the small garden behind the Mockingbird Gallery. Otherwise, it resembled those TV holding rooms: a long wooden table, four chairs, and unadorned walls. After Tess's cell phone was confiscated, we were told to wait there until Officer Janelle Davenport arrived. A moment later, Suzanne hurried in with two water bottles and a package of Oreos.

She patted me on the shoulder. "I called Andrew. He promised to let Ryan know what happened."

"Could you call David, too?" Tess asked.

Suzanne nodded before shutting the door behind her.

I reached for a water bottle and unscrewed the cap. "They probably both know we're here. Andrew's working at The Berry Basket today. Between Andrew and his mother, I'm sure even the White House has heard about us finding Cole's body."

After a while, the noise from outside our door grew to a roar. I thought I recognized Gillian's voice, followed by Max's. The door suddenly flew open, and Piper stuck her head in.

"This is madness!" she shrieked. "What in the name of God is going on?" Piper looked thoroughly distressed, and I was touched by her concern for us.

Before we could answer, she was unceremoniously yanked away by an unseen hand, and the door banged shut. This time the sound of the lock clicking followed. The next two hours were filled with people banging on the door, raised voices in the hallway, phones ringing, doors slamming. I began to feel relieved that Tess and I were locked in this room. It seemed like the calmest place in the police station. I spent a lot of the time apologizing to Tess.

That all changed with the simultaneous arrival of Janelle and Elaine Snow. When both women entered the room—each wearing an officious expression—I could feel the estrogen level in the room spike. Janelle was the more muscular of the two, an Amazon in police uniform. But Elaine towered over her with the help of designer stilettos, and her cool self-confidence trumped Janelle's attitude. There was a brief power play when Elaine demanded time to confer privately with her clients, a request that was reluctantly granted. But soon enough, Janelle was back in the room, Officer Bruno Wykoff in tow. They sat across the table from the three of us, and the questioning began.

We repeated what we'd told the police back at the

Bowman house, only this time our statements were written down.

"Now, after you broke into Mr. Bowman's house—"

"My clients did not break into the premises," Elaine said. "Miss Jacob is a good friend of Mrs. Bowman and has been a guest at the residence numerous times. Being such a good friend, she was aware Mrs. Bowman often left the Florida room door unlocked. It has been four days since Mrs. Bowman disappeared. Therefore, it's natural for Miss Jacob to be concerned about her welfare. And it's my understanding that Miss Jacob asked the police if she could accompany them into the house to ascertain if anything looked out of place. Miss Jacob was denied that request."

"This is a police matter, and we intend to handle it without outside interference."

Elaine waved a perfectly manicured hand. "If a missing person's loved one or friend is willing to assist the police, I hardly think it qualifies as interference. Especially if they ask the police to accompany them while they search the missing person's home."

Janelle decided to focus her attention on me; she wasn't getting anywhere by squaring off against our attorney. "And was this illegal search of yours worth it, Marlee? Did you uncover something the police and Natasha's husband missed during our search?"

"As a matter of fact, I did."

Janelle looked startled. "What did you find?"

"It's what I didn't find. Natasha is obsessed with her dreams. She keeps a notebook next to her bed in which she writes down her dreams as soon as she wakes up. And in her walk-in closet, she has three dream dictionaries to help her interpret those dreams."

"What's missing? The dictionaries or her dream notebook?"

"Both."

"And what does that tell you?"

"That Natasha is alive. She might be willing to take off without her clothes or even her car. But Natasha would never leave those dictionaries or her notebook behind."

Janelle nodded. "Then you've come to the same conclusion as the police. Natasha Bowman is not a victim of foul play."

"That's true. I no longer think she is. She planned her escape. And I suspect Natasha wants everyone to think something terrible happened to her."

"Why?"

"You don't have to answer this," Elaine began.

"But I want to." I took a deep breath. "Natasha is afraid of Cole. It was an abusive marriage, and it was only a matter of time before she would be seriously hurt or killed. But she needed to find a way to make her escape without Cole coming after her. She needed a diversion."

"And her disappearance is the diversion?"

"No. The announcement of the sale of the Fields property is. The day of the OPBA meeting, I think she told Keith VanderHoff all about this secret deal Cole had worked out with the Chicago developers. Then she instigated an argument with Cole earlier that day in their store. She even whacked him across the nose for good measure. Given their history, Natasha probably hopes people will think she's hiding from Cole until his anger cools. Which makes the immediate search for her less urgent." I gave Janelle a cynical look. "You can't deny the police have not been all that diligent about tracking her down."

"I'm the one asking the questions here."

I had given this a lot of thought while drinking water and munching Oreos, and I was convinced I was right. "If her disappearance were to look too suspicious, the police would have put out an APB as soon as possible. They might even have tracked her down within a day or two. And she obviously doesn't want that. So in the beginning, it looked like she was hiding somewhere to avoid her husband. Meanwhile, Cole would be distracted from going after her by the whole Fields property announcement. But I think she has another goal in mind."

Everyone turned to me with curious expressions, including Tess and Elaine.

"What is Natasha's ultimate goal?" Janelle asked.

"To punish Cole. And to see that he can never harm her again. If she stays missing, eventually, suspicion will be raised that he got rid of her. After all, Cole choked her in public this past Valentine's Day at San Sebastian. There were dozens of witnesses. The longer she remains missing—especially since her clothes and her car are still here—the more likely it will be that the police might suspect Cole of murder."

"But there would be no body."

"Like you told me yesterday, Natasha is a survivor. She may have planned something to indicate he killed her. A trail of her blood, for example."

"So you think she planned to frame Cole for her murder?" Officer Wykoff asked.

"Probably." I felt disloyal for saying this.

"Maybe she decided to take no chances and killed Cole herself." Janelle leaned forward.

Elaine put her hand on my arm. "This discussion is beyond the purview of either of my clients."

I ignored her. "She didn't kill Cole."

"You know that because . . ."

"Because whoever killed Cole tried to kill me on Friday." I was as certain of that as I had ever been of anything. "And Natasha would never harm me."

"There is no proof anyone harmed you on Friday." Janelle put on a familiar long-suffering expression.

"Because you aren't taking Marlee seriously," Tess said with force. "You just assume she was drunk and somehow hurt herself. Yet she was struck on the side of the head on Friday, just like Cole was. That points to the same perpetrator."

Janelle narrowed her eyes at me. "What I find interesting is that Cole was killed by a blow to his left temple. Something you mentioned at the OPBA meeting last week, Marlee, as is clearly audible on the YouTube video. Maybe someone who was at the meeting or watched the video found your information far too helpful."

I had already thought of this, and the idea made my stomach turn. Was I somehow responsible for Cole's murder? "What I said at the meeting wasn't meant as a tutorial. Cole had just accused Natasha of trying to kill him by whacking him on the nose with a pizzelle maker. And I said that his left temple was the spot she would have struck had she meant to finish him off. Natasha told me about his childhood injury earlier that day."

"Seems a little too pat," Janelle said. "Natasha

explains how best to kill him, and then he dies in just such a fashion four days later. It looks like she had all this planned. I believe that warrant for her arrest may have to include a murder charge. Or at the least, an accessory to murder."

My head throbbed. I also might be willing to murder for a couple of Tylenol right now. "Everyone at the OPBA meeting heard me talk about Cole's left temple. Not to mention the thousands of people who watched that stupid YouTube video." I looked inquiringly at Janelle. "By the way, has anyone figured out who's posting that stuff?"

"Not yet. And as of an hour ago, both videos of the OPBA meeting were taken down."

"I bet the killer did it," Tess said with obvious dismay.

"We don't know who put it up or took it down." Janelle didn't look happy about this.

"The police do not seem to know a great deal," Elaine said. "They certainly don't know enough to hold my clients on a charge of breaking and entering or suspicion of murder."

Janelle nodded at Wykoff, who got to his feet and left the room. "I probably could stretch the breaking and entering charge if I tried, Ms. Snow. But I have more serious matters on my plate than punishing Miss Jacob for playing Nancy Drew."

I bristled at that and was glad when my attorney said, "Yes, and one of those serious matters should be the attack on my client last week."

The door opened and Officer Wykoff returned, carrying a small object in a plastic bag. He sat down beside Janelle once more and laid it on the table before us. My mouth fell open. Inside the bag was a metal muddler. And it was stained with blood.

"Where did you get that?" I bent close to get a better look at it.

"Do you recognize this object?" Janelle asked.

"It's a stainless-steel muddler. I sell them in my store. Wooden muddlers, too."

"Did this come from your store?"

"You don't have to answer," Elaine said quickly.

I saw no point in taking the Fifth on this. "It looks like the brand I carry. But I sell muddlers every week. I sold about six at the Strawberry Moon Bash. And I doubt I'm the only shop along the lakeshore that sells muddlers."

"True. But it does seem likely that whoever handled this muddler last used it to kill Cole Bowman. We're running tests on the blood sample right now."

"And you think I was the last one to use it?"

"No. We've just arrested the person who was in possession of this muddler," Janelle announced with an air of satisfaction. "It was found in the suspect's vehicle, wrapped in a towel."

Tess and I exchanged fearful glances. We were about to find out not only who killed Cole, but also who probably tried to kill me.

"Who was it?" I asked. "One of the zoning commission members?"

Janelle looked grim. "No. It was the mayor's wife. Piper Lyall-Pierce."

Chapter 10

If Janelle had said Santa Claus killed Cole Bowman, I would have been less surprised. Tess burst into nervous laughter, which in another moment threatened to turn hysterical. As for me, I found nothing funny in the situation. Having been thrown into the middle of a murder case once before, I knew how quickly things spiraled out of control. Murder was a game changer, and no one walked away from such a terrible thing unscathed.

"There's no way Piper killed Cole," I said. "It's out of the question."

Elaine tapped her pen on the table. "Keep quiet. You might incriminate either yourself or Piper Lyall-Pierce."

Ignoring Elaine's irritated sigh, I leaned forward. "I've known Piper since I was born. She may be pushy, controlling, and far too entitled, but she is not a murderer."

"Marlee's right!" Tess chimed in. "No one in the county gives more to charitable causes than Piper and her family. Everything she's ever done is for the benefit of Oriole Point."

"Exactly," Janelle said. "And on Thursday evening, she learned Cole Bowman had gone behind her back and bought the Fields property, a property she was set on acquiring for herself. Even worse, he convinced the zoning commission to not only rezone the land, but to permit franchises, something she was violently opposed to."

"Everyone at the meeting was upset with Cole over his plans," I said. "Including me."

"But the mayor's wife is the only one who physically attacked Mr. Bowman."

Tess shook her head at Officer Wykoff. "Piper would never kill Cole. She would never kill anyone. Someone must have put that muddler in her car."

Janelle seemed unmoved by our defense of Piper. Instead, she pointed to the bloodstained muddler lying on the table between us. "Ms. Jacob, for the record, did Piper Lyall-Pierce purchase a muddler from you at the Strawberry Moon Bash?"

I pretended to mull this over, even though I did sell her one shortly after Gillian and I opened our booth. "Maybe. I can't be certain. Especially if she paid in cash. My memory remains a little fuzzy after my own attack that night."

She shot me a jaundiced look. "Luckily, we do not have to rely on your fuzzy memory alone. We questioned Gillian Kaminski ninety minutes ago. She confirmed selling the mayor's wife a stainless-steel muddler Friday evening at your booth along the river."

"A number of customers have bought muddlers from my store," I muttered.

"True," Officer Wykoff said. "Which is why we want you to compile a list of everyone who purchased one from The Berry Basket. Accompanied by a receipt, if possible."

"I'll need time to go through my computer records. And keep in mind that I'm not the only store with muddlers for sale."

Janelle cleared her throat. "Yes. We've learned Cole and Natasha's kitchen supply shop had several in stock."

"Which only proves that lots of people have muddlers," I insisted.

"Lots of people do not keep a bloodstained muddler wrapped in a towel in the backseat of their Hummer," Janelle said. "A Hummer found parked at Ruth Barlow's beach house on Lakeshore Drive just thirty minutes after we received your call about finding Cole's body."

"Wait a minute." Tess sat up even straighter. "I know what Piper was doing there. She and Ruth Barlow are organizing next month's Blackberry Road Rally. Now that the Strawberry Moon Bash is behind us, that would be the next thing for Piper to obsess about. And she wouldn't waste any time getting to work on it."

"Absolutely." I wanted to hit myself for not remembering this, especially since I feared Piper expected me to do quite a lot of volunteering for the berry-themed event. Anything in the county that involved berries was certain to somehow involve me, whether I liked it or not. "The road rally's been on the OPBA agenda for months. Everyone in town knows Piper and Ruth are in charge. Piper would naturally be spending a lot of time at Ruth's, getting things ready."

Janelle wasn't impressed. "Quite a coincidence.

The murderer attacks Cole. Then he or she just happens to drive by Ruth's property when Piper's Hummer is conveniently parked on the road, allowing the killer to toss the murder weapon inside."

"Don't forget Piper owns the only Hummer in town," I said. "Hell, she may be the last person in the state who still drives one of those things. It would be easy for the killer to keep track of her whereabouts. And only tourists lock their cars around here. You know that."

"What seems more likely is that Piper Lyall-Pierce killed Cole Bowman, threw the weapon in the car, and drove to the beach to dispose of it in the lake," Janelle said. "Only she had to make certain no one was at home at the Barlow beach cottage. She was knocking on the front door of the Barlow home when a squad car drove by and found the Hummer with the muddler inside. What I need to know is if you recognized the voice of the person Cole was speaking to before he was killed." She looked down at our written statements. "You claim to have been skulking on the stairs when you heard the door open."

I resented the term *skulking*, although it was precisely what I was doing. "As soon as I heard Cole say something, I went to hide in one of the bedrooms. When I came down a few minutes later, Cole was dead. And the killer was gone."

How could I be embroiled in yet another murder in just a few short years? And one involving people I knew far too well. "This—this is all circumstantial evidence," I went on. "And it doesn't explain who struck me on the head last Friday. It wasn't Piper. She was on her yacht with about twenty other people when I was pushed into the river. And I maintain that whoever killed Cole is the same person who attacked me."

Janelle looked as if she had been waiting for me to say just such a thing. "Maybe that person is Natasha Bowman. Maybe it's Natasha who is framing Piper."

I shook my head. "But Natasha has no reason to kill me. It doesn't make sense. I'll tell you who might be behind it. One of those zoning commission members. Like I said on Thursday, Cole must have known something nasty about a few of them. Maybe all of them. Why else would they agree to such a destructive development deal? I bet one of them is the murderer."

Elaine Snow gave my wrist a painful squeeze. "Don't say anything further, Miss Jacob."

Ignoring her, I turned back to Janelle. I was tired of the police jumping to the wrong conclusions. "Think about it. Someone wanted to get rid of Cole because he probably knew something damaging about them. And it would help to get me out of the way, since I accused them of being bought off at the meeting."

"She's right," Tess said. "I thought it was unwise of her to say such things publicly. In fact, I pulled Marlee back in her seat and told her to keep quiet."

"And Piper was as vocal as I was about the deal and determined to get to the bottom of it. She even punched Cole, she was so furious. Now someone has framed Piper for the murder. And there will probably be another attempt on my life. Which means I should have police protection until you track down the real killer."

"Absolutely," Tess agreed. "Marlee needs police protection."

Both officers looked at each other and literally

rolled their eyes. Janelle and her buddies on the force were not taking me seriously. Where was Police Chief Hitchcock when I needed him? Off in Seattle, enjoying the ocean air and the best seafood in the world, that was where!

I wagged my finger at Janelle and Wykoff. "No matter what you both think, the murderer is not Piper or Natasha. Give Piper a lie detector test. Then you should give a polygraph to each of the zoning commission members and see if anything suspicious turns up. I'll take a polygraph test myself. But if you ask me if I'm unhappy that Cole is dead, you won't like my answer. He was a detestable human being, and I'm not surprised someone did him in. I'm only surprised it took so long. I don't blame Natasha for finally striking back last Thursday with that pizzelle maker. Let me tell you, if I'd been married to him, I would have hit him over the head long ago."

Elaine turned to me with a furious expression. "Miss Jacob, will you please shut up!"

Janelle shook her head. "Ms. Snow, your client is fortunate that we are not charging her with a crime today. Which is good news for you, Marlee, since you're free to leave. I suspect if you keep on talking, you'll incriminate yourself so much, we'll end up arresting you for the Jimmy Hoffa disappearance."

Oriole Point hadn't been in such an uproar since reenactors accidentally blew up the historical museum with a cannon on loan from Fort Michilimackinac. Half the village seemed crammed into the police station, with the lights of two local news teams visible over the sea of heads. Luckily, David and Ryan were part of this mob. As soon as they caught sight of us, both men hustled Tess and me out of there with the speed of Secret Service agents.

Twenty minutes later, the four of us sat at one of the bistro tables at The Berry Basket, visibly shell shocked. Even though it wasn't yet closing time, I locked the shop door behind us as soon as we entered. Because Gillian had also been questioned by the police, she was slumped at a nearby table, nursing her second iced tea. Of course, Andrew and Dean had peppered us with questions ever since we'd escaped to the safety of my shop, but I didn't mind. It helped to talk about the murder without the disturbing presence of the police.

Someone banged on the door again. I pitied any tourists in town this afternoon. Not a single shopkeeper would be able to focus on anything but Cole's murder and the arrest of Piper.

"Can't they see the CLOSED sign?" David complained. Tess laid her head on his shoulder, causing him to look down at her with concern.

I craned my neck and caught sight of red hair and a blue T-shirt. "It's Max."

Ryan frowned as Gillian let Max in. I'd already spoken with Max on the phone, with instructions for him to find out the latest as to Piper's predicament.

"Did the judge set bail for Piper?" asked Andrew.

Max nodded. "A steep one. Luckily, she and Lionel can afford it."

"Thank God," I murmured.

Dean opened up the refrigerated unit where we kept bottled water, and pulled out one for himself. "What Piper can't afford is being viewed as a cold-blooded killer. I've never been a Piper fan, but I have to say I'm feeling pretty bad for her right now. Lionel too."

My head was pounding worse than ever, and once in a while a few spots swam before my eyes. Surely this wasn't what the doctor had meant when she told me to relax and recuperate.

Max must have noticed my distress because he turned to Dean. "Give Marlee that water and something to eat. She's looking a little pale. So is Tess."

Tess lifted up her head. "I wouldn't mind a muffin. We haven't eaten anything since breakfast. Except for a bag of Oreos that Suzanne gave us at the police station."

"The Oreos must be from my mom's secret stash there. She's supposed to be on a diet, but I'm guessing she's snacking at work." Andrew hurried behind the counter and came back with a plate heaped with muffins, along with a smaller dish of chocolate-strawberry cookies. When he put them on the table, Tess and I fell upon the sweets like ravenous dogs.

Max frowned. "You need some protein. Let me run down to the diner for sandwiches."

"Right now we need to keep our sugar high going," I said between mouthfuls.

Max grabbed an empty chair, turned it around, and straddled it. "By the way, the police brought your bikes to the station. Bruno loaded them into my van, so I can drop them off at both your houses later on."

Tess smiled and said, "Thanks," but Ryan shook his head. "I have my truck. I'll take Marlee's bike with us when we go home."

Max shrugged. "Suit yourself."

Gillian busied herself for a moment before coming to our table with a bowl of fresh strawberries. She popped one in her mouth. "At least this is natural sugar," she said.

"Is Piper still at the police station?" I asked.

"Yes, along with what looks like an army of lawyers fighting to be on her Dream Team." Max glanced over at Tess. "Your brother's wife is one of them."

"I'm not surprised. Piper should hire Elaine to lead the defense. My sister-in-law is a combination of Lucrezia Borgia and Susan B. Anthony."

David nodded. "She scares the hell out of me."

"I watched her during the coverage of the Howard murder last year," Andrew said. "She wore Prada every day. Fabulous woman."

"A woman who isn't so fabulous at the moment is Ruth Barlow," Max said. "They brought her to the police station in hysterics. When she learned Piper had been arrested, she passed out. At least according to Suzanne, who at the moment is my eyes and ears in there."

"Honestly, Mom is the biggest gossip in Oriole Point," Dean remarked.

I laughed. Talk about calling the kettle black. Like their mother, the Cabot brothers had passed on rumors about everyone in Oriole Point since they were in grade school. Some of their tales were untrue, but it didn't stop me from listening to them. I enjoyed their company—and the secrets they imparted—far too much to discourage them. Tall, cute, and auburn haired, they brought to mind the prank-loving Tarleton twins from *Gone with the Wind*. The only difference between them and their fictional counterparts was that they weren't twins. Although having been born just eleven months apart, they qualified as Irish twins. Their father's people even hailed from Cork.

"I think one of the zoning commission members is responsible for killing Cole, and for bashing me on the head." I took a moment to eat a few strawberries. "Have either of you heard anything about the members that sounds suspicious?"

Andrew frowned. "I haven't had much time this year to gather new information. Who knew floral design was such an exhausting occupation?" After graduating from college three years ago, Andrew had tried his hand at massage therapy, dog grooming, and yoga instruction. A good-looking floral designer in Saugatuck caught his eye back in February. Now he split his time between The Berry Basket and designing floral centerpieces at Beguiling Blooms. At least he had managed to find another business to work at that shared my own shop's initials.

I turned to his brother. "How about you? I read your blog every day. When you're not giving lifestyle advice, you write about the residents along the lakeshore. I'm shocked no one has tried to sue you yet."

"They can't sue me. I never use real names. Besides, I'm less interested in putting gossip on the site than imparting the flavor of what our unusual village is like. I present Oriole Point as an edgy Lake Wobegon. By the way, *The Dean Report* was named one of the top fifty blogs in the Midwest by *Chicago Magazine*."

"Do you know anything edgy about the zoning commission members?" I asked him.

"They're a pretty dull bunch as far as Oriole Point characters go. Drake Woodhill is probably the oddest duck. British Olympic runner, professional astrologer.

No romantic life to speak of. I still don't know if he's straight or gay."

"He's gay," Andrew said.

"You think everyone is gay," Dean said with a laugh. "Even me."

"You are. I'm just waiting for you to realize it."

"Ignore him. He thinks Obama is gay, too." Dean turned to me. "I've never heard about Drake getting hooked up with anyone along the lakeshore. Of course, his website does claim he's a witch. Nothing shocking about that. After all, the Biermann family were once Scientologists."

"How about Crystal Appeldoorn?" I grabbed another strawberry muffin.

"She left town right after high school, then returned years later with an adorable toddler. I heard she got married and had a baby, but her husband died in a car accident. Don't know why she stayed away from Oriole Point so long. There's a rumor she had a drug problem once upon a time."

Ryan smirked. "The same could be said of half my friends in high school."

"She's dating a former marine from Grand Haven," Andrew added. "Quite high on the cute meter. His name is Eric Dowell. Things look serious between them. He paid for an underground sprinkling system at her house last month. And he's taking her and her daughter to Disney World later this summer. They have reservations at Wilderness Lodge."

Max laughed. "I thought you had no time for gossip."

"I make time for a little bit of gossip. Just to keep my hand in."

"What about Mike Gerringer?" I asked.

"Muffin Mike?" Dean shook his head. "No news about him. Except his health goes from bad to worse. You'd think a man with a serious heart condition would sell vegetables, not pastry. I don't like his muffins, anyway. They're too dry. The Phantom's muffins are so much better. Good thing you snagged the best baker in town for your store, Marlee."

I was too busy eating one of the delicious muffins of Theo Foster, aka the Phantom, to answer, but Max jumped in with his own question. "Was there bad blood between Cole and Mike when they lived in Chicago? After all, both their businesses went belly up there."

"There was bad blood between Cole Bowman and everyone he ever knew," Dean said. "But I don't think Cole had anything to do with Mike's misfortune in Chicago."

"Misfortune" was an understatement. Mike once owned apartment buildings in Chicago, most of them on the South Side. Several of his buildings burned down due to fire code violations. The last of those fires took the lives of five people, three of them children. During the ensuing scandal, Mike's wife committed suicide. Soon after, Mike declared bankruptcy and moved to Oriole Point.

"We know Mike was a criminally negligent landlord," I said. "And Cole was a big shot Chicago real estate developer. Their paths must have crossed."

"What if they did?" Tess asked. "It's no secret Mike's negligence was responsible for that fire and those tragic deaths. From what I've heard, his court costs drove him into bankruptcy. He paid an even bigger price when his wife killed herself. It seems to me we already know terrible things about Muffin Mike. What's left to blackmail him over?"

We were silent for a few minutes, during which Tess and I finished off the muffins.

"The only zoning commission member left is Juliet Haller," Gillian said finally. "And I can't think of a sweeter person in town, unless it's her husband."

She was right. Juliet and Franklin Haller were upstanding citizens of Oriole Point. They served on even more volunteer committees than Piper. And their civic zeal didn't seem due to any feelings of duty or obligation. Juliet and Franklin were genuinely kind people.

I sat back, feeling exhausted and a bit sick to my stomach from an excess of muffins and cookies. "It's blackmail. Cole knew something unsavory about the four members of the zoning commission. They must all be hiding something."

"Maybe it was a total stranger who killed him," Gillian suggested. "Or someone who knew Cole back in Chicago."

"Then who knocked me on the head last week and pushed me in the river? And don't even try to tell me that I fell into the water because I was drunk."

"It's true," Tess said. "Both she and Cole were literally bashed on the side of the head. There's a murderer in Oriole Point. And blackmail does seem the most likely motive."

David squeezed her shoulder. "There is another possible suspect in all this: Natasha."

"The resourceful Russian," Ryan muttered.

"Natasha wouldn't hurt me. And if the police would start searching for her, a lot of this mystery might be cleared up."

"You've gotten your wish, marzipan," Max said. "When I was at the station, I learned the police finally put out an APB for Natasha. But not as a missing person. She's now wanted for questioning in the murder of her husband."

This made my spirits plummet even further. Although I wasn't sure if it was murder that was making me feel ill or all the sugar I'd consumed. All I knew was that I'd had my fill of both today.

Chapter 11

When I awoke the next morning, I feared I'd been drugged. That was my only explanation for sleeping until nine thirty. Granted, yesterday had been draining, but my internal clock got me up early regardless of how little sleep I had enjoyed the night before. I suspected Ryan snuck Benadryl in my herbal tea to ensure I got enough rest. And while I was glad Gillian was scheduled to open the shop, I had already missed too much work due to the attack on the dock.

Flinging aside the bedcovers, I wondered what would happen to my store lease now that Cole was dead. And who now inherited all those properties? I'd been so distracted by Cole's murder that I hadn't thought about what his death would mean for my business and all the other store owners along Lyall Street whose properties he had owned. Maybe that half brother of his in Atlanta would take the buildings over now. Or Natasha. After all, she was Cole's wife. Wouldn't his will naturally bequeath everything to her? Unless the Bowmans had a prenup. But if she did inherit everything, her motive to kill him just got a lot stronger.

I made my way to the bathroom. After turning on the shower, I was about to pull off the T-shirt and boy shorts I slept in when a shriek sounded from downstairs. I shut off the water.

It couldn't be Ryan. Not even his concern over me would stop him from heading off to the family orchards by nine. There it was again. A cross between a shriek and a squawk, followed by a loud whistle. A woman said something in response, followed by a strange voice crying, "Keep quiet!" Aunt Vicki must be here, accompanied by a rescue animal with feathers.

Marching downstairs, I was already framing my argument to her. She had tried for two years to convince me to adopt one of her rescue animals. I insisted there was no time for pets with my schedule, and my recent experience fostering an ill-tempered ferret had not changed my mind. However, the aroma of fresh-brewed coffee did make me sigh with pleasure.

When I followed my nose to the kitchen, I found my aunt frying bacon on the stove; a carton of eggs stood open on the counter beside her.

"Hey, you're finally up." Aunt Vicki gave me a quick smile before reaching for the eggs. "I thought Minnie was being a little too vocal, but once she gets talking, it's hard to quiet her."

I filled my mug with coffee, then scanned the sun-filled kitchen. All I saw was the normal clutter on my counter, along with the blue vista of Lake Michigan outside my windows. "Where is this bird you mistakenly think I'm going to foster?"

"In the living room." Aunt Vicki expertly cracked several eggs into a frying pan. "Picked her up on the way home from the rally yesterday. A family in Niles is moving back home to Australia. They can't take the bird with them. There's some regulation against exporting exotic animals. Don't know why they bothered to buy a parrot if they knew they were returning to Melbourne one day. Especially an African grey. They live a long time."

I peeked into the living room. A large gray bird with patches of white about its eyes sat on a four-foot-high wooden perch. Cocking her head, she greeted me with "Nice to meet you."

I lifted my mug. "Nice to meet you, too. But don't get comfortable in here. Aunt Vicki will find you a lovely family to live with."

"Minnie is pretty," the bird replied. She then made a sound that sounded exactly like a doorbell, followed by "What's for breakfast?"

I couldn't help but laugh, especially since I have a fondness for birds. My childhood was spent with a trio of cockatiels, although none had a vocabulary like this. I walked closer to examine the two metal bowls attached on either end of her perch: one filled with water, the other with fresh vegetables. To the right of my fireplace, I also spied an enormous bird cage filled with hanging toys. I once rented a studio apartment in NYC that was roughly the same size.

"I hope you're not going to bite me, like that ferret did."

The dark eyes of Minnie stared back at me. "You're a doll," she said.

Okay, this was much better than the ferret. I held out my arm. After a brief hesitation, the bird hopped onto it. She weighed considerably more than any of my cockatiels. Then again, she was much larger. "Has Aunt Vicki been coaching you?"

"What's up, mate?"

Walking into the kitchen with her, I waited to see if she would fly away, but she didn't. "Are her wings clipped?"

My aunt spooned scrambled eggs onto a plate that held several strips of bacon. "Yes, but they're close to growing out." She looked up with a grin. "She's a doll, isn't she?"

"Actually, that's what she called me. How large is her vocabulary?"

"According to the family, over three hundred words. They've had her five years. Got her when she was just a chick." Her smile deepened. "As soon as I saw her, I thought of you. I remembered those cockatiels you had when you were a kid."

"I do miss my little babies." In fact, I'd taken them with me when I moved to New York, where they eventually died of old age. I smiled at the African grey perched on my arm. "I will admit this one is adorable."

"You know all about keeping birds, Marlee. There would be no learning curve. And you won't have to take her for a walk or clean up fur balls. You'd hardly know she was here."

Minnie announced, "Peek-a-boo. I see you."

This parrot was becoming more endearing by the minute. "I'm sure Minnie will always make her presence known. And we both know birds need as much attention as a cat or dog." I scratched the top of Minnie's head. She closed her eyes in blissful contentment. "Okay, I surrender. I'll keep her. But only as long as you promise not to bring me every rescue parrot in the county."

"I knew you'd love her." Aunt Vicki hurried out of the kitchen, only to return with the tall perch. She placed it by the kitchen window. "Let's put her back on the perch so you can eat."

"Time to eat," Minnie called out.

I picked up a piece of scrambled egg and offered it to her. She nibbled at the egg eagerly. "Why did they call her Minnie? The bird is over a foot tall."

"The little girl in the family named her. Apparently, the grandparents in Australia have a macaw, so this bird looks mini compared to that parrot." Aunt Vicki held out her own arm, and Minnie hopped on. A second later Minnie was back on the perch by the window, her attention diverted by the sight of seagulls flying past outside.

I sat on one of the stools at the kitchen island and tucked into the eggs and bacon.

My aunt looked at the bandages on the side of my head. "Does it still hurt?"

I chuckled. "Only when I laugh."

She took a seat across from me. Unlike most people, my aunt wasn't afraid of long silences. Maybe because she spent so much time around animals, who valued companionship over conversation.

I was the one who finally spoke. "Have you heard from my parents? They sent me an e-mail last week from Auckland."

Not only had my English professor mother, a die-hard Tolkien fan, read and reread his books, but she'd also watched those Peter Jackson movies at least a dozen times. Their trip to New Zealand was devoted to retracing the locations of *The Lord of the Rings* and

The Hobbit movies. I hope she realized Gandalf wasn't likely to make an appearance while she and my dad were there.

My aunt nodded. "I got an e-mail from them, too. They're headed for the mountains next, so I don't expect to hear from them again for a while." She took a long sip of coffee. "By the time they get back, I hope this murder business has been cleared up. Otherwise I'll have to tell them about what happened to you last week at the marina. I'm not happy I had to find out about that from the Cabot brothers. Good thing I bumped into them on Lyall Street this morning. You should have called me from the hospital. I would have driven straight back from D.C."

"There was nothing you could do. Besides, Ryan's been staying here since the attack."

She thought a moment. "I've got a highly aggressive Rottweiler in one of my kennels at the moment. I should bring him over. The Freeport dog whisperer is working with him so I can eventually get him adopted. But he'd be a great watchdog, assuming you didn't spook him."

"No vicious guard dogs, please. Besides, Minnie would probably alert me if someone broke into the house."

"True. But she wouldn't tear out an intruder's throat like the Rottweiler would."

"Forget it."

Aunt Vicki sighed. "I phoned Piper this morning, but she's not taking any calls. Suzanne Cabot told me Lionel picked up a prescription for Xanax yesterday at the pharmacy."

"Honestly, the Cabots should be working for the NSA. And the Xanax must be for Piper. She has to feel humiliated by the arrest. I plan to stop by her house after work."

"I've heard there are news vans parked outside her gates. You may never get in, Marlee."

"I'll get in. Lionel left a voice mail last night, asking me to come over. I'm sure he and Piper have a million questions. After all, I was at the Bowman house while Cole was being murdered." I shuddered at the memory of his lifeless body in the doorway.

"The trouble you've gotten into since I left. If you didn't look so frail in those bandages, I'd give you a whopper of a lecture." She paused. "Who do you think killed him?"

After refilling my coffee mug, I launched into my explanation about the zoning commission members and their possible motive to want Cole dead. She listened intently.

"Seems reasonable," Aunt Vicki said when I was done. "Although, if it wasn't for the attack on you last Friday, I'd think it more likely someone from Cole's past is responsible. I've known him a lot longer than you have. He hasn't made many friends along the way."

"No doubt he was as ruthless professionally as he was in his personal life."

"Ruthless?" She snorted. "He should have been arrested for a few of the things he pulled. But somehow he—or his crazy rich uncle—bought his way out of it. And he certainly should have done jail time for the way he abused his girlfriends and wives."

I sat back in surprise. "Wives? Cole had another wife before Natasha?"

"When Cole was nineteen, he married the daughter of a Chicago heart surgeon he met when the family summered here. He got the girl pregnant, hence the hasty marriage. The wedding was held in Chicago, after which Cole and his bride moved to an apartment in Wicker Park. Few people in Oriole Point were even aware of the marriage. I knew only because the daughter and I volunteered at the Presbyterian camp that summer and became friends. A sweet girl. Her name was Samantha."

"I assume they divorced."

"The marriage ended the following year, shortly after her miscarriage." She frowned. "Some people suspected she miscarried as a result of his violent temper."

I recoiled at the horror of it. Cole grew more repellent by the minute.

"At the time there were rumors the heart surgeon hired someone to beat the crap out of Cole," she continued. "And I believe it. When he returned to Oriole Point, his nose looked like it had been broken. Before that, he had quite a nice profile."

"How do you know so much about Cole Bowman?"

"You keep forgetting I'm much younger than your dad. I'm forty-nine, the same age as Cole. We went to school together, and I saw how he treated the unlucky girls he dated. He pushed my best friend out of a moving car when she tried to break up with him. Her family brought charges against him, but Cole's mother and uncle paid them off."

These stories were ruining my appetite. "You never told me any of this."

"No reason I should have. Oh, I was tempted to say something when Cole moved back with his trophy wife. But since she'd been married to him for several years, I figured she knew the kind of brute he was.

Poor Natasha. I hope he isn't responsible for her disappearance."

"I'm afraid they think she's the one responsible for Cole's death. They're circling Piper because she was found with the murder weapon. But the minute Natasha turns up, she'll probably be in handcuffs, too."

"With Cole dead and Natasha missing, I'm glad now I wasn't able to find that dog she wanted." Aunt Vicki laughed at the confused look on my face. "I know. Natasha Bowman doesn't seem like the pet owning type. But she asked me last Christmas if I ever had Pomeranians or Yorkies brought to the shelter. The next time I did, she said she wanted to adopt it. In fact, Natasha asked me more than once about the dog, but the county is largely rural. Few people own those teacup Yorkies or little Poms. Fewer still give them up for adoption."

I had a hard time picturing the high-maintenance Natasha taking care of anything aside from her manicure and pedicure appointments.

"The funny thing is about two weeks ago," my aunt went on, "a family surrendered their deceased mother's Yorkie to my shelter. Cute little thing. Thought it would be perfect for Natasha, but when I called her, she said she no longer wanted a dog. I still have the pup, so if you know of anyone who'd like a sweet Yorkie . . ."

"Why would Natasha ask you several times about adopting a particular dog, then turn you down when you found one for her?" I pushed my empty plate away. "I'll bet at some point in the past few months, Natasha decided to escape from Cole. And taking a dog would have complicated things."

"Do you think Natasha killed her husband?" she asked in a stage whisper.

I shook my head so vehemently, the movement made me grow dizzy for an instant. "No. Whoever killed Cole also bashed me on the head. I can't believe Natasha would hurt me." I finished off my coffee, the caffeine unable to keep my mood from growing sad. "And if she is responsible for the murder and the attack on me last Friday, I'd rather not know about it. I trusted her. I'd hate to think my instincts about people were so off base."

Aunt Vicki began to clear the counter. "Look on it as a life lesson. I've made excellent choices where friends and animals are concerned. But I have the worst instincts when it comes to romance. How else do you account for that ex-husband of mine?"

"Sorry to remind you, but you have two ex-husbands."

"The second marriage was annulled. He was a Catholic. Technically, there's only one ex."

"Talk about splitting hairs."

"And my boyfriends haven't been much of an improvement, although at least I've made sure to not have any of them move in with me." She winked at me. "Nothing wrong with a little healthy sex and some male companionship now and again. But my priorities have always been my boys and my animals. Men come third. And a distant third, too."

Indeed, given Aunt Vicki's devotion to her sons and rescue animals, it was amazing she made room in her life for anything else. And her sons had inherited my aunt's love of animals. Her eldest was a veterinarian, and her youngest a zoology major at MSU.

"You can trust a dog or a cat," Aunt Vicki said

while rinsing dishes at the sink. "None of them will empty your bank account or make you feel bad about yourself because you've put on a few pounds." She slapped her ample backside. "At least my latest boyfriend likes his women on the large side. Voluptuous, he calls it. Well, that's me. Voluptuous, independent, and with an endless supply of opinions. Not many men can handle that combination."

Because my aunt often had an admiring male in her life, I took that with a grain of salt. I wished I knew how she did it. At least sixty pounds overweight, Aunt Vicki wore makeup only at weddings or parties. And she lived in jeans and faded T-shirts. Despite the lack of concern about her appearance, men seemed drawn to her. Maybe it was because she didn't make the slightest effort to win their favor. Vicki Jacob was an intelligent, strong woman who enjoyed the company of men but had no intention of making them the center of her life.

Sometimes I wondered if I was more like her than I admitted. Two men before Ryan had proposed, and I hadn't hesitated before turning them down. Yet I had accepted Ryan's proposal instantly. That must mean he was different than the other men. Or maybe I had changed. Maybe I was finally ready to spend less time obsessed with work. If so, why was I unable to picture myself walking down the aisle in January?

As if she was thinking the same thing, Aunt Vicki asked, "How's the winter wedding coming along? Your mom says you still haven't picked out a dress."

"I have a good idea of what I want. I'm more concerned about what happens after the wedding. Ryan wants to build a farmhouse for us near the orchards. He's even got blueprints for the house—energy efficient with thermo-nuclear heating."

After letting out a piercing whistle, Minnie announced, "Here comes trouble!"

We both laughed before Aunt Vicki turned her attention back to me. "Sounds nice. But I'm guessing you don't want to give up your view."

I looked out at the sweeping vista of Lake Michigan outside my kitchen windows. My house held a prize spot along Lakeshore Drive. Right across the narrow road was the bluff overlooking the lake. It took me only thirty seconds to walk from the front porch, cross Lakeshore Drive, and reach my Adirondack chairs and hammock. And if I wanted to swim, a quick jaunt down a nearby flight of long wooden steps led to my private beach. That was the best part of living along Lakeshore Drive. Everyone had a private beach attached to their property.

"Of course I don't want to give up my view. It's the greatest view in the world. I love this house, even the drafty bedrooms and the noisy plumbing. It even has a ghost, although I've never seen any sign of her. I'll never understand why you traded the farmland for this."

The lake house had always been handed down to a Jacob daughter, and my aunt had inherited it when Grandma Jacob died. It surprised everyone when Aunt Vicki offered the lake house to her brother in exchange for the orchard farmhouse we were living in. Even though I was only seven, I had been as thrilled as my parents to move into the blue house with the wrap-around porch, front turret, and second-story balcony. Best of all, it overlooked the lake. I never tired of falling asleep to the sound of lapping waves outside our windows. And it was always a thrill to watch the sunsets and track the storms as they swept over the water. As fun as it was to play in the orchards, I had never loved anyplace as much as the lake house.

"What would I do with a fancy house like this?" She shrugged. "It has such a tiny backyard. Where would I keep all my animals? I couldn't let them run free along the bluff. They need fenced fields. Besides, I've got no daughters to pass it on to. And that farmhouse I traded with your dad came with two dozen acres. Every square inch has come in handy."

She wasn't kidding. A state-of-the-art animal shelter had been constructed on the property, along with enough kennels and outbuildings to house a small zoo. Something I feared my aunt might one day decide to open. Especially with her youngest son soon to be a zookeeper.

I gazed with pride at my kitchen, its warmth enhanced by the yellow walls and terra-cotta tiles. "I love my Painted Lady as much as you love the farmhouse. I don't want to move."

"Sweetie, Zellar Orchards is only a twenty-minute drive from the lake. No reason Ryan can't move in here after you two get married."

"Ryan seems pretty set on that farmhouse."

"Like I said, I've been married one or two times, depending on how you look at it. And I've learned marriage is impossible without compromise. Which is why I got divorced. Just remember that compromise is fine as long as one partner isn't the only one doing it. Maybe it's time to see how much Ryan is willing to compromise for you." She now scrutinized me with the same intensity as Minnie had. "Are you sure it's the house that's bothering you? Could be you're not ready to get married."

"I'll be thirty-one in December. If I'm not ready now, when?"

"Age has nothing to do with it. Some people simply aren't suited to married life. Like me." She paused. "Or maybe you haven't met the right person yet."

This conversation made me uncomfortable. "I love Ryan. I really do."

"I'm betting he isn't the first man you've loved. And if you're having doubts, he probably won't be the last. Don't go rushing into this marriage if you aren't rock-hard certain. It wouldn't be fair to either of you."

I bit my lip. Some days I was euphoric at the thought of making a life for myself with Ryan. Other days, the idea seemed completely preposterous. Was I really not cut out for wedded bliss? A marriage proposal had already spelled the end of two romantic relationships. Back in high school, Max Riordan had surprised me with a ring and a marriage proposal the day before our senior prom. Shocked, I not only turned him down, but had also refused to go to the prom. Thankfully, my family moved to Chicago that summer, and I no longer had to deal with Max's hurt feelings or my dismay at being asked to marry him after only a few casual months of dating.

My second marriage proposal occurred when my first boyfriend in New York popped the question over a romantic dinner at Bouley, my favorite French restaurant. But I'd been so busy fielding calls and texts that night from the network about the Amish Stripper scandal, I barely noticed he'd put a ring in my chocolate soufflé. His mood had turned irate when I kept taking work-related calls, but I'd been equally resentful he didn't understand how much pressure I was under at the network. By the time the bill arrived, both the meal and our romance were over. After that, I'd relied on work to provide consolation and meaning in my life. And it had . . . right up until Evangeline Chaplin poisoned her husband.

I stood up and stretched. "I don't have time to think about weddings or marriage right now. I need to shower and get my butt over to The Berry Basket. But first I want to call Gemini Rising and ask Drake to do my horoscope."

"Since when are you interested in all that New Age stuff?"

"What I'm interested in is finding out what Cole might have blackmailed the zoning commission over. May as well start with Drake. Only I have to make certain to keep my questions discreet. If one of them is the murderer, I don't want to alarm them."

"Well, you're alarming me. You stay away from the zoning commission members until the killer is caught. I'm serious. Someone pushed you into the river last week. Who knows what they'll do next? You should hop on a plane today and join your parents in New Zealand."

"I'm not running off to New Zealand. Given the skill of our police department, they may not catch the murderer for months. Maybe years! Am I supposed to become an exile because some dangerous creep is running around Oriole Point? No way." I walked over to the gorgeous gray bird preening herself in the morning sun. "What do you think, Minnie? Will I be able to figure out what Cole knew about the commission members that they want to keep secret?"

She peeked over at me. "Kiss me."

"I can think of at least one thing everyone on the zoning commission has in common," Aunt Vicki said. "All four of them spent years living somewhere other than Oriole Point."

"Exactly. And who knows what trouble they all may have gotten into? Look at Muffin Mike's sordid adventures in Chicago."

Aunt Vicki frowned. "Hate to think anything bad of the others, especially Juliet. I've always liked her, even if she does make a ridiculous fuss over that husband of hers."

"Drake garnered a lot of media attention when he was an Olympic medalist. If there was something he could be blackmailed over, how could he keep it secret?"

"Sweetie, even presidents and kings have skeletons in their closets."

"I guess. Did you ever hear anything suspicious about Crystal?"

"Nope. Then again, I'm not one for gossip. I figure if you live long enough, everyone probably has at least one thing in their lives they're not proud of. It's none of my business."

"Unless it results in murder." I held out my arm for Minnie to hop aboard once more. "And if the same person who killed Cole also tried to kill me, I'd better make it *my* business."

The bird cocked her head at me. "You got that right, mate."

Chapter 12

A chill went over me when a customer purchased a muddler. I even hesitated before taking it from her. To think that such a small metal baton had ended someone's life. Did the killer buy a muddler from me last week? And was this what I'd been hit with on the dock? I quickly rolled the muddler in tissue paper, then slipped it into a bag. The muddler I'd seen at the police station was identical to this one: nine inches long, stainless steel, and banded with a rubber grip.

With a forced smile, I handed the bag to my customer while answering her question about the best place for dinner in the village. After she left, I had a line of customers also waiting to cash out. Gillian was busy scooping ice cream, and the shop grew more crowded by the hour. This was unusual for mid-afternoon on a Tuesday, even in high season.

Perhaps some of these visitors had been drawn to Oriole Point due to the news coverage yesterday and today. We didn't have many murders in the small, picturesque towns along the lakeshore. When we did, they were usually drug related; the community surrounding us was rural, and crystal meth was the drug of choice. I couldn't remember the last time there'd been a murder in Oriole Point. Possibly before I was born.

It was no surprise the Oriole Point police were ill equipped to handle such a high-profile case. And if Chief Hitchcock didn't head back to town soon, I would lose all respect for him. He had over twenty years of law enforcement experience behind him. We needed that experience now. As for Janelle Davenport, I didn't care how tough she appeared in those aviator sunglasses, she was in over her head. I felt overwhelmed myself. It had taken hours for me to fall asleep last night as the image of a bludgeoned Cole kept surfacing in my mind.

An older gentleman held up one of my containers of fresh strawberries. "Excuse me. Do you have strawberries that aren't so ripe? We'd like them a little green so they'll last longer."

"Strawberries aren't like bananas, sir. After they're picked, they don't continue to ripen. To keep them from growing moldy, place them in a bowl of vinegar and water. Drain the berries, and when they're dry, keep them uncovered in the refrigerator. They'll stay fresher longer." I smiled. "Those berries arrive daily straight from the orchards. Taste one."

He must have liked what he ate, because he soon got in line, holding two containers of strawberries. But I noticed that yet another customer bought a muddler. A quick look at where my wooden and stainless-steel muddlers were displayed told me that too many people seemed interested in that particular kitchen tool today. Were all these people buying muddlers because they had heard a man was murdered with one yesterday? A sick feeling swept over me.

Five minutes later, my worst fears were confirmed. Two teenage boys came up to the counter, each holding a muddler.

"Is this what that Cole Bowman guy was killed with?" one of them asked with an excited smile.

I could barely nod.

"Cool!" he said and threw down a twenty-dollar bill.

His friend already had his money out to do likewise.

As soon as the crowd thinned, I hurried over to the shelves and removed every muddler. After tossing them all in the back room, I turned around to see Gillian watching me.

"I'm glad you took them off the floor," she said. "Way too many people are interested in muddlers today. It's sick."

"Sick but profitable. I think I've sold about ten muddlers since lunch, and we're lucky to sell that many all month."

"I don't think we should put them out again until this murder case is solved."

"Nope. Not even then. I've sold my last muddler." I sighed. "Murder might be big business for the media, but I refuse to profit from anyone's death. Even Cole Bowman's."

As the largest private home between here and the Indiana border, Lyall House was Oriole Point's version of Monticello. Since I didn't agree with the sentiment "Bigger is better," I viewed Piper's house as a nineteenth-century McMansion. Built by the Lyall family in 1891, it stood on a cliff visible to anyone driving by on their way to Oriole Beach. My own house also overlooked the lake, but I lived on the other side of the river, an area settled by prosperous businessmen, not tycoons. Piper's side of the river belonged to the lumber barons and shipbuilders of Oriole Point, and the ground groaned with the weight of houses built to impress.

When I drove up the winding road, I noticed the news vans. I didn't know what they expected to happen. Piper was not likely to come running out of her mansion for an impromptu interview. As always, the black wrought-iron gate leading to her driveway was locked. But I'd been here before for charity functions. Leaving the engine running, I stepped out of the car and walked over to a small metal box attached to one of the brick columns on either side of the gate. A moment after pushing the button on the call box, I heard the voice of her housekeeper Carmen.

"State your business."

"It's Marlee Jacob. I'm here to see Piper and Lionel."

The gates slowly swung open. I hurried back to my car and drove past before they shut again. The closer I got to the mansion, the larger it loomed. I found it an interesting house—five stories, Italianate architecture, stained-glass windows—but not interesting enough to warrant the many photos of it for sale in Oriole Point, including postcards. Lyall House was big, ornate, and somewhat out of place amid the surrounding sand dunes and beach grass. It brought to mind a woman dressed up in an evening gown and a tiara for a family picnic.

Once I parked, I did a quick brush of my hair and reapplied lip gloss. A visit to the Lyall-Pierce manse required a pristine appearance, as well as a gift. I had spent the last hour at the store putting together an impressive basket of goodies for the couple. As I took the wicker basket from the backseat, I looked around for the Hummer. It was nowhere to be seen. I wondered if the police had impounded the vehicle. If so, Piper would miss it. She loved driving it around town, and I suspected she took special pride in the fact that a Hummer got only eight to ten miles per gallon. Despite her charity work, Piper also enjoyed the wretched excesses of being filthy rich.

Walking to the front door, I gave a last tug to my short denim wrap dress. Piper didn't approve of denim, but it was a Diane von Furstenberg, so it should pass inspection. Before I could ring the bell, Carmen swung open the wide door.

"Please come in, Miss Jacob. The mayor and Mrs. Lyall-Pierce are in the library, waiting for you."

I followed the petite housekeeper down first one hallway, then another. Her heels clacked on the polished tiled floor. Wearing a crisp summer shirtwaist, with her black hair swept back into a perfect chignon, Carmen Munez looked nothing like what one expected of a housekeeper on duty. First, I had never seen her in anything but heels, which I would not have thought conducive to housekeeping chores. She also had elegant manicured nails, which led me to doubt that she did much cleaning. Carmen's job was probably to tell the other servants what to do. Piper had a staff of six, although I couldn't imagine what they did all day. Carmen seemed like a live version of that Hummer: a decorative and expensive toy.

"Miss Jacob," Carmen announced when we reached the sun-drenched library.

Lionel hurried over to greet me. Taking my hands, he gave me a kiss on the cheek. "So happy you could come see us, Marlee. The past twenty-four hours have been a complete nightmare. To think anyone would dare arrest my Piper. It hardly bears thinking about."

"There is a herd of lawyers in our study at this moment who are being paid to think about it," Piper said. "Please come here, Marlee." Her voice came from the direction of a bottle-green wingback chair turned toward one of the floor-length windows. It was like being ushered into the throne room of an unhappy empress.

"She's not taking this well," Lionel whispered as he led me to his wife.

When I reached the chair where she sat, Piper eyed me with disdain. "It's rude to keep me waiting all day. I can't imagine what you had to do that was more important than coming here to discuss Cole's murder with me."

"I came as soon as I could," I said. "But I do run a business. I had to work."

"Let's not get grandiose. You own a little shop that sells fruit and things decorated with berries. You're hardly the CEO of Amazon."

"Piper." Lionel's voice grew even deeper. "The past few days have been difficult for Marlee, as well. Don't make things more difficult. You're too fine a person to behave like this."

Piper suddenly looked like a chastened child.

Interesting. Who knew the gentle giant she was married to could curb her arrogance with only a few words? "Forgive me. I'm not accustomed to being arrested and charged with murder. It's unsettled me." She gestured at the identical wingback chair across from her. "Sit down."

I held out the basket. "I brought over some items from my store that I know both of you like." Lionel took it from me with a gracious nod. His smile widened when he saw the bottle of organic boysenberry syrup and the bag of raspberry trail mix, two favorites of his. "There's also a loaf of Theo's strawberry-nut bread. He baked it special this morning for you."

Before I sat, I took a quick look around, having never been in the library before. The room smelled deliciously of lilacs; crystal vases of fresh blooms sat on several antique writing desks. And the room held enough rococo furniture to decorate The Hague.

"I apologize again for coming late, Piper, but I was working at the store. It may not be Amazon, but that little berry shop is how I make my living."

"I thought you hired people to do that."

I chuckled. "C'mon, Piper. Give me a break."

"At least you can go back to your store as if things are normal." She let out a long-suffering sigh. "I've been publicly humiliated and unjustly accused. Do you know the police hauled me out of Ruth's house as if I were Lee Harvey Oswald? The blundering fools."

"How is Ruth? I heard she fainted when they brought her to the police station."

"I have no idea why she carried on so. I was the one in handcuffs. Handcuffs! And all because that nosy officer Bruno Wycoff peeked into the Hummer while it was parked in the street. Without a warrant, I might add. As if it would be difficult for the murderer to throw the weapon into an unlocked vehicle." Piper lifted a skeptical eyebrow. "And what kind of lunatic uses a muddler to kill someone? I mean, really."

"Whoever struck me on the head the night of the Bash probably used a muddler, too. Maybe the very same one."

"How are you feeling, Marlee?" Lionel asked with genuine concern.

"Better. This is the first day I haven't had a headache."

"We've all been marked by the awful events this past week," Piper said. "And some of us have worse things to contend with than a slight headache."

No point in reminding her that I almost drowned a few days ago. Piper was Piper; not even a murder charge would change that. Unlike her obviously exhausted husband, she appeared the same as always. Hair styled to perfection, makeup impeccable, face unlined and brimming with Botox. And she was dressed as if for a photo spread in *Town & Country*. I marveled at her aplomb. Especially since the one time I saw her yesterday, she seemed completely frantic. Perhaps it was time to remind her of that.

"When Tess and I were being held at the police station, you banged open the door at some point and demanded to know what was going on. Then we never saw you again."

Her blue eyes narrowed. "I'd just learned I was being charged with murder. And that you were being detained at the station, as well. Something about you breaking into Cole's house and finding the body. Which didn't make sense but sounds like something you might do."

Ignoring the veiled insult, I proceeded to tell her and Lionel about my search of the Bowman house, the missing dream dictionaries, and how I discovered Cole's body.

"You didn't see or hear who Cole was talking to?" Lionel asked.

"No, but both Tess and I heard a car pull away right before I found the body." I shot Piper a sympathetic look. "I couldn't believe they arrested you for the murder. It's absurd. And the weapon tossed in your Hummer is an obvious attempt to frame you."

Piper reached over and gave my hand a squeeze. "Thank you, my dear."

"The problem is the muddler was found in your Hummer *and* you punched Cole last Thursday. That all points to motive and opportunity."

"As if I would dirty my hands—and risk my freedom—by killing that cretin."

"I agree. I don't believe you killed him. Any more than I believe you hit me on the head last Friday night. But I think the same person did both. That means someone wants you and me out of the way. And after last week's OPBA meeting, I believe we know why."

Piper gave her husband a vindicated look. "See, Marlee agrees with me. Someone is trying to prevent us from discovering the truth about the Strawberry Fields rezoning."

"She's right, Lionel. It's the only thing that makes sense. First, they try to kill me. Then they actually kill Cole because he must have known too many secrets.

And placing the blame for Cole's murder on Piper gets her out of the picture entirely." I leaned forward. "Who on the zoning commission would do that?"

"I think it's Gerringer, that dreadful muffin person," Piper said with distaste.

"I've contacted people in Chicago to investigate Michael Gerringer's past. He once owned a number of ramshackle apartment buildings in the city. At least four of them burned down, and several people died. He should have been jailed for being a criminally negligent landlord. Instead, he was only fined." Lionel paused. "Arson was suspected in each fire. And Gerringer's insurance policies meant he was the only person who would profit from such a terrible thing."

"Arson." This was something new to consider. If a man deliberately set fires that endangered innocent people, he would have no qualms about killing someone like Cole Bowman. "If Cole knew about the arson, he might have been blackmailing him. But Muffin Mike can't be the only member on the commission he was blackmailing. After all, the decision to rezone was unanimous. And at the OPBA meeting, I saw the expressions on their faces when we demanded to know why they had agreed. They all looked—"

"Guilty," Piper said, finishing for me. "Indeed they did, the cowardly worms. When this mess is cleared up, I plan to see that each and every one of them never sits on a village committee again. If I make life unpleasant enough for them, maybe they'll leave Oriole Point for good."

"Piper," Lionel warned. "It will seem malicious if we seek revenge after this."

"Revenge? I view it as justice."

I thought it best to keep the conversation confined to the suspects, and not their fate once this was all over. "I plan to do a little digging around myself. I'm having Drake do my horoscope, and I hope to ask him a few questions when we meet. He must have a secret or two."

"Oh, that stupid witch thing." Piper rolled her eyes. "No one's going to be driven to murder because they danced in the moonlight during the summer solstice. This isn't Salem."

"I think we can cross Juliet Haller off the list, too," Lionel said.

"Granted, they all seem harmless. But Cole had to know something about them that they want to keep hidden." I felt terrible thinking such awful things about the Hallers, but evil sometimes wore an innocent face. Until Evangeline Chaplin poisoned her husband, I would have sworn the most aggressive thing she was capable of was whisking eggs.

"Marlee's right," Piper said. "Don't you think it odd the Hallers seem to have no immediate or extended family? I know Juliet was unable to have children, but I've never heard them mention a single relative. Were they both orphans? That seems unlikely."

"There's only one more zoning commission member to consider, and that's Crystal Appeldoorn," I said. "All I've heard about her is she may have dabbled in drugs when she was younger. And I learned that only yesterday."

Piper and Lionel exchanged looks. "She did a lot more than dabble," Lionel said.

"I realize you were off in New York, Marlee, but I

can't believe you didn't know about Crystal before this." Piper seemed exasperated.

"How would I know about Crystal?"

For the first time ever, Piper looked embarrassed. Nothing embarrassed Piper. Now I was worried.

"What should I know about Crystal?" I asked. "She is four years older than me. I don't think we ever said a word to each other growing up. And she left town right after she graduated. We chat at yoga, but we're not friends. Why would I know about her personal life?"

"Her drug use was heavy," Lionel said slowly, as if weighing his words. "At first, only marijuana and hashish. But by her senior year, there was talk she'd become addicted."

"To what?"

"That's the ironic thing, given her name," Lionel remarked.

"Crystal meth?" This didn't make sense. Our high school graduating classes averaged a hundred students; that meant most kids knew far too much about their fellow classmates. "How did no one around here know about this? How did you find out?"

"Lionel and I have been busy since the OPBA meeting. Last Friday we hired private investigators to look into the backgrounds of the zoning commission members. And yesterday we also hired a detective to track Natasha Bowman down."

"You have moved fast." I was both relieved and alarmed to hear this.

"Did you think I was going to make bail only to sit around crying? I need to clear my family name. And Natasha Bowman is the wild card in all this. Either she is a victim herself or she's behind Cole's murder, the attack on you, *and* my arrest."

I knew Piper was determined, but I was beginning to think she was a Marvel superhero. "And your investigators confirmed that Crystal was a meth head?"

They both nodded.

"I still don't understand why you think I would know about this."

Piper gave her husband a weary look. "You tell her."

I turned to Lionel with growing dread. What in the world was I supposed to know?

Lionel pulled a nearby ottoman over and sat down between Piper and me. "Crystal became addicted during her senior year in high school. Most people in town don't know about her addiction because as soon as she graduated, her parents sent her to rehab in Texas."

"So?"

"She was sent off with another teenager from Oriole Point who was also a crystal meth addict. In fact, this teenager was the person who introduced her to the drug."

"Do I know this person?" I asked.

"I'm afraid you do." Lionel's expression grew even more somber. "It was Ryan."

Chapter 13

The temperature at dusk hovered around eighty, yet I sat before my fire pit, trying not to shiver. If I stared into the flames long enough, maybe I could understand how I'd had no idea Ryan was once a crystal meth addict. Although gossip was the topic of choice in Oriole Point, I was sure there were all sorts of secrets in our village that none of us guessed at. And the Zellars were an important family in the community, one of the most successful orchard growers in Michigan's famed fruit belt. Of course they wouldn't want it known that one of their sons was a drug addict.

As the evening's first fireflies glimmered among the beach grasses, I mulled over this latest news. Lionel had said Crystal and Ryan went off to rehab in Texas right out of high school. I'd been only fourteen that summer, with all my attention focused on a family vacation to Disney World. I had no memory of Ryan being gone, not that I ever paid much attention to Ryan back then. Although I briefly had a crush in middle school on his younger brother Barry.

I wondered how the Zellars had explained why one of their sons left during harvest season at the orchards. Then again, there were five Zellar sons. Ryan wouldn't have been missed that much, especially if the family saw this as a chance for him to get well. And was it really all that terrible? Two kids had foolishly played around with crystal meth and got hooked, something I heard was easy to do. I wouldn't know.

Not only was I not much of a drinker, but I also had never touched a drug in my life. I hadn't even opened the bottle of Vicodin prescribed for me following the attack at the marina. Of course, some of my friends here and in New York smoked weed or popped a few pills; a few enjoyed a line of coke now and then. But crystal meth was hard core. I couldn't imagine my laid-back fiancé being so strung out on drugs that he had to be packed off to rehab. And why had he never told me any of this? Shouldn't people know all about each other before they got married? Otherwise, it was like forming a partnership under false pretenses. I really didn't need this information right now. Not with everything else going on.

Lying back in my Adirondack chair, I turned my gaze to the moonlight shimmering on Lake Michigan. Because my Painted Lady sat on a bluff, I had a bird's-eye view of the water, which was accompanied by the sound of gentle waves. When weather permitted, I loved to relax in the grassy area across the road from my house, Here is where I kept my patio furniture, stone fire pit, and a charcoal barbecue grill. A few yards away were the wooden steps that led down to my family's private beach. I briefly considered walking down the thirty steps to the sand and water below, but I felt too tired to make the return trip. Besides,

I had to figure out how I was going to broach this subject with Ryan. I wasn't looking forward to it.

The sound of my screen door creaking open across the street told me I'd better figure it out fast. Ryan was home, and he had brought pizza with him. I could smell the pepperoni and melted cheese as he approached.

"I saw the fire pit and figured you had to be out here. I've got pizza and root beer." After leaning over for a kiss, Ryan sat down on the Adirondack chair beside me and flipped open the pizza box. "I noticed we have a gray bird and a cage as large as a small barn in the living room. I assume we're fostering him for Aunt Vicki."

"It's a her. An African grey by the name of Minnie." I gave a rueful chuckle. "And I'm not fostering her. I'm her mama now. I never could resist birds. This one's pretty special, too."

He grinned. "I agree. She told me to kiss her."

"I'd like to pretend she won't be any trouble, but I suspect she's going to be a pretty vocal member of the household."

"Hey, anything's better than that ferret. Sorry I'm late. Dad wants to spray the blackberry bushes. We might be in for another wave of root weevils—the same ones that screwed up the harvest big-time four years ago. There's no way we can afford a repeat of that."

Ryan handed me a slice of pizza with a napkin, and I took it eagerly as he launched into a critique of these root weevils compared to ones in the past. The first bite of the still hot pizza made me groan with pleasure. My favorite food in the world.

When he finally ran out of root weevil facts, I said,

"Don't worry about being late. I got back from visiting Piper and Lionel only about an hour ago."

Ryan must have been even hungrier than I was. He'd already wolfed down two slices and reached for another. "What happened at Piper's?"

"Lionel hired private investigators to track down Natasha." It was best to lead off the conversation with this. I needed to ease into the crystal meth discussion.

"Good idea. They'll probably find her before the police do. Oh, I bumped into Denise Redfern when I was picking up the pizza. She says Chief Hitchcock is flying back tonight."

"Thank God."

Ryan suddenly jumped out of his Adirondack chair. He waved his pizza slice at an insect buzzing around his hand. "Get away. Get away, damn it! Marlee, this isn't a bee, is it?"

I sat up. "I think it's a firefly. See." With a sigh of relief, I watched the firefly glow for a second, before heading off for something less animated than Ryan.

He sat down in the chair again. "This afternoon I swear a bee chased me right out of the raspberry patch. Like it had a vendetta against me or something. I ran all the way to the barn."

"I hope you had an EpiPen with you."

"I forgot it. Yeah, I know. I should carry it all the time."

"If you're nervous, I'll go in the house and get the one I keep in my purse. Although it's really too late for bees to be out and about."

"No, I'm fine." He swigged his root beer. "Anyway, how did Piper seem today?"

"Vengeful. She and Lionel are determined to find

out if the zoning commission members are hiding something. The three of us are on the same page about that. I made an appointment to have my horoscope done by Drake this Thursday. While I'm there, I'll see if I can find out anything useful from him."

"Leave the commission members alone." Ryan looked at me with disapproval. "In fact, stay out of the investigation altogether. You're lucky the police didn't charge you with breaking and entering."

"But if I hadn't broken into the Bowman house, I would never have learned that Natasha's dream dictionaries were gone."

"Which means the Russian beauty queen is probably alive." He paused. "And a murderer."

"You're saying that only because you don't like her. You and most of the people in Oriole Point."

"With reason. She's a phony gold digger who got what she deserved when she married Cole."

"What a terrible thing to say. And you don't know what you're talking about. Natasha is sweet and funny. Generous too. I think everyone's jealous because she's so beautiful."

He laughed. "You've got to be kidding."

"Natasha didn't kill Cole, and she didn't try to kill me. But those zoning commission members are another story. I bet they're hiding something."

"Stay out of it, Marlee. The police chief is coming back. And they've already charged Piper with the murder. Let the authorities figure out what's going on. Stop getting involved."

"Excuse me, but I am involved, whether I like it or not. Or did you forget someone tried to kill me last Friday?"

"Exactly. Which is why you shouldn't be anywhere

near people you suspect of being the killer." He finished off another slice. "Although I don't think the zoning commission members had anything to do with Cole's murder."

"Why else would they rezone the Fields property?"

Ryan turned to look at me, the flames from the fire pit playing over his face. He didn't look happy. "They agreed because it makes sense. Why shouldn't there be franchises here? Oriole Point gets over two million visitors in the summer. Why send them off to Holland or Grand Rapids if they have a sudden urge to eat at Olive Garden?"

"But it will cut into the profits of all the small store owners here. None of us can compete with a national chain. Half the shops on Lyall Street would go out of business."

He shrugged. "That's capitalism, babe."

I sat back as if he had punched me in the stomach. "Think of all the mom-and-pop stores that go out of business whenever a Walmart opens up. You can't possibly want to see such a thing happen in Oriole Point. I thought you cared about the welfare of our village."

"Every season three or four downtown stores go out of business, and new ones take their place. It would only be a little worse if the town allowed national chains."

"You say that because Zellars won't be affected by any of the chains. I bet you'd change your tune if a company like Dole decided to go into the fruit-growing business around here."

"If Dole wants to plant fruit trees here, let them. The Zellars haven't stayed in business for generations without knowing how to fight off the competition."

I shook my head when he offered me another slice of pizza. This conversation had killed my appetite, and I hadn't even brought up the crystal meth yet. "You're wrong about the franchises coming here and wrong about the zoning commission members. I bet if I dig around, I'll find out some very surprising things about all four of them."

"If they do have secrets, what gives you the right to expose them?"

"Because one of them might have murdered Cole *and* tried to murder me."

Ryan tossed the pizza box on the ground. "I love you, but sometimes you can't see what's right in front of you."

"What are you talking about?"

"The police have already charged someone with the murder. Now, I don't think Piper did it either. It looks like a frame-up to me. But it makes no more sense to accuse the zoning commission members. What about any of them is the least bit suspicious? Drake is a former Olympic athlete. If he had anything sinister in his background, don't you think it would have come to light by now?"

"That's why they're called secrets, Ryan."

He made a face. "And the Hallers? There's not a duller couple in the county. Yeah, Muffin Mike was a slimy slumlord back in Chicago. But he paid a big price for it when his wife committed suicide, don't you think?"

"What about Crystal?"

"What about her? She's a single mom who's worked hard and built up a solid business."

"Even you admitted she fooled around with drugs when she was younger."

"She was a kid then. Don't act like she was dealing drugs or something. I can't believe you would even consider Crystal as a murderer. You obviously don't know her at all."

"I see her at yoga every week. And we often talk when I stop for coffee at her shop. I like Crystal, but I think she needs to be honest about why she voted to rezone Strawberry Fields." I stared hard at Ryan. Exactly how many secrets was he keeping from me? "It's clear you like Crystal, too. Did you date back in high school?"

"Really? You're going to start asking me about my high school girlfriends now?"

"Why not? You never stop talking about Max. Why are you and Crystal off-limits?"

Ryan got to his feet. "What should be off-limits to you are the private lives of the zoning commission members. All of them, but especially Crystal."

"A man is dead, and someone nearly killed me. I can't believe you expect me to carry on as if nothing has happened."

"And I can't believe you're ignoring the Russian elephant in the room. No one had a better reason to want Cole dead than Natasha. And she's been missing since the day of the OPBA meeting. Seems pretty suspicious to me."

I shook my head. "That would mean Natasha is responsible for bashing me on the head."

"Yeah. It would. Marlee, what do you really know about Natasha Rostova, except she was in a beauty contest and likes rich older men?"

"I know she's not capable of murder."

"Maybe she isn't. But maybe she knew people willing to get rid of Cole for her."

I bit my lip, remembering what Janelle had told me the other day about Natasha having family members in the Russian Mafia. "If so, why would I be attacked, as well?"

Ryan shrugged. "Maybe to throw the police off. The same reason someone put that muddler in Piper's Hummer. I don't know, but you don't either. So stay out of it."

"I have to do what I think is right," I said. "But don't worry. I won't talk about the murder investigation around you again. In future, we'll keep our discussions confined to capitalism and root weevils."

He stalked back to the house. The screen door slammed behind him. Obviously, this wasn't the best time to ask Ryan if he had ever been a crystal meth addict.

Chapter 14

I hated Downward-Facing Dog. It was my least favorite yoga pose, especially today, when it sent my head injury throbbing. Otherwise, my beach yoga class was a pleasure. The thirty-minute yoga sessions were held five days a week, and I tried never to miss one. I peeked over at the blond woman lying in the final Corpse pose several yards away. Crystal Appeldoorn was a regular attendee as well.

Closing my eyes, I heard nothing but the soft murmur of the nearby waves, the cries of gulls, and the soothing voice of our instructor, Rowena, as she led us into the closing meditation. A welcome breeze from the lake ruffled my hair. The sand beneath my yoga mat had not yet turned hot from the summer sun. Early morning was the perfect time to come to Oriole Beach. Most tourists were either still asleep or having breakfast.

Ryan was gone by the time I pulled on my yoga pants and tank top. I already regretted our entire conversation the night before. I had enough trouble in my life at the moment, and I didn't need to add a

fight with my boyfriend. That was why I had been
relieved to see the note left on the kitchen island.
It read,

> *Sorry about last night. Let me make it up to you*
> *with a San Sebastian dinner. Reservation @ 7.*
> *Love you, Ryan.*

Thinking about the note put a smile on my face,
and by the time Rowena brought our yoga session
to an end, I felt completely relaxed. The twelve of
us exchanged pleasantries as we rolled up our mats.
After we said good-bye to each other, most of the
group headed for their cars in the public parking lot.
Those of us lucky to live near the lake began to walk
along the water in either direction.

Crystal's red Craftsman house was about five blocks
from the lake on my side of the river. She walked to
the public beach from home, as I did, so I would
have at least fifteen minutes to speak with her during
the return trip. Yoga mat tucked under one arm,
Crystal set off for home. I trailed after her. I always
came to the beach yoga sessions in my bare feet and
walked right along the shoreline. I enjoyed feeling
my toes sink into the sand while the cool lake water
washed over my ankles. It took weeks for the lake to
warm up. If the temperature stayed balmy, the lake
water should be perfect by mid-July. Otherwise, swim-
mers would be wincing all the way into August every
time they waded into the chilly waves.

"What's the hurry?" I asked Crystal as I caught up
with her.

She looked over at me in surprise. "After what
happened at the OPBA meeting, I didn't think you'd

want to walk with me. You seemed pretty angry that night."

I kicked at an incoming wave, sending a spray of water into the air. It looked to be the beginning of a gorgeous day: clear skies, low humidity, the lake looking as blue as the Caribbean. How sad that it would have to be marred by a discussion about murder.

"I was angry. I still am. And shocked." I tried to keep pace with Crystal, who was nearly six feet tall. "A lot of us don't understand why the zoning commission agreed to undermine our business community by green-lighting national chains and franchises."

"It's complicated, Marlee."

"It doesn't seem complicated to me, or to anyone else who owns a business in Oriole Point. What it seems is suspicious. Especially since the zoning commission decision was unanimous." I paused. "Did Cole Bowman bribe all of you?"

I knew this would startle her, and it did. She stopped and stared at me with eyes the exact color of the lake today. "Bribe? How could you accuse us of such a terrible thing?"

I stared back. "Letting a flood of national chains into our little village is a terrible thing, too. You were born and raised here, Crystal. You know this town is completely dependent on tourism. And what they love best—what keeps them coming back year after year—is our untouched charm. Our historic homes, the lighthouse, the unusual boutiques and bakeries, the local artists, the homespun quilt shops, and the country kitchen cafés. The last thing we need here is a McDonalds or a Bed Bath & Beyond. You know what this decision means for Oriole Point."

"Like I said, the decision was complicated." Crystal turned away. "But none of us were bribed. I can't believe you would think such a thing of us. Of me! I love Oriole Point. Why else would I come back home to raise my little girl here?"

"Then why do something that will hurt the town?"

"You don't understand. We didn't mean to hurt anybody." She swept back her hair, which the breeze kept blowing in her face. It suddenly struck me that she resembled Ryan: tall, lanky, straight blond hair, blue eyes. However, the result wasn't quite the same. Ryan was handsome, too handsome for his own good probably, while Crystal was a rather nondescript person. The only thing remarkable about her was her height and her slim, muscular physique. I had the feeling that she actually tried to seem forgettable, that she somehow preferred people didn't pay attention to her. I was certain she did not want my attention now.

"A lot of hurtful things have gone on this past week," I said. "Including murder."

"What a terrible thing to happen. I can't believe Cole was murdered. I was shocked when I heard the news."

"Many of us were." Now would be a good time to see if she had an alibi for the time of Cole's death. "When did you hear he'd been killed?"

"As soon as I got back to Oriole Point. I drove to Blue Lake early that morning to drop Alyssa off at music camp. Because I stopped at the mall in Muskegon, I didn't arrive back here until around three. By then, it was all anyone in the village could talk about."

Blue Lake was only a little over an hour away. If she had dropped her daughter off at camp that morning, it would have left plenty of time for Crystal to return to Oriole Point and bash Cole over the head. "Who do you think killed him?"

Crystal looked at me with obvious consternation. "Piper, of course. The police found the murder weapon in her Hummer."

"I don't care if they found Cole's body in there. She didn't do it."

"But you saw her at the meeting. She was furious with him. Piper knocked him out in front of us."

"We all would have stood in line that night to hit Cole. Piper got to him first. And throwing a punch is a lot different than murder."

I decided to remain silent for a few minutes. Give Crystal time to realize that Piper as the prime suspect in Cole's murder was not such a sure thing. Looking to my right, I gazed at the lake, which glittered all the way to an endless horizon. Somewhere on the other side lay Wisconsin, but from where we stood, all that stretched before us was water. First-time visitors to the Great Lakes were often amazed at the sheer size of the lakes, apparently forgetting that they had been named "Great" for a reason. They were our inland seas—Midwestern oceans, if you like—only without the taste of salt in the air. And I wouldn't trade Lake Michigan or Lake Superior for the Atlantic and the Pacific combined.

"'Perhaps the truth depends on a walk along the lake,'" I said finally.

"What?"

"It's a quote from the poet Wallace Stevens."

"Does that mean you think I'm not telling the truth about the zoning decision?"

"I think you're concealing the truth. If Cole didn't bribe the commission, that leaves only one alternative. Blackmail."

"That's even worse than accusing us of being bribed."

"Is it? If you'd been bribed, it would mean you sold out the town for personal greed. But if Cole knew something you wanted to keep hidden, then it was an act of self-protection. Not an admirable response, but one I could understand."

Crystal's expression turned stony. "Do you really believe all four members of the zoning commission have secrets they're hiding?"

I remembered how my Amish cooking show star had turned out to be anything but Amish. And had anything about the marriage of Evangeline and John Chaplin been real? "After what I went through in New York, I believe almost everyone has a secret or two they'd prefer to keep buried."

"Even you?"

It was a challenge I met squarely. "Maybe."

"Maybe you killed Cole. Maybe he was blackmailing you."

"Then I'd like to know how I hit my own head twice before ending up in the river. Whoever killed Cole Bowman also tried to kill me last Friday."

Crystal was the one to finally break our gaze. She looked out at the lake with a frown. "There's nothing in my life anyone could blackmail me about."

"That isn't what I heard."

For the first time, she seemed rattled. "What have you heard?"

I gave a great sigh. I needed time to work up my courage because I was about to tell a whopper. "You forget I'm engaged to Ryan Zellar."

Now she looked genuinely panicked. "So? What has he said?"

If I framed this right, I might not have to tell a lie at all. "I know both you and Ryan were addicted to crystal meth back in high school. And that he introduced you to the drug."

Crystal collapsed onto the sand. I sat down beside her. The water lapped about us, dampening our yoga pants, but I didn't think she noticed. "Don't blame Ryan," she said finally. "I was already popping pills, smoking hash, skipping class. And anything one of the Zellar brothers did had to be cool. It wasn't his fault. I made Ryan give me a hit while he was high himself. Plus, we were seventeen, which means we were stupid and afraid of nothing."

"He doesn't like to talk about those days." Indeed, he had never said a word about any of this to me.

"Ryan promised he would never say anything. But you two are getting married. I understand why he told you. A married couple shouldn't have secrets between them."

This made me feel worse. "Ryan wants only the best for you. He feels quite protective." That certainly was true. "And I know all about Texas."

She closed her eyes. "I should have thought about that once you two became engaged. You'd want to know about his first wife, and Texas would come up."

I remained quiet. What did Ryan's ex-wife have to do with Texas? I knew that her name was Laura McCoy and that she was born and raised in Phoenix. Ryan had told me they met when she came to Oriole

Point on a vacation with her girlfriends. After a whirlwind romance—almost as speedy as Cole and Natasha's courtship—they got married nine years ago. And divorced less than three years after that. She moved back to Arizona. Except for a few blurry photos of their wedding in Jamaica, it was as if Ryan had never been married. He answered any questions about her with the briefest reply. To be honest, I didn't ask him much. She'd been out of the picture so long, I didn't see the point.

"A lot seems to have happened in Texas," I said.

"Too much. Like Ryan told you, we both went to rehab there, although he needed only one time to kick his habit. Took a lot longer for me. That's why I stayed away from Oriole Point. Even though I had put them through hell, my parents kept paying for me to go to rehab until it finally worked. I only wish it hadn't taken so long. Otherwise, I wouldn't have met my husband. Ted was there, trying to get clean. He was a crack addict as well." She shook her head. "And I'm responsible for Ryan meeting Laura. I still feel guilty about that."

"He doesn't blame you." And as far as I knew, he didn't.

"Ryan's a sweetheart. But he should blame me. Every time I went into rehab, he flew down to Texas to serve as cheerleader for my recovery. One of those times, he met Laura. She was in rehab for alcoholism. They clicked right away. And why wouldn't they? He's a hot guy, and Laura was even hotter. As soon as he laid eyes on her, he was a goner. Ryan has a thing for redheads, especially if they look like a Victoria's Secret model."

I blinked. This was the first I'd heard about his fondness for gorgeous redheads with killer bods.

Crystal seemed to remember that I was a B-cup brunette and quickly added, "Obviously, his tastes have changed. For the better. You're nothing like Laura or any of the girls he dated in high school. You're good for him. Honest, down to earth, hard-working. And you don't spend every waking minute worrying about how you look."

I hoped my appearance wasn't as haphazard as this comment seemed to imply. I was still trying to digest the fact that Ryan's first wife was a recovering alcoholic.

"Anyway, when Laura got out of rehab, she flew up here to visit him. I tried to warn him that she wasn't serious about her recovery. I was afraid she'd get him back to using again. But Ryan is stronger than I gave him credit for. You're marrying one tough man."

I nodded. He might be tough, but he also was far too secretive. Did I know anything at all about Ryan Zellar, aside from his date of birth and what he did for a living? Was I stupid or too trusting? I feared I was both.

"At least the marriage didn't last long enough to cause any real damage," I replied.

"Yes. As I'm sure he told you, Ryan is the one who wanted the divorce. She fell off the wagon, no surprise to me. And they fought all the time. Last I heard, Laura was back in rehab, this time in California. I also think she's on her third marriage."

"You and Ryan should be proud of yourselves. Both of you beat your addiction."

"It wasn't easy for either of us. Harder for me. Luckily, Ryan ended his bad marriage pretty quick.

I stayed married to Ted far too long. Then again, we had a child together, and I wanted to make it work." Crystal shuddered. "Another mistake. At least I got out of there when Alyssa was only two. She doesn't remember her father at all. Which is the way I want it."

She grew silent. I wasn't certain how to get her to continue without exposing how little I actually knew. "I don't have to tell you what Ryan thinks of your ex-husband."

"You got that right. He hates Ted. Ryan has always looked on me as a sister, especially since he has only brothers. He warned me to steer clear of Ted Jones from the beginning. Ted was a triple threat—an addict, a dealer, and an armed robber. When Alyssa was two, he added murderer to his résumé. That was the end of the marriage for me. Not that the divorce really mattered. He was sentenced to life in prison without parole." Her expression turned even more bitter. "Texas judges don't look kindly on cop killers."

Talk about still waters running deep. Who would have guessed that quiet, nondescript Crystal Appeldoorn was once an addict with a murderer for an ex-husband?

"You know Ryan would do anything for you and your daughter."

"He's been such a good friend. Never judges me, even when I'm screwing up big-time. Thankfully, I cleaned up my act, which involved a lot more than kicking drugs. My entire life changed because of Alyssa. She's been the reason for my existence from the moment I learned I was pregnant. Oh, Ted tried to get clean again right after she was born, but it lasted only a few months. After that, we hardly saw him. A girlfriend moved in with me and the baby to help pay the rent." She sighed. "He's ruined his life in so many ways, but I think he really cared about Alyssa. As much as he was able to care about anybody."

"Even now?"

"The Ted I first met in rehab—the one who wanted to get clean and sober—is gone. By the time he shot those policemen, I don't think he was capable of feeling anything but rage." She suddenly straightened. "I've told Alyssa that her dad died in a car accident right after she was born. And in many ways, Ted did die then, the last of the old Ted, anyway. My parents and sister know the truth, and my best friend, Katy. Ryan too. Now you."

I felt uneasy to be included in this trusted group. "Then no one else knows about your addiction. Or that your ex-husband is in prison for murder."

"I recently told Eric. He's a good man, and he's been through a lot in his life. You don't spend two tours of duty in Baghdad without seeing horrible things. Like Ryan, he isn't judgmental. Besides, things have gotten serious between us. If he ends up being Alyssa's new daddy, I need to be completely honest with him." Crystal placed her hand on my arm. "You understand. After all, Ryan told you the truth about our addictions and his first marriage. That's the way it should be if you love someone enough to marry them."

"It should." I didn't know whether to be angry or depressed that Ryan hadn't been honest with me at all. Did he not trust me? If so, why in the world did he want to marry me? And now that I knew how much he'd kept from me, why did I want to marry him?

I stretched out so that when the next waves came in, my legs would get soaked. I needed the chill of the lake water to make me feel something right now aside from sadness. "You're not afraid your daughter will discover the truth one day?"

"Alyssa is nearly ten. The only memories she has is of living here in Oriole Point with me and my family. All of us have lavished nothing but love on her every single day. Fortunately, her father's last name is a common one—Jones. I explained that I changed my name back to Appeldoorn because I hadn't known her dad long before he died, and I felt more like an Appeldoorn than a Jones."

"But if someone looks too closely at the name and when you lived in Texas, they might stumble on the truth."

I now understood Ryan's misgivings about prying into people's secrets. I'd hate to have a child's world turned upside down if she found out her father was alive and in prison for murder. The Chaplin case had taught me that murder sent out a large and dangerous ripple.

Crystal turned her attention back to the lake. "When I was eight months pregnant, the two of us went to Idaho. Ted had a friend there who smuggled contraband over the Canadian border. This guy left to take part in some deal in Alberta, and we stayed at his house while he was gone. I ended up going into labor three weeks later, which means Alyssa's birth certificate says Boise, Idaho, not Austin, Texas."

I wondered if Lionel's detectives would discover the truth. Until I was convinced Crystal was guilty, I planned to keep this information to myself. Yes, I wanted to clear Piper's name and catch whoever it was that had attacked me. But I hoped I wouldn't have to upset an innocent child's life to do it. But Lionel's detectives might. I debated whether I should warn Crystal.

"Even if Alyssa does find out one day, I think she'll be fine. It might be a shock, but—"

Crystal got to her feet in one swift motion. "No one will upset my child's life with ugly memories of the past. No one! I made one bad choice after the other from the time I was seventeen. How could you possibly understand what it's like to be strung out on drugs in your teens and early twenties? You've no idea about some of the things I've done."

"But this is a murder case, Crystal. Piper has been arrested. She and Lionel will do anything to prove she's innocent. All anyone is looking for is the truth."

"The truth? If I have to explain the truth about her father, I'll also have to tell her about how I lived my life until the day I learned I was pregnant. My pregnancy is what got me clean. My child is what gave me the courage to leave Ted, along with the motivation to start a business that guarantees her future. Alyssa's happiness comes first, and I won't allow anyone or anything to disrupt my child's life. Not you or Piper or—"

"Or Cole Bowman?" I asked.

She glared down at me from her great height. How could I have ever thought Crystal was a quiet, unremarkable woman? Once she was roused, I suspected she could make even Piper back down.

"Be careful, Marlee. Things might end badly if you push some of us too far."

Crystal picked up her yoga mat and marched away.

I watched until her figure was a considerable distance down the beach. Only then did I begin to make my own way home. If Cole had blackmailed Crystal, I had just learned why. My relaxed state of mind following yoga had vanished. Instead, I was left with the fear that Crystal would do anything to keep her secrets from her daughter, including murder.

Chapter 15

Ryan was late. There wasn't much traffic on our country roads, so I knew he wasn't being held up due to rush hour congestion. But it was past seven thirty and still no sign of him. Ryan and I hadn't spoken since the night before. Despite the friendly note he had left, asking me to dinner, I wondered if he *was* feeling friendly toward me. My own feelings were a jumble. All day I had thought of little else but what Crystal had revealed on the beach. Even more startling than her own past were the heretofore unknown details about my fiancé. What else didn't I know about Ryan? Good grief. Was his real name even Ryan?

I suspected his tardiness was meant to punish me. Ryan loved eating at San Sebastian as much as I did. It was why he'd offered to make the reservation this morning. And since our name was on the reservation list when I arrived, he had indeed done just that. Pulling out my cell phone, I was about to text him, then decided not to. Last time I thought I was texting Ryan, Max ended up being the recipient. I wondered if I had done that subconsciously. I certainly felt more comfortable around Max, especially lately.

I'd bet anything that Crystal had spoken with Ryan today. Which meant he was pissed. For all I knew, he had no intention of even showing up for dinner.

Well, I was hungry. Whether Ryan was here or not, I planned to eat. Things were so busy at the store that I had missed lunch entirely.

Looking around for my server, I took in the elegant decor of San Sebastian: polished teakwood tables and chairs, curved booths of burgundy leather, skylights in all three dining rooms, along with a pebbled fountain a few yards from where I sat. Tess thought the restaurant slightly pretentious and too expensive, but it served the best food I'd eaten since a long-ago tasting tour of Tuscany. It also had sexy Diego Theroux presiding over the kitchen. Diego frequently walked through the restaurant in his chef whites, stopping to exchange a few words with his contented diners. Any opportunity to appreciate his considerable good looks was welcomed as much as his Andalusian paella and slow-roasted sweet onions.

As though I had sent a psychic message to Diego, he suddenly entered the dining room, platter in hand. I was surprised to see him head straight for me.

"Marlee, my servers told me that you have been sitting here for forty minutes and have not ordered a thing. I can't have that." He set the platter on the table. "Here's a tapas sampler plate to coax you into eating." His large brown eyes gazed at me with concern. "We've all been worried about you since the night of the Strawberry Moon Bash. And I heard you were the one to find Cole's body. Are you feeling all right?"

My mouth salivated at the sight and smell of a dish filled with piping hot cheese and shrimp. "I'm fine, Diego. I'm waiting for Ryan. He was supposed to meet me here at seven." I picked up a tapa. "But thank you so much for this. I'm starving."

"The Manchego cheese ones are my favorite, but they're all something new I'm trying. Let me know what you think. Because you're my test audience, it's on the house."

I quickly ate the cheese tapas and nearly swooned. "Delicious. I'll be your culinary guinea pig anytime."

He slid into the booth across from me. With a head of tousled black hair and cheekbones to make a supermodel green with envy, Diego was movie star handsome. He'd already cut a swath through the young women along the lakeshore—tourists and locals—and I wondered if any of them would ever tempt him to settle down. He'd never made any romantic overtures to me, and I had never entertained any fantasies about him. With men that attractive, it was best to admire them from afar. Besides, I enjoyed our easy friendship; it often resulted in free appetizers.

"You're dressed up too nice to be a guinea pig." He looked at my turquoise summer dress, which sported a flirty short skirt and spaghetti straps. I never dressed casually when I came to San Sebastian. The restaurant didn't have a dress code, but I felt its high prices and haute cuisine deserved a bit of formality. Tonight I was honoring that cuisine with an expensive Michael Kors outfit, one of many designer clothes I'd bought during my NYC years. I'd also taken more time to style my hair, which tonight I wore loose about my shoulders, with a few carefully placed waves that had taken nearly an hour to perfect with a curling iron.

"I always dress up for San Sebastian." I reached for another tapa. "A girl's got to show a little respect for food like this."

"I appreciate that. And I also appreciate a beautiful woman." He smiled.

I raised my eyebrow at him. "So I've heard. Quite a few."

He shrugged. "They're like my sampler platters. I need to explore what's out there before deciding what will really satisfy my hunger."

"If one of those women comes close to your tapas, grab her quick." I lifted what remained of the last artichoke tapa. "This is my favorite. Are these tapas purely Spanish, or is there a French component?" San Sebastian gave equal attention to the cuisines of both countries.

"Basque, which means they're both. About a third of our new summer menu is Basque."

"Are customers surprised you're adding Basque foods?"

"Don't know why they should be. After all, I'm Basque. The name of my restaurant is Basque, too."

"I didn't realize that."

"San Sebastián is the Basque village my family comes from. Denise Redfern did the same thing with her shop. Tonguish is the Potawatomi word for her hometown. And Rowena's yoga studio is called Karuna, which is the Sanskrit word for 'compassion.' A lot of the names people choose for their businesses reveal what's important to them." Those dimples deepened again. "Like you care a great deal about berries."

"The Berry Basket doesn't seem quite as meaningful as Karuna," I said.

"Am I interrupting something?"

Startled, Diego and I both turned to see Ryan standing beside the table. He wore jeans and a casual shirt, which surprised me. Like me, he normally dressed up for San Sebastian.

Diego pushed himself out of the booth. "I was keeping your lovely fiancée company until you arrived."

I gave Ryan a cool smile. "I didn't mind you being late. He brought me free tapas."

Ryan only glowered at me as he pushed past Diego to slide into the booth.

"I'll leave you two alone to order dinner." Diego winked at me. "The special tonight is Catalan Chicken, and I hear the chef recommends it."

"Sounds wonderful. Thanks, Diego," I said.

After he left, I reluctantly turned my attention to Ryan. There had not been a welcome kiss, a smile, or even a hi. I noticed he had his jaw firmly clenched. A sign he was angry. Well, I could play this game, too.

"I was wondering when you were going to show up."

Ryan only stared back at me. Our server appeared just then, probably relieved that he could finally get the order for this table rolling. In summer, San Sebastian became increasingly crowded. By eight o'clock, the wait for a table could be as long as three hours.

Without opening the menu, Ryan said, "Just a bowl of gazpacho."

"That's all you want for dinner?" I asked.

He nodded.

The hell with him. I was hungry. I didn't have to look at the menu, either, since I had enjoyed almost everything on it during the past two years. Plus, tonight's special sounded enticing. "Perigord salad and the Catalan Chicken." I handed both menus to the waiter. "And a glass of Riesling."

"Domestic?"

I named my favorite local vineyard.

As soon as the waiter left, Ryan said, "Do you really think you should be drinking wine? Things didn't end well the last time you had alcohol."

"I'm going to need it for our conversation. In fact, you should order a drink, too."

"No. One of us should be sober."

"Don't worry. What happened on Friday was a rare event for me." I paused. "Unlike your ex-wife, I do not have a drinking problem."

He swore under his breath, then leaned forward. "Are you drunk already? Or are you just trying to make me mad?"

"Make you mad? You came in here ready to argue. I will tell you that I'm not in a good mood myself. Or do you think I enjoy being lied to?"

"You've got some damn nerve after the way you lied to Crystal this morning. Pretending I told you all about the crystal meth. And Laura and Ted. What's the matter with you?"

"Me?" I spoke so loud, several patrons turned in our direction. Luckily, the restaurant wasn't yet filled to capacity, and the tall leather sides of our booth kept us partially hidden from the dining room. "You're the one who's been lying to me," I continued in a lower voice.

"I can't figure out how you knew to ask about all

this in the first place," he said, ignoring my last comment. "Are you binge watching *Breaking Bad*?"

"Lionel and Piper told me."

His expression went from angry to shocked. "How do they know?"

"They're hell-bent on fighting the murder charge against Piper. The best way to do that is to find the real killer. Unlike you, Piper and Lionel think the zoning commission members were blackmailed by Cole. That's why they hired private detectives to look into their backgrounds."

Ryan sat back as if he had been shoved. "You told me they hired detectives to track down Natasha. You never said they were prying into the zoning commission members' lives. That's terrible."

"It's a lot more terrible for an innocent person to go to prison for a crime she didn't commit. Are you so protective of Crystal that you're willing to sacrifice Piper?"

"Are they making this information public? I've got to tell Crystal as soon as possible. She was upset enough when she called to tell me about your conversation with her. But this will make her physically ill. Poor Crystal."

"You're not even listening to me. A man has been murdered, someone tried to kill me, an innocent person has been arrested, and the real killer is still on the loose. Instead, you're only worried that Crystal might be upset." In a day of unwelcome surprises, this was yet another. "Are you in love with her, Ryan?"

He looked at me as if I was a lunatic. "Crystal's like a sister to me. We've been through a lot together. No one understands me better, and no one cares more about my welfare. Just like I care about her and her child."

My hands began to tremble, and I clasped them before me on the table. "Crystal cares about you more than I do?"

"Sometimes I think she does." He lifted his chin in defiance.

I couldn't speak for a stunned moment. "Wow. First, I learn you were a drug addict. Then I find out you met your ex-wife in rehab, and not during a whirlwind courtship during her vacation in Oriole Point. And that you ended the marriage due to her alcoholism, not her infidelity."

He took a deep breath, as if debating whether to tell me the truth even now. "She did cheat on me. Laura spent a lot of time in bars. And she often went home with whatever guy she was drinking with. But the drinking was the real reason it all ended. It was too much."

My cell phone rang. Since I had placed it on the table, I could see it was Gillian calling me. But whatever she had to say was less crucial than the conversation I was having with Ryan.

"Why didn't you tell me any of this?"

"I don't like talking about that time in my life. And I don't see how it concerns you."

My mouth fell open. "I'm not some casual acquaintance. I'm the woman you asked to marry you. And at this moment I don't really understand why."

He looked over at me with an inscrutable expression. "I thought I could trust you."

"Clearly, you didn't. You've kept some pretty big secrets from me."

"None of this has anything to do with us." Ryan seemed exasperated, which served only to exasperate me.

"Oh, if you learned I had been in jail or had given up a child for adoption, you would be fine with me keeping that from you?"

"Yes. It would have nothing to do with our present or our future."

I slammed my hand down on the table. "That's the biggest lie you've told so far. You never stop bringing up my high school romance with Max, and that was nothing—nothing!—compared to what you've kept from me. Is there even more I don't know? Is our whole relationship as riddled with secrets as John and Evangeline Chaplin?"

"I'm glad to hear you haven't forgotten the Chaplins, Marlee. But maybe my book has jogged your memory," a familiar voice said.

I believe I went into temporary shock, because for a moment I could neither speak nor move a muscle. Then again, maybe I was hallucinating. How else to explain that April Byrne stood two feet away from me?

Chapter 16

As bad as Friday the thirteenth had been, this day was shaping up to be even worse. April Byrne was in Oriole Point! The last time we had been in the same room together was three years ago, during the Chaplin murder trial. Now that she was two feet away, I could feel my dread meter rise. She looked the same. Her white jeans were a little too tight, and her lavender tank top was even tighter. Although her shoulder-length brown hair now held blond highlights, she still wore it with the same sleek side part. And that baby face of hers made her look like a high school sophomore rather than her actual age of twenty-six. She regarded me with a mocking expression.

Why was April at San Sebastian? And how did she even find me?

Trying to recover, I finally said, "April, this is a surprise. The food here is good, but I didn't expect you to fly all the way from New York for a bowl of gazpacho."

"Don't pretend you aren't shocked to see me. But it's a nice display of bravado, Marlee."

I was actually shocked April knew what *bravado* meant. Writing a book—or hiring a ghostwriter to do so—must have improved her vocabulary.

"Not only didn't I expect to see you, but I also have no desire to do so."

"That's because you feel guilty about ruining my life." She waved her hand at Ryan, who stared at her as if he had just encountered a unicorn. "Move over, pretty boy."

Too surprised to do anything else, Ryan automatically scooted over.

"I don't want you at my table," I said. "In fact, I don't want you in Oriole Point."

She settled back. "What else don't you want? Is there a list?"

"If there is, not being lied about in your book would be at the top of it."

"You obviously haven't read *Sugar, Spice, and Vice*. If you had, you'd know every word I wrote about you and that creep of a producer Elliot was true. You both ratted me and John out to Evangeline."

"April, the rat in that situation was the home wrecker I'm looking at right now. Along with the cheating husband." I paused. "May he rest in peace."

"I should have known you were the same meddling, destructive—"

Her response was cut short when our server arrived with my wine and salad and Ryan's water.

April pointed at my wineglass. "Bring me whatever she's having, as long as it isn't the cheap stuff."

"Make sure to bring it in a carryout cup," I added. "She's not staying." The server couldn't leave our table fast enough.

April turned to Ryan, who still seemed stunned.

"Is this the man I heard you're engaged to? He's one good-looking country boy." She nudged him. "I can see why Marlee snatched you up. Of course, people also say you and your family are the orchard kings around here. Which means you're cute *and* you have money." She threw me a sly look. "That sounds like Marlee."

I counted to ten. No way was I going to give her the satisfaction of losing my temper. "I don't know why you're here, but I have nothing to say to you. Although after I read your book, you may hear from my lawyer."

"You like talking to lawyers, don't you? I remember everything you said to the lawyers at the murder trial. All of it lies."

"Elliot and I told them exactly what happened. You and John were having an affair and didn't care enough to be discreet about it. If we'd wanted to expose the two of you, we could have done it much earlier. Instead, we tried to keep Evangeline from finding out. As the producers, we were protecting her *and* the show. The only reason we finally went to her is that an item about you and John was about to appear on Page Six the next day. Evangeline would have known the truth either way. We wanted to break it to her ourselves before it hit the papers."

"It was none of your business, bitch! This concerned only John and myself!"

"And his wife, you brainless slut!" So much for keeping my temper under control.

Ryan held his arms out. "Ladies, keep it down. People are watching."

I turned to see a sea of faces looking back at us. Why was this woman coming back into my life now?

"Ryan's right. We're making a scene in a really nice restaurant in a town I call home. I don't know or care why you're here. I want nothing more to do with you. Nothing. So you've wasted a plane ticket."

"Do you really think I would fly out here just to see you? I'm on a book tour. Chicago, Detroit, Denver, Salt Lake, Seattle, San Francisco."

Grabbing my wine, I took a large gulp. That infernal book. Would I never be free of my association with the Chaplins and April Byrne?

"Isn't Oriole Point a little out of your way?" Ryan asked.

"Marlee liked to talk about her hometown when we were working at the Gourmet Living Network, and I knew it was only a two-hour drive from Chicago. Peter drove me here. He's my personal assistant." She nodded toward the waiting area of the restaurant, where a tall man with oversize sunglasses stood watching us.

"You have a personal assistant?" I asked. "Whatever for?"

"Haven't you heard? I'm a best-selling author." Her smug grin grew wider. "One who is going to appear on a new reality show later this year. It's called *Surviving Scandal.*"

I groaned.

"We're on the way to Grand Rapids and then Detroit," she went on. "But I had to stop along the way to visit you. I've been keeping track of you and that awful Elliot. After all, both of you wrecked my life and helped to kill John. Imagine how pleased I was to learn you're involved with another murder. Did you help to kill this latest man, too?"

"I was not responsible for John's death, and you

know it. Nor did I have anything to do with Cole Bowman's murder. And if you publicly imply that I was, I will sue you."

She shrugged. "Please do. It will be even more publicity for my book. Can't you see the headlines? 'Marlee Jacob, former producer of *Sugar and Spice*, once again associated with a sordid murder case.' I'm sure I'd be asked about it every time I was interviewed. And I could also tell them how this Cole Bowman guy was about to shut your business down. How coincidental that a few days later, you happen to be at his house when he's killed. I still can't figure out why they arrested the mayor's wife instead of you."

"The Bowman murder is still pretty much a local news story, at least for now," Ryan said. "How do you know all this if you just got here?"

"How do you know when I got here?" April took her wine from the server, frowning at the fact that he had followed my orders and put it in a plastic cup.

Ryan and I looked at each other. He appeared as troubled by this as I was.

"When did you get to town?" I asked.

"It's none of your business." She sipped her wine and made a face. "This isn't very good."

"As if you would know what a good vintage is." The only thing April had ever ordered when the crew went to a bar after work was Jell-O shots.

I looked up to see Gillian dodging servers and tables as she headed for us. Today we began our late summer hours at the store, and Gillian was working until eight o'clock. I didn't understand why she was here.

When Gillian reached our table, she glanced over at April before turning to me. "Marlee, I tried to call you, but you didn't answer your phone. I wanted to warn you this woman came into the store looking for you." Since she was out of breath, Gillian must have raced to get to the restaurant. "I recognized her right away as April Byrne."

April looked pleased at that. "Of course you did."

"Naturally, I didn't tell her where you were," Gillian went on. "But Odette was in the shop, and she happened to see you go into San Sebastian. So she told her."

"It's fine, Gillian."

April laughed. "Apparently, I'm more famous than I thought. Even in Oriole Point, everyone has heard about me."

Gillian bent down and whispered in my ear, "Odette said she saw April in town a few days ago."

This was unwelcome news. "April, were you in Oriole Point last week?"

"Like I told your man candy, it's none of your business." She took another sip of wine. "I can come and go as I please. I certainly don't have to give you my itinerary."

I tugged Gillian down again and whispered, "There's a tall guy in the waiting area, wearing a lime-green shirt and huge sunglasses. That's Peter, her personal assistant. Ask him when they arrived."

After a last disapproving look at April, Gillian hurried away. Luckily, April didn't turn to follow her exit and missed seeing Gillian stop to talk with her assistant.

"If you don't want to tell me when you arrived, how about a clue as to when you're leaving?" I asked.

April's smile disappeared. "I will leave when I get what I came for."

"Which is?" Ryan asked.

She ignored him. "You ruined my chance at happiness with John, and you can never make that up to me, Marlee. How can you? The poor man is dead, and his murderous wife is trying to get her sentence reduced. I have no intention of letting the world forget how John was stolen from me."

"I thought this book of yours was supposed to do that. It seems a perfect vehicle to let you spread your strange version of the truth, just like you did at the trial." I met her iron gaze with my own.

"Oh, the book is only my first step. Now it's time to make it personal."

"What are you talking about?"

She downed the rest of her wine before replying. "Did you forget that John and I planned to marry?"

"So you say."

"Yes, I do say. But John was poisoned by that jealous madwoman he was married to. And here I am three years later, all alone. I've been keeping tabs on you. I learned you moved back to this village and started up a little business. Quite a successful one. Some of your products were mentioned in *Vogue*. *Vogue!* And now I discover your perfect little life is about to get even more perfect. You're going to marry a sexy country boy." She shook her head. "Except you're not going to play the happy bride-to-be, not as long as I can ruin it for you as much as I can."

Ryan and I exchanged worried looks. "What do you plan to do?" he asked.

"See that justice is finally done." April slid out of the booth. Once she stood over me, her expression grew so hard, she finally looked her age. "Try to

enjoy your wedding plans while you can. I have a
feeling you're going to be distracted."

"Is this some kind of threat?" I asked.

But April was already striding away from me as if
she were a runway model. Gillian passed her on the
way back to our table. April didn't give her a second
look.

"What the hell is she planning to do?" Ryan asked.

Gillian sat in the booth beside him.

"What did you learn?" I asked.

"He said they flew into Chicago last Friday, about
one o'clock, rented a car at the airport, and drove to
Saugatuck. They're staying at the Rosemont Inn."

The Rosemont was one of the most popular B and
Bs along the lakeshore. Saugatuck was only ten miles
away. April was much too close for comfort. And if
they'd flown into Chicago at one o'clock, it would
have taken them less than three hours to drive to
Saugatuck. Which meant April had been here during
the Strawberry Moon Bash.

"He also said they made a day trip to Chicago yesterday for a book signing and a few interviews. But
they drove back here last night."

"Good work, Gillian. I'm surprised he told you
that much."

She took off her wire-rimmed glasses and polished
them on the edge of her Berry Basket apron. "I said my
dad was the editor of the *Oriole Point Herald* and
wanted to know how long April Byrne would be in
the area. I hinted that he might want the paper to
interview her."

I signaled to our server to bring a menu for
Gillian. "I owe you dinner for this."

Gillian put her glasses back on. "I asked her assistant why they were here, and he didn't know. But he

said she's always talking about you, Marlee. April hates you and that other producer, Elliot, from the show. He was really nervous waiting for her while she was at your table. I don't know what he expected to happen."

"Maybe it's already happened. April is determined to ruin my life. What if she wanted to end it instead?" I sighed. "We just learned she was here the night of the Strawberry Moon Bash."

The server brought a menu to our table, along with a glass of water for Gillian. He looked confused, and was probably praying for us to leave soon.

"Do you think she was the one who attacked you the night of the Bash?" Ryan asked.

"Maybe. April never did have a firm grip on reality. She's out for revenge now that Evangeline is trying to get her prison sentence reduced. Then she learns Elliot and I have done well for ourselves since the Chaplin murder. April regards this as payback time." My heart sank at the thought of this latest twist.

"But if she was the one who tried to kill you, then she was also the one who . . ." Gillian's troubled voice trailed off.

"Exactly. If April tried to get rid of me last Friday, she would have soon learned I was still alive. She's been here for days and must have heard all the OPBA meeting gossip and watched the YouTube videos. She'd know about the argument between Cole and me. What if she killed Cole, with the intention of blaming it on me?"

"Then why put the muddler in Piper's car?" Ryan shook his head. "It doesn't make sense. Someone is framing Piper for the murder, not you."

He was right. "I don't know," I said finally. "But the

fact that April's been here since Friday makes me uneasy. It can't be a coincidence that she arrived the same week someone tried to kill me and did succeed in murdering Cole."

"Please be careful, Marlee," Gillian said. "You may have a murderer after you, as well as this crazy woman. Maybe you should leave town for a while."

"Absolutely not. Oriole Point is my home. If anyone leaves, it will be April. No one is going to scare me away."

I hoped my announcement reassured Ryan and Gillian. But as April would say, "A nice display of bravado." If I'd been nervous before I arrived at San Sebastian, I was downright afraid now. It didn't seem at all fair that I had to contend with an unknown killer *and* April Byrne.

Especially since I wasn't sure which one posed the greatest danger.

Chapter 17

I never thought I'd say this, but April Byrne was responsible for one good outcome. After our encounter with her, Ryan and I agreed to put aside our argument over Crystal, his drug past, and his ex-wife. The murder of Cole Bowman and April's threats once again took center stage. And as troublesome as April was, I first needed to figure out who had tried to kill me at the Bash.

Although my appointment with Drake was for noon tomorrow, I hadn't had time to look into his past. Andrew was scheduled to work at The Berry Basket the next morning, and I called him when we returned from dinner. Not surprisingly, he'd already learned that April Byrne had shown up at San Sebastian. Our server was an old boyfriend, and he had texted Andrew while April was still at our table. After satisfying his curiosity, I asked him to research the title of the *Romuva* book that I'd found in Cole's office, while I directed my efforts to Samhain, which had been scribbled on a notepad on Cole's desk. Between the two of us, something interesting had to turn up.

By the time I arrived at the store the next day, I wasn't as optimistic. And I'd forgotten I had a jam-tasting event scheduled that afternoon. The Berry Basket stocked a wide variety of berry jams, many of them not usually seen on store shelves. Once a month, I set up a tasting table where such jams were available for spreading on fresh crumpets baked by the Phantom. We also served berry cider and juice. Since both the jams and the cider were free, I was always busy on those days. And it required more prep time than people realized.

Andrew and I spent the first hour selecting jams for the tasting: gooseberry, huckleberry, barberry, currant, cranberry, bilberry, and salmonberry. Then we paired each jam with its complementary cider or juice.

"How about the saskatoon berry jam?" Andrew asked. "Are we putting that out?"

"Nope. There are only two jars left on the shelves and none in the back room. I have to order more today." I scanned my jam and jelly shelves one more time to be sure.

"Excuse me. Did you say saskatoon berry jam? I've never heard of saskatoon berries."

I turned to see a sunburnt woman wearing a bright orange cover-up over her bathing suit.

"Saskatoon berries look and taste a lot like blue-berries, but they contain more protein and nutrients. Saskatoons are popular in Canada, where the native tribes have been growing them for centuries. We won't get any fresh berries until July and August, when

they ripen, but we carry saskatoon jams year-round."
I smiled. "And we have only two left. They sell out
fast."

She turned to the man checking out the berry
wines on the opposite wall. "Should we try a jar of
saskatoon berry jam?"

"If they're as good as she says they are, buy two."
He peered over his sunglasses at me. "My wife has a
real sweet tooth. She eats her jam with a spoon right
from the jar."

Not only did she buy the last two saskatoon berry
jams, but her husband bought two bottles of rasp-
berry-honey wine and a bottle of elderberry red wine
with a dark chocolate finish. It appeared his wife
wasn't the only one with a sweet tooth.

I was pleased at how busy we'd been this morning:
over five hundred dollars in sales in less than ninety
minutes. But it hadn't left any time for Andrew and
me to discuss Drake's past or our research. We were
both relieved when the store was briefly without a
customer. Suspecting it was only the lull before the
storm, I hurried to my laptop behind the counter.

"Let me tell you what I found out about Samhain.
By the way, it isn't pronounced Sam–hane, but Sah-
win." I clicked on my file of research notes. "Like I
thought, Samhain was the beginning of the Celtic
New Year, falling on what we now call Halloween. It's
an ancient festival of the dead, and spirits were
thought to be able to cross over into this world more
easily at that time." I went on to rattle off a history of
Samhain and the rites associated with it.

"We know Drake is a witch because he mentions it
in his blogs," I continued. "As a member of Wicca, he

would have celebrated Samhain as one of the yearly seasonal sabbats, or festivals. I couldn't find any specific reference to Drake Woodhill and Samhain, but maybe Cole discovered something bizarre. What if Drake was involved in a strange ritual on Samhain and someone died during it?"

Andrew adjusted the diamond stud in his left ear. "It's just an old Irish version of Halloween. If a weird Samhain ceremony did occur involving Drake, we'd probably know about it. The man won a bronze medal at the Olympics. How could he get away with sacrificing animals or virgins? Celebrities don't have secrets. Not anymore."

"He must have at least one. Something Cole could blackmail him over. What did you find out about Romuva?"

He rolled his eyes. "That was a dreary subject to give me. It's basically a Baltic pagan religion that worships nature and ancestors. Some Lithuanians still practice it. Romuva was recognized as an official religion in Lithuania in the nineties, but the Soviets didn't care much for it. They suppressed the religion when they annexed Lithuania. And secret groups devoted to Romuva existed in the Soviet labor camps." He shrugged. "That's basically it."

I scrolled through my research notes. "Look here. Drake's grandparents on his mother's side were Lithuanian. They lived and died in Lithuania, too. It was his mother who moved to England, where she met and married his father. What if they were members of Romuva?"

"Could be. It might explain how Drake became part of the whole pagan/witch thing. But it doesn't help us figure out what Drake could be blackmailed over."

I drummed my fingers on the counter. "Maybe the blackmail had nothing to do with his pagan background. What if there's something fishy in his racing career?"

"I checked. Drake Woodhill is like the Boy Scout of runners. Not a bad word said against him, even by his competitors. And his brother Ian was as well respected as he was."

"I know. When I looked into Drake's background, I saw his brother was a marathon runner."

"An identical twin, too." Andrew grinned. "I love stories about brothers. One is always more talented than the other, even with twins. Case in point, me and my much less gifted brother."

I remembered what Diego had told me at San Sebastian last night. That the name a person chose for their business often indicated what was most important to them. "In astrology isn't the sign Gemini represented by twins?"

"Yeah. Are we in astrology mode now? Are we done talking about blackmail?"

"Drake's store is called Gemini Rising. He named his store after astrological twins. Therefore, being a twin must be important to him."

He gave me a weary look. "Duh."

I glanced down at the Samhain section in my research file. On his notepad, Cole had scribbled *Samhain* in caps. I had automatically assumed it was one word. Especially since it matched a word for a pagan festival. But what if it wasn't one word at all? What if it was two?

Customers came into the shop, and Andrew went

to greet them. Hunched over my computer, I began typing in my search engine. In twenty minutes I had a meeting with Drake. With luck, that would be long enough to find the connection between Drake Woodhill and someone called Sam Hain.

To enter Gemini Rising, customers first walked through a walled herb garden dotted with celestial metal sculptures. Set back from the street, the store had once been the private home and studio of a painter. Despite the incense that was always kept burning in the shop, occasionally I caught a whiff of long-ago linseed oil and paint. It was a lovely combination, and I enjoyed the feeling of peace that accompanied the perfumed air of Gemini Rising.

Today was no different. Flute music sounded from a hidden CD player, and the midday sun pouring through the stained-glass front window gave the store's interior a fairy-tale aspect. Looking like a fairy-tale character herself, shop clerk Paige Lindstrom sat behind the carved oak counter, engrossed in a large leather-bound volume. When I entered, she looked up.

Paige and I had gone to school together, and she'd been a mathematical whiz. Everyone had expected her to use the math degree she'd earned in college for some high-tech profession. Instead, she'd gone off to Oregon to study hypnotic past-life regression and numerology. She had come back to Oriole Point within months of my own return, accompanied by a carpenter husband and a four-year-old son called Jonah. Many people in town didn't understand how she'd gone from math nerd to free-spirited numerologist with pink hair, multiple body piercings, and a dozen tattoos. But Paige was one of the happiest people I knew. Maybe more of us should spend time in an Oregon rain forest, studying numerology.

"Marlee, you're right on time. Drake's waiting for you upstairs."

"Thanks. And I like the new hair color." Paige's short, wispy hair had always been a dazzling platinum blond, but she recently colored it a soft pastel pink. With her delicate features, almond-shaped eyes, and tattooed fern along her neck, she resembled a woodland elf.

I pointed to the lettering on the front door to the shop. "I see Drake has his summer hours posted. Six days a week, from eleven to eight."

"Yep. And closed on Mondays."

"Then you were closed this past Monday?" I could save myself a lot of time and effort if I knew where all four zoning commission members were during the time of the murder.

"Of course. But we're closed year-round on that day regardless. Drake works at home on his blog on Monday. He doesn't like to be disturbed then, not even with a phone call."

"Good to know." This meant no alibi for Drake. And Crystal had been driving back alone from Blue Lake after dropping her daughter off at music camp. No alibi for her, either.

Eager to see Drake, I quickly climbed the narrow stairs in the corner of the shop.

A previous owner had taken down the dividing walls, turning the second floor into one large, airy space. Since the windows had no curtains and the walls were painted white, it was quite bright upstairs. Drake's downstairs shop was crammed with books, crystals, CDs, and New Age jewelry. But the second-floor office was Shaker-like in its simplicity: bleached wood floors, a wooden table with two chairs, a bamboo-framed couch with off-white cushions, and a long bookshelf holding neat stacks of astrology books and several crystals.

Drake sat at the table, looking over a sheaf of papers. "Marlee, please come in. I was reviewing your chart. You didn't give me a lot of time to work this up, but I understand the sooner you have a little guidance, the better." He waved at the chair across the table from him. "Would you care to sit here for our consultation, or do you prefer the couch?"

"The table is fine." I pulled out the wooden chair and sat down. It was more comfortable than it looked, with carved armrests and a contoured seat. "I'm glad you could fit me in."

Indeed, Drake Woodhill was the author of two best-selling books on astrology, and he ran a popular astrology blog. Many tourists who came to Oriole Point each summer were here specifically to have their charts done by Drake. He held astrology seminars twice a year in Chicago and an annual one in Salisbury, England. I watched as he shuffled through the papers. He resembled a debonair Englishman seen in old black-and-white movies: neatly trimmed mustache and goatee, and clipped dark brown hair that showed no hint of thinning, although Drake was just shy of forty-five. Even when dressed casually, he looked like Prince Charles's tailor had outfitted him. I'd never once seen him in jeans. Not surprisingly, he'd kept his thin and sinewy runner's physique, helped by the fact that he still ran five miles each morning.

As Andrew had mentioned, there seemed to be no romantic interest in his life, at least for the ten years he'd been a resident in the village. Appropriately enough, he lived with several cats in an English-style cottage near the river. I suddenly hoped that I was wrong, that Drake had no skeletons in his closet, no mistake he was desperate to conceal. And I wished for the millionth time that Cole Bowman had never moved back from Chicago. Considering what had happened, I was sure Cole would have wished for the same thing were he still alive.

Drake cleared his throat. "You asked for a predictive horoscope that focuses on your current status. Understandable. Recent events in your life have been rather turbulent and troubling. Normally, I compile a general astrological chart for a client coming to me for the first time. However, I've included all your planetary positions and aspects, allowing you to get the benefits of both a predictive and a horary reading."

I nodded, even though I wasn't certain exactly what he meant.

"Now, your sun sign is Capricorn, which denotes a tireless capacity for hard work. There is no sign of the zodiac that is as dogged or persistent. If you have a goal, nothing will stop you from accomplishing it. When other sun signs may tire or lose heart, a Capricorn will be ruthless about achieving their ends, no matter how long it takes or what it costs them."

He got that one right. It might be better for Drake and the other zoning commission members if I wasn't a Capricorn. Drake continued for some time about my sun sign, then moved on to my moon, which was in Leo. I was trying figure out how to question him about Sam Hain.

"Your Venus is in Aquarius, which is not the best position for that planet, especially for a woman. Romance has never been a priority for you. Therefore, you do not put forth much effort to make it succeed. It appears you've had serious problems with romantic partnerships your whole life. And your chart indicates that this should continue for the immediate future." He shook his head. "This year is not a harmonious one for you, romantically speaking."

That got my attention. "Drake, you know I'm engaged," I said with a nervous laugh. "Is this something you should be telling a bride-to-be?"

"Your chart shows difficulties that need to be addressed. If not, that relationship will probably fail." He looked up at me with those pale blue eyes, which had so spooked Natasha. "I can tell you what you want to hear, or I can tell you what the stars indicate. Because this is costing you a lot of money, I would prefer it if you wanted the truth."

"Go ahead." I'd never paid much attention to astrology, but maybe there was more to it than I had imagined. I feared Ryan and I were not as well matched as I had hoped.

Drake continued describing my Venus in Aquarius and all that it meant for me, especially this year. I was getting rather depressed when he shifted gears and moved on to another subject.

"Now your ascendant, or rising, sign is Gemini, which means that—"

I sat up straighter. "Wait. My rising sign is the same as the name of your shop?"

"Yes. And Gemini is a versatile sign because—"

"Why did you name your store Gemini Rising? Is it because that's your rising sign, too?"

"No. But my sun sign is Gemini."

He'd given me the opening I needed. "How serendipitous for you. Your sun sign is symbolized by the twins, and you have a twin yourself. An identical twin brother, I believe."

Drake paused. "That's true. My brother Ian and I are twins."

"Wasn't he a track-and-field athlete like you? Amazing that two brothers would both compete in the Olympics. But didn't he compete in a later Olympics than you did?"

"He ran the marathon in the Olympics four years after I competed. But my events were the eight-hundred-meter and the twelve-hundred-meter races. Getting back to your rising sign—"

"Why did you compete in different events? Was it because you didn't want to go up against each other?"

"No. I was a middle-distance runner because that's where my athletic talents lay. It became evident from the time we were twelve that we both had a talent for running, only in different specialties. By the time we got to university, we'd been competing successfully in our separate events for years." He looked confused. "I don't understand why you're interested."

"I've never known anyone who was an Olympic athlete. It's fascinating. And I'm curious as to why you competed only in one Olympics. Yes, you won a bronze medal in the eight-hundred-meter event, but you were still quite young. You might have gone on to win a silver or a gold in the next Olympics. I'm curious why you didn't compete four years later, especially since that Olympics was the first time for your brother." I shook my head. "A shame he never medaled."

"Yes, it was a shame." I felt the cordial atmosphere in the sun-filled room fade.

"Then again, it's understandable why your brother competed in just one Olympics himself. He has multiple sclerosis, doesn't he? How terrible for someone who was once an Olympic athlete. I read that he was diagnosed right after the Olympic Games. It's fortunate he was able to compete beforehand. Especially since the disease progressed so quickly."

Drake grabbed the sheaf of papers and threw them in a folder. He slid them across the desk at me. "It's apparent you are not interested in what the stars have to tell you, Marlee. Something I should have guessed from looking at your planetary aspects. Of course, I could also have surmised this from your recent conversation with Crystal about her own past."

The surprise must have been apparent on my face.

"Yes, Crystal told me about your conversation on the beach. The four of us who sit on the zoning commission are feeling rather embattled just now. First, you accuse us of being bribed or blackmailed at the OPBA meeting. Due no doubt to your accusations, the police have taken all of us in for questioning."

"I didn't know that."

"And why should you? Last time I checked, you were a shop owner, not a member of the FBI or MI6." He shook his head. "Then Piper and Lionel have the audacity to employ detectives to rummage about in our lives for dirty secrets."

"How did you find out about that?"

"When strangers begin to question family and friends, it's only natural they would contact me. That is a trait known as loyalty. Something, I fear, you have no inkling about."

"Hold on. Maybe if you'd been hit over the head and left to drown in the river, you'd be less concerned about loyalty. And why should I be loyal to the members of the zoning commission? I don't owe any of you a thing. But the commission does owe me and this town an explanation as to why you voted the way you did. If you weren't blackmailed, then the whole pack of you is greedy and unethical."

"Keep your voice down." After scraping back his chair, Drake hurried over to the door and shut it. "You Americans are so bloody loud."

"And we also get angry when something as underhanded as this Strawberry Fields deal is put into place," I said. "All of it enacted without a word to the people it will most affect."

"The zoning decision was a legal one." He sat back down.

"Obviously. Otherwise about sixty business owners would be issuing court injunctions right now. But what's behind this decision? That's what Piper and I want to know. And more than the commercial success of Oriole Point store owners is at stake. Now we're talking about Piper's freedom and my life!" I crossed my arms and gave him my own steely stare. "If you want to continue in this vein, you're going to need a thicker door for the rest of our conversation."

"What do you want me to say to you? I didn't kill Cole Bowman, and I don't know who did. What I do know is that the zoning commission members are being harassed. By you, the mayor, his wife, the police. And probably the press in another day or two."

"Can you blame us? The four of you unanimously voted to approve acres of village property to be rezoned for retail *and* franchises. All this on land owned by Cole Bowman. A man who was universally despised. It doesn't make sense that all of you would

240   *Sharon Farrow*

suddenly agree to allow such a thing. The members had to be coerced somehow."

"Maybe we believed it was a decision that made economic sense."

"No way. Only last year, you and Juliet led a petition drive to prevent a Detroit developer from opening a multiplex in our township. I remember how you kept saying such a thing would destroy our small-town charm. Now, a few months later, you, Juliet, and the others are willing to welcome companies like Burger King and Walgreens! What happened?"

He steepled his hands in front of him. "What is it you expect me to say?"

"I expect you to realize that any secret you have would not be difficult to uncover, not if the stakes were high enough." I took a deep breath. Drake would be more difficult to fool than Crystal, but I had to give it my best shot. "I know about your brother."

He started. "You know nothing at all about my brother."

"Pretend I'm Cole Bowman, a violent man with no scruples. He wants something from you that he knows you will refuse him. Being the greedy bastard he is, Cole probably tries to bribe you. But I don't think you can be bought."

Drake smirked. "I guess I should be grateful for that."

"So Cole starts to look into your past for any hint of vulnerability. The obvious thing is your pagan beliefs. Even in the twenty-first century, there are lots of people, especially in the Midwest, who might feel uneasy about anyone who calls himself a witch. Like me, Cole probably wondered why you became a witch in the first place."

He continued to watch me with narrowed eyes. "Continue. This is almost amusing."

"But it seems you've been a witch from the time you were a child. Well, not exactly a witch. A pagan. According to your blog, you didn't become a follower of Wicca until you were eighteen. Before that, you followed the faith of your mother. Romuva."

Drake's jaw literally fell open. "How in bloody hell did you find that out?"

"Cole had a book on Romuva in his home office. I saw it there on Monday. Romuva is a Lithuanian pagan religion. Given that your mother was Lithuanian, it wasn't hard to figure out where your belief system comes from."

"And you think Cole was blackmailing me over such a thing?" Drake shook his head. "How absurd. Do you believe I was also being blackmailed because I'm an astrologer?"

"No, I don't think Cole was blackmailing you over any of that. He obviously was looking for something sordid and strange, like satanism or animal mutilation. But there was nothing shocking about your pagan background. Cole must have moved on to your racing career."

"I never took a single performance-enhancing drug," Drake said in a bored voice. "If you're heading in that direction, I'll spare you the journey. I loved racing too much."

"There seems to be one thing you loved more." I took a deep breath. "Your brother."

He and I stared at each other. The silence grew so long, I grew nervous. I was the first one to blink.

"I'm sorry, Drake. But if I could find out about your brother and Samuel Hain—"

Drake stood up so quickly, his chair fell to the floor. "What do you know about Hain?"

"I found his name on a notepad in Cole's office." Here was where I had to start bluffing big-time. "I found other information, too. Information about Samuel Hain and racing. And your brother." I hoped I was right. Otherwise I had just revealed how little I actually knew, along with angering Drake. Who might or might not have murdered Cole.

I watched as he paced about the room. He stopped abruptly and turned to face me. "Did you tell this to the police?" he asked.

"No. But if I could find this out in such a short amount of time, how long do you think it will take Piper and Lionel's detectives to uncover it? And they'll make it public if it shows you had a bigger motive to kill Cole than Piper did."

Drake walked back to the table, righted the chair, and sat down. "I don't care what it will mean for me. I never did enjoy the attention that came with winning an Olympic medal. I only raced for the satisfaction of seeing how fast I could run, how far I could push my body. I competed with myself, no one else. But Ian will care. It will destroy my brother."

"I have no intention of saying anything," I answered. "But Piper is another matter."

He sighed. "I don't blame her. She's fighting for her freedom. I'd do the same. And Lionel is trying to protect her. As I have tried to protect Ian." Drake muttered to himself, something I couldn't understand. "You don't know what it's like to be an identical twin. To see yourself reflected in the person beside you from the moment you're born. And Ian and I were identical in so many ways, except he was not quite the runner I was. Initially, I *was* a long-distance runner, but I always beat Ian. Every single time. He pretended it didn't matter, but I knew it bothered him. So I became a middle-distance runner and left the longer races to him. And it worked. He began to win. Not as often as I did, but enough so he felt we were almost equals."

"But he didn't qualify for the Olympics that you competed in."

Drake shut his eyes, as if the memory was still painful. "It crushed the spirit out of him. Bad enough I made the Olympic team, but I took home a bronze medal besides. And the English love to make a fuss about their athletes. Honors, awards . . . I even met the Queen. Ian had to smile through it all, pretend to be happy for me. And he was. But he also wanted it for himself. Ian was there the whole time at the Games, cheering me on. He never let on by a single word how jealous and unhappy he felt that he couldn't have the same success in his racing career. But I knew. He was my twin. Of course I knew."

"I read that you helped train him for the next Olympics," I said.

"I'd had enough fame and glory. Instead, I became his coach. It was important for him to qualify for the Olympic team. He didn't care about winning a medal. Ian only wanted to be able to say he was an Olympian . . . like his brother." Drake seemed to fight back a sob.

"But he became ill."

"Months before the Games began, there were troubling instances of numbness in his legs. We thought it was just overtraining."

"When you say 'we,' you mean yourself and

Samuel Hain?" I offered up my last real piece of
information.

"Yes, Sam had been our coach and trainer since
we were at university. He was like family. And we both
knew something was wrong. Ian was determined no
one should suspect he was ill. That's why we took him
to South Africa to see a specialist. We thought it would
be safe since the doctor was Sam's father. Sam was
named after him. Unfortunately, Dr. Hain diagnosed
Ian with progressive-relapsing multiple sclerosis. His
symptoms were becoming more frequent, making
it next to impossible for him to compete for the
Olympic team." Drake looked off into the distance.
"That was a terrible day for all of us. Especially Ian."

My cursory research had shown only that Samuel
Hain was the Woodhill brothers' trainer. I had no
idea the reason Cole wrote that name down was due
to the father.

"That's when I decided Ian Woodhill *would* be an
official member of the next Olympic team. Even if I
had to run his races for him." He took a deep breath.
"Which I did."

This was a scenario I had suspected but thought
impossible to pull off. Apparently, Drake had found
a way. "Weren't you terrified someone would guess
the truth?"

"Ian and I look so much alike, we often fooled our
own parents. And I'd kept in training up until the
previous year, when I decided not to enter the Games.
That meant I was in good enough shape to compete,
especially since I once was a long-distance runner.
And now I was running for Ian, who soon would be
confined to a wheelchair, unable to even walk. It

helped that Sam was one of the Olympic coaches. He literally watched our backs."

"And Ian didn't mind?"

"At first he was opposed. If fate dealt him an unlucky hand, he would be man enough to play it. I was the one to insist. Ian was in the best shape of his life before his symptoms began. He would have qualified for the team. I have no doubt of that. But the illness prevented it. All I did was volunteer to be his legs. This way he would be an Olympian."

"And no one guessed?"

"Ian attended the Games as Drake Woodhill. We look and speak exactly the same, so whenever the press wanted to interview Drake, he was able to pull it off. As I was able to convince everyone that I was Ian. People see only what they expect to see."

"Don't they do blood tests on competing athletes?"

"The tests run on me would produce the same results on Ian." He shot me a rueful smile. "You still don't understand. Identical twins are clones of each other, the same in every way, including our blood. Only the most sophisticated DNA marker test would discern a difference."

"You almost won a medal, too. Fourth place."

"I'm glad I didn't medal. It wouldn't have been fair to the other athletes. And Ian didn't care about winning a medal. He only wanted to be regarded as fast enough to make the Olympic team." Drake threw me a challenging look. "And he was."

"But if the truth came out now . . ."

"They would take away my bronze medal. I could live with that. But Ian would be stripped of his Olympian status. And the shame and dishonor would be too much for him. He no longer is able to walk.

And lately there are problems with his speech. All he has left are the memories of his racing days, when he had the strong, fast body of an Olympic runner. I will not let anyone strip away the only happiness he clings to."

"If Cole blackmailed you with this information, that gives you a motive to kill him."

"Then you'll have to find a way to prove it." Drake handed me my horoscope. "Our consultation is over. I suggest you read your predictive horoscope when you get home, especially your current transit chart. Your Saturn is already in transit. It's rather alarming."

"Drake, I don't mean to meddle. And I won't say anything unless I have to."

His eyes narrowed. "I strongly recommend that you leave now. My Mercury is in Scorpio, and I doubt you want to be the recipient of any further comments from me."

I was out the door before any more of my planets had a chance to transit.

Chapter 18

From homicide to huckleberries, I thought as I spooned out jam. As expected, the shop bustled with customers for my afternoon tasting, most of them happily surprised to be offered free berry cider, crumpets, and jam. Of course, Andrew wanted to know what had happened during my appointment with Drake. I explained that there were unfounded rumors about his brother's qualifying races. I left it vague, and Andrew assumed I meant some sort of drug infraction.

Perhaps I was being silly. If Piper and Lionel's detectives uncovered the truth, it would become public knowledge. But I suddenly feared the consequences of revealing such things. Uncovering people's secrets sounded fine in theory, but once you felt their distress, witnessed their fear and pain, it was not that simple to expose them. Maybe Ryan was right. I should leave the policing to the police, despite what I thought of their methods and results.

And Andrew had news. The state police had been brought in. I hoped this meant the focus of their investigation would extend beyond Piper and Natasha.

Even better, Chief Hitchcock was back in town. He'd been policing Oriole Point my entire life, and I respected his judgment. Except for his misguided faith in Officer Janelle Davenport.

The jam tasting went well; I sold out of gooseberry. By four thirty, the crowd had thinned, and I cleaned up the sample table, leaving a platter of crumpets with an open jar of cranberry jam. Gillian would arrive soon for her shift, and I welcomed the end of the workday. I felt drained after my talk with Drake, and uncertain of what to do.

As I finished clearing the table, Andrew announced, "Marlee, you have a visitor."

Looking up, I saw Hitchcock, our police chief, walk through the door. Even if he hadn't been in his police uniform, Gene Hitchcock would be hard to overlook. At six feet five, he usually towered over everyone in the room. As a child, I remembered Officer Hitchcock being rail thin, with a mop of sandy brown hair. He was fifty-three now, graying, and a good forty pounds heavier. What hadn't changed was his deceptively casual expression paired with an unnerving gaze. It made him intimidating and charming at the same time.

"Marlee, could I speak with you?" His tone was friendly, but he wore a poker face.

"Sure, Chief Hitchcock. We can go in the back and talk in my office."

"I think it's better if we do this at the police station."

I looked at Andrew, who seemed both worried and excited. "Fine. We can go right now."

A moment later, I set off down Lyall Street with the police chief. We must have stood out given his uniform and his height, and the fact that I still wore my blue Berry Basket apron over my jeans. I hoped no one would think the police were hauling me away to jail. Then again, I *was* being hauled off. Hitchcock's request to come to police headquarters had been made politely, but I didn't fool myself that it was anything other than an order.

"Glad you're back in town," I said as we side-stepped the outdoor display of metal turtles and frogs in front of Nature's Carnival. "I can't believe it's only been a week since the OPBA meeting. A lot's happened since then. But I'm sorry you had to cut your vacation short."

"It wasn't a vacation. My father had a stroke." Hitchcock stopped before the always bubbly Mia Norris, who held a tray of sample popcorn by the open door of Popping Fun. He chose a small paper cup filled with buttered popcorn.

"Now I'm even sorrier. No one told me you had a family emergency. I hope everything is all right." We continued our way down the crowded sidewalk.

"Dad's doing better. My mother is the one who needed most of the attention. She doesn't handle stress well." Hitchcock took a deep breath. "Anyway, this isn't why I wanted to talk with you. It seems you've been in the thick of things all week. Accusing the zoning commission members of being black-mailed or bribed at an OPBA meeting. Being hit on the head and pushed in the river. Discovering Cole's body after you broke into his house."

"Technically, I didn't break in. You see, I—"

"We dusted the house for prints. Yours were found in every room, including on the kitchen window frame." He shook his head at me. "Where I assume you made your illegal entry."

I felt my cheeks flush with embarrassment. "I am sorry. I should have told the police, but I intended to use the Florida room door. Only it was locked this time. And Natasha never locks it. Otherwise, I wouldn't have resorted to lifting off the kitchen window."

His gaze was withering. "You are extremely fortunate to have Vicki Jacob as an aunt. If she and my wife weren't best friends, I'd charge you with breaking and entering just to teach you a lesson. And your buddy Tess would be charged as an accomplice."

I must have looked appropriately contrite, because he added, "But I don't think you killed Cole. I also don't have the time to hassle you about breaking into the Bowman house. Not with the mayor's wife under arrest for murder."

"She was framed. Piper didn't kill him."

"We'll see." He munched his popcorn.

"Chief Hitchcock, I hope you haven't stopped looking for the real murderer. I know Piper had the weapon in her car, but it must have been planted there by the real killer. The police should be looking into all the other suspects."

"Let me guess. The zoning commission members?"

"Absolutely. I've spoken with Piper and Lionel. We all agree the commission members were bribed or blackmailed. Most likely blackmailed, or else why kill Cole?"

"Then why try to get rid of you, as well?"

"Because I threatened to expose any blackmail at the OPBA meeting. And Piper would have been right beside me while I did it. Which means someone tried to kill me, then went on to frame Piper for Cole's murder." I shook my head. "I can't believe the police don't see it. I hope the state police are more on the ball."

He lifted an eyebrow. "I now understand why Officer Davenport finds you exasperating."

"Look, I'm not trying to be obnoxious, but I don't want the killer to have the chance to murder me again. Call me crazy, but I have a problem with that."

"Well, well, well. Good to see you, Chief Hitchcock." Sheila Sawyer stood on the front step of her shop, Sweet Dreams. "I'm relieved to see you're back in Oriole Point. Things have been out of control this past week. Along with certain people." Her gaze fell on me.

"Yes. I'm back now, and my officers and I will try to get everything sorted out."

"I'm also glad you seem to have taken Marlee into custody," Sheila went on. "She has caused endless problems, which include stumbling over Cole's dead body. Many of us want to know why she and that friend of hers were at the Bowman house, anyway. Very suspicious. I hope you're arresting her. Both she and Piper were probably in on it together."

"I'm right here, Sheila," I said. "Don't talk about me as if I were already locked up."

"With luck, that will be soon. You've caused enough harm."

Hitchcock held up his hand. "Marlee is not under arrest. She's simply coming with me to the station for a little talk." He took my arm. "Let's go."

"If you want to know the truth, I'm going to the police station to lodge a complaint about your store," I called back. "I've heard rumors a mouse was found in one of your candy bins."

Sheila's expression turned to one of outrage, but Hitchcock hustled me off before she could respond.

Hitchcock bit back a grin. "Be careful, Marlee. You already have at least one person in town who wants you dead. I don't think you need to add the Sawyers, too."

"I'm already on their hit list. Only they don't have the brains to do it."

"Speaking of people who don't wish you well, I've been told the young woman from the Chaplin murder trial is in town. April Byrne."

"She and her assistant are actually staying in Saugatuck, but yes, she's in town. And for the express purpose of making my life miserable." I stopped, and Hitchcock looked at me. "She checked in at the Rosemont Inn in Saugatuck Friday afternoon. Which means she could have been at the Strawberry Moon Bash that night."

"You think she may have been the one to hit you over the head?"

"Maybe. April has a long memory and a short fuse. For all I know, she's also the one who killed Cole."

"Why implicate Piper? Why not you?"

"April's like a live grenade. Who knows when she'll detonate, or why? She surprised Ryan and me at San Sebastian yesterday and warned us of unpleasant things to come."

He nodded. "I'll send a car over to the Rosemont today and bring her in for questioning." While relieved to hear this, I knew it would probably spur April into some fresh mayhem.

The white clapboard police station came into view. "Have you heard anything about Natasha? Piper and

Lionel hired a private detective to track her down, but I don't think they've been successful yet. I'm really worried about her."

He held open the station door. "You worry too much."

Suzanne Cabot sat at her reception desk, looking more agitated than ever. I feared this past week had been filled with too much gossip even for her. "Marlee, it's absolutely incredible, isn't it?"

"What's incredible?"

"Let me handle this, Suzanne." Hitchcock steered me into his office before I could find out what she was so excited about. He shut the door behind us.

A state trooper got to his feet.

"Marlee Jacob, this is Detective Greg Trejo. He's heading up the Bowman murder investigation for the state police."

"Miss Jacob." Trejo nodded. He looked to be in his late thirties and had moderately attractive Latino looks: light brown skin, straight black hair, dark eyes. Back in the day, he would have been the exact type of guy who sent Tess's heart racing. How odd that she had ended up with a green-eyed Dutchman with spiked blond hair.

Hitchcock pulled out a chair in front of his desk. "Let's all sit down."

I thought it best to take the lead. Certain questions had been nagging me. "Chief Hitchcock, I never heard why Cole was at his house on Monday. When I biked through downtown that morning, I saw Cole put out his OPEN flag in front of Kitchen Cellar. Does anyone know why he returned home right before lunch?"

Trejo sat on a chair beside me. "Mr. Bowman had an appointment at noon," he answered in a brusque voice. "We learned this from his employee, Joan Meyerlink. She works evenings at the shop and was surprised when Mr. Bowman called and asked her to come in early that day."

"Did she know anything about the appointment?" I asked.

"Only that he was meeting someone at noon," Hitchcock said. "Bowman never told her where or with whom. We checked his phone for messages. None were pertinent to our inquiry." He pulled out a folder. "Detective Trejo and I want to go over your statement to the police. It's regrettable that none of my officers thought to separate you and Tess following your discovery of the body. Witnesses should never be allowed to see each other until each has been interrogated separately." He sighed. "One of the few downsides in having a police force that rarely handles a murder."

"It's likely Mr. Bowman's appointment was at his house." Trejo sat back in his chair. "We questioned all the neighbors in the cul-de-sac. Several stated they saw you and Tess Nakamura ride your bikes down the street earlier in the morning. Three of them also recall hearing two cars drive past their house just before noon. One right after the other. They then heard a single car drive past again about three minutes later. Two of them caught a glimpse of the vehicles and swore one of them was Cole's. As for the car following him, the best description they could give is that it was a dark color, black or maybe midnight blue. Given the time of day and the fact that the road is a cul-de-sac, it's almost certain the car was driven by the killer."

"Their accounts corroborate what Tess told the police about hearing two cars pull up to the house, followed by the sound of one car leaving again a few moments later," Hitchcock said.

Now I felt as agitated as Suzanne. "The dark car was probably the same one that tried to run down Cole last Thursday on Lyall and Iroquois. I told the police about that, too." I gave him a knowing look. "By the way, Piper's Hummer is white."

"I know." Hitchcock turned his attention back to the folder. "Now let's go over your statement once again."

An hour later, we were finally done. I regretted not taking some popcorn samples from Mia at Popping Fun. Because I met with Drake during lunch, I'd had nothing to eat all day except crumpets and jam. And I was parched. I prayed the police would let me out of here soon. I was tired, hungry, thirsty, and still curious about what Suzanne thought was so incredible.

I smoothed my apron. "If we're done here, can I go?" Without waiting for an answer, I got to my feet. Hitchcock and Trejo followed suit.

"I understand Piper is the focus of the investigation right now," I said. "But please don't forget about Natasha. And not as a murder suspect, either. I think she ran for her life last week because she was terrified of Cole. And I'm worried sick about her."

Both men exchanged inscrutable glances.

"What?" I asked.

"Like I said, you worry too much." Hitchcock opened the door, letting in the sound of ringing phones, chatter, and a radio turned to the news channel. "Come with me."

Trying to control my exasperation, I followed Hitchcock out into the station. "Where are we going? I thought we were done with my statement." I looked over at Trejo, who fell into step beside me, but he stared straight ahead. "I don't understand. Do you have something terrible to tell me about Natasha? Please don't keep it from me. I have to know. Is Natasha all right?"

Hitchcock halted before the closed door to the interrogation room. "Would you please calm down? I never knew you Jacobs were so excitable. You must get it from all those Italians on your mother's side of the family. Natasha is fine. In fact, your friend is alive and well." He flung open the door. "And right here waiting for you."

I didn't know when I'd been so happy to see someone as I was Natasha. She was even more thrilled to see me. For ten minutes we embraced, crying and blathering on about how worried we had been about each other. At least I assumed that was what Natasha was saying. She was so filled with emotion, she temporarily forgot how to speak English.

At last we calmed down and sat next to each other, holding hands, like girls setting off on their first school field trip. It was only then I noticed that someone beside Hitchcock and Detective Trejo was in the interrogation room with us.

I stared at Cole's uncle, who sat tipped back in his chair, fiddling with a fishing lure.

Glancing up at me, he lifted an index finger, as if in salute.

"What is Old Man Bowman doing here?" I asked Hitchcock. Most people in town called Cole's uncle Old Man Bowman, so I wasn't worried he would take offense.

"He was with me." Natasha squeezed my hands. "Uncle Wendall helped me get away. Marlee, he is my knight in pretty armor."

I turned again to look at him. The wiry seventy-year-old did not seem like anyone's idea of a knight in shining armor. As always, Old Man Bowman wore his long white hair in a skinny twisted ponytail that hung down his back. And he sported his typical outfit: cargo shorts, a loose cotton shirt, and Birkenstock sandals on his bare feet. Only the first snowfall convinced him to add a jacket and some socks to his wardrobe.

"You ran off with him? Natasha, where were the two of you?"

She finally let go of my hands to stroke Old Man Bowman's cheek. He gave her a little wink. "We were in the Higher Up, in a cabin by the Mountain of Iron." She hadn't regained her command of English yet.

Confused, I looked over at Hitchcock. "They were in the Upper Peninsula, staying at a cabin near Iron Mountain," he said. "Wendall owns four cabins in the UP."

"Had five, but the one in Manistique burned down years ago," Old Man Bowman said. "I'll have to build myself another one up there when hunting season is over."

"It is over," Trejo reminded him.

Bowman shook his head. "Not hunting season for

Bigfoot. There ain't no limit to chasing him down. I missed my early summer hunting at Tawas, but Natasha here needed my help."

"Be careful, Wendall." Hitchcock stared hard at the old man. "I don't want to hear you've been shooting at any two-legged creatures in the forest. And it doesn't matter whether they're hairy or not. You hear me?"

"Oh, I hear you." Old Man Bowman held his fishing lure up to the light. "But I hear lots of things. Don't mean I take them all to heart."

I didn't care about Old Man Bowman's obsession with Bigfoot. Especially now. "But how did you get to the Upper Peninsula? And how long did you have this planned?"

Natasha turned back to me, and I finally took a good look at her. She seemed remarkably well for someone who had left Oriole Point in fear for her life. Her wavy dark hair was piled atop her head in a style that only looked careless but which, I knew, took Natasha ages to perfect. Noticeably tanner than she was last week, Natasha must have been in the sun more than usual. Or she'd found a tanning salon up north. And she wore a pair of white shorts and a knit halter top of emerald green. The outfit was new to me, as were her gold crescent earrings and the gold bangles on her wrist. Apparently, she had managed to fit in a little shopping while she was gone.

"I go to Uncle Wendall in February and tell him I must run away from his devil of a nephew," Natasha began. "It was after Cole chokes me on Valentine's Day. I know if Cole put his hands on me in public, things will get worse when we are alone. And they did. He almost drowns me that night."

My mouth fell open. "Drowned? How? In the lake? Wouldn't it have been frozen?"

"*Nyet*. In the bathtub. Because Cole choked me, my throat hurt terrible. I thought the warm water will help. Only when I get in Jacuzzi, Cole begins to yell like I had been the one to choke him. I tell him to leave me alone, but he grabs me and holds me under water. He holds me down a long time." Her beautiful face hardened at the memory. "I think, this is my last night on earth. *Da*, and when it is not, I decide to run away. But I must leave so Cole cannot find me. That is why I went to Uncle Wendall. He knows Cole is crazy man."

"Nasty son of a bitch," Bowman muttered. "He always was, even when he was a kid. Meaner than a trapped badger. I blame his mother for never putting a leash on that boy. Well, look what it got him. With his head smashed in on his own front porch." He shrugged. "Never did like him. I gave him money all those years ago only because his silly mama begged me to. I hoped he'd take the money and go off to Chicago. He did, too. Only he ended up losing it all. After his mama married again and came into money from that second husband, she was fool enough to sign over her Michigan properties to Cole. Bet you that's what got the mean bully killed. Mean and stupid, that's all I can say about my nephew. Just because he's dead don't mean I'll change my mind, either."

"But how did you get out of Oriole Point with no one seeing you?" I asked Natasha.

"I make Cole angry, so he thinks I am hiding from him. It gives me time to get far away."

"Then you deliberately started the fight with him at Kitchen Cellar?"

She nodded. "I even hit him on the nose with that Italian thing."

"Why didn't you take your car or any of your clothes?"

"I want to disappear. Poof, I am gone. I hope maybe the police think Cole did something terrible to me."

"You wanted to make us believe you were a victim of foul play?" Hitchcock said.

"*Da.* At least until I get far, far away." She gestured to Old Man Bowman. "Uncle Wendall pretends he leaves to hunt Bigfoot a week before. But he comes back Thursday and meets me at those strawberry fields. We know no one will see us there."

"It was you who told Keith VanderHoff about Cole owning the Fields property, wasn't it?" I asked.

"Of course. I text him while I was in your shop last week. It was right before the OPBA meeting, and I know Keith will announce it that night to everyone." Natasha seemed pleased with herself. I didn't blame her. I had suspected as much, but I was glad she confirmed it.

"It caused an uproar. Piper ended up punching him."

She looked wistful. "I wish I had seen such a thing."

"Many people did. Someone put it on YouTube. I'm surprised you didn't know about it."

"I leave everything behind. Even my phone. Uncle Wendall says if I take it, the police will find us."

"No one should have a cell phone," Old Man Bowman growled. "The government spies on everyone who uses those damn things."

I gave her another hug. "You didn't leave everything, though. I went to your house a few days ago and noticed your dream dictionaries and notebook were gone."

"Oh, I would not leave my dream books. *Nikogda.* Never. And you are right about my strawberry dream. It did mean good luck for me. Cole is dead, and I am home again." Her grin was enormous.

Natasha had to learn to keep certain things to herself, especially when the police were listening.

"Until I discovered the dictionaries were gone, I feared you were dead," I said quickly. "I understand you needed to escape Cole, but I wish you had told me."

"And I wish you had told the police about your husband trying to drown you," Detective Trejo said. "We may have been able to prevent the whole Upper Peninsula caper."

"I do not know what a 'caper' is. But the police did not help me when we lived in Chicago. Twice I go to them for help—twice!—but Cole only got a hit on the hand. And I got in worse trouble after. So, no police. *Nyet.* I must get away without Cole finding me. And Uncle Wendall has cabins in the north where I can stay until I make my second escape."

"Second escape?" I asked.

Old Man Bowman guffawed. "What do you think? Natasha was going to spend the rest of her life fishing in Lake Superior? Nah, I only wanted her to lay low until I got a friend with a private plane to fly her over the border into Canada."

Natasha stretched out her arms, sending her bracelets jangling. "I think maybe I will run away to Vancouver. I have a friend there. She was once Miss Bulgaria."

"How did the police find you?" I looked over at Trejo and Hitchcock.

"We didn't," Hitchcock said.

"I went to town to buy some propane Tuesday night." Old Man Bowman now seemed bored. "When I got there, I checked the newspapers and saw Piper had been arrested for the murder of my nephew. After I told Natasha, we decided to head back, since Cole was not there to hurt her. We got back to Oriole Point late last night and came to the police station this morning. And we've been here all day, answering questions. Damn fool nonsense." He lifted his eyebrows, which were jet black and naturally arched. Sometimes he looked like a charcoal drawing.

"You must have been shocked to read he'd been murdered," I said.

Natasha nodded. "But I think maybe I know. Every night after I leave, I dream it is raining. The night before Wendall hears about Cole, I dream the rain stopped. It means I am safe now." Her face grew serious. "And I am. Cole cannot hurt me again."

"Weren't you afraid the police would think you killed Cole?" I asked.

"We had what you call an alibi."

"She's right." Hitchcock leaned his tall frame against the wall, arms crossed in front of him. "Both Wendall and Natasha were seen in the UP. We have three reliable witnesses who saw them sitting outside his cabin on Monday, around noon, the same time Cole was murdered here. Therefore, they're not being charged with murder."

"That doesn't mean you weren't involved." Trejo stared hard at Natasha and Old Man Bowman. "Neither of you is remorseful about his death. A jury might be persuaded that one or both of you arranged for someone to kill him."

"And people say I'm crazy for believing in Bigfoot." Old Man Bowman leaned his head back and closed his eyes. "Wake me up when this dog and pony show is over."

"He is right." Natasha pouted. "We could have stayed in the north. But we came back as soon as we heard. And now you think we killed Cole. That is foolish. If I want to kill my husband, why would I leave? It makes me look guilty."

"That's true." I lifted my chin in defiance at Trejo. "She isn't responsible for Cole's death any more than Piper is."

"I do not know." Natasha shrugged. "Piper could have killed him."

I groaned.

"We should tell them about the service," Trejo said.

"As everyone learned at the OPBA meeting, Cole had a half brother called Alan Klimek," Hitchcock said. "He flew in last night from Atlanta. He's made arrangements for Cole's burial at the Oriole Point cemetery Saturday morning, at ten. He asked for a combination memorial service and burial. But I'm not sure how many people will want to pay tribute to Cole."

"I will be curious," Natasha said. "No one liked him. Especially me."

"Do you mind that his brother has taken over the funeral arrangements?" I asked her. "After all, you're still his wife."

"Widow, not wife. And I do not care. His brother can do what he likes. But I will be there. I want to make certain Cole is really dead."

A troubling thought occurred to me. I turned to the police chief. "The press is camped out by Piper's house. If they hear about the burial, reporters might turn up at the cemetery."

"I'll have my officers there to make certain the press remains outside the gates."

I was still uneasy at the prospect of the service. Would the murderer also be there?

"Okay. That's enough for today." Hitchcock opened the door. "Everyone is free to go. But, Wendall and Natasha, both of you are to stay in Oriole Point until the investigation is over."

Old Man Bowman shook his head. "If this keeps up, I'm never gonna get over to Tawas to look for Bigfoot. They're migrating right now, and I'm missing it."

Natasha kissed me on the cheek. "I am sorry you worry about me. You are my best friend. Better than sister. Of course, I do not like my sister."

"Come home with me, Natasha. You can stay at my house for as long as you like."

Her brown eyes grew wide. "The killer of Cole is not in jail. Until they find him, I must stay safe with Uncle Wendall at his lake cabin. He has a tree house out back. With a bedroom and electricity!" She giggled. "If you pull up the rope ladder, only a monkey can get up there."

Natasha swept out of the room arm in arm with Old Man Bowman.

Hitchcock, Trejo, and I stood speechless for several minutes.

"I hope you're relieved Natasha is alive and well," Hitchcock finally said. "Like I said, you worry too much."

"I'm still worried." I sighed. "If Old Man Bowman and Natasha have become a couple, anything is possible. Hell, that means there probably is a Bigfoot."

Chapter 19

By the time I returned from the police station, it was six o'clock and Gillian was now manning The Berry Basket. Greeting me at the front door to my shop was Tess, who sat astride her yellow ten-speed. Since Cole's murder, she and I had biked to and from work together. Neither of us wanted to be caught alone on a country road just now.

"You look rather forworn," she said as we pedaled down Lyall Street.

"Forworn? You haven't resorted to archaic English in a while. But yes, I'm exhausted."

"Bad news in your horoscope?"

"More than the stars seem to be aligning strangely in Oriole Point."

I didn't want to say more until we had ridden out of the downtown area. Once we headed along the road toward our neighborhood, Tess drew up beside me. "What happened?"

For the next few minutes, I related what I had learned from Drake. She seemed appropriately upset.

"I can't believe Drake would do such a dishonest

thing. The British regard him as a sports hero, like Sebastian Coe. How disillusioning to learn he cheated."

"But he doesn't regard it as cheating. His brother means the world to Drake, and he did it all for him. I understand it in a weird way. Although I'd never have the nerve to pull it off."

Next, I briefed her on what I had learned about Crystal, and she grew even more somber. I left out Ryan's drug use and the revelations about his ex-wife. At the moment, I didn't have time for the conversation that would prompt.

"Crystal and Drake both have secrets Cole could have blackmailed them over," Tess said as we began to pedal once more. "I hate to think what Cole knew about Juliet Haller and Muffin Mike. Don't know how many surprises I can handle this week."

"Get ready for another one. Natasha's back."

Tess skidded to a stop. She refused to go farther until I told her the whole story about Natasha's escape with Old Man Bowman. Ten minutes later we were finally on our way again, but Tess was so troubled that her bike veered several times into the curb. I was relieved when we reached the corner where Tess made the turn for her own house two blocks away.

"Will you be all right?" Tess asked. "I can ride with you to your front door."

"Don't be silly. Besides, people are returning from work now." Proving my point, my neighbor Doug Washington beeped his horn as he drove past in his silver Prius. "See? And Ryan should be there. He swore he'd get there by six."

With a last wave, Tess headed for home. As I got

back on my bike, I hoped Ryan was true to his word. I was famished, and he had promised to stop by the market and pick up a rotisserie chicken. With the spinach and fresh strawberries I already had in my kitchen, it would take no time at all to put together a chicken and strawberry-spinach salad. When I reached the section of Lakeshore Drive where I lived, I felt grateful for the canopy of tall trees now overhead. It was another hot day, and the shade was as welcome as the sight of the blue lake stretching to my right over the bluff. I shut my eyes and flung my head back, enjoying the breeze against my face.

A second later, I opened them again, only to feel a wave of horror. A car was heading right for me! With a startled cry, I swerved to the right. I'd been pedaling so fast that I flew over the curb and barely missed hitting a stand of beech trees. After plowing through a bed of black-eyed Susans, I finally braked. Heart pounding, I stood, gripping my handlebars.

"Marlee, my goodness! I'm so sorry. Are you hurt?"

I looked over. The car had screeched to a halt, and I spotted an alarmed Franklin Haller through the open window on the passenger side. Juliet had to be the driver; she ran over to where I stood among the crushed flower beds. "Marlee!"

"I'm okay. But how could you not see me?"

Juliet looked as upset as I felt. "Franklin and I stopped by your house, but no one was home. We were returning, and all of a sudden there you were. Driving straight toward us with your eyes closed! You could have been killed."

"Yes, I—I shouldn't have closed my eyes." However, I wasn't certain that Juliet hadn't pointed her vehicle right for me.

Feeling nervous at being alone with the Hallers, I walked my bike back to the road. This was the second time in the past week a speeding car seemed bent on running someone down. I cast a suspicious eye at the Haller's dark blue Chrysler.

"I'm surprised you found no one home. Ryan should be there."

"There's a Zellar Orchards pickup in your driveway," Franklin said. "But no one answered the door when we knocked."

"He might be in the shower. Why were you coming to visit me?"

Juliet looked over at her husband. "I think it's better if we do this somewhere private. Seeing that you're on the way home, could we drive back to your house so we can talk?"

My mind raced as I tried to figure a way out of this. I didn't care to be alone with the Hallers. Still, if Ryan's truck was in the driveway, he must be home. "Follow me," I said finally.

But as I pedaled down the road, I grew worried. If Ryan was at the house, had the Hallers gotten to him first and done something sinister? Two of the zoning commission members had secrets worth killing over. Did the Hallers have a secret, as well? And was I the next person to be gotten rid of?

I caught sight of the front corner turret of my house. Coasting up my driveway, I sighed in relief at the sight of Ryan's parked truck. Before the Hallers could get out of their car, I ran up the steps to my front porch. The door was open. So much for Ryan keeping an eye on things. I scanned the living room, which was empty, except for Minnie in her cage.

Minnie looked up from her food dish to announce, "Mommy's home!"

For the past three days, she'd regaled me with one startling phrase and sound effect after another. If this kept up, I wouldn't be surprised if she began singing like Beyoncé.

"Ryan, are you here?" I hurried into the kitchen and noticed a rotisserie chicken sitting on the granite counter. Typical of him not to bother to put it in the refrigerator. When I turned to do it myself, I spied a note on the fridge door.

Got the chicken. Feeling sweaty. Went for a swim.

If he was down at the beach, he wouldn't be any protection against the Hallers, who were now in my living room. Maybe I could convince them to talk outside on my chairs overlooking the lake. Then again, if their intentions were violent, did I really want to be that close to the edge of the bluff?

"Marlee, is it okay if we sit down?" Juliet said from the other room.

"Sure. Be right there." Even from the kitchen, I could hear Minnie do a perfect imitation of my cell phone's ringtone.

Grabbing a bamboo tray, I placed three glasses on it and a dish of sliced lemons, then removed the pitcher of iced tea I always had at the ready in the refrigerator. When I walked back to the living room, both Hallers were sitting side by side on my tartan love seat.

"Where's Ryan?" Juliet asked.

"Outside." I set the tray down on the coffee table. "If

you're thirsty, please help yourself. The tea is already sweetened."

As I took a seat on my glider rocker, Minnie asked, "Who took the cashews?"

Franklin pointed at Minnie, who began preening herself. "That's an amazing bird."

"Yes. Minnie's quite the talker. I adopted her last week from Aunt Vicki."

"Hello, Minnie," he said. "Are you a pretty bird?"

She cocked her head at him. "What's up, punk?"

"Maybe I should take her into the kitchen so we can talk." I jumped to my feet. Minnie's vocabulary was a lot more colorful than I had imagined. If she let loose with a few swear words, I'd start laughing. Not the best thing to do if I was entertaining a murderer. But although Minnie eagerly jumped onto my wrist when I opened the cage, she refused to hop onto her perch by the kitchen window.

"Give me a kiss," she ordered, tightening her grip on my arm.

I had no choice but to return to the living room with the parrot. This time, she climbed onto my shoulder, which no doubt gave me a piratical air. I sat back down on the glider.

"Sorry. But Minnie's been alone all day while I was at work. She needs a little attention."

"Mommy loves me," Minnie said. This was followed by a loud series of kissing noises.

"I've never heard a bird talk like that," Juliet said as she poured a glass of iced tea.

"Neither have I," I said. "I've dated men with smaller vocabularies."

Juliet handed the tea to Franklin, along with a napkin and a slice of lemon. Everyone knew Juliet catered to her husband's every need. It was a bit retro, but perhaps understandable given that she never had a child to fuss over.

"Aunt Vicki claims she can say about three hundred words. But I'm starting to suspect it's closer to a thousand." *Enough with the chitchat.* "Exactly why did you want to see me? Is something wrong?"

Juliet leaned forward, her hands clasped over her knees. I had never seen her look so worried. "Drake called us," she began. "He told us you came to his store today and asked all sorts of personal questions. We also know you spoke to Crystal."

Were the zoning commission members in constant contact? This seemingly innocent village organization was starting to sound like a cabal.

"We're not fools," Franklin said. "You wouldn't be grilling Drake or Crystal about their pasts if you weren't determined to prove the commission members were bribed or blackmailed. Juliet figured it was only a matter of time before you came to her with questions, too. If you did, we thought it should be done privately and not at Neverland, in front of our customers."

They were making me feel defensive about all this. "I'd like nothing better than to stop sticking my nose into everyone else's business. Believe me, I'm not happy to be involved in Cole's murder. But I was attacked at the Strawberry Moon Bash, and Cole was murdered three days later. And please don't bring up that muddler in Piper's car. We all know Piper didn't kill Cole. But someone did."

Minnie let out a loud catcall whistle. I shot her a reproving look.

"And you think it was me?" Juliet shook her head.

"Marlee, I run a children's book and toy store, I volunteer at the library, and Franklin and I lead kayaking tours for the nature center on weekends. Do I seem like a person who would commit murder?"

"Well, someone is a murderer. And the same person probably tried to kill me. I need to find out who did it and have them arrested before another attempt is made on my life. But all I have to go on is a possible motive. You know the decision by the zoning commission was a nasty shock to everyone at the OPBA meeting. All four of you seem to be decent people who care about Oriole Point. Which begs the question, why did you give in to Cole's demands?"

"You think my wife was blackmailed?" With his drooping jowls, sad eyes, and large ears, Franklin resembled Eeyore, the gloomy donkey from *Winnie-the-Pooh*; today he appeared more morose than ever.

"Yes, I do. Since you already know about my conversations with Crystal and Drake, I assume you also know both of them have something to hide."

"Which means you think I do." Juliet seemed even sadder than her husband.

"I'm sorry, but yes."

"Give Minnie a cashew!" my parrot ordered.

"I don't have any cashews," I muttered to her.

"The police questioned us yesterday," Franklin said. "They found nothing suspicious. If you don't believe us, you can ask Chief Hitchcock or that detective from the state police."

"But did you tell them the whole truth? Did Crystal? Did Drake? I doubt it. And the police and I aren't the only ones looking into the lives of the zoning commission members. Piper and Lionel hired private detectives."

Both Hallers turned ashen. Franklin set his glass down with a clatter. "No one told us."

"Not many people know . . . yet. Whatever they find out will be handed over to the police. Make no mistake. Piper is not going to jail for killing Cole Bowman. But if we can figure out who did it, all this will be over. I'd be thrilled if Juliet had nothing to do with Cole's death. If you have an alibi for the time of his murder, you have nothing to worry about. For the record, Crystal and Drake do not. He was at home, and she was driving back alone from Blue Lake. But I have no idea where you were. Or Muffin Mike."

"Mike collects antiques," Franklin said. "Grand Haven holds an antique fair on the third Monday of every month. I know Mike went this past Monday, because he came back with a set of nineteenth-century muffin molds. He put them on display in his shop."

"When did he leave?"

Franklin shrugged. "Don't know for sure. But Mike was in his store when I stopped by for a muffin at ten. He must have left later that morning. The fair runs from nine to three."

I sighed. "And Grand Haven is forty-five miles away. Like Crystal, his exact whereabouts at the time of Cole's death are uncertain. It's not much of an alibi."

Juliet finally smiled. "Well, I do have an alibi. I was working at Neverland when Cole was murdered, and I can prove it. I ordered a turkey wrap from the Lyall Street Grille, and Marilyn walked it over to me. She got there at eleven thirty, and we talked at my store for over an hour."

That was a relief. But the Hallers weren't out of the woods yet.

I looked at Franklin. "If you don't mind me asking, where were you?"

He stiffened. "I do mind you asking. For the record, I was transplanting bushes on our property. But I'm not on the zoning commission. So how did I get dragged into this?"

"If your wife was blackmailed, it could involve anyone she was close to."

Juliet patted him on the arm. "We may as well tell her. If Piper and Lionel are digging into our past, it will come to light eventually."

"And why should we tell Marlee rather than the police?"

"Here comes trouble!" Minnie called out.

"Because I won't say anything to the authorities unless it's absolutely necessary. I'm only trying to figure this out for myself, and maybe point the police in the right direction. Like I said, I'm not going to wait around until someone makes another attempt on my life. After speaking with Crystal and Drake, I now understand what Cole could have blackmailed them over. If you've all been in contact with each other, you probably both know, as well."

They seemed insulted.

"Of course we don't," Juliet said. "Yes, we know Cole put pressure on the four of us so we would approve the rezoning, but we have too much respect for each other's privacy to ask for specifics. That doesn't seem to be the case for you."

"I can't afford scruples. My life's in danger."

Juliet took her husband's hand. "If Marlee doesn't find out on her own, Piper will. Let's get it over with."

"Damn it all," Franklin cried. "I can't believe you want to tell her."

"Damn it all," Minnie repeated. "Where are the cashews?"

He closed his eyes. "Go ahead then."

I tried to ignore Minnie, who was now murmuring "la-la-la-la-la" in my ear.

Juliet took a deep breath. "You were right to think Cole was blackmailing us. He came to the commission in November to discuss a possible rezoning of property. At the time we didn't know which piece of land he was referring to, and he wouldn't elaborate. He said only that a number of acres within town limits might become available soon. They were currently zoned as residential, but he needed the property to be commercial lots. He further surprised us by asking that we lift the restriction against franchises and national chains." She frowned. "He was so vague about where this property was, we turned him down immediately. We were especially irritated by the franchise stipulation. All four of us made it clear we would never agree to such a thing."

"How did he take the decision?"

"You know what Cole was like," she said with obvious distaste. "He flew into a rage and stormed out. We didn't hear any more about it until this past spring. He asked for a closed door meeting with the commission and once again made his demands. This time, we learned he'd recently inherited the Fields property from his mother. Again, we turned him down. Only he had something else with him that night—four sealed envelopes. He told us to take the envelopes home, read the contents, and meet him again in two days. Cole felt confident we would change our minds by then."

Franklin put his arm around her. "The slimy bastard."

"It's hot in here," Minnie complained. "Where are the cashews?"

I wished I did have some cashews. It might shut her up. "So after all of you turned down his request in November, Cole set about trying to find some dirt to threaten you with?"

She nodded. "We didn't want to approve those changes. It broke our hearts. But it would have been much worse if the information in those folders had come out. The four of us made the only decision we could live with."

"Okay, Cole knew your secrets and blackmailed all of you," I said. "But what would prevent him from doing it again? What if he wanted something else from the commission in the future? One of the members may have feared it was too great a risk to leave Cole alive."

"Of course that occurred to us," Franklin said. "But Juliet and I didn't kill him. And we can't bear to think it was one of the other three members. They're our colleagues and friends."

I didn't think it could be anyone else, but I wasn't going to argue the point. "What were you so afraid he would reveal about Juliet?"

Tears filled her eyes as Franklin said, "I'm the cause of all this. I'm the problem."

"No, you're not." Juliet clutched at him. "You're a wonderful man, the kindest man."

"But a man with something to hide," I added.

"Oh, the hell with this. Yes, I have something to

hide." Franklin looked at me with sudden defiance. "When I was nineteen, I went to jail for five years. Not here in Michigan. In California, where Juliet and I are from."

"What were you sent to jail for?"

Juliet closed her eyes as Franklin answered, "Rape of a minor."

As Minnie let out a loud whistle, I stood up. I felt sick to my stomach. Suddenly I didn't want to know these things. I preferred to take people at face value. I liked regarding Julie and Franklin as a pleasant couple who sold toys and books and taught crafts to children during the holidays. *Wait a minute.* Franklin worked with children! This was terrible. Shouldn't customers who brought their children to Neverland be informed that he was a child molester or a pedophile or whatever the hell he was?

"You should both leave," I said in a shaky voice.

"It isn't what you think," Juliet cried. "He would never hurt a child."

"I don't understand."

"It was me. I was the so-called child." Juliet's face flushed with emotion. "I met Franklin when I was fourteen. He was eighteen and worked at a local fast-food place. He had already graduated and was trying to save money to go to community college. I developed a crush on him right away. He was the most attractive boy I'd ever seen, with the most beautiful eyes."

"Bee-yoo-tee-ful," Minnie sang out.

Franklin kissed her on the forehead. "She was like Shakespeare's Juliet to me. And as young as Juliet, too. That's why I tried to keep my distance whenever she came by."

"I was shameless, though. Eventually, I wore him down."

"I couldn't help it," Franklin said in a quiet voice. "I fell in love with her. Given her age, I tried not to. But it happened, anyway."

"We became lovers the following year. Being fifteen, that meant I was underage. But we planned to marry when I turned eighteen. We needed to keep our relationship a secret until then."

"Blame me. I should have stayed away until she was legally of age. I did try to date her officially. I went to her house and talked to her dad. But he wouldn't hear of it. And it wasn't only because I was nineteen and she was fifteen. He didn't like that I was some guy working a fast-food drive-through, with no future that he could see." Franklin pursed his lips. "Then there was my pedigree. I'm a foster child. No real family to speak of. He didn't think I was good enough for his only daughter. And I wasn't."

"Don't say that." Juliet patted his cheek. "No man could have made me happier."

I found myself both touched and disturbed by this conversation. "What happened?"

"After my father refused to let Franklin date me, I continued to meet with him in secret. Then I got into some silly argument with my best friend. She told my parents I was seeing Franklin after school. Even worse, she told them I was sleeping with him."

"He went to the police and had me arrested," Franklin said. "In California, having sex with a minor who is three years younger is a felony. I served five years for statutory rape."

"After I graduated from high school, I went off to college," Juliet added. "A year later, Franklin was released. I was there to greet him as soon he walked free. We got married and haven't spent a day apart since."

"Can you fly?" Minnie asked us.

I didn't know what to think of their story. "What did your parents do?"

"They broke off all contact after I married him. I haven't heard from them for decades. For all I know, they're both dead. But I still haven't forgiven them, especially my father. There was no need to have Franklin arrested and sent to jail. It was done out of spite."

I felt confused. "In the grand scheme of things, this doesn't seem like the worst secret in the world. After all, the two of you are married. And it's been over thirty years."

"Statutory rape is still a rape charge," Franklin insisted. "People will hear only that I was in jail for raping a minor. They won't care about the details. That's why both of us changed our names before moving to Michigan. How long do you think we could continue owning a children's store in this lovely small town if my past became common knowledge? There are more than a few narrow-minded people who would insist I pack up and leave."

"This is our home now," Juliet said. "The people here are our only family. We've never been able to have children of our own. But we've tried to make up for that by owning Neverland. If we had to give up everything we've built and leave Oriole Point, I don't know how we could bear it." Her eyes filled with tears once more. "I'm sorry, Marlee. But I'd rather see a hundred franchises and national chains open in

Oriole Point before losing the happiness Franklin and I have known here."

She began to sob, prompting Franklin to hold her close. I sighed with frustration when Minnie began to imitate her. I was glad neither Haller seemed to notice my "crying" bird.

After a few minutes, Juliet raised her head. "Don't you see? He's paid such a high price for loving me. It was my father who sent Franklin to jail for five years. Now I've become a victim of blackmail because I'm a member of the zoning commission. Me, not Franklin! That means his life could again be ruined because of me. I cannot allow that."

"Shhh, darling. It isn't your fault. None if it is your fault," he murmured.

I heard the back screen door open. "Marlee? You home?"

"Daddy's here!" Minnie extended her wings as she sat on my shoulder. "Stttrrretch!"

Ryan walked into the living room, wearing a wet bathing suit and toweling his damp hair. "Oh, hey, I didn't know you had company." He exchanged brief pleasantries with the Hallers. "Let me grab a quick shower, and I'll be right out. Are you two staying for dinner?" He looked over at me. I gave a gentle shake of my head.

The Hallers got to their feet as Juliet tried to compose herself. "No. We only wanted to know if Marlee would be attending the memorial service for Cole on Saturday. Reverend Alison from Unity Church called to inform us. We thought Marlee might want to be there. But we're leaving now."

After a quick good-bye, Ryan headed for the stairs. As soon as he was gone, I turned to the Hallers. "For what it's worth, I think you're wrong. I believe the people of Oriole Point would stand by the two of you if the truth came out. But if it does, I won't be the one to reveal it."

"Where are the cashews?" Minnie asked again. I made a mental note to buy cashews after dinner.

Although Franklin didn't look convinced by my assurance, Juliet gave me a watery smile. "If you talk to Mike Gerringer about Cole, please be careful," Juliet warned. "Mike has serious heart problems, and he's already reeling from the stress. I don't think he can take much more."

"Don't worry. I have no plans to upset him or anyone else."

I had made up my mind. I was done playing detective.

Chapter 20

I had never liked Cole Bowman. Since he was a good twenty years older than me, I hadn't had much contact with him when I was growing up. Widely regarded as a disagreeable man who nursed grudges, he had few friends and too much money. It should have come as no surprise when someone murdered him.

But it had been an unholy surprise when I first saw Cole's lifeless eyes staring up at me, blood running down one side of his face. Although shocked to find him dead, I immediately had to deal with Tess's terrified reaction. Everything that followed—the police interrogation, commiserating with Piper, my personal hunt for clues and a murderer, April Byrne's unexpected arrival—had distracted me from the chilling crime at the center of it.

Taking a seat on one of the folding chairs placed before Cole's casket suddenly reminded me of what had happened. Someone in Oriole Point drove to Cole's house on Monday, walked right up to him, and bashed him over the head with a metal muddler. And they knew to strike him in the exact spot Natasha had told me was vulnerable to injury. The same part of his skull I revealed was his weak point during the OPBA meeting last week.

Filled with remorse, I looked at the coffin placed before the entrance to the Bowman family plot and sent a silent apology to the dead man. As much as I disliked Cole, I had never wished him dead. But someone had done more than wish for his death. The increasing chatter around me indicated that most of the graveside chairs were now filled. I feared one of those chairs was occupied by the murderer, and I was grateful to be sitting between Tess and Max.

"I didn't expect so many people to show up," Max said. "I assumed Cole was friendless."

I looked over my shoulder. Cole's brother had requested a graveside memorial service rather than a viewing at the funeral home. The funeral director had set up thirty white chairs, all of which were occupied. Behind the last row of chairs stood dozens more Oriole Point residents, all dressed for a funeral. Although, the owner of the Sandy Shoals Saloon wore cutoffs and a red T-shirt emblazoned with the words DRINK MORE BEER.

"Except for Piper and Lionel, everyone in OPBA, the zoning commission, and the city council seems to be here," I said. "Chief Hitchcock and that state police detective are standing in the back, too. But it's mostly store owners. Even if we couldn't stand Cole, it's only proper we all show up." I didn't mention the other reason everyone was here. Like Natasha, they probably wanted to make certain Cole was really dead.

Tess waved away a buzzing mosquito. "David couldn't come. He's consulting with a client from Charlevoix this morning about a special order."

"Andrew and Dean were desperate to be here, but I refused to change the schedule. They're at The Berry Basket, where they'll have to get the funeral gossip from their mom."

Suzanne Cabot sat in the third row, texting non-stop on her phone while whispering to her companions.

"Janelle's here," Max added. "But she's not in uniform."

I scanned the crowd again. Max was right. Janelle Davenport sat in the back row, her expression unreadable behind those aviator sunglasses.

"Why is she's wearing sunglasses?" I faced forward once more. "It's overcast today."

Max grinned. "She told Louis she keeps her sunglasses on so suspects can't tell what she's thinking."

"Next thing you know, she'll be wearing disguises to hand out speeding tickets."

"Is Piper coming this morning?" Tess asked me.

"No. I went to her house yesterday to let Lionel and her know about the memorial service. But Piper is not such a hypocrite that she'd pretend to grieve for Cole. Aunt Vicki refused to attend as well. She's disliked Cole since they were in high school."

I didn't bother to tell Max or Tess the rest of my conversation at Lyall House. Or that Piper's detectives had unearthed the truth about Crystal and her ex-husband. In fact, they planned to give the information to Chief Hitchcock later today. While I hinted to Piper that I'd also discovered the truth about Crystal, I had refrained from mentioning what I learned from Drake and the Hallers. Let the private detectives earn their lucrative fees.

I had more than enough to do. I spent the days

following the Haller visit working at my store and trying to fit the pieces of this murderous puzzle together. Three of the zoning commission members had a reason to want Cole dead. As for Muffin Mike, I didn't even want to speak with him now. Detective work was not as enjoyable as I had thought it would be.

I glanced over at Mike, who sat across the aisle from us. His cherubic face seemed glum, or maybe he was just tired. His heart problems, coupled with his weight, often hampered his breathing. Still, he was not a weak man by any means. Over six feet tall and nearly three hundred pounds, Muffin Mike had the physique of an old-fashioned strong man. All he needed was a handlebar mustache. He certainly had the strength to smash Cole hard enough to kill him, even if he hadn't been aiming for Cole's left temple. Then again, both Olympic medalist Drake and tall, athletic Crystal were strong enough to do the same. And Franklin Haller was a stout but muscular man who spent every free minute kayaking. No doubt his upper-body strength far outstripped mine, despite our age difference.

I sighed. A shame to spend such a lovely Saturday morning at the cemetery. Seventy-five degrees and cloudy, this was the kind of summer weather I enjoyed most. I'd lived in the Northeast and the Midwest my whole life, and too much sun oppressed me. I reveled in balmy, sunless days, warm with a hint of mist rising above the flower beds and ferns. It was a day like this that I missed most when the lake-effect snows arrived each winter.

Tess pointed to the three empty seats in the front row ahead of us. A white satin ribbon stretched across them. "I assume that's reserved for family. Do you think Natasha changed her mind and decided to stay away?"

I shrugged. Tess, Max, and I had agreed to come together this morning, and I called Natasha to ask if she wanted to ride with us. But she had preferred to arrive with Old Man Bowman. I also asked Ryan if he wanted to join us; he announced he'd rather be Tasered than attend. I thought he was being silly. Sitting here beneath the oak trees wasn't a terrible way to while away an hour or two. St. Michael's was the oldest cemetery in the county, boasting acres of rolling green lawns, lavish beds of blue hydrangeas and white rhododendrons, six historic mausoleums, and a remarkable bronze statue of a woman gazing upward, with hands cupped before her. Photos of this statue, called *The Lady of Oriole*, were sold in many stores downtown.

The chatter around us stopped. We turned to see Natasha and Old Man Bowman walking arm in arm down the aisle. She wore a sleeveless white dress that ended twelve inches above her knees. Her long hair was swept up in a side ponytail with small white flowers threaded through it. Old Man Bowman sported what amounted to formal wear for him: white cargo pants, a black cotton shirt, and black Birks on his bare feet. They looked like a disturbing bridal couple.

When they sat down in front of us, Max whispered, "Are they a couple for real?"

"I hope not," I said.

Natasha turned around and gave us her sunniest smile. "So many people are here."

Old Man Bowman snorted. "Give the people what they want, and they'll show up."

She hit him playfully on the shoulder. "Be quiet. His brother will not like us to joke."

"Where is Cole's half brother?" Tess asked. "Have you met him yet?"

"Yes. Alan comes to the tree house yesterday to talk to me." Natasha scrunched her nose in disapproval. "He is younger than Cole, but I see a resemblance. So I do not like him."

"What did he want to talk to you about?" Max leaned forward.

"What do you think Cole's brother would want to talk about?" Old Man Bowman said. "Money, of course. He wanted to know if we'd seen the will."

"Have you?" I asked.

Natasha shook her head. "The family lawyer in Grand Rapids calls me. We have a meeting Monday. That is when he reads the will. A cousin flies in from Florida tonight, and some aunt comes tomorrow."

"That's his mama's sister Kelly," Old Man Bowman said. "Don't know why she'd be in the will. Unless there's some weird codicil or something."

"Did you have a prenup, Natasha?" I had long been curious about this.

She seemed taken aback. "Am I a stupid peasant girl who marries a rich man and settles for nothing? *Spasiba, nyet.* There is no prenup."

Tess and I looked at each other. We were thinking the same thing. Even if the Bowmans didn't have a prenup, that didn't mean Cole had left everything to Natasha. Given how mean he was, I wouldn't be surprised if the estate went to his half brother. And part of it to whoever this cousin and aunt were. Or else why was the lawyer waiting until Monday to read the will?

Natasha craned her neck. "I see Alan's car. He is here."

"Is the press still waiting outside the cemetery gates?" Tess asked.

"Nah. The damn vultures are gone. Chief Hitchcock's officers chased them all off." Old Man Bowman turned back to the front with a grunt.

Reverend Alison Beck went to stand before the assembled group. Cole had not belonged to any religious denomination, but Unity Church of Oriole Point had volunteered to officiate. Behind her sat the closed casket, with a single enormous spray of white gladioli laid across it. Because the floral tribute came from the shop Andrew worked at part-time, I knew it had been paid for by the city council. It was sad but telling that not a single relative or friend had arranged for flowers to be sent.

Reverend Alison gestured to the empty seat beside Old Man Bowman. I turned to see a tall, brown-haired man hurrying down the aisle. In his dark business suit, Cole's half brother was easily the most formally dressed man here. I caught only a glimpse of Alan before he sat down, but I could see the resemblance that Natasha had mentioned. Although Alan was at least ten years younger than Cole, the brothers shared the same high forehead, prominent nose, and thinning hair. Alan even walked slightly hunched over, as Cole had done.

Now that the Bowman relatives were seated, Reverend Alison cleared her throat. "I welcome you all here today to celebrate the life of Cole Joseph Bowman. Although his life was cut short, we should remember instead the way he lived and not the tragic manner in which he died. Cole was a loving son and brother, and a devoted husband."

I was sure I wasn't the only person who made a face at hearing that.

Natasha took offense, as well. "Why is she saying such a thing? Make her stop."

Old Man Bowman whispered in Natasha's ear. Poor Alison Beck. Hired by the church only two months ago, she was unaware of how vile Cole had been. As she went on about how he would be missed by all, a few snickers could be heard from the so-called mourners. Someone should have told her the truth. Instead, she thought she could make up for her lack of knowledge about the deceased by uttering the usual platitudes. For most people, this would have worked. But she had the misfortune to be officiating at the funeral of a man who was about as likable as an SS officer.

She seemed visibly relieved when it came time to introduce Cole's brother, Alan Klimek. He walked to the front with his head down. I wondered that he wanted to speak at all. I hadn't been aware that Cole even had a half brother, and I'd never seen him in Oriole Point before.

He took a moment, staring at the ground. In the resulting silence all that could be heard were blue jays screaming from the trees.

"I did not know my brother well," he began. "And we rarely saw each other, largely because we lived so far apart. But we shared a mother, whom we loved. And I come here today as much for the memory of her as for Cole."

Alan now lifted his head and looked out at us. I saw that he did not have the same hooded eyes as his brother, thank goodness. "My mother would be heartbroken that one of her sons died so young. But even worse than his premature death would be the knowledge that her son had been murdered. Cole was not robbed. He was not in the wrong place at the wrong time. Indeed, he was standing on the steps of his own house when he was brutally cut down. And for what? Why was my brother killed?" He paused. "I think some of you know."

Tess and I snuck peeks at each other.

"I am aware that the mayor's wife has been arrested for this crime. But too many people I've talked to believe she is not guilty. If that's true, the real killer of my brother is still free." His accusing gaze swept over us. "Maybe the killer is here right now, thinking to enjoy the sick victory of my brother's death. Whoever you are, you will not have much more time to enjoy your freedom. I plan to do all I can to see that the murderer is caught. And if Piper Lyall-Pierce is the killer, she may have had an accomplice. Rest assured, I shall make certain that person is brought to justice, as well." He suddenly looked straight at me.

When he returned to his seat, I whispered, "Why did he look at me when he said that?"

"I don't know," Tess whispered back. "But if he thinks you're an accomplice, he probably thinks I'm one, too. After all, we were both at Cole's house when he was killed."

Reverend Alison cleared her throat. "If no one else wishes to speak, I would like to—"

"Excuse me. I wish to speak."

My heart sank. I didn't have to turn around to know who that voice belonged to.

"Is that who I think it is?" Max asked.

All heads turned to stare as April Byrne marched down the aisle. Even for those who didn't know who she was, April had caught their attention. For one thing, she was the only person here wearing all black. Tess and I unintentionally wore similar outfits today: black summer skirts with short-sleeved white tops. But April's funeral ensemble—black silk jumpsuit, black Kate Spade shoulder bag, black stilettos, and black pillbox fascinator—was apparently her version of mourning attire.

I groaned. "What is she up to now?"

She went to stand before the coffin, forcing Reverend Alison to jump back. April glanced over at me in the second row, her eyes as unfriendly as her tight smile.

"I could not let the memorial service of this poor man go by without speaking. While I never met Cole Bowman, I do know what it's like to lose a loved one to murder. Three years ago, the man I adored was killed in cold blood. Poisoned by his jealous wife. I'm sure you are all aware of this awful tragedy. For those who don't recognize me, I am April Byrne, and the man I lost was John Chaplin, the celebrated chef of *Sugar and Spice.*"

A buzz rose up from the crowd as everyone began to speak. Half the attendees glanced over at me. Max took my hand in his and squeezed. Tess held my other hand for support.

Natasha turned around. "This woman should not be here. I will stop this." She started to get up, but Old Man Bowman pulled her back down.

"I feel for Alan Klimek, who grieves the loss of his murdered brother," April continued. "Because even if the murderer is caught, there are often other people responsible for the victim's death. And it's painful to realize they have escaped justice, even if the real murderer is no longer free. Your mayor's wife may be the killer. I do not know. If she is, I'm glad she's been arrested and will go to trial. But what if there was someone who helped her? Someone who also had a grudge against Cole Bowman."

"I hate this woman so much," I muttered. Max squeezed my hand again.

"I have information about certain people here in Oriole Point. One person in particular. This same person was also involved in the murder of my beloved John. I find it most suspicious that she is once more connected to a murder. Especially since Mr. Bowman was known to be hated by two of her close friends. One of them his own wife."

Both Natasha and I shot to our feet at the same time.

"You are the most unrepentant liar I have ever met!" I shouted.

"Yes. *Lzhets!* Liar!" Natasha pointed at April. "And we know who you are. Everyone knows. You are the whore who sleeps with the famous cook when he is married to another famous cook! Now you write a book and pretend you are not a woman who cheats and lies and wears black to a funeral of a man you never met. *Svin'ya!* Pig! You only want to be famous. You do not care about justice! And you do not care about my husband. No one cared about him. He was terrible man. And he would punch you in the face if he were not dead!"

Old Man Bowman's shoulders shook with laughter.

"Leave, or I will punch you, too!" Natasha moved toward her. "*Ukhodi!* Go away!"

Chief Hitchcock strode up the aisle and planted himself between the two women. "This is a memorial service, Miss Byrne, and you are not a family member or a friend of Cole Bowman. If you are not here to eulogize the deceased, I must ask you to leave."

April nodded with an apologetic smile. "You're right. This isn't the time or place."

Readjusting that silly feathered hat, April brushed past Hitchcock. I noticed she took care to avoid looking at Natasha. But halfway up the aisle, she stopped and turned once more. "But I have arranged for a more proper time and place. If anyone, including the police, wishes to hear what I have to say about this murder, they should come to the Fields property Monday, at two o'clock. A press conference will be held regarding this very matter."

My mouth fell open. This was the nasty business April had planned. This was why she was here. To ruin my reputation and my happiness in the only place I had ever regarded as home.

Hitchcock frowned. "Do you have permission to film on the Fields property? If not, you and the reporters will be refused access."

Alan stood up. "I gave her permission."

At this rate, I feared the casket would fly open and Cole would sit up and deliver yet another shocking revelation.

"In case everyone has forgotten, the Fields property was being managed by the Taylor Investment Group, which was founded by my mother and entrusted to Cole. My brother and I sat on the board. Since he is now dead, I am in charge of the property, at least until the will is read and we know how Cole has legally dispersed of the property."

Hitchcock looked at me, and I saw regret in his eyes. He was trying to help me, but the law was the law.

April gave me her most poisonous smile. "I will see everyone on Monday, then. Don't forget. Two o'clock at the Fields property."

She flounced off as if she was leaving a party, but Detective Trejo stopped her. He was joined by Hitchcock and Janelle, all of whom led April away to a quieter area. Their discussion seemed heated. I prayed April would get them so agitated, a little police brutality would ensue. I'd love to see April knocked into an open grave.

Max, Tess, and Natasha crowded around me, offering consolation in English and Russian. Even old Man Bowman patted me on the shoulder. At least April's appearance had ended the memorial service. Reverend Alison looked slightly shell shocked. I wondered if this was her first memorial service. Considering how it went, it might be her last.

Not surprisingly, the Sawyers looked pleased at what had occurred. Crystal never glanced in my direction as she left, but Drake allowed himself a solemn nod. The Hallers were hand in hand, as usual, but both seemed as regretful as I was at what had occurred.

Juliet leaned over the empty chairs. "Marlee, Mike would like to speak with you for a moment." She pointed to Muffin Mike, who stood about sixty yards away.

"Remember what we said about his heart," Franklin cautioned.

"Why must you talk with this muffin man?" Natasha asked.

"Let me find out." I gave everyone a reassuring smile. "I'll be back in a few minutes."

I was relieved to be able to question Muffin Mike in clear view of my friends. Especially since I still had no idea who had killed Cole. But being in the cemetery reminded me of one thing. If I wasn't careful, I could be the next inhabitant here.

Mike pointed at two headstones as soon as I reached his side. "Look at that," he said. "Timothy and Frances Russell, husband and wife. Both dead at the age of twenty-two in the year 1879. Couldn't have been much more than newlyweds when they died. Maybe a terrible sickness swept over the village that year. Tragic, don't you think?"

"I'm sure the cemetery has lots of tragic stories like this."

He now turned his attention to me. His eyes seemed bloodshot, as if he had not had enough sleep. "Nothing tragic about Cole's death, though, was there? In fact, most people in Oriole Point look on it as a good thing. Few people liked him."

"That seems pretty tragic to me. To die and have no one really miss you. The only person who would genuinely have mourned Cole was his mother, and she's gone. His brother seems to be here more for her memory than for Cole."

"Ah, yes, the avenging brother. Out for justice—or something." Mike gestured to the bench by the grave of the most famous inhabitant at St. Michael's. "Do you mind if we sit?"

Luckily, the wooden bench was wide. Mike's girth took up a good deal of it. "I was always curious why one of the first lady pilots moved to Oriole Point," he said, referring to the celebrated Helena Dotrice, whose grave we sat by. "Or did they call them avia-trixes then?"

"I learned in school that Dotrice was born in France but moved to Chicago to teach other women to fly." The breeze picked up, and I brushed a strand of hair from my eyes. "She flew over Lake Michigan, landed in Oriole Point, and must have liked what she saw. I read she lost her husband right before then. She probably wanted a fresh start."

"It seems an awful lot like my own story. After my wife died, I couldn't think of anywhere else I wanted to go aside from this beautiful village. I regret we didn't move here many years ago. Lorraine would still be alive if we had." He fell silent.

The silence stretched, and I grew uncomfortable. "You wanted to talk to me?"

"Juliet told me you've been questioning the zoning commission members. I figured I was next on your list. What better time to have our talk than at Cole's memorial service."

"A pretty dismal memorial service. Even without the last-minute surprise guest."

"Murder casts a wide net. Innocent people often get caught up in it. This April Byrne woman won't let you put the murder of John Chaplin behind you. Now that Cole's been murdered, I find my own past being dredged up. Chief Hitchcock and Detective Trejo paid me a visit yesterday, and I told them everything they wanted to know about Chicago."

He shot me a resentful look. "But now you have questions, too."

"It's more than morbid curiosity, Mike. Someone tried to kill me. Most likely the same person who murdered Cole. And you and I both know it wasn't Piper."

"I don't share your high opinion of Piper."

"You don't have to. But Piper's anger over the re-zoning of the Fields property doesn't seem a strong enough reason for murder. But blackmail . . ." I raised an eyebrow at him. "People might kill to keep their secrets."

"Depends on the secret."

"I've learned some interesting secrets the past few days."

"From my fellow zoning commission members? If so, that means you believe I also have a secret. One that would allow Cole to blackmail me about the Fields property."

"I do."

Muffin Mike shook his head. "I thought everyone knew the ugly details of my years in Chicago. It's a matter of public record. I owned several buildings in Chicago's less desirable neighborhoods. Quite a profitable business investment for me, as long as I put as little money as possible into the upkeep of those properties. The consequences, of course, were not good. Especially for my tenants."

"You were a slumlord." I heard the contempt in my voice, but he didn't seem to notice.

"Yes, I was a slumlord. Amazing what a building owner can get away with in a poor neighborhood—rats, lack of potable water, faulty wiring, toxic mold, stairways with broken bannisters. I might still be in

Chicago if I'd kept those properties habitable. Instead, I paid off building inspectors to look the other way."

"I heard some of those properties burned down. In one of those fires, people died."

He grimaced sharply, and I worried he might be having chest pains. "Five people died, three of them children. Even after that, I could pay off inspectors or bribe the police. But I couldn't hide the truth from myself. Or from Lorraine. I suffered a heart attack within days of that last fire. My bad luck to survive. In the end, Lorraine was the one who paid the price for my greed. She committed suicide."

"I'm sorry."

"No, I'm the one who's sorry. She shot herself in our apartment, and our son Billy found her. Can you imagine the horror of that? He has to live with that memory for the rest of his life. And all because I was a dishonest bastard." Mike shook his head. "I don't blame him for never wanting to see me again. I don't blame him at all."

"He may change his mind one day."

"It's been years since I've seen him. He lives in Ohio now and wants nothing to do with me. Billy hates me so much that he legally changed his last name. And why shouldn't he? I'm responsible for his mother's suicide. After the fire took those lives, the papers and TV news were filled with accusations against me. Reporters exposed the violations in my properties, and charges were brought against me. I never did jail time, but the settlements I paid to the victims' families drained my bank account. I was also accused of arson, but they only found proof of negligence. That was enough to ruin me. And enough for Lorraine to want to end her life."

"Is that when you left Chicago and moved here?"

"I lost Lorraine, my son, and my money. What did I have to keep me in Chicago any longer? Lorraine and I had vacationed here. We always loved it. I thought Oriole Point could heal me, help me to sleep at night once more."

"Did it?"

"Eventually. But it took a long time. Fishing along the river, walking on the beach, starting my bakery. My grandfather was a baker, and I used to work for him when I was a kid. Baking muffins was a welcome change from what I did in Chicago. I almost forgot my life there ever happened." His face darkened. "Then Cole moved back three years ago."

"Did you know him in Chicago?"

"Our paths crossed now and again. We both were involved in real estate. But his development projects were all high ticket, so we didn't have much contact. And neither of us cared for the other. There was no reason for us to spend time together after he returned."

"But you both ended up on the OPBA board. Although your position as a fellow board member probably didn't interest him as much as your seat on the zoning commission." I turned to face him. "That's why he blackmailed you."

He smirked. "Over what? I'd been publicly accused of being a slumlord and forced to pay restitution. What could he blackmail me over?"

"Lionel and Piper uncovered rumors of arson and insurance fraud."

"Rumors? You need more than rumors to blackmail someone."

I threw up my hands. "I've spent the past week

talking to the other zoning commission members.
They all have something to hide. And Juliet admitted
that Cole was blackmailing her. Therefore, I have to
assume he was blackmailing all of you."

"Just because he blackmailed Juliet doesn't mean
he had anything on me." He suddenly seemed to
grow short of breath. Good grief. I didn't want to
send him into cardiac arrest.

"Mike, you asked for this talk, not me. I believe the
four of you were blackmailed by Cole. And it's possible one of you killed him over it. I'm just trying to
get at the truth. So is Piper. Between us and the
police, the truth will come out eventually."

"The truth?" Then he surprised me by bursting
into tears. It was an unsettling sight.

"I didn't mean to upset you. Please stop crying.
This can't be good for your heart."

"The truth?" he repeated as his shoulders shook
with sobs. "What do I know of the truth? I've never
told the truth. I don't dare. You want the truth? Here
it is. I *am* guilty of arson. That was why Lorraine
killed herself. It wasn't the publicity. What pushed
her over the edge was learning I was responsible for
all those fires, including the one that killed those
children."

I felt dismayed and saddened by this latest unsavory
secret. "And Cole knew?"

"Cole heard something when he was in Chicago
that tipped him off. Then he waited for the right
moment to use it."

"Did you tell Chief Hitchcock you committed
arson?"

Mike took a moment to get himself under control.
"There's no statute of limitations for a felony arson.

I'd be sent to prison. And with my heart problems, I wouldn't last long. But if I die in prison, it would be justice served. Only I've hurt and disgraced my son so much. He's married and has a family. If I'm convicted of arson, this would all become public again. It would shame my son, and there are grandchildren now." He grabbed my hand. "Please, Marlee, do not tell the police. I swear on my grandchildren that I did not kill Cole. I pray the real killer is caught soon. Otherwise the ugly truths all four of us are trying to hide will be revealed. And it will cause so much unhappiness."

How were police officers and Catholic priests able to listen to confessions without growing disillusioned and depressed?

"Mike, I'm going to let the police do their job. I decided that yesterday, after talking with Juliet and Franklin. I have enough to handle right now with April Byrne being in town. And now this damn press conference." I once more stood up.

With a great sigh, Mike labored to get to his feet, as well. "You should know that Miss Byrne has talked with some of the zoning commission members."

"What!"

"Drake called me on Friday. April had just been to see him. I also know she talked with Crystal. She hasn't come to me or Juliet yet, but it looks like she has questions for all of us. Just like you do."

"But why? What is she asking questions about?"

"Not what. Who. She's asking questions about you, Marlee."

My temples were throbbing again. "April will not be happy until she ruins my life."

"I'm sorry. If she comes to see me or if I find out she's talked to Juliet, I'll let you know." Breathing hard, Mike began to walk back to where the memorial service had been held.

I fell into step beside him. "Sometimes I feel I'll never be free of the Chaplin murder."

"Like I said, murder casts a wide net. I only hope it doesn't take both of us down."

Chapter 21

I spent the rest of the day wishing I'd gone to law school. Right after the memorial service, I ran off to buy a copy of April's book. After highlighting anything I suspected could be termed slander or libel, I called our family attorney at home. I needed to know which one I could sue her over: slander or libel. Maybe both. Because I was going to sue April for something. A lawsuit might be the only way to slow down her revenging rampage. Did she really imagine she could get me charged with Cole's murder?

The day following the memorial service, I decided to once again talk to the zoning commission members. I needed to know exactly what April had asked them about. But in the summertime the Hallers closed Neverland on Sunday to go kayaking, while Muffin Mike spent his Sundays in South Haven, at the weekly meeting of the historical society. Gemini Rising was open for business, but Paige informed me that Drake was in Pentwater, participating in some sort of symposium on the upcoming summer solstice. That left Crystal.

Taking a quick break from my own store, I darted down Lyall Street to buy lattes for Dean and myself at Coffee by Crystal.

As soon as I entered the popular coffee business, Crystal spotted me. Even while pouring steamed milk into a glass of espresso, she shot me a look as cold as the iced mocha lattes I had come for. With eight people in line in front of me, I didn't reach the cashier to place my order for another fifteen minutes. During that time, at least six Oriole Point residents stopped to ask me questions about the memorial service, Cole's murder, April's book, and if it was true that Natasha was having sex with Old Man Bowman in his tree house.

By the time I reached the counter, I felt even more uneasy with the image of Natasha and Wendall cavorting among the trees. It couldn't be true. Could it? Once I placed my order, I moved down the long wooden counter to where customers were watching the baristas put the drinks together. I was relieved Crystal was busy making an iced chai, which meant my order would be prepared by another barista. Given the way she looked at me, I wasn't comfortable with Crystal preparing my food and drink at the moment.

I inhaled the enticing aroma of coffee beans, bags of which lined the shelves of the store. Coffee by Crystal was also a café, with tables scattered about its three rooms, although its menu was limited to a daily soup, a hummus plate, baked egg dishes, and sandwich wraps. Since coffee and pastry are inextricably linked, Crystal also sold pound cakes, scones, and cookies. But everyone really came to Coffee by Crystal for the gourmet coffee drinks, the free Wi-Fi, and the laid-back atmosphere. If you sat down with a latte and a laptop, you could remain there undisturbed from open to close, even at the height of tourist season. Although, given how Crystal kept throwing unfriendly glances at me, I suspected today I might be hustled right out the door.

When my drinks were ready, it was Crystal who grabbed them. She held out the plastic cups. "Two grand iced mocha lattes."

I took them from her. "Crystal, could I talk to you for a minute?"

"No. You talked enough a few days ago." Leaning on the counter, she added in a low voice, "And you also talked to the police about me. I'll never forgive you for that."

"I didn't talk to them, at least not about you." We were surrounded by a milling crowd of thirsty tourists, but there were enough locals within earshot to give me pause. "Crystal, come outside for a minute. Please."

For a second, her stubborn expression seemed set in stone. Then she said, "Wait there."

A few moments later, she came out from behind the counter and gestured for me to follow her outside. We walked down the block until we reached the post office. Since it was Sunday, the building was closed and fewer people were in the immediate vicinity.

Crystal crossed her arms and faced me. "After the memorial service yesterday, Chief Hitchcock asked me to come to the police station. I thought he wanted to question me again about the zoning commission, but he and Detective Trejo knew about my past. Everything. From my time in rehab to my marriage and divorce. Marlee, they even have Ted's name and what he went to prison for. You and I talked about this on Wednesday, so I find it too much of a coincidence that the police know everything now. I can't believe you would do this to me. Or Alyssa." She looked like she wanted to slap me. "Have you no shame? To wreck a little girl's life just because someone hit you on the head last week."

"I didn't say anything to the police about you. Not a word. Piper and Lionel hired private detectives to look into the backgrounds of everyone on the zoning commission. And it didn't take long for your past and that of your ex-husband to be discovered." I shook my head with exasperation. "This isn't just about you. A man has been murdered. Yeah, he was a creep no one liked, but the police are going to solve the crime no matter how unpopular he was. And whether you like it or not, you're involved."

"So are you. I'm not the only one that people are suspicious about. Your old friend April Byrne told me you're trying to frame the zoning commission members for Cole's murder."

My spirits plummeted even farther. "Why? Because I supposedly killed him?"

"She claims you and Piper did it. After all, the weapon was found in Piper's car. And you were actually at Cole's house during the time of the murder."

"Ridiculous. Why not include Tess? She was at the house when I found Cole's body."

This seemed to throw her off momentarily. No one with a functioning brain would ever think the upstanding Tess Nakamura capable of murder. "Why not?" she asked defiantly. "You, Tess, and Piper could have gone in on the murder together."

"You make it sound like we were planning to buy a shower gift or something. Crystal, I came to see you today because I need to know what April talked with you about. But I should have guessed. She told you I was a sociopath *and* a ruthless killer."

Crystal only stared back at me.

"Except you have more of a motive to want Cole dead than I do. So do the other zoning commission members. Yes, he was going to kick me out of my store, but do you really think I'd murder him over something like that? You can't be serious." I sighed. "Is it true she wants the zoning commission members to be at the press conference tomorrow?"

"April wants us to tell the reporters how you've been badgering us to admit we've been blackmailed. The better to throw attention away from you."

I swore under my breath. "And is everyone going to be there?"

Her expression turned from unhappy to incredulous. "Are you insane? The last thing any of us want is to have our names linked with blackmail. That really would get people looking too closely into our lives. Drake and I turned her down flat. And Juliet called last night, after April spoke with her. Juliet and Franklin won't be at the press conference, either."

"How about Muffin Mike?"

"I called him on the way to work today. He'd just heard from April and refused her as well. But he's really upset by this whole business. Then again, we all are." Crystal suddenly looked defeated. "April intends to mention these blackmail claims whether we're there or not. That means we're screwed. All of us. Including you, Marlee."

This was the first thing she'd said so far that I agreed with. We were all screwed.

I was going about this all wrong. Why worry about whether the zoning commission members showed up at the press conference or not? Or what April wanted to talk with them about? Instead, I should go to the malicious moron who had started it all. That afternoon I began to leave messages for April at the Rosemont Inn. By the time I went to bed, I'd left over a dozen. And still no response. No doubt April was enjoying this tremendously. My suspicions were confirmed when April finally called me the following morning.

"Is there some reason you're leaving me all these pathetic messages, Marlee?" she asked. "I have a press conference to prepare for, and I don't have time to spare for you. Unless you want to beg me to call it off. I'll make time to listen to you squirm."

"April, we need to talk. This is getting out of control."

"It's been out of control since John was murdered. No reason for things to calm down just because you're the one in trouble now."

"I'm not the one in trouble, April. But you might be." I hoped some kernel of logic would penetrate her scheming brain. "I've talked to the zoning commission members. Apparently, they're supposed to show up at the press conference to back your claim about me harassing them into confessing to the murder."

"What's your point?"

"Hasn't it occurred to you that one of those four

people could be the murderer, with blackmail the likely motive? None of them want to have accusations of blackmail tossed out in front of reporters. Especially the killer. You might frighten this person into killing again. Only you'll be the target now. That should frighten you."

She laughed. "You're the one who seems frightened."

"Damn it. There's no reason to hold a press conference, except to cause trouble for me."

"Seems reason enough. Now, if that's all you wanted to say—"

"April, please meet me this morning. There are things we need to talk about privately. No reporters, no boyfriend, no personal assistant. Just you and me." I swallowed my pride. "Please, April. I'm begging you."

An excruciating long pause followed. "On one condition," she said finally.

"Name it." No matter what she wanted, I'd agree. Anything to have a chance to convince her to call off the reporters.

"If I agree to meet you this morning, you must promise to be at the press conference."

Now it was time for me to hesitate. The last thing I wanted was to be there to serve as April's punching bag. But if I could meet with her privately, maybe I could get her to cancel the whole thing. Especially since my lawyer had assured me I would be able to sue her for slander. The threat of a costly lawsuit directed against April and her publisher might be enough. And I had an official writ from the attorney to show her. "All right. But we need to meet a couple of hours before the press conference. I don't want to do this last minute."

"You're such a demanding bitch. But I'll humor you. Meet me in ninety minutes."

I sighed in relief. "Where? Do you want to come to my shop? Or I can drive to Saugatuck and meet you at the Rosemont."

"Not a good idea. We shouldn't be seen together before the press conference."

I assumed this was because she had all sorts of wild accusations to hurl at me then. "Okay, where? It's tourist season. There aren't many places we won't be seen."

"The Strawberry Fields property. The reporters won't come to set up until around noon. Peter and I scouted the location when we were looking for a place to hold the press conference. It's covered with overgrown weeds and bushes. No one will see us. Park near the old house."

It didn't seem wise to meet April alone in the middle of a deserted property, especially since she was still on my list of suspects. I'd have to get someone to come with me. "Fine," I said. "I'll see you at Strawberry Fields in ninety minutes."

After I hung up, I hoped this whole idea wasn't a mistake. Maybe April's press conference was preferable to what could happen. Especially if April arrived for our meeting brandishing a steel muddler.

Because of the press conference, I scheduled Gillian and Andrew to work at The Berry Basket on Monday. Despite the fact that I wasn't the favorite person of the zoning commission members, I decided to risk irritating them once again. I had to make certain none of them would show up for the press conference if I wasn't able to get it canceled.

Crystal groaned out loud as soon as she saw me, but gave a curt "No!" when I asked if she'd changed her mind about being there.

Drake scowled when I interrupted his horoscope reading with Stan Luft, the grocer. "I have no intention of going anywhere near those reporters," he said in a cold, clipped voice. "Now take your transiting planets out of my office."

Juliet Haller was more cordial when I visited her store. "I told April yesterday that Franklin and I have no intention of attending the press conference. But she called again just a few minutes ago. She won't stop hounding me." She grabbed my wrist. "If you could find a way to get her to cancel it altogether, we would be forever grateful."

That left Muffin Mike, who I caught at his busiest time of the workday, just after opening, when both locals and tourists streamed into his store for fresh hot muffins, doughnuts, and urns of free coffee. The free coffee did not endear him to Crystal. Although Mike wore a jolly expression, I noticed he was more out of breath than usual. Fortunately, he employed twenty-two-year-old Brianna Evers, who had no problem racing about the shop, bagging muffins, making fresh coffee, and pulling baking pans out of the oven.

"I heard April called you about the press conference," I said as he rang up a customer.

"She called me again about ten minutes ago. I told her I wanted no part of it."

This wasn't a good sign. Juliet had said the same thing. If Drake and Crystal had been in the mood to talk to me, no doubt they would have concurred. April seemed determined to go ahead with this press conference, despite my pleas.

"Let me see if I can get her to call it off," I said.

"Good luck." He took another labored breath. "She seems bent on turning Cole's murder into her own drama. We're all just supporting players."

"Except for me. It looks like I'm the star of this media circus."

After checking the time, I called Tess as soon as I got in my car. "Are you up to playing lookout again?" I asked. "I know it's last minute, but I'm meeting April at Strawberry Fields. I promised I'd come alone, but I'd feel better if you and David tagged along. All you have to do is wait in the car while I talk to her. Can I swing by the store and pick both of you up?"

"I wish you'd told me sooner. David and I are in the middle of a complicated piece right now. We can't leave for about two hours. Can you wait until then?"

"No. She's probably already there."

"Don't go alone, Marlee. I don't trust April. She may have reporters waiting for you. It could be an ambush."

I hadn't thought of that. "She might. But I need to convince her to call off this press conference. And I've got legal papers with me that may help persuade her."

"Just be smart. Remember the YouTube video of the OPBA meeting."

"Do you think April may somehow record our meeting?"

"I don't know. But if she does, don't get caught twice."

After I hung up, I felt even more uneasy. Filming me secretly sounded like something April would do. Or she might have reporters already there waiting for me. I called Ryan next. He might not approve of my involvement in all this, but I knew he'd come with me to the Fields property. As usual, he didn't answer his phone. There were times when I wondered why he even bothered owning a cell phone.

I had no sooner tossed my own phone on the car seat beside me when it rang. It was Natasha. I quickly put her on speaker.

"Marlee, I have most wonderful news!"

"What's happened?"

"The will. The lawyer read it to us. Cole left me everything! I own the house and all the properties in town. I own your store! This means you can stay in your berry store forever!"

I was so thrilled by this news, I couldn't speak for a moment. "That's incredible. Perfect, in fact. But what about Cole's brother, and those two other relatives who were flying in?"

"Alan gets land in Atlanta. What do I care about that? And those relatives only get jewelry and furniture from Cole's mother. It is old and ugly stuff I do not want. But I have the Oriole Point property! All of it. Including Strawberry Fields."

"Natasha, this is even better. I'm driving there right now to meet with April. I wanted to persuade her not to hold that awful press conference today. Now I can tell her she has to clear off the property. The new owner won't allow her to be there."

"*Da!* Tell her Natasha Bowman says she cannot have reporters on *my* property. If she does not leave, I will have the police go there and force her off!"

Relief washed over me. "I'll call you right away if she refuses."

"Do not worry. I dream of bells last night. This means a new life begins for me. You too!"

With luck, it would be a life without April Byrne in it. I ended my call with a promise to stop by the tree house to visit Natasha as soon as I was done.

By the time I pulled up the long gravel driveway to the Fields property, I was primed to be on the look-out for any sign of a reporter or a photographer in the bushes. But there were lots of bushes and tall grass to skulk in. Hortense Fields had lived for a century in the weathered farmhouse, and it looked as if it had been a hundred years since any maintenance was done on the building. I also doubted a gardener had been employed on the property for a good decade. The windows of the house were completely hidden by towering spruce and wild rosebushes.

A black Ford Focus sat parked on the driveway directly in front of a ramshackle toolshed. The Chicago license plates meant it must be April's rental car. When I parked behind the Focus, I could see it was empty. I turned off the engine. With an uneasy sigh, I opened the door and got out.

"April!" I called. I heard nothing but chickadees, cardinals, rose-breasted grosbeaks, and the hammering of a woodpecker. Batting aside branches of prickly bramble bushes, I went over to the parked car. It was locked.

I looked around. Where could April possibly be?

Maybe Tess was right. What if April was waiting for me with a reporter or two in tow? I walked to the back of the boarded-up house. The breeze rustled the tall grasses around me, and something scurried along the ground a few feet away. I hoped it wasn't a rat.

I slowly circled the house, looking over my shoulder

the whole time. It felt like the opening scene of some teen slasher movie. I almost expected a crazed lunatic to jump out of the grass, waving a chain saw at me. A shame the property had been left untended so long. Once upon a time, the gardens here must have been lovely. The remnants of them were still evident, all the flowers having gone wild. This many flowers drew numerous bees, which were buzzing so loudly they nearly drowned out the birds. A good thing I hadn't asked Ryan to come with me.

The property seemed deserted. If April was here, she was hiding. But why? My nerves on edge, I retraced my steps until I reached the driveway once more. As I scanned the area, I caught sight of red berries along the ground. Stretching for yards to my left lay a strawberry patch, overgrown and left to grow as wild as the flowers. However, it took an expert eye to glimpse the low-lying strawberry plants. A variety of bushes towered over them; their foliage nearly concealed the berries. Being wild strawberries, the fruits were small and almost jewel-like. I plucked one and popped it in my mouth. Perfect stage of ripeness.

It was incorrect to call this place Strawberry Fields in June; like pumpkins, strawberry plants grew in patches. Still, the impulse to name it after the famous Beatles song was irresistible. There were certainly enough strawberry plants in evidence to justify it. And with no one to scare away the wild animals, the property also saw its fair share of deer, coyotes, raccoons, and opossums. The neglected acres had turned into a rambling meadow, with an impressive array of monarch butterflies and ruby tiger moths.

Any other time, I might have enjoyed exploring the meadow. But reporters would soon be arriving in their vans. I had to wait for April to appear and talk some sense into her. If that failed, I'd call the police to throw her off what was now Natasha's property.

"April, where are you?" I called again.

Was this some sort of trick? Or had the killer beaten both of us here? But unless I had been followed, how would the killer know where I was? Aside from my friends, only April and Juliet knew I was coming here. The danger seemed minimal. Still, where was April?

I looked at my phone. I could call the police, but what would I say? April was supposed to meet me, but she didn't show up. What if that black car didn't even belong to April?

With a start, I recalled that the car that almost killed Cole on Lyall Street had been a dark color. Not that the car's color was much of a clue. The Hallers nearly ran me down the other day in their dark blue Chrysler. And at the funeral, I noticed Drake drove a black BMW, while Crystal had arrived in a navy blue midsize car. I had never spotted Muffin Mike driving, but Andrew assured me that Mike owned a black Honda Accord. And none of them had strong alibis as to their whereabouts during the time of Cole's death. That meant all four of them had motive, opportunity, and owned a black or dark blue car.

I hadn't felt this frustrated since the Chaplin murder trial. At least there was never any doubt as to who had killed John Chaplin. But I still couldn't figure out who had murdered Cole. Each of the zoning commission members had a reason to want him dead. A good reason, too. They were all trying to protect someone they loved. A family member whose life would be thrown into total upheaval if the truth came out. I stopped in my tracks. Except that wasn't quite true. My mind raced back over my conversations with the people Cole had blackmailed. One of those stories was slightly different from the others. Different enough that the reason given for the blackmail didn't hold water. Different enough that I now knew with chilling clarity who had killed Cole Bowman.

At that moment, a gleam of silver caught my eye at ground level about ten yards away. Batting away the overhanging branches, I searched for what had caught the sunlight.

The birdsong suddenly seemed to stop. But that was probably due to the fear that swept over me. I saw then what glinted in the sun's reflection. It was a stainless-steel muddler. And two feet away, lying facedown in the patch of wild strawberries, was April Byrne.

Chapter 22

This had to be a joke, some sick prank of April's. She couldn't be dead. I stared in horror at the muddler lying at my feet. It was an exact copy of the muddler found in Piper's car. The same type I sold in my shop.

Kneeling down, I reached out my hand. But I was suddenly afraid to touch her. If not for the sun reflecting off the steel muddler, I never would have seen her. Overgrown barberry bushes surrounded us on all sides. And April's olive-green pants and green print shirt worked almost as well as army camouflage.

I gently touched her shoulder. "April, are you all right? April!"

She remained as still as the ground I knelt on. *Oh no. Please. Not another dead body.* I hadn't gotten over the shock of the first one. I gently turned April on her side, hoping for a groan, the slightest movement, but nothing. I choked back a sob when I saw that her eyes were shut. And there was a large, ugly contusion on her left temple. Just like Cole's.

I shot to my feet, cursing Hortense Fields for not

taking better care of this land. The entire property had been left to turn into a meandering, overgrown field, one that could conceal a dead body. Or two. Was it concealing the killer now, as well? My heart began racing.

I stood for a second, trying to prevent myself from spiraling into a panic attack. *Calm down.* After all, I wasn't in the middle of a state forest or on a lonely stretch of beach. Right down that winding driveway was Penniman Road. If I concentrated, I could hear the distant sound of cars driving past. All I had to do was get to my car or the street and wave down someone. I remembered the cell phone still clutched in my hand. I must call the police. But just then, I heard footsteps scuffling on the dirt path.

"Put the phone down, Marlee."

I looked up as Muffin Mike ambled toward me. His enormous girth caused the thorny branches of the bushes to slap him as he approached. He seemed oblivious. Indeed, his concentration was on me. Mine focused on the gun clutched in his hand.

"Drop the phone!" His breathing, as always, was short and labored. But his voice seemed as steely as the muddler lying beside April. "Do it, or I'll shoot you."

With a regretful sigh, I looked down at my cell phone, my last hope of salvation. I'd been so close to keying in the number for the police.

"Drop it!"

After a long, tense moment, I let the phone fall from my hand onto the dirt path.

"Now pick that up." He gestured to the muddler with his gun.

"Do you plan to frame me for April's murder, just like you framed Piper?"

"Yeah, I do."

Fear and disgust rolled over me in equal measure. "Sorry, Muffin Mike, but I'm not putting my finger-prints on it just because you asked."

He cocked his head to one side, causing his chin to triple. Sweat poured down his face and neck. How could I ever have thought he looked cherubic? At this moment, in his brown pants, shirt, and porkpie straw hat, he resembled a Mafia hit man.

"Muffin Mike," he said with scorn. "I always hated that name. Even though none of you in town said it to my face, I knew everyone called me that."

"Apparently, we should have been calling you a murderer." If I ran straight through the bushes and kept zigzagging, would he be able to get off a clean shot? I knew I could outrun him. Then again, I had no idea how good a marksman Muffin Mike was.

"You should have kept your mouth shut. If you and Piper hadn't created a scene at the OPBA meet-ing, I wouldn't have involved either of you. But you two had to make a stink, especially you. Accusing the zoning commission members of being blackmailed."

"I was right."

"That you were. But wrong on what the outcome would be of threatening to expose us." He frowned. "Dead wrong."

"I'm not going to wrap my prints all over the mud-dler and make it easy for you. You're the one who's wrong about that."

He shrugged. "I'll wait until after I kill you to put the muddler in your hand. Either way, the police will find April, dead from a lethal blow to the head. And you lying beside her, the weapon still in your hand."

"I presume I'll have died from a gunshot wound." I pointed to his handgun. "If that's registered, even the Oriole Point Police will be able to trace it to you."

"Of course they will. I'll be the one who calls the police."

"What?" Was fear causing me to hallucinate now?

"After all, poor Miss Byrne requested that I come to give her moral support for this meeting you forced her to agree to. A meeting you insisted she come to alone. Very suspicious. Naturally, I came to look out for her. Given the recent murder in town, I thought it best to bring my registered handgun as added protection. When I arrived, I discovered you'd bashed April over the head. You tried to come after me next, but you didn't expect me to be carrying this." He lifted the gun. "Lucky for me. Not so lucky for you."

"Don't you think the police might find it suspicious that the town muffin man shows up packing heat?"

"Not at all. Miss Byrne has been in constant contact with me this past week. Ever since she appeared on that morning talk show, plugging her book. We've become quite the bosom buddies. I even managed to convince her that you gave Evangeline Chaplin the idea of poisoning her husband. Of course, she hated you so much, it wasn't all that difficult to do."

"Are you kidding me?" I'd never entertained the idea that the killer and April were working together.

"Oh, she and I were entirely serious about bringing you down. You left me no choice after those threats you made at the OPBA meeting. I mean, really. Accusing four people of being blackmailed in such a public forum. You have the brain capacity of a gnat, young woman. If a person can be blackmailed, that means they have something to hide. And they'll kill anyone who threatens to expose them, even if the person is not the original blackmailer."

At this moment, I was worrying about my brain capacity, as well. "So it was the OPBA meeting that gave you the idea to kill Cole and me?"

"When Cole came to the zoning commission with evidence to blackmail us with, we knew we had no choice but to give him what he wanted. Although I only turned him down the first time to piss him off. I never could stand the man. They can stick strip malls and fast-food joints all over Oriole Point for all I care. But I do care that Cole had information that could send me to prison. I couldn't let him hold that over me. Who knew what he might ask for next? I was counting the days until I figured out when and how to get rid of him." He smiled. "The OPBA meeting served as the perfect trigger."

I threw a quick glance at the cell phone at my feet. If I could just snatch it up and make a run for it. "When Piper and I reacted so strongly to the news about the rezoning, you must have seen your chance."

His breathing grew more labored as he paused. Maybe the summer heat—and the obvious excitement he derived from murder—would send him into cardiac arrest, which always seemed a few short breaths away for him. "The pair of you were in fine form. And Piper punching him was a delightful ending I never expected. After the YouTube video surfaced the following morning, I knew it was time to put my plans in place."

"A stroke of diabolical luck, at least for you."

"It was neither. I'm the OPBA's public relations chair. I've had every meeting since I took office filmed by Brianna."

"Wait. That sweet girl who works at Muffins and More is the one who put the video on YouTube?"

"I pay Brianna forty dollars to film the meetings, in case trouble crops up, like it did last year. You weren't on the board then, but two shopkeepers came to blows in the audience. There were depositions taken and legal crap I had to deal with. I've had all the meetings filmed since then to cover my ass." He laughed "The next morning, I told Brianna to post the video of Piper on YouTube. I paid her extra to keep it between the two of us. She did the same with the video of you fighting with Cole. I asked her to post that one the day after the Bash."

I was now sweating as much as Muffin Mike. If he intended to shoot me, why was he putting it off? Not that I was complaining about still being alive, but did he have something else unpleasant planned? Although I didn't know what was more unpleasant than being murdered.

"Who did you want to frame? Me or Piper?"

"Piper. I had other plans for you. After all, you told us you were going to uncover the truth behind the zoning commission decision. I wasn't going to let you stick around, any more than I wanted Cole alive and well." He shook his head. "I could kick myself, looking back. I had the two of you in my sights a few hours before the OPBA meeting. I was about to drive home when I saw Cole hurrying down the street. A street that was deserted because of the coming storm. It was a stupid thing to do, trying to run him over with my car, but I lost my temper and drove straight for him. The bastard jumped out of the way at the last minute. I almost hit you." He wore a rueful grin. "If I'd known what was going to happen that night at the meeting, I would have aimed for you instead."

I felt sick as everything fell into place. "You're the one who tried to kill me at the Strawberry Moon Bash."

"Guilty as charged, only I won't be charged with it. Or any crime. I struck you pretty hard, too, but I couldn't even knock you off your feet. You must have the hardest head of anyone in town. I finally had to push your sorry ass into the river." He let out a weary sigh. "Then your old boyfriend came along a minute later and fished you out. I couldn't believe it."

"Really? You thought it would easy to kill me right out in public?"

"I watched you all night, waiting for an opportunity. You were drunk. In fact, you were so drunk, I was able to sneak around the back of your booth and steal a muddler. Gillian was busy making drinks, and you were busy drinking them. You made it easy."

If I survived, I made a mental note to never touch a drop of alcohol again while working. "That was how you got the weapon you used to kill Cole."

"Cole was a dead man, no matter what," he continued. "I called him last week to reveal that Crystal was thinking of going to the police about the blackmail. It wasn't true, but it made him nervous enough to agree to meet with me at his house. I knew Drake always stayed home on Mondays. Crystal was supposed to drop off her kid at some music camp that morning, which meant she'd be driving back alone at the same time Cole was killed. No way to prove they were where they said they were."

"Except for Juliet. She was at her store."

He smirked. "Of course you know that. You've been playing Sherlock. Then you also know her sickeningly devoted husband has been busy laying sod and transplanting shrubbery on their property all week. No way to prove he was where he says he was, either."

"If you intended to make the police focus on them, why frame Piper?"

He shrugged. "Why not? She had a motive for killing Cole. And the upcoming road rally is our next village event. I knew she'd be at Ruth's house that day, working on it. No one locks their car in Oriole Point, which meant I'd be able to throw the weapon into her Hummer. Ruth's property is huge. Her nearest neighbor isn't for a half mile." A look of satisfaction crossed his damp face. "I worried the police might think she'd been framed. Imagine my pleasure when they actually arrested her. Even if they find Piper innocent, the police still have to track down the killer. And who will they turn their attention to? The zoning commission members."

"Which includes you." Maybe he wasn't as smart as he thought he was.

"But I have an alibi. Miss Byrne and I were together that morning at my house, talking over the Chaplin case and agreeing about how terrible a person you are, Marlee." He shrugged. "Of course, now that April is dead, she won't be able to contradict me. Neither will you."

"You're a despicable pig." Hell, if he was going to kill me, what did it matter if I made him angry? I was pretty angry myself. "Here I was, feeling sorry for you. What with Cole blackmailing you about the arson rumors, and your wife committing suicide."

"Don't be an idiot. Do you really think I'd give a shit if Cole brought up my wife's suicide or the arson? It was all over the Chicago news channels and papers for months."

"But Cole was blackmailing you."

"And there was plenty to blackmail me with. Although his hands were as dirty as mine back in Chicago. In fact, he sold me one of those sinkholes I turned into apartment buildings. Certainly, he knew the arson rumors were true. He also suspected the truth about my wife."

"What truth?"

"Lorraine didn't commit suicide. She was murdered." He paused. "By me."

I didn't think he could surprise me again, but he did. "You murdered your wife? Why?"

"She guessed that the fires were deliberately set. And that I'd done it for the insurance money. Lorraine was unhappy about the whole setup, but it paid for our penthouse apartment on the Gold Coast, so her guilty conscience didn't bother her too much. Until the fire that killed those kids. She couldn't live with herself after that. Lorraine told me she was going to the police with proof that I had committed arson and insurance fraud." He nodded toward the gun. "And that was the end of her threats."

This was literally too much to take in. For a moment, my head swam. From fear, the heat, too many sordid tales of murder. "I should have figured out it was you much sooner," I said with resentment. "Especially after you claimed you submitted to Cole's blackmail because the truth would devastate your son and grandchildren. Except you also told me your son hasn't spoken to you in years. In fact, he legally changed his name and moved away. The other zoning commission members were trying to protect people whose lives might be destroyed by the truth. That's not the case with your son at all."

He smirked. "Don't blame me for your stupidity."

Mike was right. I was stupid for not realizing the truth earlier, and even stupider for agreeing to meet April at the Fields property. I had to get out of here. I still couldn't figure out why he hadn't shot me yet. If he'd killed his wife, he certainly wouldn't hesitate to shoot me. I must have made a jerky movement, because he took a step closer.

"Don't even think about moving, Marlee. Unless it's to pick up the muddler, like I asked." He waved the handgun. "Pick it up. Otherwise I'll shoot you more than once. And the first two bullets will only cause you extreme pain. Why do that to yourself?"

"Maybe you don't want to shoot me," I replied. "Maybe there's some reason you haven't killed me yet. You seem to be a man who plans everything out. I figure you planned this, too."

"True." A thoughtful look crossed his face. "If you must know, I'm waiting."

This made me even more afraid. "Waiting for what?"

"The reporters." He chuckled. "Oh, there's so much you don't know, for all your small-town detecting. When you called April this morning about meeting you here, she contacted me immediately. Her next call was to the reporters. She promised them a big scoop about you threatening her and the zoning commission. And told them that they should arrive earlier than planned."

"She rescheduled the press conference?" Even with April dead, I still felt a wave of dismay about how she had tried to ruin my life all the way to the end.

"Like I said, April and I have been talking for over a week. In fact, I'm responsible for her being in Oriole Point. When I watched her on the morning talk show, I saw how angry she was at you. It was clear she wanted revenge. I wanted to get rid of you, and what better way to distract you from nosing around than by bringing an old enemy to town?"

"How in the world did you contact April? She was in New York City."

"They have this new invention called a phone. I called my wife's cousin who works at the network there. She put me in touch with April's agent within the hour. Right after my conversation with April, she booked a flight to Chicago that afternoon. To make the trip legit, her agent set up a book signing in Chicago. Hell, I was the one who got her a room at the Rosemont Inn." He looked immensely pleased with himself. "I even invited her to the Strawberry Moon Bash. Told her you'd have a booth there, so she could watch you from afar without you guessing a thing."

Now I understood. "She was your safety net. If I had died at the Bash that night, you had two suspects set up to take the blame—a blackmailed zoning commission member and my old friend April."

"Even you see the beautiful symmetry of it. If Piper was exonerated, one of the zoning commission members would have been accused of Cole's murder. I would have seen to that. The same member would be blamed for attacking you at the Bash *and* framing Piper."

"Then why was April still here after I survived your attack? What purpose did she serve except for making my life hell?"

"April's book and recent TV appearance prove how much she hated you. And no one would blame you for hating her, wishing her dead even. Especially when April comes to your hometown and threatens to make wild accusations about you during a press conference." He sighed. "You snapped, Marlee. You couldn't take the pressure. What with almost drowning, then finding Cole's body. Now the press conference. It was too much. You arranged to meet her in this isolated field, hoping to scare her into calling off the press conference. When April refused, you struck her."

"And why would I kill her with a muddler?"

"Like I said, you snapped. All the zoning commission members will attest to how you harassed them into confessing to Cole's murder. In fact, you actually believed your good friend Piper did kill Cole. You've been trying to protect her."

I shook my head. "People might think you're that crazy, but I doubt they'll think I am."

"C'mon, everyone knows you're still suffering the effects of your head injury. Then there was that drunken display you put on at the Bash. Personal problems at home perhaps. Combined with the awful fact that you were about to be kicked out of your store. You'd become quite unbalanced. That's why you brought a muddler with you. In your state of mind, you thought you needed to protect yourself from April. Instead, the two of you began to argue. I heard part of the argument as I was walking here.

I arrived just in time to see you strike April with the muddler. When you saw me, you tried to come after me, as well. I was forced to shoot."

"No one will believe this." Although I wasn't sure this was true.

"Are you kidding? Oriole Point will eat it up. Especially when you factor in your involvement in the Chaplin murder trial. With reporters putting their own spin on the story, this will make the national news. Too bad April's dead. She would have loved all the attention." He glanced at his wristwatch. "It's almost time. Pick up the muddler."

My mind raced. He was too far away for me to make a grab for the gun. What if I took him by surprise? Charged him maybe. Or threw myself into the bushes. Suddenly I heard a noise. Mike heard it, too. It was a moan, and it came from where April lay among the strawberries. My God, April was still alive!

Mike took a step closer. With his gun trained on me, he looked over at April's prone body. *Now or never*, I told myself. I bent down quickly and snatched up the muddler. When Mike turned toward me, I flung it at his head the minute he fired off a shot.

Hurling myself to the ground, I saw the dirt a few inches away explode from the bullet. I rolled. As he fired once more, I dug around in my messenger bag, which was slung across my body. Crawling through the strawberry plants and thorny bushes, I heard Mike behind me. He fired again. It was a wild shot. He couldn't see me, not with all the overgrown vegetation. I was a lot more agile than lumbering Muffin Mike. I got to my feet but stayed crouched down.

If I could get behind him for a second. It was all I needed. Suddenly, there he was. A foot away. I lunged for him at the same time he raised his gun. Again, a shot went off, but in the wrong direction. Grabbing his damp shirt collar with one hand, I plunged the EpiPen into his neck with the other.

He reeled back, looking startled. "What the hell did you do?"

"Epinephrine." I held up the now empty EpiPen.

Mike began to gasp for air. He dropped his gun, then clutched at his chest. "My heart!" His breathing was now rapid and wheezy. "What's happening, you bitch? Help me!"

I stepped aside as he fell to his knees.

"I can't breathe!" He turned white with fear.

While the epinephrine took full effect, I ran to check on April. She had rolled onto her back and was still moaning. "April, it's Marlee. You're going to be all right."

Her eyes fluttered open. "Marlee," she said in a weak voice. "What happened?"

"Way too much." I took her pulse. "Lie still while I call for help."

Mike collapsed onto the crushed strawberry plants, struggling for air. He looked in no condition to search for his gun. In fact, if he didn't get to a hospital soon, he would die.

I picked up my cell phone where it still lay undisturbed after I dropped it. I sent up a prayer of thanks to see that it wasn't broken. Especially since I had turned on the video camera right before Mike ordered me to put it down. With shaking hands, I called 911. But right before I did, I checked to see if the video camera on my phone was still running.

It was.

Chapter 23

Muffin Mike was right. We made the national news. The publicity began when EMS arrived at the same time as two of the local news teams. April revived enough by then to manage a brave smile for the cameras before she was carried into the ambulance. I made certain to get on board, as well. Mike was on an oxygen tank with heart fibrillation; he might not make it to the hospital. But in case he survived, I refused to let him out of my sight.

Since he was in cardiac arrest, Mike was wheeled off as soon as we got to the hospital. I remained with April when she was taken to a curtained cubicle to be examined. Joining us were Chief Hitchcock, Officer Janelle Davenport, and Detective Trejo, who were all waiting at the hospital when we arrived.

"Marlee, what's going on?" Hitchcock barked. "I heard your nine-one-one call. Something about Mike Gerringer trying to kill you and April."

"And you stuck him with an EpiPen?" Janelle shook her head. "Where the hell did you get an EpiPen?"

I collapsed onto a chair near the gurney where

April was being examined. The stress and fear of the last half hour were catching up with me. "I always carry one in my purse. Ryan's severely allergic to bees."

"But why stick the pen in Mike?" Hitchcock asked.

"He has a heart condition. Epinephrine makes the heart race faster." I took a deep breath to steady my own racing heart. "It was the only way to stop him from shooting me."

"Why did he want to kill you?"

I pressed PLAY on my phone's video camera and held it out to them. I watched as their expressions changed to one of amazement and satisfaction. Hearing my recorded conversation with Muffin Mike brought home the horror of what had just happened. I looked over at April, who was now being examined by Dr. Sankar. But April seemed oblivious to any injuries she had suffered. Instead, she was listening to what was coming from my phone as avidly as the police were.

I would forever be grateful that Tess had reminded me about the video that was secretly filmed at the OPBA meeting. Determined to be the one in control this time, I decided to use my phone video camera to record my meeting with April. It was why I had walked about the strawberry fields with the phone in my hand. I intended to hit PLAY as soon as I saw her. Instead, I had done so when Mike ordered me to drop the phone. Although the phone's video showed only the sky overhead, the audio was clear as a bell.

When the video ended, Hitchcock and Davenport looked at each other.

"So Mike killed Cole," Hitchcock said. "The son of

a bitch." He looked over at April. "Did you hear any of this when you were out there? Or were you unconscious the whole time?"

April's brown eyes grew wide, and I could see the wheels turning in her head. "I woke up early in the conversation," she said in that girlish voice she employed when trying to appear winsome and innocent. "I didn't move, though. I remember feeling confused, disoriented. And I could tell something dangerous was going on. So I just kept still."

"But you eventually made a sound," Hitchcock said.

The three of us looked at her. I was curious to see what she would come up with.

"I could tell Marlee was in trouble. I thought if I moaned, it would distract this Mike fellow from hurting her." She reached up to touch her bruised temple. "He'd already tried to kill me. In fact, he was waiting for me when I arrived. Gave me quite a scare when he just popped up. I didn't see his car. But he told me there was a back road through the property. He parked out near the old silo."

"Why would he do that?" Janelle asked.

"He said that Marlee had just been to his shop and that she was on her way. He didn't want her to know he was there." April sighed. "I was stupid enough to think he was doing this to protect me while I talked with Marlee."

"Because I'm such a dangerous individual," I said.

She had the grace to look uncomfortable. "It's not my fault. That terrible man lied to me, saying that Marlee was in on Cole's murder with the mayor's wife. And that she was trying to make everyone think the zoning commission members were being blackmailed.

I mean, you can't blame me. After all, Marlee caused all kinds of problems for me and John."

I started to protest, but Hitchcock put up his hand. "None of us want to hear about the Chaplin murder again. We're interested in the murder of Cole Bowman." He gave her a stern look. "And in the attempted murder of both you and Marlee."

That seemed to sink in, because she nodded. "I'm sorry. You're right. This is more important. If Marlee hadn't made Mike chase after her, I might be dead now in those fields. It's a terrible thing, Chief Hitchcock, being involved in two murder cases. You have no idea."

Hitchcock allowed himself a small grin. "I have some idea, Miss Byrne."

She now looked at me. "Marlee, this feud between us has gone on long enough."

"Fine with me. I was never a willing part of it, anyway."

"Now here I am," she went on, as if I had never spoken, "once again in the middle of a murder case. At least I know how to handle the press better than I did three years ago. I have so much to tell the public about this latest chapter in my life. In fact, the next edition of my book will have to include everything that's happened here. How my love for John led me on a misguided quest for revenge. How I learned to forgive my enemy." April gave a gracious nod in my direction. "Although not all my enemies. I still want Evangeline to rot in prison."

"Let's just worry about getting the murderer of Cole Bowman into prison," Trejo said.

Hitchcock nodded. "After the doctor is done, we'll

take you to the station. You need to give us an official statement."

"Then allow me to finish my examination." As she did last Friday, when she treated me, Dr. Sankar didn't bother to mask her irritation. "And I've scheduled a CT scan to make certain there's no internal bleeding. Everyone please wait outside so I can do my job."

April gave a little wave from her exam table as I left with Hitchcock, Davenport, and Trejo. When the curtain closed behind us, two more police officers were waiting. One of them was Officer Wykoff, who informed us that Mike Gerringer's heart rate had been stabilized. Although in serious condition, he was expected to live. I sighed aloud in relief. I only wanted the bastard to be caught and punished. I didn't want to be the one responsible for his death.

"I think we should pay a call on Mr. Gerringer," Detective Trejo said to Hitchcock.

When Trejo and Hitchcock walked off, Janelle Davenport turned to me. "I watched you while April was giving her side of the story in there. You looked surprised. Was she telling the truth? Was she awake the whole time and just pretending to be dead? After all, her version of the story makes her out to be quite the clever heroine."

"I have no idea if she was awake or not. She certainly was out cold when I found her. But she could have regained consciousness. I was busy trying to stay alive, so I wasn't paying much attention to her." Maybe it was the stress of the day and nearly being killed, but I was willing to give April the benefit of the doubt. She could be telling the truth.

After all, there was a first time for everything.

* * *

A press conference was held later that day, but this one took place in front of the hospital, not at Strawberry Fields. I was part of it, along with the police, Piper, and April. It was like watching two rock divas perform onstage at the same time. I didn't mind being overshadowed. I was just the person who had brought the killer down. Me and my EpiPen. All that mattered was that I'd been able to stop Mike's rampage without suffering anything more than a few scratches from the thorny bushes. As soon as I was done with the press and the police, Piper and Lionel drove me home. I didn't have the energy to go back to the Fields property to retrieve my car. I'd send Ryan to pick it up later.

But if I thought I could relax on my front porch, I was mistaken. So many cars were parked outside my house, it looked like I was holding a garage sale. Scattered throughout my living room were Tess, Ryan, Max, Natasha, Andrew, Dean, Gillian, David, Denise Redfern, and Aunt Vicki. Even Old Man Bowman. This didn't surprise me. But also milling about the room were the Hallers, Crystal, and Drake. Once my friends were done greeting me with hugs and kisses, the four of them came up to me.

"We're sorry you were almost killed today, Marlee," Drake said as he and the other three gathered around. "We never thought our rezoning decision would lead to murder."

"It wasn't the rezoning," I said. "It was the blackmail. Cole knew Mike killed his wife. That's why Cole is dead."

"But we all had secrets to hide," Juliet said mournfully. "It could have been any of us."

"Except none of you did murder him over your secrets. None of you ever would."

Juliet, then Franklin, gave me a hug, and Crystal reached for my hand.

Drake winked at me and said, "Your planets seem to be in much better positions now, Marlee."

"I thought I felt a shift," I replied with a smile.

"Kiss for Mommy!" Minnie called out. I went over and took her from the cage. As she perched happily on my arm, I obliged her with a few quick kisses.

Piper clapped her hands for attention. Everyone in the living room stopped talking. "Thanks to Marlee and her EpiPen, that murderous muffin man has been brought to justice."

Ryan put his arm around my shoulders. "Aren't you glad I have a life-threatening allergy?"

Minnie gave her best imitation of a police siren.

"I never did like his muffins," Andrew added.

"And my name has been cleared, and my family's honor restored," Piper continued.

I suspected that was the most important thing to Piper.

"But let's put this sordid business behind us. We don't want Oriole Point to be known as a place where a muffin man goes about killing people." Piper spread out her arms. "Our village is all about natural beauty and artists and historic charm. We should redouble our efforts to make visitors forget about this messy murder as quickly as possible."

"Here comes trouble!" Minnie announced.

Piper threw a nervous glance at the bird. "Now that everyone is here," she continued, "this is the perfect time to officially launch the Blackberry Road Rally. Although Ruth Barlow and I are in charge of the event, Ruth broke her arm when she passed out at the police station last week. Who better to take her place than our own berry girl herself—Marlee!"

Groans rose up.

"I disagree. This is not the time to worry about the road rally," Drake protested. "Good grief, Marlee was nearly killed today."

Natasha chimed in. "Yes, let our poor Marlee rest!"

"Poor Marlee," Minnie repeated. "Poor Marlee."

I scratched my bird's head. "I don't mind. In fact, working on the road rally will help get my life back to normal."

Piper nodded in approval. "Just as I thought. That's why I brought a folder describing my plans to promote the rally. If everyone will take a seat, I'll pass them out."

The room was filled with grumbling as we sat down. I, however, was feeling quite lighthearted. I caught a murderer today. And had saved my own skin, as well as April's. A road rally was an enjoyable piece of cake after that. Besides, it reminded me that strawberry season was almost over. At the moment, strawberries held a few too many unpleasant memories. But blackberries sounded like the perfect antidote.

After all, no one had ever been murdered during blackberry season. At least not yet.

Recipes

Sharon Farrow

Strawberry-Banana Smoothie

Smoothies are The Berry Basket's most popular beverage during the summer. But whipping up a strawberry-banana smoothie is always a good idea, no matter the time of year. Because the bananas and strawberries are sweet enough, the chocolate is optional. Then again, chocolate is always an option for some of us.

    1½ cups milk (dairy, rice, almond, or soy)
    1 cup frozen or fresh strawberries, stems
        removed if fresh
    1 cup chopped ice
    1 medium banana, peeled and cut in half
    ½ cup vanilla or strawberry frozen yogurt
    1 heaping tablespoon cocoa powder, or
        20 to 30 chocolate baking chips (optional)

Place all the ingredients in a blender and pulse until the consistency is smooth. Pour the smoothies into two glasses and serve at once.

Makes 2 servings

Strawberry-Spinach Salad

Both spinach and strawberries are high in anti-inflammatory components, making this salad not only tasty but healthy. Even Muffin Mike could enjoy this without guilt. If you'd like to include some protein, simply add shredded cooked chicken to the salad.

Salad:
   2 cups fresh strawberries, stems removed and sliced
   1 bunch fresh spinach, rinsed and torn into small pieces
   1 small red onion, thinly sliced
   8 ounces feta cheese
   4 ounces sliced almonds

Dressing:
   ¼ cup olive oil or vegetable oil
   2 tablespoons white wine vinegar
   1½ teaspoons poppy seeds
   ¼ teaspoon paprika
   Granulated sugar, to taste

Toss the strawberries, spinach, and onion together in a large bowl. Set the salad aside.

Next, whisk together all the dressing ingredients in a small bowl. Pour the dressing over the salad and toss. Sprinkle with the feta cheese and almonds, and serve at once.

Serves 4

Strawberry Smash Muffins

These are the muffins that tempted the poor boy Marlee saved after he suffered an allergic reaction to strawberries. For those who aren't allergic, bake and enjoy. Since each muffin is less than 180 calories, these are a guilt-free treat, as well.

> 1⅔ cups fresh strawberries, rinsed and stems removed
> ⅔ cup granulated sugar
> ⅓ cup vegetable oil
> 2 large eggs
> 1½ cups all-purpose flour
> ½ teaspoon baking soda
> ½ teaspoon salt
> ½ teaspoon ground cinnamon

Preheat the oven to 450°F. Line the cups of a 12-cup muffin tin with paper cups or grease the cups.

Smash the strawberries in a large bowl with a fork. Stir in the sugar, oil, and eggs and mix well. Next, add the flour, baking soda, salt, and cinnamon and mix until moistened.

Spoon the batter into the prepared muffin cups. Bake for 15 to18 minutes, or until the muffins are light golden brown or a toothpick inserted in the center of one comes out clean.

Makes 12 muffins

Strawberry-Nut Bread

When Marlee visited Piper and Lionel, she brought a gift basket filled with their favorite things from The Berry Basket. The only baked good that was included was this delicious strawberry-nut bread, baked by her skilled baker, Theo Foster, also known as the Phantom. Luckily, this is such a simple recipe, you won't need your own resident baker to pull it off.

  One 16-ounce bag frozen whole strawberries, thawed and drained, or 2 cups fresh strawberries, stems removed
  2 cups granulated sugar
  ½ cup canola oil
  4 large eggs
  ¾ cup unsweetened applesauce
  3 cups all-purpose flour
  2 teaspoons ground cinnamon
  1 teaspoon baking soda
  1 teaspoon salt
  1 cup chopped walnuts or pecans

Preheat the oven to 350°F. Grease and lightly flour two 9 x 5-inch loaf pans.

Gently mash or chop the strawberries in a medium bowl and then set aside.

Mix together the sugar and the oil in a large bowl. Stir in the eggs. Add the strawberries and mix until thoroughly blended. Next, add the applesauce, the flour, the cinnamon, and salt and stir until the mixture is moistened. Fold in the nuts.

Pour an equal amount of batter into each of the prepared loaf pans. Bake for 60 to 70 minutes, or until a toothpick inserted in the center of one of the loaves comes out clean.

Let the loaves cool for 15 to 30 minutes, and then loosen sides of the loaves with a knife or a spatula. Remove the loaves from the pans and finish cooling them on wire racks.

Makes 2 loaves